PRAISE FOR *THE BOB WATSON*

"Greg Bardsley has a keen sense of the absurdity of everyday life, particularly Corporate America. But he gets the real things right, too, like all the messy stuff that makes us human. My advice: ditch your next meeting, find a coffee shop, and start reading. You won't regret it."

—Matthew Norman, author of
We're All Damaged and *Domestic Violets*

"Likably wry and dementedly screwball, *The Bob Watson* is a novel full of both sharp wit and genuine emotion."

—Lou Berney, Edgar Award–winning
author of *The Long and Faraway Gone*

"Fasten your seatbelt. *The Bob Watson* is a madcap race against time and conflicting priorities in California's go-go Silicon Valley—a raucous parody of the valley's twisted family and corporate values."

—Al Riske, author of *Precarious*, *Sabrina's
Window*, and *The Possibility of Snow*

"Does the ever-modernizing, depersonalizing corporate world make you want to stop and yell time-out? Bardsley warns us to be careful what we wish for in a fresh satire that is spot-on and hilarious—at least for those of us standing on the sidelines."

—Tim Dorsey, *New York Times* bestselling
ɔadkill

"*The Bob Watson* is worbsurd,
and sidesplittingly funny. oning
friends, family, and work–

—Mark Richardson, author of *Hunt for the Troll*

ALSO BY GREG BARDSLEY

Cash Out

THE
BOB
WATSON

A Novel

GREG
BARDSLEY

HARPER ● PERENNIAL

NEW YORK ● LONDON ● TORONTO ● SYDNEY ● NEW DELHI ● AUCKLAND

HARPER ● PERENNIAL

THE BOB WATSON. Copyright © 2016 by Greg Bardsley. All rights reserved. Printed in the United States of America. No part of this book may be used or reproduced in any manner whatsoever without written permission except in the case of brief quotations embodied in critical articles and reviews. For information, address HarperCollins Publishers, 195 Broadway, New York, NY 10007.

HarperCollins books may be purchased for educational, business, or sales promotional use. For information, please email the Special Markets Department at SPsales@harpercollins.com.

First Harper Perennial paperback published 2016.

Designed by Leydiana Rodriguez

Library of Congress Cataloging-in-Publication Data has been applied for.

ISBN 978–0–06–230479–7

16 17 18 19 20   RRD   10 9 8 7 6 5 4 3 2 1

For Jennifer and her beloved nephews,
Jack and Dylan

I don't have to be what you want me to be.

MUHAMMAD ALI

THE
BOB
WATSON

FIND INSPIRATION

I'm in a meeting imagining the attendees having sex.

This is what I do when people force me to attend their use-less meetings, when I'm waiting for the perfect moment to ditch them. Like today. Here I am sitting listening to Janice from Finance blabber about "L-Docs in the P-FID," her generous hindquarters aimed at us as she jots hexagons and acronyms onto a whiteboard, her tiny shoulders hunched. This whole meeting has nothing to do with me, of course, so I just sit there and imag-ine her getting it on with Blake the tiny intern. Right here on the table, and it's getting really disgusting and ass-cracky, and people are groaning in agony as they're forced to bear witness. And let me make this clear: This pornolizing is not a turn-on; it's just amusing as hell. I mean, there's Janice in this superbizarre position, limbs pointed in all directions, and she's snarling like an animal as sweet little Blake from Pepperdine pounds away with this bewildered look on his face. And there's Louis from FP&A just totally disgusted. Yeah, he's so grossed out, he's to-tally projectile-vomiting onto the lovers, and I mean gallons and gallons. And of course, I might as well throw in that dejected-looking guy over there with the bushy mustache. Yeah, have him mount the intern. Oh, and yeah, let's add a moaning Ted Koppel as he nears climax. I mean, hell, why not? Right? Because this meeting blows. So hell, let's go ahead and toss Nancy Grace into the mix. Oh, and here comes Hillary Clinton with an enormous "prosthetic," if you know what I mean, and she's saying, *Well well well . . . What do we have here?*

I smile. *This is getting good.*

Which is when a text message snaps me back into reality.

It says . . .

OK

And it stops my heart a sec.

The tabletop orgy begins to fade. Hillary snaps, *Rick, we're just getting started.*

I stare at the name on the phone, feel my jaw drop. I shake my face and blink. Look again. I actually have a text message from the woman I've daydreamed about, have secretly stalked on Facebook, have tried to flirt with, have imagined cuddling up to on cold Sunday nights, have envisioned sliding my face across her body and into her open mouth, have fantasized about watching her laugh uncontrollably at my jokes. I actually have a text from the beautiful creature who for years has pushed me away with a gentle smile. I actually have her name—*Audrey (nanny)*—illuminating my screen.

The moment is so rare, it's like wining the Lotto.

Or seeing a whale breach in front of your kayak.

Or making a verified Chupacabra sighting.

Or running into Burt Reynolds at 7-Eleven.

It's Audrey. Sweet and luscious Audrey with her supersmooth

skin and the sweetest smile on Earth. Texting me—ME!!!! It's so much, I almost forget I'm in this useless assembly I'm planning to ditch.

At the whiteboard, Janice from Finance says, "We must P-FID the L-Docs."

I imagine Audrey letting loose at a lounge—giving in to my bongo playing.

"And we need a BFO for the EDOs."

I bring my phone under the table and text back: OK what?

"And the P-FIDs. We need to R-Doc the P-FIDs."

The incoming text makes my phone shake, sends a ripple to my crotch.

> The Greek. . . . . Tonight.
> . . . . OK

I gaze at Janice and pretend to be engrossed.

The Greek? Tonight? OK?

I twist my lips in thought, feel my brows wrinkle.

What the hell is she talking about?

I cock my head and squint at Janice's blue marker, my face suddenly coming to life as new icons and acronyms flood the whiteboard. Janice glances at me, grins in victory as traces of comprehension invigorate my face. I scoot to the edge of my seat and straighten, pulling on my lower lip, checking my logic one last time as Janice watches, brimming with pride.

The Greek. She's talking about the Greek Theatre in Berkeley, hands down the best concert venue in Northern California.

My eyes widen and bulge.

Janice nods to me. "Yes, that's right. We must scrub the P-FIDs."

But tonight?

Again, I feel my face twist into thought, and Janice frowns.

Janice erases the whiteboard. "Let me explain it for you another way," she says, and everyone groans. I'm thinking so hard, I don't even pretend those are sex groans. Janice populates the whiteboard with cylinders and hexagons and arrows.

At which point, I jump out of my chair, victorious.

Janice yelps in delight.

Tonight! Tonight at the Greek. The English Beat—tonight, at the Greek. They're playing at the Greek. Tonight.

And then . . .

Me and Audrey. Together. Just the two of us. At the Greek. With my favorite band ever, the English Beat.

Blood gushes south, and I stare into space with a giggle.

Janice watches, nearly sings, "There we go."

The English Beat at the Greek. I had mentioned it to Audrey maybe a month ago—it probably was the eighty-seventh time I'd suggested a date over the years. I lose track and forget—I've always considered Audrey a long-term project, and I am nothing if not stunningly shameless and persistent. And she's always declined with that smile—not so much a rejection as a *maybe next time*. But this time . . .

Janice caps her marker, grins at me, swelling with pride. "That's the look of someone who finally gets it."

Then I think of something.

After all these years, why now?

My phone vibrates.

But on 1 condition.

Hmm . . . Maybe she actually digs the disheveled look.

I tap back: Anything, baby.

Janice babbles, and I imagine sitting at the Greek with

Audrey, the sun setting on the bay, the scent of ganja in the air, our hands slipping into each other's as we wait for Dave and the band to take the stage. The air crisping, the energy building, as I prepare to stick my tongue into her happy, wanting mouth.

> Think about today. . . . What's happening today? . . .
> Think and get back to me.

• • •

For the next fifteen minutes, Janice from Finance gets pink in face as she fails to explain the P-FIDs to me. A bead of sweat rolls down her temple as she scrawls out one final P-FID on the whiteboard, glancing back at me, hoping it finally registers.

I'm perched at the end of my seat. Thinking hard.

Audrey asked, What's happening today? . . . Hmmm.

Janice attaches an arrow to the hexagon, glances back.

Oh.

Janice stops and straightens. "You got it?"

I stare into space, nodding, a smile forming as I finally realize what Audrey is hinting at. I produce an exaggerated, surprised overbite as I run the logic one last time.

Today. . . . Oh crap, I forgot. . . . Today.

Janice addresses the rest of the room. "Let's move on to the SERVPRO."

Today is the last day my sister and her family will be in the United States.

Janice clears the whiteboard. "The SERVPRO is tiered."

How could've I forgotten?

Tonight they leave for Argentina—overseas assignment for the husband, Samson James Barnard IV. Their eight-year-old son, Collin (my nephew), a cool little Renaissance man, isn't too happy about it. We haven't hung out in a while, but my sister gave me the lowdown a month ago: Collin is bummed about losing his live-in nanny—the beautiful Audrey—who's remaining stateside. Hell, I can understand; Collin has been one lucky little bastard all these years, having Audrey cuddling him and loving him and being there for him. I will admit to being a tad jealous over the years, especially since Audrey always seems just within my reach, but not really. She always just laughs and runs a hand down my arm, calls me by my full name and looks me in the eye, an eyebrow lifting ever so slightly. "Rick Blanco," she says in mock shock, her hand hitting my arm, then trailing down to my wrist. "What are you doing asking me out? I'm too busy taking care of your nephew. You should think of doing that once in a while."

I gaze at her, transfixed. "What's that?"

She lets go and pinches me lightly. "Spending time with your nephew, you goof."

I stare at Janice's whiteboard and imagine lazing in bed with Audrey on a Sunday morning, her silky skin sliding against my hairy legs as we giggle about something really stupid. That easy smile. Just hanging out. And she says, getting closer, *Rick Blanco, you freaking dork. Why do you make me so happy?*

I tap away. I got it.

Janice babbles and my cell vibrates. Good. Tell me.

> My sis and fam are leaving tonight.

My phone shakes.

> And what about that, Rick Blanco?

Janice glances at me. "Follow me on this."

I give Janice my serious look and tap back. They need a ride to the airport?

LOL. . . . . Try again.

Janice scribbles.

You need help moving out of my sister's compound???

"If you're not careful, you can get lost in the SERVPRO."

Dude . . . . Think.

I do think, and I draw a blank.

A minute later, my cell vibrates again. Who's going to really miss you, Rick Blanco? . . . Who's always talking about how cool you are?

I tap: You?????

LOL. . . . . Think again.

I stare into space, and Janice says, "Rick. Stay with me."
And then it hits me like a happy slap to the face.
Oh!!! I tap. Collin????
Janice watches me, beams with pride.

Bingo. . . . . Now, what are you going to do today?

My lips twist in confusion. Come again?
Janice babbles and I pretend to listen. It's a long time before I get another text.

Call me when you're ready to try again. . . . Until then,
I'm officially planning to do yoga tonight.

•　•　•

I sit in the meeting glancing up at Janice as I make careful entries into my notepad, running through the facts one last time.

- My nephew digs me
- Audrey wants me to do something for him
- If I do enough, she'll go out with me tonight
- I want Audrey long time
- The kid loves "adventures"—I can do something with that
- And I can teach him how to pull a Bob Watson
- Everyone should know how to pull a Bob Watson.

Suddenly, I'm so excited I want to jump into the air. I think I have a plan that'll make the kid happy and land me Audrey. *The Bob Watson. Yes, of course. The Bob Watson is my answer.* I feel my chest swell as I realize, *Today is gonna be special.*

There's just no way I could've anticipated the riot.

VALIDATE YOUR KEEPER

So, about my special talent.

You see, I'm a serial meeting ditcher. A walkout artist. An underground pioneer of worker-bee liberty. And I've gotten so good at it that the very people running these meetings don't even realize they're getting ditched, even though I do what I do in broad daylight. I just get up and walk out—none of that exaggerated-tiptoeing bullshit. It's that simple. But of course, just like so many things in life, it's simple because I've spent years toiling away on the craft. In my journey, I've worked hard to master the tools of nuance and distraction, and I've spent a lot of time on my people-reading skills (knowing *when* meetings are most vulnerable to a successful ditch is just as important as knowing *how* to ditch them). Ultimately, all of it must come together, but when it does—when the right bozos call you into the wrong meeting, with the right conditions for a juicy little ditch— few things feel as good.

For me, it all started when I "met" Bob Watson.

In case you're wondering, Bob had no idea who I was—and

still doesn't. And I didn't really notice him, either. He was always the good-natured guy who'd make a few good comments in meetings, get good conversations going. He was such a great listener. He'd even get *me* cranked up, and soon I'd be blabbering on and on, and he'd lie back and let people dive into the heart of the matter. He'd let them have center stage—that's the kind of guy he was.

Bob was middle-aged, and had his own scene going. He'd wear these worn-in loafers, khakis, and off-white and pastel linen shirts I'd imagine on a Latin-jazz-club owner. It was like he almost didn't fit in, but did just enough. He had this relaxed way to him—not one of those too-cool-for-you attitudes, but just this inner calmness, this look that seemed nearly tickled but, again, not quite. His speech pattern was slow California native, his voice gravelly from smoking. He never took notes; in fact, he always seemed way too relaxed, just sitting there with this serene look on his face as everyone barked comments about "leveraging PLDs for the L-Docs."

Of course, this was a long time ago, back when I was a twenty-one-year-old rookie at Robards International cutting my teeth on "bottom-tier data transformation." And I'll be totally honest: I really didn't know what I was doing, and I surely had no idea how everyone else fit in. These two facts presented the perfect conditions for getting sucked into meetings that had nothing to do with me—if only I knew this is how corporate America works. And so there I'd be, stuck in these colorless conference rooms with mesh wallpaper, huddled around a long table with all these men in Dockers and women in shoulder pads, none of them showing any intention of cutting off these mind-numbing discussions about something called the Rothberg documentation process.

What did any of this have to do with me? Nothing, of course.

And so my mind would of course turn to sex. After that, I'd usually proceed to people watching. You know, the normal stuff, like *When was the last time that guy ate flapjacks?* and *I wonder what's the worst thing he's ever done.* And of course, *When was the last time she vomited?*

One day, Bob had gotten things started—"Let's pause and really think about this stuff"—and now everyone was talking about the R-Tools and the FP&A docs. You had to give it to Bob; he really knew how to get the dialog going. Even so, I could handle only so much of this stuff. It wasn't too long before I hit my max. Maybe Bob and the gang were loving it in here, but I hated it. The daydreaming wasn't working, and soon my knee was bouncing involuntarily out of pure caged-animalism. Then my heart began to pound. I felt a light sweat cool my temples. My fists balled, over and over. Inside, I was screaming.

I just have to get out of here.

I wanted to collect my things and just leave. Just leave this room and never come back. But of course, I couldn't—Bob and the others would notice. My throat tightened. And I realized, I *hate* being detained, jailed, held, trapped. I felt my body rise from my chair and pace the room. Surprisingly, Bob and the gang didn't seem to care, and I realized everyone was too busy talking at each other. I stopped in front of the window, wondering how I could take control of my life short of retreating to a shack in the mountains, where I'd have to live off worms and bark. Which was when I gazed longingly out the window and spotted Bob Watson crossing the street with a new cup of coffee in his hand, the steam wafting into the sunshine, his gait slow and relaxed, his Ray-Bans riding low on his nose. Not a care in the world as he strolled back from that coffeehouse where those gorgeous art students worked the steamers.

Wait a minute.

I stood there, dumbstruck, as I watched Bob saunter toward the building and stop to admire a squirrel scampering up a white oak.

I thought Bob was here with us in this . . .

I turned back to the conference room, and, sure enough, there were Bob's things—his notepad, his pen, his water bottle. Thirty minutes later, still no Bob—and no one seemed to care. I decided to stand up to stretch and pace the room. Soon I was pressing my face against the tiny porthole window of the conference room door, like a jailbird who's heard interesting sounds just out of eyeshot. My eyes darted around the office until they settled on Bob at his desk.

He was working.

Getting things done.

Oh. Yeah. I needed to watch this guy. I needed to attend the same meetings he attended and just soak him up—learn his moves, see how he set it all up—because I could tell right then and there: This was a kindred spirit, a corporate soul mate who could lead me to another world. Hell, another dimension, the existence of which I hadn't quite allowed myself to believe.

So I watched and studied Bob. A lot.

It seemed like he could do just about anything he wanted, with no consequences. To watch him pull off his ditches was kind of a life experience; it helped me realize that maybe I, too, had the power to control my life, even at work, even though the suits wanted me to think otherwise. And does it get more empowering than that? I guess that's why I studied Bob so closely. This was a master who'd perfected his secret craft—my job was to observe and document, and to avoid tainting anything. I was patient and persistent not only in my observation and documentation, but also in my subsequent practice.

But I couldn't stop. After I'd learned how to pull a Bob

Watson, I taught myself variations that I named in his honor. And I have many. There's the Bob Watson Classic (a straight meeting ditch), the Reverse Bob Watson (you leave, only to return five minutes later, to build trust for a future ditch), the FU Watson (self-explanatory), the Watson Solo (you ditch a one-on-one; yes, that's right: a one-on-one), and the Extreme Watson (multiple ditches, with multiple returns, each absence lasting a little longer than the previous, until you're gone and never coming back).

At some point, Bob left the company. I'm not sure exactly *when* he left.

●   ●   ●

All these years later, I am super passionate about this stuff. More than ever, I really, truly do not like it when people waste my time. So if you drag me to your unnecessary meeting and I am forced to sit there and wait for my Bob Watson moment, I *will* pornolize you (sorry). That is, I will imagine you in the middle of some kind of depraved porno—an orgy, maybe, or a gang bang, or a glory-hole marathon. And I *will* imagine everything.

But today is different. I'm on a mission.

Janice asks, "Any comments?"

I snap to attention, because here's my chance. My chance to validate, which is a critical element of the Bob Watson. You see, if you want to be like Bob, a serial meeting ditcher who never got fired, you must validate the meeting organizers and, if possible, the attendees. You must make that emotional imprint, making them feel you're engaged—and most important, that *they* are okay—so that when you are long gone, all they'll remember are your passionate comments, your supportive nods, your earnest gazes.

I raise my hand, and Janice nods. I give her my thoughtful look, raising a brow. "I just wanted to let you know that the company needs this," I say, pitching my voice high at the end, for resonance. "The J-23 Incubation Initiative is perhaps one of the most important things we can do this year." I pause, like I'm thinking about it, and scoot to the edge of my seat, my back arched, like I want to jump into the air. "But the question is, how do we drive this point through to the regions?"

Janice beams, babbles about "leveraging the verticals."

I keep the eye contact, thinking of the calls I need to make.

Janice announces that the J-23 Incubation Process is designed for adaptation in the PWC and that . . . blah . . . blah . . . blah . . . blah. She's using words like *align* and *cascade* and *value capture*, and then the acronyms tumble out. I try to say something, but she raises a finger, as if to say, *No way*. I sit and listen, and decide that Janice from Finance is even more of a control freak than I previously thought. But who am I fooling? It's not just Janice. This office is packed with control freaks. Hell, the whole world is oozing control freaks. Everyone is trying to control each other.

Do what I do.

Value what I value.

Live life my way.

Do as I say.

Change to make me happy.

Listen to me.

Attend my meeting.

Generally speaking, I tend to say, *Nah*.

Other folks take another path. Just look at my poor sister and her husband: happy subjects of a kingdom of control. Control freaks who don't even realize that they themselves are being controlled—controlled by each other, controlled by trends, controlled by the hyperactive, ultracompetitive, overachiever subculture that dictates nearly everything they do. At this point, my sister has changed so fundamentally that I can barely see the person who grew up alongside me.

This malady they have, I've given it a name—Overachiever Fever, the symptoms of which are enough to turn a staunch tee-totaler into a raging drunk. That's because with Overachiever Fever, nothing in life—and I mean *nothing*—is ever quite good enough. This means folks are always stressing out. It means competition is nuts. It means that *life mapping*—a term I never wanted to learn—is absolutely essential. And it means that looking over your shoulder is a must.

It's no way to live.

The poor bastards.

If only they could chill out a bit.

If only they knew the way of Bob.

Sitting there thinking of Audrey's assignment, I decide that teaching the Bob Watson to Collin makes all kinds of sense. I realize that in the coming years, it will be way important for my little dude to stay strong in the face of the oppressors—the over-achievers, the control freaks, the stress ballers, the elitists, the aspiring masters of the universe.

He needs to learn how to fight the power, Bob Watson style.

It reminds me of this time I asked Audrey out for a drink. She just smiled and said, "Hold that thought, Rick Blanco. Because I want to tell you about your nephew's extracurricular activities."

I thought this was an odd response, but I dig her quirkiness. "Shoot, baby."

"I mean, listen to this: There's the Mandarin-immersion pro-gram at school, the software-coding tutor at home, the personal trainer for lacrosse at the health club, the oral forensics coach, who visits after dinner on Tuesdays, the body-language coach on Wednesdays, the cello instructor on Saturdays, the personal shaman/spiritual adviser on Sunday nights, and the publicist who is on retainer."

I focused on Audrey's lips.

"He's eight years old, Rick Blanco."

I admired her hairline. "He also wants his nanny to have drinks with cool dudes."

Audrey shook her head and sighed. "Rick Blanco."

I still can't figure that one out.

DISTRACT AND LEAVE

Trapped in the conference room and thinking about Audrey's perfect lower lip, I come to an easy conclusion.

I need to get out of here.

Now my heart is racing. That's what happens when I have a plan, when I know I'm about to pull a Bob Watson. I bite my lip and tap my foot as I wait for an opportunity to initiate a Bob Watson launch sequence.

That's right. After you've made yourself visible and present, after you've validated speakers and attendees, after you've made those emotional and mental imprints, you must gently toss to the center of the room a smoke bomb of sorts—a distraction. "Cover" that allows you to slip out. Usually it's an "innocent" comment or question that quickly leads people to a subtopic so inflammable that no one can resist weighing in. Which is when you get up and leave, unnoticed.

Janice says, "Which is why—if you look at row seventy-eight on the chart printout—you can clearly see how the subtiers of the P-FID fluctuate."

I raise my hand and offer my stupid look. "But what about the SysCON?"

Janice stiffens. Everyone else groans.

The SysCON is her catnip.

"It's quite simple." She steadies herself, and her cheeks redden. "We shall—God as my witness—leverage the SysCON for the richest ROI this industry has ever seen." She turns to the whiteboard, where she starts to draw out a hexagon, labeling each corner. "And I'm talking about the L-PAR, HyperPHY, AGRO, a variety of industry-standard M24s, and the whole range of J-4s in the FOD." I notice two people fighting off sleep, three others checking email, and one poor soul somehow—against all odds—paying full attention. "We must strip it apart—do a complete K-KAR on this baby—and put it back together, but with things like the J-8s and AGRO rationalization."

Crickets.

"And we will K-KAR and K-KAR and K-KAR as long as it takes. And only then will we feed it into the SysCON."

I raise my hand. "So it really is a deep, full thrust with the K-KARs and the L-Docs?"

Janice lowers her eyelids. "We'll drench the K-KARs with L-Docs and the SysCON and B-24s, and then spreadsheet the whole thing." She seems to have transported herself to a curious, acronym-rich dimension I hadn't thought possible. "And it's K-KARs in the RAD, K-KARs in the—"

"Janice Janice Janice." I'm like a traffic cop, with my arms out—*Stop*. "Sorry to interrupt, but . . ." She's frozen, and the attendees look up. ". . . I just have to step in here. Please." I approach her and pluck the marker from her hand. "I'd like to draw something out." I move to the whiteboard under a growing din of murmurs. "Because I'm starting to feel we're thinking about this all wrong." I look at her open mouth, then at the attendees, all eyes on me—what drama, what an interesting break from normal programming. "And our problems start with the K-KAR."

You could've heard an ant burp.

"The problem is . . ." I write out K-KAR in giant letters. ". . . the K-KAR is limited in scope." I make a big show of crossing out the *K-KAR* with the marker, "slashing" it with long, dramatic swipes, adding little curlicues at the end. "The K-KAR is—forgive me—the largest Chihuahua."

Gasps.

"Here's what I think of the K-KAR." I keep crossing out the *K-KAR*, like I'm committing a crime of passion. Janice takes a step toward me, stops. Bites her lip, her chest heaving. "I'm sorry, but the K-KAR is like your grandpa's landline telephone—an out-of-date relic." I turn and look at Janice, then the others. "And yet we need the K-KAR. We all know that." I look at Janice again, giving her the serious eyes. "But we also need the SysCON and the L-Docs." I turn to the attendees. "So what do we do?"

Silence.

I wipe the board clean. "What we do is—and I'm serious—something I'll call . . ."

I make them wait a sec.

". . . process husbandry."

Hushed murmurs. Janice sways.

"Yes." In a fit of creativity, I write out the *K-KAR* diagonally. "That's right. It's time to . . ." Under the *K-KAR*, I write "SysCON" as if the former is mounting the latter. ". . . mate the K-KAR with the SysCON."

You would have thought I'd just dropped my pants to reveal a banana sling.

"We need to put the K-KAR in a room with the SysCON." I offer them the serious eyes again. "And we need to lock that door. And we won't let them out until the SysCON is knocked-up, so to speak. Knocked up with their love child—a zygote ready to incubate into a new breed." I turn and stare at Janice, then at the attendees. "I'm talking about a love child that will evolve bottom-tier data transformation into a new kind of species. I'm talking about a new era." Under the SysCON, I draw a crude, asexual orifice, and out of it I produce a waterfall of fluid. Atop the small pool of discharge, I write out a new acronym—K-CONKAR. "The era of the K-CONKAR."

The room explodes into a chorus of cheers and gasps. Janice charges, swipes the marker from my hand, lifts her lip at me, and heads for the whiteboard, taking the eraser in the other hand. People at the table are debating, excitement in their voices, as Janice works frantically to erase my explicit suggestion. Slowly, I step back, out of the spotlight, and look at my phone—nothing.

Janice is trembling as she attacks the whiteboard. "The K-KAR . . ." She shouts. "*Cannot* . . ." She stops herself, takes a big breath, and lets it out slowly. ". . . be crossbred."

The attendees hush for a moment, then explode into debate. Floyd thrusts an index finger into the air, nearly shouts over the din, "We need a committee. A K-CONKAR exploratory committee." The words are hardly out of his mouth when a cadre of K-KAR purists pounce on him, their teeth showing, their shoulders leaning forward, their eyes glaring. The notion—no, the blasphemous, perverted, nearly incestuous suggestion—of a process called the K-CONKAR has half the room foaming at the mouth, mindless of the fact that, two minutes ago, they were listless zombie slaves. Now, they're alive—their faces flushed, their hearts thumping, their throats tight as they prepare to interject a rapid, buttery flurry of L-Docs, J-23s, and HyperPHYs into the dialogue. Don't they know they are back on the bottle? Bolstered, invigorated—propped up—by a rare and short-lived tonic drawn from the very insulated, antiseptic, corporate monotony that just minutes ago had brought them to their knees, their heads bowed, their clasped hands begging for the executioner's special brand of swift mercy?

This high? This K-CONKAR high of theirs? Oh yes, it will crash. And when it does—when my poor colleagues awake in a sea of their own empties, reminded of their relapse, their obsessive-compulsive binge into bottom-tier data transformation—I will be long gone.

They bark at each other, nod, fold their arms, and scribble.

Slowly, I backpedal to the conference room door. "And once we complete the L-PAR thrust," I say, "we penetrate deeper with the HyperPHY. And we must go so deep with the HyperPHY, it hurts."

Hank says, "And once we're in with the HyperPHY, we can— and we will—pound away."

I take another step back as Janice pounds her first into her palm, creating a rhythmic listing of acronyms—"First, it's the R-PID . . ." *Fist pound.* "Then it's the L-Docs . . ." *Fist pound.* "And then it's the L-PARs . . ." *Fist pound.* ". . . and the J-22s . . ." *Fist pound.* ". . . and the A-100s . . ." *Pound.* ". . . and then that deep thrust with the HyperPHY—over . . ." *Pound.* ". . . and over . . ." *Pound.* ". . . and over again."

Floyd says, "You can't create a K-CONKAR with the Hyper-PHY."

Someone says, "We must hyperscale the HyperPHY."

"No," Janice snaps. "We must milk the HyperPHY."

"Which is why the HyperPHY must not be soiled by the K-KAR."

"The HyperPHY has no place in this discussion."

"Are you kidding? The HyperPHY might very well be our Lucy."

"Lucy?"

"The *Australopithecus* of all Robards International processes."

"Why are we even having this discussion?"

"Because the K-KAR has been R-POD'd and L-Doc'd to death."

"What the HyperPHY needs is much more of that."

"You have got to be—"

"The HyperPHY needs a good soiling by the SysCON."

"A rogering."

"Or the K-CONKAR. The K-CONKAR could do that."

"The point is—and I'm serious—the HyperPHY has been wearing a chastity belt of sorts."

"Folks. . . . Folks. . . . Guys. . . . Let's keep the tone—No need for—"

"Listen, you think the HyperPHY is some protected, virginal princess?"

"No. I *know* it's—"

"Dude, the HyperPHY is a cougar. A chain-smoking, whiskey-drinking cougar."

"I don't like your tone, mister."

"Try this on for size—I don't like you."

"Well, you can take the K-CONKAR and shove it up your HyperPHY'd—"

"Shut your trap, you raspy bag."

"SysCON hugger."

"HyerPHY dittohead."

"Hyperslut."

"Asshole."

"Prick."

"You want the SBC Office on your ass?"

"People."

"I'll HyperPHY your ass right out of this company."

"Guys. Stop."

"The K-KAR is a simple, dull sloth."

"And the SysCON is a flatulent old whore who doesn't bathe."

Janice shouts, "We need an L-Doc on the innards of the K-CONKAR ASAP."

"The K-KAR is an overfed pedophile living in a desert trailer."

Janice says, "Rick, help me with these people."

I address the group. "It seems like the L-Docs may not be aligned with the K-KAR. And maybe that's our problem."

Janice pauses, touches her chin. "I know we had a break scheduled, but I think we're getting over the initial anxiety about the formation of a K-CONKAR, and this discussion seems to be becoming productive. So we're gonna cancel the break and keep going."

But of course the door is already shutting behind me.

Gently.

Graciously.

GET SHIT DONE

The beauty of the Bob Watson is that it allows you to ditch the spreadsheeters, the bullshit artists, and the hot-potato tossers so you can actually get shit done. On most days, I'd be knocking out a series of P-FIDs and L-Docs. I'd be on the phone with Europe. I'd have the SysCON tool up. I'd be scanning in medical bills and documents, and resubmitting it all for the fifth time in three days. I'd be rebooting my PC after it once again crashed in the middle of an application for a benefits reimbursement. And yes— I'll admit it—maybe I'd be taking a few "nonstrategic" detours along the way.

Today is different. Today is all about getting the green light from Audrey.

At my desk, I lean back and tap a text to her.

> OK. . . . So . . . I guess taking him on a dump run won't do it.

No response.

Five minutes later, I tap: Is there something specific u had in mind?

My cell shakes. Just be you, RB

I lower my cell and squint into space. *Just be me?*

And then an idea strikes: When I'm with the kid—when we really just hang out—I'm not thinking of Audrey or trying to be cool. We're just ourselves. The kid and I just thumb our noses at the world, and we do what we want—not unlike pulling a Bob Watson, I suppose. We don't meet up very often, but when we do, it's pretty cool. And it's pretty clear that Collin *really* digs our adventures—it's like he never gets to be a kid, unless he's with me. Now that I think about it, I'm not sure my sister and brother-in-law care about the beauty of just hanging out and having fun.

The last time Collin and I hung out—and I'll admit it was a while ago—we just sat in the sun at the park and watched people as I tapped away on my bongos. People are always so interesting.

"Uncle Rick?"

"Yeah."

"You still haven't changed your mind?"

I admire an absolutely stunning blonde in black yoga pants.

"About what, kiddo?"

"About people."

The blonde smiles back, her face softening.

"People? Changed my mind about *people?*"

One last look at the blonde before she disappears forever.

"You know." He straightens and looks around the park, whispers. "About them."

"Them? You mean, beautiful women in God's greatest gift to humankind—yoga pants?"

"You know." Hope spreads across his face. "Neanderthals."

"Oh, yes." I bite my lip. "The Neanderthals."

He locks on to me with those intense, brown eyes. "So, you're still a speciesist?"

"Speciesist? What? No, I'm—"

"Because you think *Homo sapiens* are better than . . ." His voice cracks at the thought. ". . . everyone else."

"Well, c'mon, kid." I stop the bongo playing and give him a serious look. "You have to admit we're pretty badass."

He studies me for a very long time, and I offer my cocky meathead look.

Collin says, "What if you fell into the Arctic Ocean in the middle of the night? And you're surrounded by perfectly happy sea life as your body shuts down?"

I think about it. "I'd stick out my stomach really huge—like this—and float on my back."

He rolls his eyes.

"Or, I'd sink to the bottom of the sea."

"Exactly."

"But if I am going to take a dip in the Arctic . . ." I give him my serious eyes. ". . . I'd insist on wearing those floatie armbands they have in the kiddie pools."

"Ha . . . ha . . . ha." He's not amused. "In reality, you'd shut down and sink. And you wouldn't think *Homo sapiens* are the best species then." His chest rises and falls, and he announces, "No one shows the other species any respect."

We sit and think about it. Soon, his breathing settles, and I say, "Now. . . . If. . . . If a bunch of anteaters ever found a way to send one of their own to the moon and back, then maybe I would agree."

He pierces me with those eyes.

"But the truth is, no other species *has* gone to the moon, or created cancer-fighting drugs, or written *War and Peace*, or even gone serial with a Vine."

He looks at me, deciding if he should get mad or not. Finally, he cracks a tiny grin.

"I'm just saying, Collin-babe. *Homo sapiens* are pretty badass."

He lets out a long, annoyed sigh. "Of course we're badass, but so are other species. Have you ever heard of the *Bathynomus giganteus*?"

Collin's ability to pronounce words always blows me away. "The what?"

He sighs quickly. "Also known as the giant isopod." He waits for it to register, I offer my stupid look, and he gives up. "It's a carnivorous crustacean."

"Can you get those in the frozen-food section?"

"It lives seven thousand feet below sea level. Can you do that? No." He straightens, looks around, and throws out his arms in exasperation. "Why won't *People* magazine do a story about the *Bathynomus giganteus*?"

Another moment of joint reflection until I break the silence. "I don't want to be a speciesist." Stupid look with big eyes asking for mercy. "But sometimes I can't help being one."

This gets him, and he leans into me. "You can, too."

"It's like with the Neanderthals," I say.

His face brightens. Neanderthal talk is basically Collin's catnip.

"I'm sorry, kiddo, but the Neanderthals lost out to the *Homo sapiens*."

"Uncle Rick." Another sigh. "You just don't get it."

"When I think about Neanderthals, finally I feel like I have a hominid I can feel superior to."

He grabs my wrist, squeezes. "Why won't you listen to me?"

"I get confused."

"Look," he says, excitement coursing through his body. "We

don't know why Neanderthals 'disappeared.' We don't even know if they *did* disappear." He peers into me, waiting for it to sink in. "We're starting to learn things about Neanderthals that no one knew. I was watching this show on the Prehistoric Channel, and we're finding evidence that they . . ." He looks around, lowers his voice. ". . . are not gone."

"Wait a minute. Just what are you suggesting?"

He tries to talk without moving his mouth. "They're all over the place."

"You mean . . ."

He nods, his eyes wide. "The Neanderthals successfully bred themselves into the European population."

"So there are people who . . ."

"Have Neanderthal in them," he whispers. "And they don't even know it."

"So they don't live in their own packs?"

"We think that's unlikely, but possible. There *are* enormous, untamed forests in Russia. Very few people have explored some of these places."

I look around the park, scanning the faces and body shapes. "But you think they live among us? Like, they've slipped into society?"

He raises his eyebrows, lowers his chin, and zeros in on me. "It's possible."

"So, maybe some of us are more Neanderthal than others? Some might be pure-bred Neanderthals?"

He looks to the sky. "It's like people with red hair, or albinos. Sometimes people inherit a gene that's been recessive for centuries. We're still learning about things like that."

"So, someone might have been born with Neanderthal features, but his parents look perfectly *Homo sapien*?"

He looks away, nearly cracks a smile, and returns to me with dead-serious eyes. "Maybe."

"I think I know what we should do," I say.

He smiles, waits for more.

"I think we should go to a bigger park."

"Like Golden Gate Park, or the Presidio?"

I scratch my chin as I look at him. "Maybe Golden Gate Park. More subjects to observe."

He gets so excited, he bounces and tightens.

I add, "And I just think we should do more fieldwork."

"Just like on the Prehistoric Channel."

"Exactly. I think we need to document as many Neanderthal sightings as possible."

"Just like last time?" he asks.

"Just like last time."

Suddenly, he deflates. "Oh, but we need our stuff."

I turn and grab my backpack. "Really?" I reach in and pull out a pair of giant binoculars. Collin jumps to his feet and dances around.

"And . . ." I reach into the backpack again, pull out a small, dog-eared spiral-ringed notepad. ". . . I have our field log."

Shoots his fists into the air.

I pull out my camera. "And, of course, we need to continue our visual documentation."

He spins and jumps into the air.

"We just can't have you taking close-ups like last time, okay?"

"And we can't have you using the binoculars on female sunbathers," he says.

I put my hands out—*I promise.*

"We'll do those pretend poses with me, like the last time, and then you just zero in on them. They had no idea."

I gather our things. "Okay, let's do this."

He small-steps back to me, and falls into my lap. We hug, and he says, "Thanks, Rick."

"Of course. But first, let's do your puffs." I pull out his asthma inhaler and fasten the albuterol canister to the end—Audrey is always reminding me to do this. "We need your lungs ready, in case we have to chase down a Neanderthal." I ease the inhaler to his face, release a spray of albuterol, and he takes a long, slow breath, a hand gripping my pinkie. Then another. And then a hug—the kid is always hugging me.

His voice is soft. "Rick?"

"Yeah?"

"I love doing Neanderthal searches with you."

"Good."

We sit there awhile, letting the sun warm us.

"And Rick?"

"Yes."

"I love doing *anything* with you."

My chest tightens, and I'm slammed with a wave of claustrophobia. Old feelings, and fears. I screw my eyes shut, wishing I could pull him off me. But I just take a deep breath and hug him back.

I feel like a heartless caveman.

• • •

After all that uncomfortable introspection, I now have a plan—Neanderthals, baby.

So of course, it feels like a perfect time to take a break.

I can nearly hear a factory whistle blowing long and hard as I stand up with a giant smile, stretch like a dog (dragging locked legs), and begin my rounds. After all, if I am going to pull a

Workplace Watson—leaving not just a meeting but the office building altogether—it's important to lay the groundwork, and that means making myself visible while I'm still here.

Plus, I love hanging out with people.

I drop in on Donna in Sales Enablement, who's a good twenty years older than me, and who surprised the hell out of me last year in Tallahassee. We were in town for the Fiscal-Year P-FID Alignment Meeting, an annual acronym-laced, spreadsheet-drenched boondoggle put on by Janice from Finance, who essentially herds fifty people into a windowless motel conference room and talks at them for three days. Pulling a Bob Watson at an offsite is tricky and not for beginners, but I did manage a few sweet escapes in which I hung out across the street at a dive bar, nursing greyhounds and watching baseball.

Which was when Donna came from behind. "You '*sick*,' too?"

I'm startled, but kind of excited to have a drinking buddy.

"Nah, I just pulled a Bob Watson."

"Who?" Donna takes the stool beside me, scoots in closer, the scent of whiskey and cigarettes overpowering the Tic Tacs. "Bob who?" She waits, and I give her nothing. "Is he handsome?" She leans in and touches my forearm. "Call him."

I shake my head. "Bob slipped away a long time ago."

She turns to the bartender. "Three whiskeys. Straight."

He sets up the glasses.

"I don't think Bob's coming back."

"Really?" Donna watches the bartender finish his pours. When he's done, she slides two glasses to me. "You can drink for him, then."

Donna is still fit—shapely—and she's got thick, sexy-long hair falling over long lashes and high cheekbones. And she's sultry, with slow and graceful movements that seem to suggest nothing really surprises her. It's a sexy scene. But of course, as for all of us firmly ensnared by the aging process, there are some things she cannot control. In my own case, they're a rapidly receding hairline, an unseemly paunch, and enlarging jowls, among quite a few other things. For Donna, it's this too-many-years-of-hard-living scene—a raspy smoker's voice accented by a high-pitched granny tenor.

Maybe that's why she's got this let's-cut-the-shit attitude.

Soon, Donna has me drunk.

"It's good to know that . . ." She looks straight ahead. ". . . there's someone else at Robards who takes control of their life." She turns and glances at my lips. "Someone who likes to have a little fun. Spice things up." She nods for the bartender to pour me another. "Life's short, sweetie. We might as well enjoy ourselves, right?"

I'm feeling dizzy—good dizzy.

"You're . . ." I steady myself. ". . . a bad girl."

She releases a hearty chain-smoking granny laugh. "You like that, sweetie?" She touches my leg just so. "Or are you just lonely? Like the rest of us? And you're thinking, life is too short to *not* have a little fun. Where's this Bob?"

I hear myself say it. "Sometimes I'm so lonely I can't stand it."

"Well." She rubs my thigh. "What a great opportunity we have right now."

"Opportunity?"

"You know." Donna squeezes. "To say 'fuck you' to the whole thing."

"The whole thing?"

"You know. The P-FIDs. The loneliness. The banality. The death."

"And how do you suggest we say 'fuck you' to the whole thing?"

Donna takes her eyes off the baseball, faces me, and begins to eye-fuck me. It's clear she's done this a few thousand times over the years. She gives me these calm brown eyes that seem to say it all without one syllable of language—how in the hell can she do that? They're like assured hands slipping under my shirt and sliding up my chest, nails trailing up and around and all over. The eyes shift and expand in a nearly magical fashion, feasting on me in a slow, methodical progression, burrowing deeper and deeper, like she's taking a tour inside of me, like she's overriding my own control circuits and having her way with me, the pleasure in her eyes.

I stare back, light-headed.

Donna lifts an eyebrow.

I offer, "I have a boner."

Donna produces a motel room card key. Slides it over. Glances at me, smiles, and returns to the baseball. "Just in case you're interested. Room 515."

A year earlier, I would have taken Donna's card and sprinted across the street, shot through the corridors, and slid to a stop at Room 515. But today, even with the boner, I find a surprising level of restraint and self-control. It's not about Donna—not her age or anything else. It's about me and what I want, and for once—finally, after all these years—I know I won't get it by going to bed with Donna. For a change. I actually can see what will happen afterward in Room 515—the hole in my chest will feel even wider.

I want something deeper. I want to feel like everything is gonna be okay.

Donna was remarkably cool when I slid the motel key back to her. We hung out and talked about her sick mom, how it's nearly more than she can handle, and we also did some more eye fucking—hell, why not? Since then, we've had this fun kind of relationship. We are supercandid with each other—flirty and open, but with an understanding.

I care about Donna.

Today in her cube, I tell her about Audrey and the challenge she issued.

Donna grins. "What do you think she wants?"

"What do you mean?"

"I mean, why now after all these years?"

I stare into space awhile, feeling like an idiot. "I don't know."

"Maybe you just enjoy it and not think too hard."

I chipper up. "I'm good at that."

"But if you *do* want to think about it, are you sure there's nothing else at play?"

"Huh?"

"I'm saying, it's odd for a girl to say no all these years—and then one day out of the blue say yes. You know what I'm saying, sweetie?"

No, I don't know what she's saying. I view Audrey's text messages today much like a dog would greet an unexpected stick of salami from his owner—the dog isn't thinking, *After a lifetime of kibble, why is this guy giving me a stick of salami?* The dog is thinking, *I will take that salami, and I will go to a dark corner where I will eat it.*

Donna says, "Is there a chance she's not the girl you think she is?"

"Such as?"

"You know." Donna suddenly sounds like she grew up in back alleys. "Maybe she's dealing on the side?"

"She's not dealing, Donna."

"Maybe she needs a runner—or a patsy? Or a place to store hot merchandise."

"Donna." I laugh. "She's the nanny to my nephew."

Donna leans back and looks away. "I'm just saying—as a woman—this sounds a bit odd."

I let out a long sigh. This isn't what I wanted to hear.

"But I'm probably wrong." She traces her gold necklace with her fingers. "And you know I hope it works out."

Her scenarios suddenly have me freaked out. I mean, what the hell do I truly know about Audrey's life outside of her role as Collin's sweet, beautiful nanny? And yeah, I guess it *is* kind of weird that—after all my chasing all these years—Audrey is finally saying yes. And why is she making me do all this hoop jumping with Collin today? If I stop and think about it, it *is* a bit odd.

•   •   •

On the way back to my cube, I drop in on some accounting friends, Diana and Keith. This week they're hosting an older gentleman from the Beijing office. His name is Huang Fu, but when he works with Americans, he uses a familiar, easy-to-pronounce western name—many Chinese do this to make their American colleagues feel comfortable. I think that's a cool example of being outwardly focused.

Huang Fu has chosen the name Tyrone.

"I'm taking Tyrone out tonight," Bobby says. "We're gonna go nuts."

Tyrone produces a giant smile and accepts a series of fist bumps.

"I can tell." I look at Keith and Diana, then at Tyrone. "This guy's an animal."

Tyrone steps toward me, hands clasped. "Where do the ladies tonight?"

"I was just chatting with a lady who'd eat you alive."

Diana says, "I'm out."

My phone buzzes, and I jolt in excitement. *Audrey?* I glance at the screen and deflate—it's simply another automated text from Robards International telling me that my recent benefits enrollment application has been rejected, this time because of "missing G-29 documentation."

Keith asks, "You in tonight, RB? Three studs on the town. We'll be unstoppable."

Diana allows a smile. "Almost unfair for the other guys."

I tell them about my hot date with Audrey, and Tyrone says, "Ooooooooooh, you lady-killer," and starts laughing, his face one enormous smile. "She have sister?"

Keith says, "Is this the nanny chick you've been working since the horse-and-buggy era?"

I place a hand on Keith's shoulder. "Energy and persistence conquer all things, my child."

"Good for you, Mr. Franklin," Diana says, pointing to my mobile. "Let's see her."

Reluctantly, I pull up Audrey's Facebook.

We huddle around my phone, and Tyrone says, "Swee lee'il mama."

Diana says, "You like the all-natural type."

Tyrone pulls back, looks at me with surprise. "This pretty girl go with *you?*" His giant, round face contorts into a tapestry of confusion. "She owe you money?"

I stare down at Audrey's pic—that sweet face and long, lustrous hair. Those eyes looking back at me. "You guys know I like her special."

Keith steps back, giving Audrey some respect. "That's cool, dude. She's a really pretty girl—"

"—that you have no business dating," Diana adds.

We all laugh, and Keith grabs my shoulder, gives it a shake.

Tyrone is studying my face. "You like her lot."

I smile and nod, looking away.

Keith says, "She's got a really pretty face, dude." He sighs to himself, turns to Tyrone, and explains, "I'm a sucker for pretty faces."

Diana adds, "Keith's a face man, Tyrone."

Tyrone's lips form an O. "Face man?"

Keith says, "You know what we're saying, Tyrone? I like women with really pretty faces. We call that being a face man."

"Ahhhhh." Tyrone smiles and nods. "Keith like face."

I turn to Diana. "I think I know what *your* fancy is?"

Diana smirks. "No you don't."

"Big, strong arms?" I ask.

She laughs.

Tyrone says, "You need large—how you say?—genitals?"

"A nice smile. It tells me everything."

This seems to bore the guys.

Keith says, "I also like butts. The big ones."

Tyrone looks at us and makes the O with his lips again. "Big bottom? Kim Kardash bottom—can snap bones and crush rock." He smiles and nods. "That good. Every person diff'rent."

Diana says, "What about you, Tyrone?"

"No no no." Tyrone looks down, shakes his head. "I don't share."

"Come on, Tyrone."

"You a big-bottom man, Tyrone?"

Tyrone frowns. "Big bottom expensive to feed. And not healthy."

"He's a titty man," Keith announces.

Tyrone swats away the idea with the back of his hand. "Okay, okay, I tell you. I like lady with nice leg."

"I love a woman with great legs," Keith says. "Sexy as hell."

We sit there nodding, until Tyrone looks to me. "What about you?"

Diana folds her arms. "Rick's a mystery, Tyrone."

Tyrone studies me, thinking. "You face man, too."

"Nah." I sit on the edge of Keith's desk, look down. "I'm a bit different."

"You no different. You man."

"You see." I shift my weight and fold my arms. "It's just that every person has their own preference." I motion to Tyrone. "You're a leg man. Keith here is a big-ass man. Diana's a smile woman. Me? . . . Well this is just me, but . . . Aw, forget it."

Diana and Keith moan and complain. "C'mon, dude."

"Is okay," Tyrone says. "I don't judge. Diversity good for planet."

I look at them. "Okay, fine. This is just me. But me?" I look at them and press my fingers to my chest. "Me? Me—Well . . . Me, I'm a vagina man."

Tyrone steps back and squints as if he's made a great discovery. He whispers to himself. "Vagina man."

"But that's just me."

Diana and Keith play it straight, not even a smile.

Tyrone scrunches his face. "Is normal here? Vagina man?"

Diana says, "There's nothing normal about Rick, Tyrone."

"I call you, Vagina Man." Tyrone releases a deep and hearty *oh-ho-ho-hoooo* belly laugh. We all laugh hard. After a while, Tyrone announces, "Vagina Man come with us tonight."

I'm already leaving the cube, waving goodbye. "Sorry, guys. Hot date tonight."

Truth is, I'm not a vagina man. I mean, of course I can appreciate a good vagina. But really, I'm a feelings man—meaning, if I'm really honest with myself in a way I'd never be in front of the guys (or anybody), what really gets me is the woman who makes me feel that special way. When I'm with Audrey, I get this very rare feeling. She calms me, and I get this sense that things are going to be okay. And this smile builds within me, from the inside to the out, and I feel like I am the coolest, luckiest dude around—just because she's paying attention to me. Just because I think she kind of likes the real me.

One time I caught Audrey watching me at a barbecue, her arms folded, her face softening. "You're a funny guy, Rick Blanco," she said. "But, you know, you don't have to be funny for *me*. It's okay." And she looked at me with the warmest smile, like she knew—like she knew exactly why it's easier for me to crack jokes and be a goof than to drop it all and stand beside the cold reality of my past and present. "But funny's good, too."

She's right; funny is good. Funny medicates and redirects.

I do like the idea of not having to cover things up—with someone I could trust. But that's the last thing Keith wants to hear when we talk about girls. Hell, it's the last thing *I'd* want to hear from another dude. I mean, I'd respect the hell out of that honest dude. And I do care about my feelings more than I do about legs and vaginas (barely). But to talk about those feelings with your office buddies, it's not gonna fly.

So I'll just be a vagina man.

·   ·   ·

I call Audrey and say, "Okay."

"Okay," she mimics.

"It's about cavemen."

"A self-examination?" she says, playing it straight.

"For Collin."

"You're going caveman for Collin?"

"I'm gonna teach him how to pull a Bob Watson."

"A what?"

"A Bob Watson—an escape—and I'm gonna take him on a Neanderthal adventure."

"Oh, Neanderthals." Her voice softens. "Collin loves those."

I think of the time Collin tried to interview a heavy-browed San Franciscan on the Marina Green. "We have a good time."

"He's been talking about putting trackers on 'specimens.'"

"I don't have trackers," I say.

"Yeah, but *he* might. Last week I found him on the phone with the U.S. Fish and Wildlife. He was asking where he could buy trackers." Audrey sighs. "Collin gets focused."

"I'll make sure no one gets tagged."

She pauses, like she's thinking about it. "A Neanderthal adventure. Not bad."

"Audrey likey?"

"Audrey do likey."

"Audrey likey enoughy to go to the Greeky tonighty?"

Long pause. "You're going to do something special, right? You know, more than the normal people watching. Something special, right?"

"Special?"

"You know, something he'll always remember."

I stare into space as my brain freezes.

"It's his last day in the States, Rick Blanco." Audrey's doing this happy whisper—kind of a sexy-fun tone. "It's gotta be special, dude. More than spying on big-boned people in Golden Gate Park."

I hear myself announce, "Of course I've got something special brewing."

"Good," she says. "Lay it on me."

Thick, scratchy silence as my mind grinds to a halt.

"Well," I say. "I'm checking on a few things."

"Uh-huh." Long pause. "Let me know once you finish the checking, and maybe I'll cancel my yoga."

"You'll love the Beat."

"I know I would. I saw them live in Santa Cruz. They're amazing."

"We'll have a good time tonight."

"*You'll* have a good time tonight, Rick Blanco. Not sure if I can join you."

I offer a playful sad voice. "I'm supposed to have a good time by myself?"

Long pause. "Something tells me you're quite good at having fun with yourself."

"Well, what about you, Audrey Diamond?"

"Me?" She seems to lower her voice. "What do you think, Rick? You think I have fun with myself?"

I'm getting a boner, and my voice turns weak. "Where are you?"

"I think we're getting a little ahead of ourselves, Rick Blanco."

"Wherever you are, I can be there in minutes."

"I'm sure you could be."

"Audrey-babe. C'mon. What are you doing to me?"

"I need you to do it special."

I think of what Donna always tells me: *Sweet girls have needs, too.*

"Rick?"

I need to buy rubbers.

"Rick?"

Or, maybe she'll let me watch. And nothing more. I can do that.

Audrey's vagina floats before my eyes.

"Rick."

The vision intensifies, and I blurt, "I've wanted you for so long."

"Rick. The Neanderthal adventure. I need you to do *that* special. Not me."

"Of course it will be special," I pant. "I swear."

"Good. Ping me when you're ready to share."

MAKE NEW PLANS

I sit at my desk thinking, *What the hell is she doing to me?*

I take a pen and a piece of scratch paper and scribble, "Something special." And I stare at the words. It's like the music of my mind (lots of organ pipes and circusy flutes) grinds to a halt. It's like Audrey knew this would be something I just naturally cannot do, not unlike telling a raccoon he can eat all the crawfish he wants . . . so long as he writes and choreographs an opera.

Does she simply enjoy teasing me?

And then it hits me, and I sit up and clap my hands.

Mama. I throw a fist into the air. *Mama knows a dude.*

A minute later, I have Mama on the phone.

"Dickie," she chirps, her squeaky old-lady voice more fragile than ever. "Finally decided to come back to me and the boys?"

"Mama-babe. You know I can't do that."

"Dickie. C'mon, honey. Don't talk that way."

"You and me? We're like fire and gas," I say. "It wouldn't be good for the boys."

Here's the thing about Mama: She is not my ex, nor did we

ever mate and have children, no matter how much she might argue otherwise. But she is a friend. And she's cool. And she's lonely—an elderly empty nester who can't seem to fully accept that her husband (perhaps a guy named Dick, perhaps not) left her with two boys some thirty or forty years ago. She insists I am her Dickie, the prick who abandoned her so long ago, but I don't think she's really that senile. I think she just likes screwing with me, teasing me for looking like Dick Rayborne, the head of Human Resources at my own Robards International—and I admit that I kinda do, unfortunately.

My resemblance to Dick is the only reason I ever met Mama.

It was about a year ago, and I had pulled a Bob Watson to embark on one of my find-me missions, meaning I was putting myself "out there," physically, in hopes that maybe the woman who will change my life—and I have to believe she's out there—would discover me. Because maybe I'm not supposed to find my girl. Maybe she's supposed to find *me*. This fantasy girl who will light me up just like Audrey does. This girl who makes me feel *that way*, who will take away all my pain. But unlike Audrey, this girl who will at least give me a shot.

So I decided to go to Menlo Park and sit near the fountain outside Cafe Borrone and Kepler's Books and Magazines. Lots of cool women there. And good energy, too, if you're into that kind of thing—and I am. So I sat there sipping a vanilla latte and enjoying the people watching, the sun and water fountain medicating my soul, a smile spreading as I looked around and enjoyed everyone talking and reading and eating. And I closed my eyes and resolved to make myself open to this woman, this woman who just *has* to be out there.

"Dickie," a frail voice warbled. "There you are, you little . . . shit."

I jolted and opened my eyes. Standing before me was a tiny old lady, oily hair pulled into a gray ponytail, her body twisted into a permanent hunch, her shoulders turned in. She looked about eighty, with long, frail limbs, a heavy midsection, and yellow polyester pants revealing a massive "camel toe." Blue-veined hands worked slowly as they reached into a giant blue fanny pack that hung off her hip. She lifted her chin to inspect me through low-riding eyeglasses, her eyes enormous behind the thick lenses.

"Sorry, sweetie." I smiled and showed her my palms, gave her my innocent eyes. "But I'm not Dickie."

"Like hell you aren't," she snapped. "I've been to the library, coverboy. I've looked you up in the trade periodicals. And I've seen your pictures in there, read the articles, saw the covers."

"Covers?"

"*Headcount*. I've read it all, mister. Both spreads. Saw all those stupid pictures of you in your mansion. Saw you in the office with your 'conployees.' We all know exactly who you are, Mr. Paperwork."

Headcount?

Conployees?

"And plus . . ." She nearly said it to herself as she gazed into space. "You think I wouldn't recognize my own husband?"

I studied her face, looking for clues. "Are you okay?" I asked gently. "Are you lost?"

"Lost?" she snapped and glared at me. She reached into her fanny pack and pulled out a folded set of papers. "I followed you all the way from that shithole you call work." She unfolded the papers and tossed them onto my lap. "Take a look at these, Dickie, and let me know if you think I am lost."

I looked down at my lap and saw my face staring back at me.

It was a color photocopy of a magazine cover—*Headcount*, its masthead slogan declaring, THE PREMIER JOURNAL FOR HUMAN RESOURCES PROFESSIONALS WORLDWIDE.

What is this? A joke?

And then I realized it was actually a photo of my workplace twin, Dick Rayborne, executive vice president of Human Resources at my very own Robards International. I gazed at the cover shot of Rayborne and sighed, defeated. God, I *did* look like him. That puffy face, those brown, narrow-set eyes. That receding hairline with the pronounced widow's peak. That same weak chin.

And yet in this photo he looked a lot happier than me. He had this sly grin—this look that seemed to say, *I've got it all figured out, bub*—as he posed for the camera, standing in the center of a large, tightly clustered group of "conployees," his deep blue, pin-striped suit popping against the backdrop of their seafoam-green jumpsuits. The headline announced, THE FATHER OF CONSOURCING. I began to finger through the photocopies and discovered yet another *Headcount* cover featuring Dick Rayborne—his eyes nearly crossed, a forced smile revealing an enormous set of teeth as he tried to seem casual in the ornate living room of his peninsula mansion. The headline proclaims, DICK RAYBORNE'S NEW TARGET: THE BLOATED U.S. SALARY.

I pulled away from the articles and looked up at her. "Who exactly are you?"

"You can call me Mama."

"And why do you have a problem with me?"

"Don't play games with me, Dickie."

I looked around the plaza. *Is this a prank?* But all I saw were dozens of people eating, reading, and chatting. No one was even looking at us. She pointed to the fanned-out pages on my lap. "Two *Headcount* covers in five months? You're their little douchebag darling."

I put my palms out again. "Listen, ma'am. My name is Rick Blanco."

She shuffled closer, panting, and took the seat beside me. "Do an old lady a favor and just read those stories."

I looked over at her, and I could see the sincerity in her tired, moist eyes. I imagined how hard it must have been for her to follow me, park, and find me here by the fountain. She looked like maybe no one really checked in on her—her clothes a little too dirty, her hair a little too oily, her breathing a little too labored. Worried eyes. And I found myself saying, "Okay. Fine. You want me to read these?"

She nodded, still panting.

"And would you like a bowl of soup or something?"

She seemed embarrassed. "That would be nice."

And so I got her a bowl of chicken soup and read the *Headcount* articles. The first cover story, from September, told how Dick Rayborne had turned his dream of "consourcing" into a very real and profitable practice at Robards. It was Dick's "trailblazing idea" to hire ex-cons, parolees, and furloughed criminals into low-paying jobs at Robards, where he stationed them in a "maximum-security" building on campus. By laying off 37 percent of the regular workforce and consolidating the survivors into "ultrahigh-density work environments," Dick was able to vacate one of the buildings on campus, equip it with new security features, and locate the incoming conployees there.

Yet as *Headcount* noted, the real genius of Dick's plan was that he rejected the widely held belief that all convicts are low-skilled, high-risk employees. It turned out a substantial number of skilled ex-cons were eager to work; the problem was, employers didn't want them because they were criminals. That made them "bargain-basement cheap," Dick told *Headcount*, "and willing to work for lower wages and fewer benefits." The result? Dick had reduced payroll costs at Robards by 22 percent, and he was planning to open a new "cell block" within the next ten months, thanks to a fresh round of layoffs targeting employees with clean records. "We've found that offshoring is problematic," Dick told *Headcount*. "The labor supply can be unreliable, because other companies can—and will—hire away your headcount with better salaries and benefits. Outsourcing is no different. But with consourcing, there is no competition for my labor. And that allows us to really squeeze our human capital for maximum ROI."

Mama seemed to enjoy watching me absorb the articles. "You're a real swell guy, Dickie. Is that why you come here? So no one will recognize you?"

"You're right, I do like it that no one will recognize me here. But not for the reasons you think."

"You don't want anyone to recognize you and pour a hot coffee over your head."

"It's a childhood-memory thing," I snapped. "I don't like people staring and pointing, like I'm some community charity case. I'm done with that shit."

Her face softened, as if she knew what I meant. "Fair enough. Keep reading."

There were so many nuggets in these stories. Like how the pocketless jumpsuits worn by conployees not only prevented workplace theft but also soothed nerves and made the ex-cons feel at home. Like how seafoam green had been proven to reduce violent anxiety better than any other color. Like how Dick branded his consourcing project the "Invitation to Cooperate Program at Robards International," which had landed him a stack of public-service awards.

"Had enough, Dickie?"

I flipped the pages and scanned quickly. There were details about typical conployee jobs—everything from customer service to the always-empty Robards International day-care facility, which Rayborne kept open for the sake of PR. There was even talk of forming a conployee strategic advisory council. "Our conployees have a vitality—a passion—for getting ahead, for finding new ways to make money," Dick told *Headcount*. "They're creative, and they're eager to meet new people, make new connections. We want to capture and funnel that energy."

Mama spooned soup into her shaky mouth, swallowed. "It's funny, though. They didn't mention the spike in 'incidents,' did they? You know, the repeated cases of 'unwanted touching' across the street at Peet's Coffee and Tea. Or the rash of car battery thefts in your parking lot. Or the employee stalking cases. Or the string of lunchtime home burglaries in the neighborhood. Or that nut who got loose on the roof with a crossbow."

I peeked at the second *Headcount* story. It was about Dick "attacking" U.S. salaries with "the predatory zeal of a wolf." I didn't need to read any more; I had the idea.

Anyways, it's taken a while, but Mama has accepted that I am not Dick Rayborne—even though she still calls me Dick. That's okay with me. I really think Mama's just bored and feisty, and definitely a little lonely. So every few weeks I meet her for lunch at Cafe Borrone, and we'll hang out. And we'll chat about the news—stories of trapped miners and rogue congressmen and rich people who "screw the little guy." Sometimes she tells me how her sons never call or visit, that her house is "too empty and dead." And she cries. I'll put an arm around her and ask, "So tell me about this CEO who was taped kicking a dog." And she'll stop, sniffle, and say, "Oh, this guy's a class-A puss bucket. Listen to this."

Today, on the phone with Mama, I ask for a favor.

"I'm an old lady, Dickie. Old ladies don't do favors; they *receive* favors."

"It's about Audrey—the one I've told you about."

"That little tramp you've been chasing right under my nose?"

"Exactly. Well, she finally said yes."

"To a date? Or a fuck session?" She says it so sweetly. "I knew she was a tramp."

"So here's the thing, Mama. I need to do something special for my nephew—and I need to do it today—or the date with Audrey is off."

Mama pauses. "She's a kinky little game player, isn't she?"

"I don't know what you're talking about."

"You like that, Dickie? Kinky mind games with sweet-looking tramps? You filthy animal."

I look away and think about it. "Maybe. But that's not why I'm telling you this."

"How could I help you with a game-playing home wrecker?" She adopts this syrupy old-lady voice. "I'm just a sweet little grandma."

I tell Mama about Audrey's challenge, and my idea to take Collin on a Neanderthal adventure.

"What the fuck is a Neanderthal adventure?" Mama says. "God, you're an odd bird."

"It's this thing we do. The kid is eight, Mama. Enormous imagination."

"I don't know anything about Neanderthals," Mama says.

"But you can introduce me to someone who does."

Long pause. "My friend at Stanford?"

"I think you said he's in the anthropology department."

"Paleoanthropology," she snaps. "And it's a 'she.' You're not one for details, are you, Dickie?"

"The one who studies prehistoric humans. The one you met on jury duty?"

"Sabine?" she says. "Sabine Rorgstardt?" She laughs. "One

of the world's top experts on cavemen? You think I'm going to introduce you to Sabine Rorgstardt so she can help you dry hump some home wrecker behind my back?"

"It's not like that, Mama. You know I like this girl." I stop myself, decide to take another tack. "Plus, you know we had our run. You know it wouldn't be good for the kids if we lived under the same roof again. Acrimony. Instability. Projectiles. You and me? The passions run too deep, the emotions are too raw."

She chuckles, enjoying the role playing.

"And let's face it, Mama. You deserve more than anything I could ever give you."

Now she's laughing. "Okay, okay."

"You're gonna help me?"

"You want me to introduce you to Sabine Rorgstardt?"

"Please, Mama."

"You want her to meet your runt nephew?"

"Exactly, Mama. That's it. But it needs to happen today. You have her phone number?"

"Of course I have her phone number. She takes me food shopping."

"And you can introduce us today?"

"Yes, yes." She sighs. "God, you're needy."

I'm gushing. "Thank you, Mama. I can't tell you how much I appreciate this."

"Of course, of course." Mama adopts this breezy tone. "And are you ready to fight the system?"

"Okay, time's of the essence here, Mama. How do we do this?"

There's a long pause. "We do this by you doing what I say."

"Whatever you say, baby."

"And that starts with you meeting me in the bushes located between—now, listen to me—the north and south parking lots. You understand me?"

I feel my brows crinkle. "Bushes?"

"Do you understand English? I want you to meet me inside the large stand of bushes that separates the north and south parking lots of Robards International."

"I don't—"

"Dickie, do you want this girl?"

"Audrey?" I stammer. "Yes, I want her."

"How bad do you want her?"

I think of cuddling with Audrey. "Really very badly."

"Do you want to impress her with a caveman adventure for the ages?"

"Yes, that's it."

"So you can take her out and be a . . ." Her voice slips to a geriatric purr. ". . . filthy animal with her?"

I like the way Audrey makes me feel, and I want her in a big, meaningful relationship way. But now that Mama mentions it, yes, I also would like to be a filthy animal with Audrey. Without thinking, my throat releases a telling moan of want.

"Is she gonna let you take her, Dickie? Tonight? Finally?"

"I don't—"

"You want that?"

"*Yes*," I yell. "*Yes*." I gather myself, take a deep breath. "I want her so bad."

"Then meet me in those bushes in thirty minutes."

GO ON AN ADVENTURE

As I've said, the trick to a good meeting ditch is to let people think you're coming back. Those pencils, those pads of paper, and even that "body double" cell phone left behind with no battery or SIM card? Used judiciously, these props create an important sense of security, a false belief—an assumption—that I actually plan to return to that godforsaken conference room. Likewise, when it comes to ditching the entire workplace—the building, the campus . . . hell, the city—the same principle applies. In fact, it's more critical than ever.

And so, at my desk, I click through my Bob Watson props . . .

Disable screen saver on my PC? Check. . . . Flip on my brass reading lamp? Check. . . . Under said lamp, place large stack of reports and sketched-out diagrams featuring the latest Robards acronyms? Check. . . . Atop said stack of papers, place my dime-store reading glasses? Check. . . . Throw in a writing pen? Check. . . . Remove keys and wallet from the briefcase that is placed prominently atop my desk, and pocket said items? Check. . . . Grab a notebook and stride through the office like I'm

late for a meeting while I think about my imminent breakout?
Oh, yeah, baby.

* * *

I'm so excited, I nearly fly down the stairwell.

The plan is clicking into place. I'll meet Mama in the
bushes, get the introduction to the Stanford expert, go pull the
kid out of school via the Bob Watston methodology, take the kid
to Stanford, and geek out on Neanderthals for a bit. Maybe do
some Neanderthal searches. Hang out. Drop the kid off at my
sister's. Do some goodbye hugs. Leave with Audrey for the Greek
Theatre and the English Beat. Hang out at the Beat show with
a supercool chick. Possibly snake my tongue down her throat, if
allowed.

The only problem? Traffic to the concert will be a nightmare.

I burst through the stairwell door and onto the south-end
parking lot, the white sun washing over me in its instant warmth,
a light breeze blowing through my hair. I stop a second, take
in a deep breath. *Hell, yes. Freedom.* I gaze at the expanse of
enormous, tall bushes over there, that dense stretch of wilderness
separating the north and south lots. *Why in the hell does Mama
want to meet me inside those bushes?* From this distance, a white
mist seems to swirl above the foliage, reminding me of a jungle
in the morning sun. I find myself imagining that I'm an explorer
preparing to enter its swampy innards, not sure what I'll encoun-
ter, not sure if I'll ever return.

I look for spies and head for the bushes, cutting through the
parked cars. Halfway through, I decide to call my sister and let
her know I'd like to pull Collin out of school.

She sounds annoyed. "What are you talking about?"

"You know," I say, "just some hooky on his last day in the country."

"He's on a field trip this morning. He's not even there."

Oh no. I can practically see Audrey giving me a sad finger-wave goodbye.

"Well, what about the afternoon?"

"The afternoon?" She releases an annoyed sigh. "He has Mandarin in the afternoon."

I think of Sabine Rorgstardt. "Sure, but it's his last—"

"It's stepping-stones, Rick. Stepping-stones to getting into a *good* school. I know you may not fully appreciate this, but a *good* school is so important in today's world."

I wish I could reply, *What about helping your brother land a date with a good woman?* But I don't want Ana to know about me and Audrey—wouldn't be cool to Audrey. So instead, I say, "I thought you said you got Collin into a great school in Buenos Aires."

She laughs, then raises her voice. "I'm talking about college, Rick. The road to a *good* college starts now."

"Aren't there like tons of good schools out there?"

"A private institution. You know, Stanford. Harvard. Princeton."

My sister and I. What happened to us? What happened to the brother and sister who, as kids, wasted long summer afternoons crank-calling local businesses, watching TV, reading novels, and wandering the neighborhood looking for things to do? What happened to the teenage siblings who worked hard, who talked about right and wrong and family, the things that really mattered? What became of the kids who were proud to get into college, who worked hard and fought tooth and nail for internships and first jobs with no daddies or uncles pulling strings? What happened to the brother and sister who, as young adults, would share a few quiet laughs about the self-important snobs we'd see running around town with their kids? What happened to the sister and brother who'd look at each other and wonder, *Are these children getting what they need?*

What happened was, the brother took a job at Robards International and the sister got into a grad school, at a *good* private school Back East. What happened was, the brother got lost in bottom-tier data collection projects, and the sister married Samson James Barnard IV (Stanford MBA, class of '01), and Ana Theresa Blanco became Ana Barnard, and gave birth to a kid they named Collin James Barnard. What happened was, the sister was steadily converted into a subculture that insists all aspects of one's life must be spectacular, at all times. A subculture that somehow thinks that out of the 2,700 universities in the country, only about 20 are *good*. What happened was, the sister he loves so dearly calls only when she wants something.

I miss Ana Theresa Blanco.

Ana Barnard says, "After Mandarin, he has SAT Prep."

I'm still standing beside the wall of bushes, keeping an eye out for spies. "What if I took him *after* the Mandarin and the SAT Prep?"

She offers a defeated sigh. "I guess."

"From what I understand, he doesn't take his SAT for another nine or ten years. I'm sure he can afford to miss a prep session."

Silence again, and then, "Okay. Take him, and have a blast, okay? Just make sure he says goodbye to all the teachers and the principal's office. And you need to find out when he returns from the field trip—I think it's noon. Just call the school.

"He's got his body-language training today, but that's fast.

You'll be in and out. So if you want to bring him home after dinner, I think that will be fine. Just let me know."

"Of course."

Sympathy in her voice. "Because I want to be able to fully trust you, okay?"

"Of course."

She pauses again and sighs that way I've known all my life—a brief trace of my real sister. "Samson and I want to feel we can *truly* trust you."

"Yeah, cool. No worries. I should run."

"Because, Samson and I want to tell you something."

"Oh yeah?" I prepare for incoming yuppie insanity. "News?"

"We've been thinking . . ."

From behind, a door clicks. I spin around, see a cluster of employees leaving the building. *Shit, I can't be seen standing here like this.* I decide to push into the wall of bushes and begin my trek through the wilds of Robards, in search of Mama. In an instant, it feels like I've been transported to another dimension— indeed, in the wilds of Robards, with a thick canopy blocking the sun and a dense undergrowth requiring a slow, difficult passage. I smile to myself, shaking my head at the realization that I am stumbling through a mess of bushes, leaves, and twigs—in my office clothes—following the peculiar instructions of an oddball granny, all so I might have a chance with a woman.

It's moments like this when you understand the hole in your heart.

"Yeah?" I push forward, crunching dead leaves and cracking fallen branches. "You guys've been thinking?"

"Well, first, I just want to let you know that *we* know how much Collin cares about you. So Samson and I—we've been talking."

Incoming . . . Incoming . . . Yuppie insanity incoming.

"And we've got an idea."

Where in the hell is Mama?

"And we would like to make an offer. It's kind of coming out of left field, I acknowledge, but we have a problem with Kaarlo."

"Kaarlo?"

"You know," Ana snaps. "The house sitter?"

Oh, that's right. Kaarlo the high-end Swedish house sitter. Samson James Barnard IV and my sister don't want (or need) to sell their gorgeous, custom-made Woodside mansion, and they certainly don't want (or need) to rent it out to anyone. Not after all the refinements they've made to the house—the "spiritually cleansed" Tibetan tile flooring, the granite kitchen sink carved by Vikings circa A.D. 780, the cabinets made from ancient wood soaked in llama bile for thirty days and sanded to perfection by happy, minimalist elders in Bolivia. So they'd found Kaarlo the high-end Swedish house sitter, who's lived in the homes of some of the most powerful Silicon Valley titans.

"Kaarlo's backed out," Ana says. "He's going to house-sit for Owen Wilson on the North Shore. It's a wonderful opportunity for Kaarlo, and I can't say I blame him."

"North Shore?"

"Maui." She waits for me to be impressed. "So, we're in a pickle."

"Okay."

"We essentially need a house sitter. You know, someone who can live here, take care of things, make sure the yard staff won't slack off. Do a little cleaning and maintenance."

"Kaarlo doesn't have any friends?"

"No one we can trust." She sighs. "So Samson and I were thinking maybe you'd be interested."

I stop in my tracks.

"You could live there. You know, for the next two years."

My head is light. My eyelids flutter.

After a long pause, Ana offers, "Did I mention we'd throw in a monthly stipend for food and living expenses? Samson just wants to be sure nothing happens to the house."

My mouth opens, but nothing comes out.

"So, depending on what you want to do, I was thinking you could rent out your condo. And between the free housing at our place, the stipend, and your rental income from the condo, you probably could quit your job, take a few years off."

I feel faint.

"Didn't you want to write that book on how to pull a Bob what's-his-name?"

My face goes numb as I think of quitting Robards International, of telling Janice from Finance I am done with her meetings. I can nearly see myself in my sister's backyard, in the shade, hunting and pecking away on what will become *the* only how-to book on ditching useless meetings.

"Rick?"

I think of hanging out with Audrey in that house, of hosting poker with the guys in that house, of lazing on the sofa during a six-hour Judd Apatow movie marathon in that house, of throwing margarita parties in that house. Of making dinner naked in that house—for days and days.

"Rick?"

I snap out of it, shake my face. "I'll do it."

A hint of glee in her voice. "And there's just one other thing. A small thing, really."

My head's in the stars. "Okay."

"Samson and I are planning a trip this summer."

"Okay."

"It's been a crazy year, and we just need to recharge, you know?"

Staring into space. "Uh-huh."

"So we are planning to take five weeks in Greece this summer. Samson has his sabbatical this year, and—"

"A recharge?" I say, snapping out of it. "Five weeks?"

"Exactly. Maybe six weeks, we haven't finalized things. But the point is, this is really just for Samson and me. You know? We just really need to unplug, recharge, spend some Ana and Samson time."

For six weeks? I snap out of it. What planet do they live on? What kind of person has my sister become that she actually *desires* to spend six weeks alone with Samson James Barnard IV, who might be the most out-of-touch and boring person I know? Ana Theresa Blanco avoided bores at all costs.

"So we're wondering if Collin could stay with you until we return. Maybe Samson and I can plan a layover at SFO on the way back, and just pick him up."

I'm sure Audrey would totally get off seeing me as a devoted, cool uncle, and therefore it would be only a matter of time until she and I are in bed, and she's laughing, and her toes are in my mouth, and she's saying, *Let me take the kid for a few days.*

After a while, my sister says, "Rick?"

I hear myself mumble, "Just trying to process all this."

More movement in the bushes, but I don't care. My mind is scrambling, thinking of how I'll quit. My god, how I've wanted to quit.

Is this really happening?

"Rick?" Her voice is meek and slow, just like it always was when we were kids and she had to fess up to something. "I have to admit. I'm a little nervous about this."

"What? You mean, being away from Collin so long?"

"No." She sounds so serious. "The house."

"What do you mean, you're worried about the house?"

"I need to be able to trust you with it. You know? Nothing like that time you had those Raiders fans at your condo."

Ana Theresa Blanco was a Raiders fan.

Ana Barnard does Pilates.

"Yeah, no Raider parties," I say. "I'll honor whatever rules you want."

Really slowly, she says, "I just need to be able to trust you—to keep things secure. And I'm not talking about what you think I'm talking about."

I don't even want to think about *that*, that thing I did that changed our lives. It hurts too much to think about *that*. I blink my eyes and shake my face.

"This is all about the house. Okay? And trust."

"I understand."

I stand there and gaze into space, a smile forming. I can't believe this is happening. I am going to quit Robards International and live an easy life in a $5 million Woodside mansion, where I will pen an antimeeting manifesto for the ages.

"Rick?"

I snap out of it. "Yep, I'm here."

"In fact, maybe you could come over tonight, and we could talk about all of this. I'm sure that would do it for me."

My vision is a blur now. Still smiling. "Sure."

"In fact, if you are going to go take Collin out of school—*after* the SAT Prep . . ."

"Of course. After the SAT Prep."

". . . maybe we could talk about the plan."

"That works. Say, six P.M.?"

"Perfect."

I am practically singing. "Okay then."

"Rick?"

"Yeah?"

"I love you."

That's always great to hear.

"I love you, too, Ana."

More movement in the bushes. *Mama?* Gingerly, I head in that direction, pushing through more shrubs. "Listen, we'll discuss it tonight. Don't worry, I'll keep the house totally safe, and I'll follow your rules." Beneath the thick carpet of dried leaves, my foot slips under a rope or a cord, and I nearly fall on my face.

"Rick?"

I stand up and run my foot through the leaves, looking for the obstruction. Finally I reach down and pull up an orange extension cord—a recently bought extension cord feeding straight into that cluster of bushes over there.

What the . . . ?

"Rick, where are you?"

I follow the extension cord. "Never mind that. I'll bring Collin home tonight by six, and then you and I will put this issue to bed, to your liking. But I can't stick around too long tonight—hot date."

"Okay."

"And, Ana?"

"Yeah?"

"I'm just so—I mean, I guess I just—"

"It's okay. I know."

Which is when I push through another thicket and stumble out the other end, crashing into a sea of empty beer cans so deep I can barely feel the ground.

Someone's talking.

Daffy Duck?

A moment later, I'm sitting upright in the sea of empties. And I'm speechless.

It's so much to take in. There's the set of old mattresses surrounded by thousands of empties. There's the fat and juicy tri-tip roasting on a Weber grill. There's the homemade contraption directly above the grill—three small electric fans dispersing smoke in a variety of directions. And in the middle, placed atop a stack of milk crates, is a small television flashing remarkably sharp images of Bugs Bunny and Daffy Duck enjoying an easy conversation over Chinese takeout.

What the . . .

From under the cans, a tinny voice calls out. "Rick?"

Shit. Ana. I squint down at the cans, listening for my phone. "Rick?"

I turn right and slip my hand under the cans, feeling for my phone. And somehow, I find it. To limit the noise, I pull it out slowly. It's silent here, except for Bugs and Daffy. "Hey there," I say into the phone, like nothing's happened.

"Rick, you okay?"

"I'm fine, I'm fine."

"Where are you?"

I gaze into the air, forcing a smile. "Just the grocery store."

"That didn't sound like—"

"Just a little collision with a stack of lard jars." I force an annoyed sigh. "I've got a few cracked jars here." Another annoyed sigh. "There's lard everywhere."

"Lard jars? What kind of grocery store—"

"Listen, I should find a clerk to clean this up."

She's laughing. "Watch where you're going. See you this evening."

Too late for that, I think, as a bald, pudgy man emerges from the bushes, shooting through the empties with unsettling speed. I don't realize he's wielding barbecue prongs until he's pressing them into my neck.

Which is when I hear a series of clicks.

From somewhere unseen, Mama adopts a syrupy tone. "That's a good boy," she drawls. "You really have learned your clicks, haven't you, Ernie?"

Ernie produces a happy noise, presses the prongs deeper into my neck, and I stiffen and grimace. Determined not to move my head, I dart my eyes up to him and do my best ventriloquist impersonation. "Easy, fella. I'm not a tri-tip."

From the bushes, three metallic clicks.

He steps back and withdraws his prongs. And I finally take a breath.

Mama's shaky voice is getting closer. "What a good boy you are." Four more clicks. "Come and get your goodie, Ernie."

I turn around, and there's Mama—her body twisted into that permanent hunch, her veined hands slowly dipping into her giant fanny pack and reemerging with some type of jerky. I realize I'm just sitting there, frozen in disbelief.

"Mama, I have to say—this is a whole new level of crazy for you."

Slowly, she looks up and inspects me through her glasses, her eyes enormous. "Do I know you?"

I laugh. "Mama, c'mon. No games today. I'm here, just like you asked."

"Games?" Fists on her hips, mouth twisted in old-lady aggression. "Aren't *you* the king of games, Dickie? Paperwork games?"

I laugh. "Mama. C'mon. No role playing today. I've got way too much to—"

"And now here you are: Dick Rayborne, snooping in on my boys. Trampling through the Playroom."

"The caveman lady. Sabine Rorg-something. C'mon, Mama."

She winks and shakes head. "You really are like a pig, aren't you, Dickie? An insatiable appetite. Want want want. Take take take." She scowls at me. "Haven't you taken enough, Mr. Paperwork?"

"Mama, c'mon. What are we doing here?"

Mama reaches into her fanny pack and produces three tight clicks; they're different from the ones before, and Ernie charges across "the Playroom," sending cans everywhere, an eyebrow arched. I recoil and holler, and he slides to a stop in front of Mama. She reaches into her pack and pulls out a mini bottle of Jack Daniel's, the kind they sell on airplanes. Ernie snatches the bottle, twists off the cap, and drains it, tossing the new empty over his shoulder.

It's like she's talking to a tired old dog—slow and low. "That's my Ernie. It took a while to learn your clicks, but you stuck with it, and now look at you, earning all kinds of goodies from Mama." Ernie waits for more, but she puts a hand out as if to say, *Not yet.* Then she produces three more clicks.

"Cujo," she squeaks. "Come see Mama."

Nothing.

Ernie moans for another bottle.

She cocks her head, listening. "Cujo? Don't you worry about this mister here. Mama's gonna make sure. Mama's gonna make sure Dickie doesn't get you fired."

That gets me. I look at Ernie and realize he's wearing a seafoam-green jumpsuit, the requisite uniform for a certain type of employee at Robards International. I give Ernie another look, meet his crooked gaze—that eyebrow still arched, that little mouth turning crooked, contorting his enormous jowls as he begs for another mini. And I feel a chill.

Conployee.

"Cuuuuuuu-jo. Mama's gonna make sure Dickie plays nice."

"I'm happy to meet your friends, Mama. But I need to get my nephew. And I need that introduction to the caveman professor. You promised."

"Cuuuuuuu-jooo?"

Nothing.

She pokes into her fanny pack and pulls out a third clicker—this one's orange—and produces three wooden clicks. Ernie squeals and tiny-steps closer. She reaches into her fanny pack and produces another airline bottle—this time, Wild Turkey—and a thick, marbled cube of cured meat. Pork belly? Ernie snatches them out of her shaky hands, makes a happy noise, and plunks down onto his mattress.

"Cujo?"

To the left, a heap of leaves and twigs eases up from the earth, and I notice the large manhole underneath it. I jolt and step back as an enormous, bald-shaven man emerges, the tattoos on his scalp and neck contrasting boldly against his seafoam jumpsuit, a black beard coming to a point near his collarbones, his dark brown eyes watching me closely. He offers an uneasy smile.

"That's my boy," Mama says, stretching the words. "Come get your goodies."

Cujo approaches with caution, watching me closely—*my lord, he's huge*. He takes a bottle and a slice of pork belly, still watching me, ready to bolt.

"Don't you worry about Dickie here. Mama's gonna take care of this."

"Dude." I pull out my wallet. "I'm not Dick Rayborne. Read my driver's license."

She's shaking her head, her eyes closed. "Cujo?"

His voice is thick, deep, and wet. "Yes, Mama?"

"Do you recognize this man?"

"I suppose I do, Mama."

"And who is he?"

"Well, Mama . . ." Cujo glances at me, looks at Mama. "You're looking at the Warden."

"The Warden?"

"It's what we call him."

"Rayborne?" Mama says. "Dickie Raynorne? Your VP of HR? The king of paperwork? You call him the Warden?"

"Yes, Mama."

I'm pleading now. "Mama, c'mon. Just tell me what you want."

"Cujo?"

"Yes?"

"You seem frightened. Is there anything you want to tell Mama?"

Cujo looks at me, nods. "It's just . . ."

"It's okay, sweetie. You can tell me."

"It's just that the Warden—I mean, Mr. Rayborne. Well. It's just that we're out here, and . . . well . . . we're supposed to be . . ." He nods toward the campus. ". . . in there."

We watch as Ernie rises from his mattress, his eyes on the Looney Tunes, and stabs the tri-tip with his prongs, the meat sizzling on the grill.

"Don't worry about that, honey." She turns to me, thins her eyes. "Mama's gonna take care of Dickie here."

"Mama, I can't get fired for bad behavior. If I get pinched, my parole officer will find out, and I'll be toast. Back to house arrest." He offers some very sad eyes. "Or maybe even back to San Quentin."

I clasp my hands for emphasis. "Guys, I promise. I'm not Dick Rayborne, and even if I were him, I wouldn't rat on you." I look at Cujo, searching for a trace of reason, and offer my wallet. "Dude, look at the driver's license."

Cujo stiffens, backs up. God, he's massive—six-foot-five,

maybe, and close to three hundred pounds, with dark, curly hair sprouting out from his collar and cuffs. He offers a polite smile. "Sorry, Warden, but I'm not getting my prints on your wallet." He lumbers back to the manhole, parting the sea of empties, and squeezes in. He turns and looks up at me, his eyes hopeful. "We'll just go back to work. C'mon, Ernie. We'll go back the way we came, right back up this old pipe—it's nice and dry, so our threads never get tarnished, so no need to worry about damage to company property. Don't worry about a thing, Mr. Rayborne. C'mon, Ernie."

Mama snaps, "Boys, don't go anywhere. You might need to help your Mama today."

I look at Cujo, then at Ernie. "She's your mom?"

Cujo's frown turns into a grin. "That ain't our mom, dude." His face softens as he looks at Mama. "We were just chillin' here one day—taking a break, just for a few minutes, Warden, I swear—and Mama here just walked in on us."

Mama smiles at the memory. "I'd come to spy on this bird," she says and jerks her thumb at me.

"And I guess she just took a liking to us."

"Because it was clear," she says to me. "These boys lacked the kind of parental guidance and love that sets a man on his way for the rest of his life."

Cujo meets my eye and smiles. "Empty nester," he whispers and chuckles. "It's awesome."

Mama puffs. "And I was appalled, Dick. I was appalled at what they told me. This whole operation you created. A really rotten thing, all around."

"Mama, please. I mean, fine—I'll be Dick. But this is my last chance with Audrey."

She waves me off. "I bet your mother would be ashamed if she knew what you're up to."

That feels like a punch in the gut, and I snap, "Don't mention my mother."

Her face softens, and she mutters, "Fair enough."

My cell rings, giving all of us a jolt. I pull it out of my pocket: Audrey.

"Don't you dare answer that phone. We have work to do."

"No, it's Audrey. The girl."

"The girl?" She looks to Ernie. "Get me that phone."

Ernie rushes over, presses the prongs into my neck, and snatches the phone.

"Let me see that."

"Please don't."

He hands it to her, and she clicks the clicker, awarding him another mini of Wild Turkey.

"Please."

She pokes at the screen and puts it to her ear. Pulls it away, frowns at it, and puts it back to her ear. "Hello?"

I wave my hands and whisper-yell. "Don't say anything."

She scrunches her face and looks into space, listening. "Who's this?"

I bend over, wincing. "Please. I might be able to quit and write—"

"Yes. Well, I'm having a few words with your secret lover. . . . Yes, that's right."

"Mama, please."

"Me? . . . I'm his wife, you tramp. . . . What? Yes, his wife. Well, ex-wife, I guess. And I'm standing here with our two boys. I'm sure he didn't tell you about them, either. Did he?"

I reach for the phone, and the prongs ease deeper into my throat.

"And I wonder if you have any idea what your secret boyfriend does here at Robards International. . . . What? . . . Because I think you might be shocked to hear what he's doing to these kids, including my two boys. . . . Yes, well, I'm afraid he can't come to the phone right now. We're trying to resolve some of his behavior issues. . . . Who? . . . What? . . . Collin? . . . I don't know who that is. Sounds like one of your lover's cronies. . . . And I am afraid we have to go. . . . What? . . . No. I said he needs to pay back his debt to society, and he needs to make things right. How do you hang these things up?"

I feel nausea setting in. I take a knee in the empties.

• • •

Mama is standing over me, her camel toe way too close, but I don't have the energy to care. In one brief phone call, she's managed to jeopardize my best girl opportunity in years—the promise of finally dating the woman who turns my insides to goo, who gives me an instant boner, who makes me feel like a new person. How many times does a guy meet a woman like that? How many times does a woman like that actually agree to date a guy like me? Hell, maybe that was enough right there—that call. Maybe Audrey now thinks I'm a freak with an even freakier ex. Is it possible she might actually believe I have kids? After all these years of knowing me and my family, she couldn't possibly think I have an ex and kids. But could Audrey call my sister and tell her about my freaky friend, and could that possibly jeopardize my opportunity to house-sit and quit my job?

Okay, I'm overthinking this.

Mama says, "You want your phone back?"

We look over to the mattresses, where Cujo is splayed out talking into the phone. I can't hear everything, but he's saying things like "Do you like to party?"

I bury my face in my hands.

"If you want that telephone back," she says. "If you ever want to introduce your nephew to Sabine Rorgstardt, you need to do some things for me."

"Can't we do this tomorrow?"

Mama looks at me, then at Cujo and Ernie. "Do you want your telephone?"

I nod.

"Do you want me to help you with my friend the caveman lady?"

"Please."

"Then here's what you're gonna do." She looks at me, crosses her arms. "We're gonna take the wagon."

I laugh. "Fine. I don't want those guys in my car."

"And you're gonna take me and the boys on that caveman adventure of yours. You're gonna give them the experiences they never had. In fact, we're gonna act as a family—family wagon, family games, all of that—'cause that's obviously something you forgot about, something you don't seem to care about at Robards International."

Naturally, my brain scans through a litany of Bob Watson moves.

Cue: "Validate" and "Redirect."

I see my hand take Mama by the wrist. I look her in the eye and hold my gaze. "You know, you're right. I haven't done enough for these boys."

Mama huffs. "Darn straight you haven't."

I nod toward the conployees. "The boys are so impressionable right now. It just makes me want to do this right for them."

She squints at me, assessing.

"So I'm thinking this adventure will fail if we do something last-second, like today." I give her wrist a gentle squeeze. "I mean, we want to make a statement for these boys."

She thinks about it, cocks her head in concession. "We do."

"Here's what we're gonna do," I say. "I really think we should take the boys to the library—I mean, like, now—and research adventure options for next week. Early next week." I pause, as if I'm running through the logic. "So I think we divide and conquer today. You and the boys go to the library, and I'll take the runt to meet the Sabine lady."

She bites her lip, looks down. "We *could* get the boys engaged that way," she mumbles, more to herself. "They've got a great library not too far from here. Plus, I do need to look up some stuff on that oil executive who's wasting water."

My whole body eases.

"Boys," she shouts into the air. "We're going to the library."

Yes.

"Wait a minute. Dammit." She turns back to me. "I can't take the boys to the library."

"What?" I stiffen. "Of course you can."

"Don't you remember? I almost forgot myself. I have a shitload of honey-dos for you."

"Honey-dos?"

"Yes. I need your help. God, I forget everything these days."

"Mama. Please."

She points at me. "You want the prongs?"

"Come on."

"Honey-do number one . . ." She thinks about it, bites her lip. ". . . you're gonna break into a house with us. God, how could have I forgot?"

"Mama, the library."

"And not just any house."

Wait. . . . House?

"Because you need to show these boys some fun." She pauses, puffs out her cheeks. "And you need to do something else."

My cell rings, and Cujo looks at the screen. "Hey, dude, it's your secret lover again. I think she likes me."

I reach out to him, even though he's twenty feet away. "Don't answer that."

He's looking at the screen. "Keeps talking about some runt named Collin."

"Please," I yell.

"Maybe she'll change her mind . . ." Still looking at the phone, lost in his thoughts. ". . . if we did a little sexting . . ." More thinking. ". . . and ol' Cujo showed her what he's packing." He looks at me, his eyes serious. "This thing take good close-ups, bro?"

· · ·

We're in Mama's '76 metallic-blue Cadillac Fleetwood station wagon, parked in front of a nondescript tract house somewhere in Sunnyvale. Mama and I are in the front arguing. In the back, Cujo and Ernie are huddling over my phone, giggling at the dick pics they've sent Audrey.

Cujo tells me, "Your girl keeps asking, 'Is this you?' and I keep saying, 'Don't you recognize me?'"

As if I needed more problems.

Mama seems to be elsewhere—in a different dimension, it seems, or maybe even at another time in her life. If this is indeed some game she's playing—be it whimsical role playing or something else—she certainly *is* convincing. Her tone is softer, happier, and it's like she's known me for decades. "Listen, we're gonna have some family time if it kills you."

"I really—"

"And you're gonna learn a few things." She looks away at a thought, and her lip starts to quiver. "Because, honey, you've lost your way."

"You're never gonna help me with the Neanderthal expert, are you?"

"Oh, Dick." She looks down, shakes her head. "You really *have* lost your way. You're so focused on bringing home the bacon that you don't even . . ." She nods toward the backseat, where Cujo and Ernie fight over my phone, landing hard swats on each other's hands. ". . . you don't even know your own kids."

From the backseat, a long, wet fart—and then cackles.

"And yes, I will help you with my friend Sabine Rorgstardt. Very soon."

"I'm gonna leave very soon."

"I'll send Cujo after you."

My voice cracks. "Why are you doing this?"

"Oh, honey." She shakes her head, disappointed. "Don't you understand? These boys here, they're *our* boys." She pauses, adopts a sweet tone. "Our little ones."

Cujo releases a deep giggle.

"Listen, Mama. I don't have anyone." My throat tightens. "Don't you understand what I'm saying about this girl? I could see myself with her. For a long time."

"We need to get back to the way we were," Mama says. "The way things were."

"Listen, I'm just not gonna miss this opportunity."

"I've got my helper boys," Mama says. "My strong, healthy helper boys who do whatever I need."

"Tell them to give me my phone back."

She reaches into her fanny pack and produces three quick clicks. The slapping and cackling stop, and Cujo says, "Yes, Mama?"

She closes her eyes and cocks her head. "I need a favor."

"Sure, Mama."

"I need my helper boys to get into that house and open the front door."

Ernie squeals with glee.

She turns and gives them the serious eyes. "Now, you boys listen to me."

They look back, hopeful.

"No taking," she snaps. "You hear me?"

They whine and moan.

"You be good boys, and Mama will have a little something for you."

They explode out of the car.

• • •

Cujo and Ernie have disappeared down one side of the house.

Mama says, "It's always something with you. Late nights at the office. Weekends at the office. Nights out with the guys. Projects in the garage."

And I realize I could just leave. Just step out of this car and start walking. With Cujo and Ernie breaking into the house, they couldn't catch me even if Mama used her clicker. Hell, I could just find a gas station or something, make a few calls on a pay phone, and clear things up with Audrey and ask her to get Collin for me.

"Well, anyways," Mama says, "back to your honey-dos."

I could report my phone as stolen, have AT&T stop the service.

"And honey-do number one is, you're gonna figure out what's going on inside that house there."

I glance at the house, a very modest rancher painted light yellow with white trim. The front door is now open, and through the threshold we can see Ernie standing in the narrow entryway, grinning crookedly, barbecue prongs at his side.

"I'm not going in there."

"You are such a wuss," Mama says. "What if I told you I know the owners? They're friends."

"Really?"

She's looking at me, nodding slowly.

"I do this, and you'll have the boys give back my phone so I can call someone about my nephew?"

Mama nods.

"And you'll connect me to your Neanderthal expert?"

She looks away, nods.

"You promise?"

"Yes, promise," she snaps. "Think about someone other than yourself for a change, and join me in that house."

My heart begins to thump. "That's breaking and entering."

"The boys did the breaking. You'll just be entering. Plus, they're friends."

I look at her, then at the house, wondering what's in there. And then, *Why are we here?* My brain does what it's been trained to do.

Cue: "Distract"

"Look," I shout and point to a cross street. "A police car. We have to leave."

Mama doesn't even look. "That was pathetic, Dickie." She shows me her clicker, strokes it. "And if you try ditching me, you won't get so far as a block."

I look at her, and then at the house. "This really does have something to do with Robards International?"

"Of course." She's nearly yelling. "Look beyond yourself, Dick. Seize this moment to do something meaningful, for one day in your life. For just twenty minutes."

"This isn't some random address?"

"No," she yells. "Now come on, and start living."

And like an out-of-body experience, I hear myself saying, "Okay, fine."

BREAK A FEW RULES ALONG THE WAY

The summer before third grade, my sister and I joined forces for a project of the ages—a fort that would leave the other kids speechless.

We moved earth and scavenged wood. We sawed and hammered. We paused and schemed. In all, we worked dutifully for more than two weeks, forgoing our normal summer routines (fighting over TV channels, finding sly new ways to tell on each other, and playing with our own friends) as we relished in a rare and wonderful moment in our relationship, the outside world suddenly seeming distant and muted in the midst of our unprecedented creation, our newfound cooperation, our moment of mutual admiration. This special thing we had going—not the fort, really, but this new peace between us—it was obvious and apparent, the questions thumping heavily overhead. Why weren't we annoying each other? Why weren't we arguing over every step of the project? Why were we enjoying this?

Neither of us said a word about it. That would have ruined everything. And deep inside, I think we knew that this moment, it was delicate and fleeting, like a towering house of feather-weight cards, bound to collapse at some point. But until then . . .

About four days before the start of school, we stopped and surveyed our creation. It was nearly time to host an open house for Mama, Papa, and some of the neighborhood kids. But we both recognized a problem—the moat encircling our fort was deep enough and symmetrical, thanks to Ana's direction during the trenching. The problem was that the soil kept absorbing the water.

Ana folded her arms in that way of hers. "We need a liner."

I looked up at her. "A what?"

"A liner. A plastic sheet to keep the water from soaking into the dirt."

That night, after dinner but before baths, I slipped out and took a ride on my bike. The air was thick and cool as I glided toward the construction site near the school. They were building houses there, and I was sure I could find some sheets of plastic used to cover mounds of dirt, or something like that. By the time I got there, my heart was pounding, my skin perspiring more than it should. My breathing grew shallow as I found a long black sheet of plastic and tried to roll it up into something I could handle on the bike ride home.

Until someone gripped the back of my neck, and I let out a yelp.

A deep voice. "What do you think you're doing?"

Hand still gripping my neck, scaring me into paralysis. "I . . . I . . ."

"I'll tell you what you're doing. You're trespassing."

I tried not to cry, but failed.

"And you're stealing."

I was crying so hard, I couldn't get a word out.

"You're the one who's been stealing two-by-fours, aren't you?"

I gasped for air. "I . . . I . . ."

And then a thud, and the subsequent spray of dirt clods.

He released my neck, and I dashed away.

His voice was tight. "Okay, that's it."

I turned and got a look at him. He seemed a little older than my dad, with a big stomach hanging over tiny hips. Under the bill of a Peterbilt cap, his eyes glowered, seemed almost red. He pointed at me and yelled, "Get over here."

And then another dirt clod, nailing him in the jaw.

My sister stood atop a nearby dirt mound, winding up for another overhand throw, her upper lip curled so high it seemed to press against her nose. "Don't you ever touch my brother." Her voice may have been weak and breathless, but her body language was just the opposite. She charged off the hill and let loose with a third dirt clod, which forced him to duck. "My dad is gonna kick your ass."

We pedaled home faster than we knew we could, our legs pumping furiously, an odd silence settling in between us. Finally, as we turned onto our street, looking back one last time, Ana said flatly, "You shouldn't have done that."

It seemed to Ana that I was always doing "that"—that stupid thing that screwed everything up, that turned a good day into a bad dream, that ruined nice moments and rare instances of good fortune. My heart sank, because I couldn't disagree with her, as much as I wanted to. How could have I known that, in just a few years, I'd screw up worse than either of us could've imagined.

Back at the house, Ana kept me in the side yard so I could catch my breath and stop crying. "It's okay," she whispered and hugged me, stroking my head. I let her take me in and hugged her back, squeezing hard. "It's all over," she soothed, "and we're gonna be okay."

Me and my sister—I'm not sure we'd ever been so close.

Then, from inside the house came the sound of our doorbell.

The last four days of summer I spent in my room—grounded.

Ana spent them at the city pool with Heather Haley.

Four months later, in the dead of the winter night, I got up to use the bathroom. A storm had come in, the wind rustling trees. I stopped at the window looking out to our backyard. The hard rain came in at an angle, pelting everything. It made me feel warm and safe inside, everyone snug and settled in their rooms as the world outside fell into the cold grip of winter. I stood there and settled for some reason on the lonely, desolate shape in the far corner—our summer fort, abandoned and unfinished. Forgotten, it seemed, from a time that felt so long ago.

●   ●   ●

And now—all these years later—here I am.

Trespassing.

Again.

Hell, this is beyond trespassing. This is breaking and entering. Is this a felony? I shove my hands into my pockets; there's no way I'm leaving my prints here. I look to the family room; Ernie is on the floor in front of the television (more Looney Tunes) with a salad bowl of milk and Froot Loops. In the hall bathroom, Cujo is using my phone, talking to someone between grunts. Mama approaches from behind, slides her spindly arms around me, and presses her camel toe against my butt. "It's so nice to have you home with us for a change," she rasps with a little thrust.

I decide maybe I can get somewhere with her if I play along.

"Baby," I say. "You know that everything I do, I do it for you and the boys. Every minute I am not here, I am working hard to put food on this table."

"I guess . . ." She squeezes and thrusts. ". . . it's just nice to be in a family home—a home that isn't empty."

It definitely *is* a family home. The walls are nicked and peppered with long, dark streaks, and a bookcase is packed with photos of brown-haired children playing at the park, walking to school, splashing about in the pool, pausing to pose in front of the Disneyland gates. In the kitchen, a high chair is pressed against the table. In the family room, Ernie sits crisscross applesauce amid an assortment of Tonka trucks and Lego toys.

"Baby, why are we here?"

Mama presses her cheek to my back and moans. "It's been so long."

"Baby," I soothe, "not with the boys around. Plus, we're on a mission."

The hallway toilet flushes, and Cujo emerges from the bathroom with a skip to his step. I hear myself asking, "Did you wash your hands?" Cujo gives me a lazy sneer and sulks back to the bathroom.

Mama seems nearly breathless. "Let's put a movie on for the boys and go to our room."

Gently, I try to peel her off me, but she just moans and squeezes harder.

"Baby." I pause really long. "You know this isn't a good time."

"Fine," she says. "But there's never a good time anymore."

"You said if I came with you—if I helped you with something here—you'd connect me to the Sabine lady."

More thrusts and some quivering. "I will, honey. I will. Just hold your horses."

"Mama," I yell, "what the hell are we doing here?"

"It's not obvious to you?"

Cujo lumbers into the kitchen. "Mama, can Angel come over?"

"Obvious?" I say to Mama. "What's obvious?"

"I just called her on my new phone," Cujo says sweetly.

"Dude, I need my phone."

Cujo cackles and proceeds to the family room.

Another thrust from Mama.

"What's the point to all this?" Again, I try and fail to peel away her hands without damaging them—she seems so arthritic and brittle. "No, don't tell me. There is no point, is there?"

Mama unlocks her hands and spins me around so we're face-to-face. "Figure it out."

In a matter of minutes, I find myself searching the kitchen. I don't notice anything unusual here—standard family kitchen fare (plates, pans, spices, and cups of every kind in the cabinets, and an assortment of blue and orange Nerf gun toys strewn across the floor). Under the sink, I find a tidy stack of paper bags squeezed beside a crusty old fish tank—that's odd, but people keep things in all kinds of unusual places. I stand up and stretch, looking at Mama, hoping for a hint. Hell, truth is, there's probably no reason we're here, except for the fact that Mama is basically bonkers and I'm too desperate to believe that she'll actually help me with the Neanderthal expert.

Mama stands there, her arms folded, and sticks her chin out. "Keep looking."

Cujo lumbers in and hands me my cell. "Angel's stopping by." He yanks open the fridge. "Just for a bit." He pulls out a milk jug, twists off the cap, and starts to chug, sucking on the nozzle like a giant baby slurping on a bottle.

"What have I told you?" Mama says. "Don't do that."

Cujo keeps chugging.

Mama roars, "Use a cup."

Cujo lowers the jug from his mouth—milk dripping from his beard—and releases a massive belch that echoes throughout the house. "Next time," he says with a happy sigh and tosses the jug back into the fridge. He dance-walks out of the kitchen, leaving the fridge door open.

Mama looks away, muttering to herself. "Wild child."

My cell vibrates with a text. Audrey?

It's my sister.

> HELP! Collin alone bus w/ Chinese tourists. Can u get him?

Mama approaches from behind, reattaches herself.

I text back, What? Where r u?

Mama lets her hands wander, and I decide, *What the hell? Maybe she needs this.*

> Have appointment with dean of admissions— PRINCETON!!:) . . . Hard to resked. Can u get Collin?

Princeton? Did I mention Collin is eight?

Another text comes in: Mix-up at drop-off. . . . He lied to Jenny, said he was supposed to be dropped off at Westin Palo Alto for bus tour.

Jenny is my sister's personal assistant.

> But was a big lie. . . . Luke drop-off but NO MIND to check for REST OF CLASS—errrrr!!!

Luke is my sister's chef.

> School called, said he's missing. How EMBARRASSING!!!

The hands rub my stomach then head south. I pull them back up.

Jenny called hotel. He's on bus with Chinese tourists.

I tap back, Why the hell would he do that?
Mama gropes and moans.

No idea. . . . Can u help??? ☺ . . . He'll be on bus for
hours (headed to Vegas) unless you can get him. . . . I
have Princeton phoner.

Maybe it's not my place to say, but wouldn't the average parent cancel what they're doing and run out of the house barefoot—or in their underwear, or in whatever they're wearing—and dive headfirst into their car, and subsequently break every traffic law known to man in order to pull their child off a bus full of strangers headed to Vegas?

Hotel can tell u where to intercept.

This is not the first time my sister has asked me to do something like this.

Can u help?

None of this makes sense, or feels right. An eight-year-old child lies about a field trip, gets on a bus full of strangers headed for Vegas. Is this the behavior of a happy child who is healthy and well? Suddenly my Neanderthal project seems like small potatoes. My stomach tightens as I tap, Of course.

☺ Merci.

I let out a frustrated sigh—Ana.

Mama quakes, "You feel the fire burning, too, baby?"

Thanks Rick. . . . You know today is just insane.

Oh yeah—today. Their last day in the States.

And I stand there wondering who's going to help this poor kid for the next two years. Luke the vegan chef, who is somehow included in the relocation package? That scares the shit out of me—this kid doesn't need vegan shakes, he needs love and attention. Audrey is not coming with them. While Ana and Samson James Barnard IV were happy to foot the bill for their vegan chef, they decided they could get a decent nanny for peanuts in Buenos Aires.

Just take him to school. . . . Call hotel for bus coordinates.

"Who's that?" Mama slurs.

I tap back, OK.

I slide my phone into my pocket. "Let's get cracking here," I say. "We need to intercept a tour bus."

"You want me to introduce you to Sabine and drive you to that bus?"

"Yes," I snap and try to peel her off me. "I think we have a runaway."

Mama lets go and motions to the kitchen. "Then keep looking."

I move to close the fridge, but stop when I see an orange container in the vegetable drawer. I glance at Mama. "Is *this* it?"

"You're—"

The doorbell rings.

Oh, crap. My stomach weakens and my skin cools. *I'm toast.*

Mama seems more surprised than concerned. "No one's expected home for hours."

Cujo bounces to the entryway and opens the door. I scramble for a place to hide.

Cujo hollers. "Angel's here."

Mama whispers, "I've been meaning to talk to you about her." She sighs. "I don't think she's a good influence."

I hear myself say, "You really play house with these twerps?"

Mama deflates, looks away. "Don't judge me."

"Mama, can she come in for a while? Please?"

"I guess so." Another sigh. "As long as she follows the rules."

Silence.

"And no more alone time behind closed doors." Mama takes on a stern voice. "I mean it."

The front door slams shut. Soon the entry to the kitchen is filled by an enormous white woman in stained back-stretch pants and a giant white sweater. I'm guessing six-foot-something and at least 275 pounds. She's sucking on a sixty-four-ouncer from 7-Eleven, grinning. "Hi, Mama," she says, the straw still in her mouth.

Mama looks away, tired. "Hi, honey."

Angel gives me a long look and tongues the straw.

"You kids respect the house rules, okay?"

"Sure, Mama."

"And we're leaving soon."

Cujo pulls Angel away, says, "We never take long."

I watch Cujo lead Angel to the other side of the house and decide, *Time to get the hell out of here.* I eye the orange object inside the fridge, step forward, and take a knee. Gently, I pull out the vegetable drawer to take a closer look. "There we go," Mama says. "That's it."

Looking at the orange box, I realize it's actually a hard-plastic cooler no bigger than a loaf of bread—I didn't know they made them that small. Transparent, industrial-grade tape has sealed the lid shut, and the latch is secured by a tiny padlock.

Okay, this is genuinely weird.

I peer up to Mama. "We really *are* here for a reason."

She smiles and nods to the cooler. *What's in there?* The possibilities race through my mind, flashing before me in nasty little bursts. *Drugs. . . . Chemicals. . . . Extrajuicy organs. . . . Embryos. . . . Eggs from an extinct species. . . . A half-eaten chimichanga from Led Zeppelin's 1970 U.S tour. . . . A prehistoric fish carcass. . . . Milton Berle's boyhood tonsils. . . . Connie Chung stool samples, circa 1982 . . .* I stare into space, wondering what any of this has to do with Dick Rayborne, executive vice president of Human Resources at Robards International. Mama is nearly panting as she points to the cooler. "Take that out and put it on the counter."

I pull out my shirttails, tuck my hands underneath, and use the fabric as de facto gloves—again, I will *not* leave my prints anywhere. On the counter, I give the cooler a closer look. It appears like it could be something you'd bring to work for lunches, but I don't see any of the usual branding, or any handle or strap for toting it around. But on the side I do notice a tiny white sticker with small, typed print—I lean in and squint at the text.

"What's it say?"

I crinkle my brows. "Uganda."

"Make any sense to you, Dickie?"

Under *Uganda*, there's even smaller text:

24 kg
Grasslands
Extraction: Recovery
M // Olive

I straighten and turn to Mama. "Robards doesn't make anything that needs refrigeration. And we don't do any business in Uganda."

Mama reaches into her fanny pack and produces two thin clicks. Almost instantaneously, there's a loud thump in the TV room followed by the rapid patter of footsteps. In a blink, Ernie is sliding to a stop in front of us, panting, a crooked grin spreading across his face as he lowers the barbecue prongs to his side. Mama produces a mini of Jack Daniel's and nods to the cooler. "Be a good helper boy and open that thing for Mama." Ernie releases a happy noise and lifts the prongs. Within seconds, he's working the fork end of the prongs into the padlock's keyhole. Ernie hums to himself as he works the prongs, and Mama says, "It's awfully quiet on the other side of the house." She sighs long and hard. "Ernie, when you're done with this, Mama needs you to go on a secret mission."

Ernie works the prongs, releasing strange sounds of contentment.

"Okay?"

Ernie nods, and the padlock clicks open.

"What a good helper boy I have," Mama says, playing up the sweet, frail granny voice. She offers the mini of Jack Daniel's, and Ernie snatches it so quickly he's like a cartoon. He twists off the cap and drains the mini, humming happily before succumbing to a rapturous shudder.

"Now, Mama needs you to go on that secret mission."

He looks at her, his blue eyes enormous and eager.

She whispers. "Mama needs you to go see what Cujo's doing and come back and tell me your secret report."

Ernie makes a tight squeal. He hands me the empty mini, places the prongs on the counter, and falls to the floor to crawl under the kitchen table. On the opposite end, he reemerges triumphant, clutching a Nerf rifle, ready to fire, and tiptoes out of the room, giggling like a giddy six-year-old.

"We need to get going," I say. "My nephew snuck onto a bus headed to Vegas."

"Okay, let's get cranking." Mama joins me at the counter, breathing hard, and slides the cooler toward me. "Now that we have some privacy, let's get the show on the road."

I use my knuckles to slide it back to her. "I'm not having anything to do with this."

Slides it back. "Too late, Dickie boy. We're here because of you and your paperwork. So stop acting like a victim and open the goddamn box."

I step back, looking at the cooler. Whatever it is, I know it won't be good. Why else would Mama bring me here? I look at her and ask, "I do this, and then we get the hell out of here and we use your wagon to intercept the tourist bus?"

"Yes."

"And you call Sabine what's-her-name?"

"*Yes*," she yells.

Then I have an idea. "Mama, we both know it's wrong to leave any of *our* kids stranded."

Mama allows a grin. "After this, we'll go find Collin."

My stomach eases, and I gaze down at the cooler.

"C'mon, honey." Mama slides the cooler closer. "Before the boys start acting up."

From the back of the house, the sounds of rapid dart fire and hard thumps.

I look down at the cooler, then at Mama—she's right, we need to get out of here. With my hands under my shirttails, I find a steak knife from a drawer and use it to break the taped seal around the cooler lid. I pull out my hands and use the backs of my knuckles to lift the lid. I look in and—it's a set of vials containing clear liquid. I glance at Mama for a clue, and she's just standing there, arms folded, relishing my confusion. At which point, Ernie streaks in from the back of the house—that grin more crooked than ever—giggling uncontrollably as Angel rumbles after him in the largest thong I've ever seen, flopping and jiggling everywhere. Snarling. In the family room, she tries to corner him, but he easily slips away—again and again. Finally, Cujo emerges fully naked, still erect, clutching his own Nerf rifle, a toothy smile spreading across his face as he sneaks toward the family room.

My God, he's hairy.

Cujo double-pumps the dart gun and snickers. "Where is he?"

"Okay, that does it." Mama flips the cooler shut. "The boys have been cooped inside too long. They're going crazy with cabin fever."

I try to ignore the commotion in the family room. "But . . ." I nod to the cooler. "What's in those?"

Mama blinks hard. "We need to take the boys someplace to get their energy out."

I think of Collin. "Honey," I snap, playing up the familiarity. "You've forgotten about Collin again. We can't leave *our* Collin alone on a bus. It's downright negligent."

Mama shakes her head, disappointed in herself. "That's right." She balls her fists, lifts her chin into the air, and closes her eyes. "Okay," she roars. "Everyone in the wagon and buckled up in sixty seconds. Or they don't get a special prize from Mama."

Sixty seconds later, the boys are in Mama's Fleetwood, panting from the mad rush, and still giggling. Cujo works hard to squeeze his massive arms and chest into his jumpsuit, and when he does, the zipper chews up some of his body hair. Not that he seems to care, or even notice. Angel waddles out of the house half-dressed, clutching her shoes and stretch pants, still managing to take a pull from her sixty-four-ouncer. She brushes past me, stops, and leans through the open window on Cujo's side of the wagon, the bottom of her sweater rising to expose the thong. Her thunder fills the Fleetwood and makes the glass vibrate. "Thanks for *nothing*, asshole."

Cujo and Ernie giggle as Angel barefoots it across the street, cussing, and heaves her things into a dusty Trans Am. I lower my head and scan the neighborhood, see no one else. But God, we must be making a major scene here. I imagine dozens of busy-bodies watching from the safety of their living room windows, dialing the police or scribbling down Mama's tags. Or, snapping photos. My heart pounds at the thought. Photos of me. Photos of me participating in a felony. What if my sister found out and I lost the house-sitting gig? Standing near the back of the wagon with Mama, I realize I'm holding the orange cooler. How in the hell did that happen?

Mama opens the back of the wagon, and I notice the frayed, sun-bleached BABY ON BOARD sign on the glass. She takes a few hard breaths and nods to the back bay of the wagon. "Put that in here and take two presents from that container there."

I don't budge.

"C'mon," Mama snaps. "The boys are getting restless, and we need to pick up Collin." She opens a blue Tupperware container; it's stuffed with dozens of shoe-box-size presents, each wrapped in kiddie paper with red and blue balloon designs. She pulls out two presents, says something to herself, like she's doing math in her head and double-checking the numbers. Then she hands me a third present. "Give that to Angel for being a good girl today."

Good girl?

I follow Mama as she shuffles to Cujo's side of the wagon. "Now," she says, her voice so sweet and fragile. "You both did a *wonderful* job listening to Mama." They look up at her, silent and eager. "You picked up after yourself, you collected your belongings . . ." She nods to the barbecue prongs placed across Ernie's lap. ". . . and you were good helper boys, getting everything done in time. So . . ." She eases the presents toward the window but pauses before Cujo can take them. ". . . just one more thing before you get your presents."

Cujo moans.

Ernie growls.

"Cujo," she says sternly. "I want you to buckle up."

Cujo laughs. When he sees that she's serious, he flops and moans.

"Now, don't you pull that naughty stuff with me, mister. I'll use the pepper spray again."

"Mama," he pleads. "C'mon."

"Cujo," she snaps. "I'm gonna count to three."

"Mama. C'mon."

"One."

Cujo looks to me. "Warden, you don't care about buckling up, do you?"

I say, "Are we really having this conversation?"

"Two."

"C'mon, Mama," Cujo pleads. "Lighten up."

"Don't let me get to *three*, mister."

Silence, and then, "Mama."

"Three."

Cujo buckles up. "Gimme a break," he mumbles.

"That's a good boy," she coos and eases the presents through Cujo's window. With startling velocity, the boys snatch them out of her hands and begin to tear them open. I lean in and squint at the contents. Inside each box is a sealed slice of cured pork belly, a handful of Bazooka bubble gum, two cherry-flavored Tootsie Pops, a 7-Eleven gift card, a half-pint of Wild Turkey, a tin canister of Skoal, a crisp fifty-dollar bill, and three shiny silver dollars.

Ernie hums happily as he unwraps a Tootsie Pop.

Cujo enjoys a long pull of bourbon.

Mama closes her eyes and cocks her head, motherly. "What do you say, boys?"

Cujo pulls away from his bourbon and quakes. "Thanks, Mama." Ernie pulls the lollipop from his mouth, releases a happy squeal, his eyes twinkling, and takes a pull from his own bottle, his round little body twitching in delight. A hint of joy spreads across Mama's face as she watches the boys finger through their loot. She leans in and whispers to me, "It's important to reward positive behavior."

I scan the neighborhood again, still see no one. "We better get out of here."

Mama nods, shuts the back hatch of the wagon, and nods to the remaining present in my hand. "Give that to Angel, and I'll get the car started."

"Okay, but . . ." My phone vibrates. ". . . let me just . . ." I squint at the screen—it looks like Audrey has called nine times.

There are seven voice mails and four texts, but I'm not sure I have the stomach to go any further.

Angel starts the Trans Am, and the ground vibrates.

I stare at the phone, wondering what to do first.

"Honey," Mama snaps. "C'mon."

It's too bad about Audrey, but I have to call about the bus.

"HONEY," Mama roars.

I huff, put the phone away, and head toward the Trans Am. I'm in the middle of the street when it rockets from the curb, pulls an immediate U-turn, and accelerates toward me. I dash out of its path just in time as a monstrous arm shoots out of the driver-side window. In a flash, the present is plucked from my grasp as the Trans Am roars past me and accelerates out of the neighborhood. Mama yells from the wagon, "Honey, stop loafing around. The boys are getting restless, and we need to pick up Collin."

I hear myself explode with rage. "Okay, okay," I snarl, my tone acidic. "Just fucking relax." I stop myself, take in a long breath, and head toward the station wagon. On the exhale, I hear myself muttering, "Nag, nag, nag."

●　●　●

Mama's driving.

The boys are in the back, trading prizes.

I'm riding shotgun, talking on the phone with a clerk at the Westin Palo Alto. "We've contacted the charter company," the clerk says, "and they have spoken with the driver. They can confirm they have an eight-year-old Caucasian passenger named Collin. That's all I have."

"Can you tell me where the bus is now?"

"The dispatcher said they made a stop at the Facebook

campus and spent a lot of time there—they did a tour—so they really haven't gone that far."

"How far?"

"They're on 101, headed south. They just passed San Jose International."

I cover the phone and bark to Mama, "We need to go south on 280. That'll take us to 101, and we can jet south and maybe catch them."

Mama snaps, "You think I don't know the freeways anymore?"

The clerk gives me the number of the dispatcher. "It's a white bus with a blue stripe down the middle. He said to call if you don't catch up with them on 101, and the dispatcher can give you updated coordinates."

By the time I'm off the phone, we're already merging onto 280 South. Mama guns the wagon as she weaves through the lanes, the engine screaming, the boys hollering. "If they just passed the airport," Mama yells over the din, "we might be able to catch them near Morgan Hill. Maybe Gilroy."

It feels good that she cares, and that she's dropped the role playing for a bit. "Thanks, Mama."

"This is your runt nephew, on a bus packed with strangers. More than a few whack jobs, I'm sure. Headed for Las Vegas. Why didn't your sister fetch after him?"

"Good question."

"Why isn't she having a heart attack?" Mama glances at me. "Or is she?"

I shake my head and sigh. "She isn't."

"Does your sister have some kind of issue?"

"We all have issues, Mama."

She nods to that, says, "After this, you're gonna help me with that cooler."

I feel my chest tighten. "What about the Neanderthal lady?"

"I will introduce you to Sabine Rorgstardt once you help me with the contents of that cooler."

I look at my phone. It's already 10:55. How will I ever get everything done in time? In the next seven hours, I need to rescue my runaway nephew, help a crazy granny do something with a cooler of vials, speak with a Neanderthal expert at Stanford and convince said expert to change her plans so my nephew can have a "Neanderthal adventure," convince my nephew's nanny that he had an amazing time, get the kid home on time so I can show my sister I'm the perfect person to house-sit her mansion for the next two years, and somehow get to the Greek Theatre in Berkeley with Audrey before the English Beat takes the stage.

My phone rings—it's Audrey.

I attempt to sound relaxed and carefree. "Hey, baby."

Silence.

"Baby?"

Finally, a weak voice. "Rick?"

"Audrey."

"Is that really you?"

I cover my mouth and huddle against my door. "Baby, it's me."

Another long silence.

"Audrey?"

Her voice sharpens. "What's going on?"

"Audrey, I lost my—"

"Cool it with the dick pics, okay?"

"Audrey. That's not—"

"And who's your buddy?"

"Audrey, listen to me."

"Who's the grandma lady?"

"Grandma lady?"

"The lady who says you're treating 'these kids' poorly? It was like she knew who I was. What does that mean? Is she talking about Collin?"

"Audrey, Mama's just confused," I blurt and realize what I've done and slap my palm to my forehead, cringing.

Mama glances at me, snaps, "Confused? That's what you always say when I demand some attention, isn't it?"

"Rick, who is that?"

"Audrey." I can nearly see the gates of the Greek Theatre closing on me. "Please. I can explain."

"That's the lady who said you can't be trusted."

"No, she meant—Listen, Audrey. Yes, she's the one. But she's confused."

Mama yells, *"I'm not confused."*

"Audrey, Collin's on a tour bus to Vegas. The boys are going nuts in the back. Mama gave them too much sugar and whiskey. We have a cooler of weird liquid in the wagon. We need to intercept the Chinese tour bus. An hour ago I was talking about P-FIDs in the HyperPHY." I take a breath. "Angel came over and broke the house rules." Another big breath. "I've just got a lot going on."

Long silence. "Rick, where are you? You sound weird."

"Audrey, listen. I'm sorry about this morning. Cujo the conployee got my phone." Cujo cackles, wet and deep. "But everything is fine, Audrey. I swear."

"Who was that?"

"Audrey, I'm getting Collin, and we're gonna see an expert."

"Rick." Audrey's voice is tight. "Maybe my little challenge is too much right now. Plus, my friend Megan called—she wants to get gyros tonight. Maybe we should drop the whole concert thing—I didn't mean to stress you out. I thought you would've liked the challenge. You know, after all these years."

"No," I snap. "No. Everything is fine. Seriously, trust me."

She pauses a moment. "Listen," she says, "I really think—"

"Audrey, seriously. Believe me when I say I'm cool, we're fine. I'm getting Collin, and we're gonna have a great day. It'll be cool. I'll see you at my sister's house tonight. You'll see—we're gonna have an amazing day, something special. And we'll head out after that."

This seems to resonate with Audrey. "Okay. Well, call me in an hour, okay?"

"Of course, I should have him off the bus by then."

"Oh yeah," Audrey says. "What's this thing about Collin and a bus?"

I tell Audrey about my sister's texts, and how Collin fooled Luke the vegan chef into taking him to the Westin Palo Alto for a fake field trip with Mandarin-speaking tourists. Audrey sighs and cusses. "Your sister texted you? She's not going to get him?"

"No," I say. "My question is, what kind of moron drops a kid off at a hotel for a field trip? When there aren't any other kids nearby? And who wouldn't at least walk him to the bus so he can sign him in?"

"Rick." Audrey pauses a moment. "Luke makes vegan soufflés. That's where his wizardry ends. I would have taken him to school today, but . . ." She clears her throat. ". . . I'm moving my things out."

"That reminds me," I say. "Why aren't you staying to house-sit their place?"

There's a long pause. "I just need to . . . I just gotta move on, Rick." She clears her throat again. "I can't believe he's on a tour bus."

We approach the freeway interchange, and Mama guns us onto 101 South.

I ask, "How did he even know about a Chinese tour bus leaving the Westin?"

"We drive by there every morning. He always talks about them."

"Okay, but why would he even do something like this?"

"It's never been this bad."

"What do you mean? He's done this before?"

"Rick . . ." Audrey pauses again. "You can't see what's happening?"

"What are you talking about?"

"Do you know what he did last summer?"

"You mean the rocket propellant?"

"No. I found him in the back. He was standing atop the retaining wall. And he was trying to make himself jump."

"The retaining wall?" My stomach cools at the mere idea of Collin standing atop that retaining wall and staring down at the cobblestones a good fifteen feet below. "Collin is scared of heights."

Audrey says, "He wanted to jump."

I feel my face crinkle. "What are you talking about?"

Her voice goes tiny. "He wanted to break his leg. I found him back there, and he said he wanted to break his leg. I talked him down, and he's crying, telling me he really truly wanted to break his leg, and I'm holding him, rocking him, but he keeps saying it. Keeps saying, if he breaks his leg, if he does something big like that—like that time he split his lip and Ana canceled the yoga and spent the whole day with him—if he really hurts himself, if he breaks his leg, then his mom wouldn't just cancel her day and be with him; she'd cancel the whole week, maybe the whole month, and she'd be there when he woke up, would make him breakfast, would read to him, would help him with his homework."

My chest tightens. "I . . ."

"That was on a Saturday. Samson and Ana had left to spend the entire weekend in Calistoga. You took him that night—"

"And I brought him home that Sunday night, and they—"

"Still weren't home," Audrey says. "So you got him ready for bed and fell asleep in his little bed."

I recall a bedtime debate about whether Neanderthals would enjoy watching *Downton Abbey*.

"So when she gets home, I decide to tell her," Audrey says. "And she just stares at me. Says, 'I need you to take Collin to school this week,' and she just leaves me standing there."

"My sister doesn't know how to connect," I say. "Ever since the—" But I can't say it, or just don't want to say it. "And every year, she just closes up a little more."

"And Samson," Audrey says. "He's the perfect partner for that, right?"

"The last thing Samson James Barnard IV wants," I say, "is someone who will open up and go all-in."

It weighs on me so heavily, I feel it in my chest and on my back and over my shoulders. Sometimes I just want to wring my sister's neck. "I don't know what's going to happen to him," I say. "Ana wants to ship him back here to spend the summer with me. Maybe that's not such a bad idea."

Audrey sniffles. "So listen. When you get there, just give him a hug, okay?"

I feel weird. "Of course," I mumble. "Yeah, sure. We're gonna do an adventure."

We end the call, and I turn to Mama. "We need to reach that bus, like, yesterday."

Mama cuts off a Camry as she dives across the lanes. The boys holler and laugh. "We don't abandon our people, do we, Dickie?" Soon, Mama has the Fleetwood screaming down 101.

The boys have taken to flashing BAs at motorists, their asses pressed hard against the windows, the car starting to stink. After each surprised motorist, Ernie's teary laughter intensifies, and they take pulls of Wild Turkey.

Mama guns the Fleetwood a little more. "Settle them down."

I turn, force a stern look, and drop my voice. "Boys."

They're in another world—eyes slitted, cheeks flushed, mouths open in delight.

"C'mon. Cool it. Get back into your jumpsuits."

We come up on a Highlander, and Ernie uses the opportunity to press his privates against the glass. Cujo releases a tight cackle, and Ernie spasms in laughter until tears roll down his cheeks. We scream past a minivan of moms and toddlers, and Cujo executes something called the Teabag.

Mama leans over, says lowly. "The boys are just wearing me out."

Ernie rolls down his window, and Cujo lifts his ass into the air. My God, the hair.

Mama glances at the rearview mirror. "Don't you dare."

Cujo eases his ass through the window as we rocket past a silver fox in a Cadillac.

Mama says, "They don't listen to us. It's like they think *they're* in charge."

"Well, maybe you want to—"

"Not that I get any help from you," she snarls.

"Mama, c'mon."

In the backseat, Cujo has placed Ernie in a headlock. Ernie stiffens, crosses his eyes, and gurgles, and Cujo eases a string of drool off his lower lip, swinging it over Ernie's cherry-red face. Someone pushes out a tight fart.

"They act up because it's the only way they can get your attention."

"That's not—"

"Just tell me where I'm going."

"You're doing fine right here," I say. "We should be coming up on them soon."

"It's always about you and your needs, isn't it?"

"Mama, c'mon. Let's cut the BS here."

"What are you talking about?"

"What's the deal with the pretend family here?"

She weakens her voice, playing up the frail-granny act. "I don't understand." She focuses on the road, allows a grin. "I'm just so confused. Aren't you Dickie, my asshole husband?"

"Mama, seriously. We both know you're as sharp as a tack. You know I'm not your deadbeat ex, and that these clowns aren't our kids."

"Listen," Mama says. "I said I'd help you with Sabine Rorgstardt, and you agreed to do as I say for a little bit."

"Okay, but—"

"Honey," she snaps. "I wear the pants in this relationship. I always have, and I always will. You hear?"

I deflate in my seat. "Fine."

"Plus . . ." Mama pauses a bit. "I just . . . I don't know. Sometimes it's nice to go back to that time. To take care of little ones again."

I glance back at the boys. Cujo still has Ernie in a headlock. "These aren't little ones, Mama."

She nods reluctantly. "Not every family is picture-perfect, Dickie. You should know that."

A lump forms. I *do* know that.

• • •

The truth is, I'm packing a ton of family baggage.

After what I've done, I could never have a family—it's an easier life if I just chase women and make people laugh. Hell, in this world of countless instances of shittiness happening to countless quantities of people in countless ways, a few laughs with some cool people can really soften the edges. So what I've done is ditch the shittiness—the corporate bullshit, the assholes and phonies, the family crap.

I didn't even want to be an uncle—still don't, in a lot of ways. In fact, when my sister was pregnant with Collin, I tried to avoid her. I'm not proud of that, but if I am being honest here, I have to say that's what I did. The closer Ana got to the delivery date, the more I ditched her. There was a part of me—a childish part of me—that secretly resolved to ditch my sister and her child for years at a time. Maybe I could get away with never meeting this kid. Because if you knew the background, you'd understand why this was probably best for the kid. I had caused enough pain—for her, for me.

Never again, if I had any say in it.

Then, toward the end of her pregnancy, on the Fourth of July, in front of everyone, she took my hand and placed it lightly on her stomach. And I felt him move, the rolls, the warmth, the new life so safe and sound, so perfect. She was like a conduit—connecting me to a new dimension, to a new generation, a hundred years of love and meaning. It felt amazing, and it was like a punch in the gut. My chest swelled in rhythmic warmth—an instant connection—and I pulled my hand away so quickly it drew long stares from everyone there in her backyard. Stares from people who didn't understand. Folks who weren't there twenty years earlier. Those people looking at me like I'm crazy. Those people who were appalled by the fact I was "on vacation"—gone, nowhere to be found—when Ana went into labor. Those people, they just don't understand when you don't trust yourself, when you know you're a fuckup, when you know just how much you've already sent the world off course, how you seem to do it over and over, no matter how much you try. People tell you, *Don't be crazy. You're not like that at all. It's in your head.* But you know the truth. You know what you did. And you know you can never take it back.

And you swear to yourself. Never again.

Eight months later, Ana called me.

Her voice was weak. "You've hurt me."

"I'm sorry," I said. "And I'm happy for you. I just don't want to do anything that would put you guys in jeopardy."

"What are you talking about?"

"You know what I am talking about."

She sighed. "Rick. It's over. It's behind us."

I felt weird, so I forced a laugh. "It's not."

"It *is*, Rick. It's over. It's behind us. Way behind us."

The words tumbled out. "It can't be behind me. Ever."

"I want you to meet him."

"I don't know."

Two weeks later, I pulled a Bob Watson and headed over to my sister's house. I sat in my car, worked on my breathing for a long time. Deep breaths in, long breaths out. I closed my eyes and asked for help.

Help me. Mama and Papa. Please.

I got out, steadied myself. Deep breaths, letting them out slowly.

Help me.

Stay cool.

Deep breaths.

I found myself standing before my sister and brother-in-law's fifteen-foot-tall, six-foot-wide, solid-oak front door.

Deep breaths.

I knocked, hard.

Help me.

Finally, the door opened slowly. A woman in her late twenties was smiling at me. She seemed so at ease, so comfortable—content with herself, and perhaps with me. Her dark brown hair was pulled into a ponytail, and yellow Play-Doh was smeared into her jeans and deep green T-shirt. She stuck a foot out, wiped her forehead with the back of her forearm, and blew out a long breath. She smiled again—just an easy happiness—and her voice was light and gentle. "I'm Audrey."

The nanny.

"Rick."

"I'm so glad you're here, Rick." She opened the door wider. "And your timing is perfect."

I stepped in. "Yeah?"

"They're gone." She smiled, like she could read my mind, like she knew I'd rather not do this under the watchful eyes of my sister and Samson James Barnard IV. "He just woke from a nap and had a feeding."

Then gentle and rapid thumping.

Audrey stepped back with a grin.

The thumping got a little louder.

Audrey said it so light and sweet. "I think I *hear* someone."

The thumping got faster and closer.

Audrey looked at me, smiled. "Where's our Collin?"

And then from around the corner peered a moon-shaped face. Giant brown eyes. A shock of dirty-brown hair. Enormous round cheeks. He was smiling up at Audrey, oblivious to me. Audrey knelt down and threw her arms open. "Hey, buddy."

He giggled and thumped around the corner. But stopped short. *God, he's cute,* I thought, and I felt a smile spreading across my face. I lowered myself to the floor and sat crisscross.

"C'mon, honey." Arms still open. "Come say hi to your uncle Rick."

Collin looked at me, turned to Audrey. He shuffled to her, his diapered butt wagging and crackling in movement. He reached her and plopped himself into her lap. "That's my little man," she said and wrapped him up in her arms. She lowered her face to his, kissed him on the cheek, and looked at me. *Does she look at everyone this way?* And I noticed her hairline—so lovely.

Then I noticed his intense gaze. He was staring at me, deciding.

She softened her voice, nearly whispered. "Can you say hi to your uncle Rick?"

He continued to give me a good, long look.

Please don't cry.

I tried to make my voice soft and light, and felt like a dork doing it. "Hey there."

We looked at each other some more, and I noticed that unmistaken Blanco family forehead. Just like me, my sister, and our father. He's got that delicate chin of my mother's, and his father's lighter skin. The sweet eyes are all his own.

And I had to admit, he was beautiful.

He watched me some more, and Audrey said, "I think this is the start of something special, Collin buddy."

He gave me another long look and allowed the briefest of grins.

And I said to Audrey, "I'm sorry, but I need to go."

GAIN NEW INSIGHTS

We spot the bus just south of Gilroy.

We come up on its flank so quickly that Mama needs to pump the brakes so we don't sail past it. She grips the steering wheel and hollers, "Boys, we need your help." But they aren't listening; Cujo has Ernie in something he's calling the butt lock, and they're laughing uncontrollably.

"I'll just wave down the driver," I say. "Speed up."

Mama accelerates, and soon we are adjacent to the bus. The windows are tinted, but we can clearly see that it's packed with Chinese tourists. Some are pointing at Mama's old car and exchanging comments. I also notice the thick blue line running down the side of the bus. Collin's in there.

Mama produces three clicks, and the boys stop their horseplay. "Boys," she says, pointing to the bus, "I need you to get their attention. Can you do that?" Within seconds, Cujo and Ernie are flashing BAs at the bus. The tourists pull back from the windows, their mouths open. Then come the perplexed smiles. Then the laughter and pointing. Then come the cameras.

"*Boys!*"

Ernie giggles as he scrambles into the back bay of the wagon and presses his naked butt against the glass. Cujo sits up and eases his head out the window, flicking his tongue between two fingers. I roll down the window and make eye contact with the driver, a gray-haired fellow who looks like he could be a conductor on a steam locomotive. I show my him phone and motion for him to pull over. He nods and starts to slow down, easing onto the shoulder of 101. Mama lets off the gas and pulls in behind. When we come to a stop behind the bus—the cars screaming past us—I let out the biggest sigh of relief. *We've got him.*

"Go get your nephew," Mama tells me. "I'll keep the boys here with their new reward for being such good helpers." Slowly, she pulls out two new minis of whiskey. "That is, as soon as they get their jumpsuits on." The boys whine and complain, and Mama snaps, "I mean it."

I get out of the car and trot to the bus, the gravel crunching with each step as the doors open with a long hiss. I look up at the windows and see the faces staring, cameras snapping—but no Collin. When I reach the door and look up, the driver motions me in. "Are you Collin's dad?"

I step into the bus, and the cameras start shuttering like I'm a world leader. "I'm his uncle."

Collin is standing on the front seat, holding a microphone. He's telling the tourists something in Mandarin, and they're nodding with polite smiles. He turns and seems surprised that it's me. *Where's his usual smile?* He blinks and says something in Mandarin—I'm impressed with his fluency. The tourists offer a collective *ahhh*, a sympathetic tone, and he looks down like he's going to cry. I wave to everyone and holler, "Thanks for looking after my amazing nephew," and they smile and nod. A man in the back says, "He's a very good little boy. Very smart."

Collin says, "Where's my mom?"

"On the phone with Princeton."

"Does she know I'm on a bus giving a tour in Mandarin?" He looks at me. "For people from China?"

"Yes. Okay, let's go, kiddo. I've got something special planned for you."

He straightens and faces the tourists. "Can you take a photo of me talking to them?"

I pull out my phone. "Sure, then we have to go."

"My mom will love this." He puts the mike to his mouth and thrusts a finger into the air like he's a lecturer. "It will be great for my college application." He pauses, glances at me. "Was she worried about me?"

Which is when I notice the dark rings around his eyes.

• • •

I walk Collin to the wagon and stop him short. "Are you okay, kiddo?"

He's looking down, thinking to himself as the cars roar past us.

"Collin?"

He looks up, his face drawn, so serious, his mouth twisted tight. I've never seen him like this. "This will work out okay," he mumbles, more to himself. "Now maybe I can make it back in time for SAT Prep. I'm still scoring poorly in critical reading and math." He shakes his head. "Math is really my weak spot."

I take him by the shoulder and give a light shake. "Collin."

"I'm hoping the tour bus will score as extra credit, win me some points with my mom and the admissions boards." He looks up at me, for reaction, hopeful he's on the right track. "And maybe they'll overlook my relatively poor performance in math."

"Collin."

He looks into space. "I hate math, Uncle Rick. So much pressure."

I nod. "Whoever invented math was a sadist."

"My mom says she's getting me a math coach. Three hours a day all summer."

I look at the rings around his eyes. This is a new thing. "Are you sleeping okay, kiddo?"

He turns and looks at me, deflated. "The greatest achievers don't need a lot of sleep. That's what my dad says."

"All I know is, you're a very smart and talented boy."

Collin snaps, "That's not good enough."

I bite my lip and smile. "Listen, how about a Neanderthal adventure?"

This seems to really depress him. It's like he's about to cry. "I don't have time for Neanderthal adventures, Uncle Rick. I'm eight. I need to start thinking about activities that will help me with the college admissions boards."

"Your mom said it was okay."

This reaches him, and his eyes brighten. "Really?"

"Really."

He pinches his chin and thinks. "But I can get to school in time for the SAT Prep. It will look better on my final school record—I helped a busload of Mandarin-speaking tourists, and I still made it back for SAT Prep. That will look good." He thinks about it, adds, "Did I tell you that Ping and Xiùy ng said they'd write letters of recommendation for me? They're gonna say what an amazing Mandarin-speaking tour guide I am?"

God, does this kid need a Bob Watson.

"Listen." I square him toward me and look into his eyes. "What if I told you you could get credit for attending SAT Prep and still go on a Neanderthal adventure? All at the same time?"

An eyebrow lifts. "I *do* still love Neanderthals . . ." He looks at me, eyes so serious. ". . . even if my mom says there's no time for them."

I direct him toward the wagon. "I think it's time you learned how to pull a Bob Watson." The bus pulls away with a goodbye honk. "Plus, I have some people I want you to meet."

● ● ●

I can tell Collin doesn't know what to think of Mama and her old Fleetwood station wagon. And he's a bit suspicious of Ernie's happy silence. But there's no question that he loves Cujo. Suddenly, Collin's eyes are alive, and the vein on his neck is showing. He looks at Cujo, then at me, and then back to Cujo, then back to me. His voice awash in awe, he says, "I can't believe you did it."

I buckle Collin beside me in the front seat, and Mama pulls us back onto 101. "What are you talking about, kiddo?"

Collin looks up to me again. "You're amazing," he gushes and leans into me affectionately. "The best uncle in the universe."

"Feel free to tell Audrey that, if you want. Today. Okay?"

His eyes are full of wonder—this is the Collin I know. "How'd you do it?"

"Do what?"

"Get me one."

"Get you what?"

He looks at Cujo again and shakes his head in happy disbelief. "You know."

"No, I don't know. What are you talking about?"

"How'd you . . ." Collin pulls me close, whispers into my ear. ". . . get me . . ." He takes a big breath and he looks at Cujo again. ". . . a real . . . living . . . breathing . . ."

Cujo shifts and announces, "I'm bored."

". . . Neanderthal."

Nean——

I turn back and glance at Cujo and note the stocky build, the heavy brows, the slightly smaller skull, the plentiful body fur. "Oh, no, Cujo is—"

"Thank you." Collin leans into me, hugs me with all his might. "Thank you so much, Uncle Rick."

"Collin, honey, you need to under——"

"Uncle Rick?" Collin gazes up at me, his eyes enormous.

Suddenly, I realize I don't have a car seat for the little guy. *Crap!*

"Uncle Rick, I just knew it."

"Knew what, kiddo?"

"I just knew I'd see you one last time."

"Of course."

"I just knew we'd go on one last adventure."

"Just be sure to tell Audrey how awesome it is."

"I just never could've guessed this." He releases me, throws his hands up in the air, squints into space a moment. "It's like *Danny and the Dinosaur,* only better."

Mama asks, "Ever done a cash transaction, Dickie?"

"Me? Of course."

"For forty-five thousand dollars?"

Collin announces, "We need to find a lab that can do DNA testing."

Mama coasts the Fleetwood to the next exit, drives us across the overpass, and gases us back onto 101, northbound. "Get ready to do some counting," she says.

"Wait a minute," I snap. "What about Sabine Rorgstardt?"

"Help me with the forty-five thousand, and I'll get you Sabine."

"But you said—" My cell vibrates. It's Audrey. I press the

phone to my ear, plug the other ear with a finger, and hunch down. "Audrey?" I say. "I have him."

She sounds relieved. "Is he okay?"

"He's fine now." I look at Collin, who is straining to turn and look back at Cujo. "When he came off the bus, he just seemed so focused and wound up. And he's got rings under his eyes. Is he sleeping?"

Audrey says, "He's exhausted and stressed out. Has he been talking about the admissions boards?"

"Oh, so that's a normal thing now? Lovely." I pull the phone off my ear and shake my head, take a breath. "Do you feel comfortable slapping my sister and her husband back into reality? They'd listen to you. Plus, you're a short-timer. It's your last day. What could they do if you pushed them around a little?"

She laughs, says, "I don't want to think about that." She clears her throat. "How's he doing now?"

Collin has unbuckled his seat belt and is climbing over to join Cujo and Ernie in the backseat, nearly whacking Mama in the jaw with his heel. I stiffen in horror at the risky move in a speeding relic. Cujo and Ernie giggle and buckle Collin into the spot between them.

"He's doing pretty well," I say. "So I was wondering, what time should we leave tonight for the Greek?"

"Oh." Her tone is so apologetic. "Well . . . I guess I'm still planning to go to yoga tonight. Sorry."

"What?" I laugh. "Have you no faith?"

"Well, I guess I really meant it when I said it needs to be special—what you do for Collin. And I guess I haven't seen that yet."

I imagine sending Audrey a selfie of me and Collin with Sabine Rorgstardt, Collin's eyes bright and happy, his cheeks flushed with excitement. "Audrey, I promise that will happen today. Just keep your phone close, okay?"

"Well, call me when you have an update," she says, "and I can always cancel on yoga."

Mama glances at me and frowns. "Tell that tramp to retract the claws for a few hours, will ya?"

Audrey says, "Who's that?"

My face heats up as my mind grinds to a halt.

Mama leans right, pulls an arm off the steering wheel, and snatches the phone out of my hand. She fumbles with the phone before getting it to her ear—only she has it upside down. "Listen, you slutty little home wrecker. Do you think you could find it within yourself to stop the phone fucking for a bit so Dickie here can help me with the boys and handle the forty-five K?" She pulls the phone off her face, looks at the screen, and presses the hang-up button. Tosses it back to me, adds, "And do you think it's possible to *not* think about yourself for a change and focus on the family?"

I try to call Audrey back, but it goes to voice mail. I sit back and close my eyes.

Mama says, "Just manage the boys while I drive."

"Where are we going?"

"Don't worry about that."

In the backseat, Collin's little voice drips with empathy. "Cujo? Do you ever feel . . . you know . . . misunderstood?"

Cujo scratches his beard, straightens his back, and squints into space, thinking. "Misunderstood? You mean like people don't know the real Cujo?"

Collin's eyes twinkle as he looks up at him. "Exactly."

"Totally, little bro." Cujo squints out the window and mumbles, more to himself, "People don't understand the real me."

Collin turns to me, his eyes intense, the vein on his neck popping. "See? It's exactly what I was telling you. Specism is real."

Cujo says, "You think I like being shoved into this little piece-of-shit uniform? It's like my body can't breathe. I mean, hell, it needs air. You know, ventilation." He stretches and unzips his jumpsuit to the stomach, exposing large curls of body hair. "A cool breeze of mercy."

Mama asks me, "Do you have access to a firearm?"

"Me?" I turn back, look at Mama. "No, I don't have a firearm. What the hell are you talking about?"

"Well, we've got the boys, I suppose. You know, in case things go tapioca."

My phone vibrates—text from my sister. Have Princeton in sec. . . . Remember: vegan snacks ONLY. Whole Foods good option. I'll repay.

Collin gazes up at Cujo. "You feel like you can't be you."

"I've always had a lot of hair," Cujo says, his voice tight, "but it was never a big deal, until now." He shoots a look at me. "It's like the Warden and his folks—It's like they're saying there's something wrong with my body."

Collin snaps, "There's nothing wrong with you."

Cujo says, "It's like the suits think the real Cujo needs to be covered with this little outfit in this stupid color. A color for gomers and dandies." He twists his mouth and grumbles, "Wage earnin'."

Collin takes a big breath, lets it out slowly. Finally, he looks up at Cujo. "Do you know about Darwinism?"

"Dar-what?"

"You know, survival of the fittest?" Collin says. "The so-called scholars use that term when . . . when they talk about your . . . your . . . you know . . ." His voice lightens. ". . . your kind?"

"Survival of the fittest?" Cujo shifts and ruminates. "Hell yeah, little bro. That's exactly what I'd call it." Cujo wipes a droplet of sweat from his scalp, and Ernie listens eagerly. "My kind? We're supposed to run wild and free. I mean, there was a day when I'd take what I wanted, when I'd do what I wanted—and yeah, you could call it survival of the fittest." He cocks his head, licks his lips, and smiles at a thought. "And damn did we have a fucking blast."

"Hey, dude. Watch the language."

"All those times, all those years," Cujo says. "It was like I was expressing myself. Like I was saying, 'This is me, eggheads. Now try to stop me.'"

Mama takes the ramp for 280 North.

"Where are we going, Mama?'

"Shut up and mind the boys."

"See, Uncle Rick? The idea that these people have been naturally selected into extinction is an utter fallacy. They live among us still." Collin bounces in his seat, smacks his hands. "Where did you find him?"

I don't have the heart to ruin the moment, so I'm selective. "I found him—You're not gonna believe this, kiddo. I found him in the bushes near my work. You love it in the bushes, don't you, Cujo?"

Cujo chuckles, licks his lips quickly. "I do."

"As much as he tries," Collin announces, "the wild side still calls for him."

"I tried," Cujo says. "I really wanted to change."

Collin yells, "Don't apologize for your existence. If your kind needed to evolve, it would have happened a long time ago. If you weren't equipped to survive, you would be extinct."

"I appreciate that, little bro." Cujo shakes his head and sighs. "I'm trying to settle down a little, trying to get off the streets, stop making a living off survival of the fittest and start earning a steady income." He pulls at his jumpsuit and huffs. "Parole officer got me this gig. Some new 'Invitation to Cooperate' program for ex-cons. Okay, fine. Give it a shot. But now? Now that I'm here in this fucking uniform, all I can think is, *This ain't me*. And the longer I live this life—the more I 'cooperate'—the more I just want to hightail it back to those bushes and just be me."

Collin sounds like he's teaching a college course, presenting Cujo to his students. "The world has never understood your kind."

"The fucking world wants to change me."

"*Dude*," I yell. "Language."

"I'm a survival-of-the-fittest guy," Cujo says. "Invitation to Cooperate? It's more like Invitation to Lick the Warden's Cornhole."

Collin is aglow. "You want to do it the old way, don't you? You know, caveman style."

"Caveman style?" Cujo chuckles and looks down at Collin. "I like you, little bro."

"Perhaps we can stay in touch. I'd like track your movements, your migration patterns, if you don't mind. I mean, especially if you decide to go back to the caveman style."

Cujo says, "Have you ever dropped some heat in the wild, dude?"

"Huh?"

My sister texts, Also feel free to practice math facts in Mandarin.

"You should try it," Cujo says. "Shitting in the bushes is actually kinda cool. It's like it's *my* way of reconnecting with my wild side." He raises an eyebrow. "The primal Cujo." He fingers his beard and grins into space. "The Cujo that squats in a bush and does what comes natural."

& please be open to giving him leadership opportunities.
Great practice. Thanks ☺

Collin says, "But you guys can do anything we do. In fact, many of your kind mated with our kind. It's just that you prefer to be wild."

Cujo puffs his chest out, searches for the right words. "It's like I'm a house cat, but kinda feral."

Collin twinkles up at him. "You're very self-aware."

● ● ●

We're sailing up 280 when my phone vibrates again. I brace for more Overachiever Fever insanity until I realize it's actually a pic from Audrey. I tap on the thumbnail, and it blooms into full-screen wonderfulness. It's a pic of her naked feet, crossed at the ankles, her lovely calves and lower legs showing, skin as smooth as the finest silk. Nothing risqué or exhibitionist, but sexy as hell and maybe a little flirty. And I wonder if it's my man brain that is making this pic seem so sexy. It's basically a pair of feet on some type of ottoman.

A caption comes in: Did my nails red and white, just like Beat colors ☺

I should have noticed, but I hadn't. I look again, and indeed she's got the colors of the English Beat (red, white, and black) on her nails—her big toes even bear the band's signature checkered black and white pattern. How freaking cool is that? I tap back, Is this ur way of saying we're on for 2nite?

My phone buzzes. No. . . . It's my way of saying I'm pulling for u.

I stare at the pic some more. She's killing me.

From the back, Cujo says, "Whoa." His voice is nearly shaky. He slumps in his seat and swats Ernie on the knee. "Dude, check it out." Ernie looks, sees what Cujo sees, and ducks, encouraging Collin to do the same thing.

Collin is popping, he's so excited. "What is it?" he rasps.

Which is when I notice the Datsun 120y coupe and its occupants, coming up on our right. They're wearing seafoam-green shirts. Long sleeves. Zip-ups, just like . . . Or, actually . . . Jumpsuits? My heart sinks as I give them another look, my mind scrambling for a reason—any reason—to believe that we're not being tailed by a carload of conployees.

I give them one last look.

They're smiling at us. But not really.

● ● ●

Mama says, "I thought I told you to stop hanging out with those boys."

Cujo slides a little lower, and Ernie grips his prongs.

Collin whispers excitedly, "Who are they?"

"Did you hear me?"

The Datsun is loaded down with so many conployees, the rear bumper is inches from scraping the road. I don't want to look over, but I do for one final assessment. Of course, they're all staring at me, and I jerk away, but the vision sizzles.

Shaved heads, with lots of ink work.

Expectant eyebrows.

Steady eyes.

Toothy grins.

My scalp tingles, and my face flushes. "Hit the gas, Mama," I say. "Let's lose these guys."

Mama huffs. "I'm not running away from a bunch of over-grown burnouts." She frowns, glances at me. "What kind of ex-

ample is that for the boys? Letting their bully friends dictate what
we do, letting them have control over our lives?"

Cujo says, "C'mon, Mama. Listen to the Warden. Let's lose
these guys."

"I told you to stop associating with these losers."

Collin reddens. "Neanderthals are *not* losers."

"Mama, you don't understand." Cujo twirls his beard and
nearly whispers. "At Robards, these guys kind of run the show."

She laughs. "Is that true, Dickie?"

"I—"

"No," Cujo says. "I mean, they run the sideshow. Not like the
Warden and his suits run the office shit. I mean these guys kinda
run the side businesses in the Little Big House."

"The what?"

"You know, the Little Big House. The conployee building at
work. It's like a little big house—you know, a little prison—on
account of all the ex-cons working there. For a lot of guys, it
kinda feels like the old days in prison. You know, with gangs and
posses and guys who call the shots inside."

Collin says, "We always figured they had a hierarchical social
structure, but now I have documentable proof. Uncle Rick, did
you bring our field log?"

We approach the Sand Hill exit, and I motion for Mama to
take the exit.

"So these guys run the show amongst the cons?"

Cujo says, "They run the show for one of the crews in the
Little Big House."

"And you and Ernie don't play with these boys?"

"Nah." Cujo kinda mumbles. "We're friendly with the
Robards Syndicate. But these guys here are the Robards Clown
Posse."

"Interesting," Collin says, more to himself. "They don't have the classic look—the pronounced brow and massive bone structure—that we see here in my new best friend, Cujo."

Mama takes the Sand Hill exit, and the Robards Clown Posse falls in behind. "Cujo, your father and I want you to be one hundred percent honest with us."

Silence.

"You hear me?"

"Yes, Mama."

"Why are these boys following us?"

"Mama, I swear. I don't know." Cujo leans forward, as if to punctuate the point. "Ernie and me, we kinda keep it low-profile. We don't run any action in the Little Big House. Not like the Robards Clown Posse."

Mama scoots up on her seat, bites her lip. "Where am I going, honey?"

I squint into the side-view mirror, and the Robards Clown Posse is right up on us, the Datsun nearly kissing Mama's bumper. "Okay, pull a right here."

"Where in the hell am I going?" she yells.

"Take this right," I snap. "Right here."

Mama growls. "These boys are really starting to piss me off." She guns the Fleetwood, and we jerk forward. "Who do they think they are?" Another growl. "No respect."

We're on the four-lane Sand Hill Road. "Stay in the right lane here, Mama."

The Datsun dives into the left lane and makes a run up on us. Mama cusses and jerks the Fleetwood to the left. The Datsun skids and veers farther left. "Little punks," she mutters and keeps the Fleetwood over the lane dividers.

"Mama," Cujo says. "I wouldn't piss these guys off."

Collin suddenly looks a little scared.

"I thought I told you," she roars. "I don't tolerate bullies. And neither should you."

We come up on the first light, and I say, "Turn in here."

"Where?"

"Take a right," I snap. "Here. Right here."

Mama pulls a sweeping right, with no brakes, and the Fleetwood screeches and grazes the corner curb. "How many times have I told you I'm not a goddamn mind reader?" she says. "Some things never change. Where in the hell am I?"

The Datsun is right behind us.

"Rosewood Sand Hill."

"What?"

I yell into her ear, *"The goddamn Rosewood Sand Hill."*

She skids the Fleetwood to a halt, and the Datsun swerves to avoid slamming into us. She turns and lowers her head as she glares into my eyes. "Don't you *dare* yell at me. How many times have I told you?"

I deflate, look away. "Sorry. I'm just worked—"

"What an awful example for the boys."

"I know. I'm just—"

"To speak to the mother of your children that way."

Okay, this is getting really weird.

I close my eyes a moment. "You're right. I'm sorry."

She jerks the Fleetwood forward, and the Datsun self-corrects and follows.

Softly, she asks, "Now, where are we?"

"A very fancy hotel." I motion for her to roll into the front check-in area, where bellhops are waiting. "Just pull in here. I'm sure there are cameras everywhere."

"Yeah, they won't try anything here," Cujo says and glances back at the Datsun. "Not with all this security."

I know we are quite the scene here. The Rosewood Sand

Hill has become *the* meeting place for venture capitalists, billionaires, and all other types of Silicon Valley elites and their associated ecosystem. Situated in the rolling foothills of Menlo Park, the Rosewood is where one might hook up with a rich sugar mama or daddy. Where one may gawk and play rich. Porsches and Teslas and Fiskers populate the valet parking areas.

And here we are—our motley crew—pulling up in a forty-year-old station wagon, followed by a Datsun packed with inked-up ex-cons. For a moment, the Rosewood staff seem a bit baffled— just standing there, staring at us—but they recover and spring into action, gliding toward us, smiling, ready to open doors.

"Now," Mama says, "I want you boys on your best behavior."

A happy young man opens her door. "Welcome to the Rosewood."

Mama looks to me. "What the hell are we doing here? We have to get the merchandise."

Another man opens my door, and I say to Mama, "Let's go into the lobby. They aren't going to screw with us here. I'll get you guys situated, then I'll take the Fleetwood to Collin's school so he can get his things and pull a Bob Watson."

Mama looks into the rearview mirror. The Robards Clown Posse are piling out of their car, stretching and straightening out their seafoam-green jumpsuits. One of them tosses the keys to a bellhop. "And what about these boys? You expect me to handle these clowns while you and the runt enjoy a Sunday drive to the school?"

"No. Let's all go the lobby, have a seat, and figure this thing out. Then Collin and I will go to the school. You and the boys can have a drink, and we'll come back and pick you all up."

The Clown Posse has fanned out and circled the Fleetwood, and one of the bellhops has tucked his chin into his lapel, whispering into a tiny microphone, his jaw tight.

"Fine." Mama shuffles to get out of the wagon. "Cujo, be a good helper boy and get Mama that little orange cooler from the back." Cujo twists, reaches, and turns back with the cooler. "Thank you, sweetie," Mama coos, and Cujo swings it over the front seat and into her lap. "Now you boys do as I say, okay?"

"Yes, Mama."

We step out of the wagon, and a large, well-dressed man from the hotel approaches with a grimace. He's wearing an earpiece, and he's scanning the Clown Posse. "Welcome to the Rosewood."

"Thanks." I pull out my wallet and finger through my bills. The smallest is a twenty. *Oh, what the hell?* I hand it to him. "We're just having a drink in the lobby. And oh . . ." I turn to the bellhop on the driver's side. ". . . I'll be back out in a few minutes, so you may want to park it nearby." I nod to the collection of polished roadsters and sedans on display forty feet away, failing to suppress a grin. "That cool?"

"Certainly, sir."

One of the Clowns steps forward, his eye gleaming. He's got a small black Nike bag slung over his shoulder, and his jumpsuit is partially unzipped, revealing a massive, heavily inked chest. "Same with us." My God, his voice is gravelly. He sounds like Wolfman Jack with a touch of Larry King. "We'll be quick," he adds, and his buddies chortle, puffing their chests out and grinning.

I say, "I think we can be professional about this, guys."

Nike Bag gives me a long look, and his face softens. He turns to his buddies, whispers something, and they turn back to me with true fear on their faces. "Mr. Warden," he says, startled. They back up, and he points over his shoulder with a thumb. "We can take off, Mr. Warden. I mean, we didn't know you were involved."

"I'm not the Warden, guys."

"Of course he's the Warden," Mama says. "You've seen his picture."

I feel my chest rise. "I'm Rick Blanco, and all I want to do is go to the Greek with my nephew's nanny."

Their worried eyes tell me they don't believe.

"We're sorry, Warden. We didn't know this was your side action. We thought this one was fair game. I mean, like you say in those videos, the company *wants* us to show our entrepreneurial side."

"Entrepreneurial side for Robards International," I say. "Not yourselves."

"Yes, Warden. You're right. Well, maybe we could give you— er, I mean Robards—a part of our cut."

"The Warden doesn't want a part of your little cut," I snap, marveling at how easily all of this is spilling out, how easy it is to be Dick Rayborne, EVP of Human Resources at Robards International. "The Warden makes tens of millions of dollars a year. Do you think the Warden cares about your side action?" They step back, listen intently. "The Warden cares about lowering the cost of total head count."

Nike Bag puts his palms out. "Whatever the Warden wants to do, we're cool." He tries to gauge my eyes. "If the Warden would prefer we just got back in our car and returned to work, that's fine with us, too."

"Guys, let's just go inside and figure this thing out. Whatever 'this thing' is."

Nike Bag is so pleasant. "Whatever the Warden wants."

Cujo approaches from behind and puts a huge arm around me. "You probably can tell already." He squeezes. "The Warden's a doofus."

The Clowns ease up, crack a few smiles, and exchange a few more whispers.

Mama yanks the barbecue prongs from Ernie's grasp. "Boys," she barks. "Come with me. All of you." She marches into the hotel, her head down, clutching the cooler in one arm as she lifts the prongs into the air and points forward. "We're gonna straighten this out right now."

.   .   .

We're seated across from the Robards Clown Posse, which is squeezed into a lobby sofa. Three Clowns are trying to stare me down, trying to get under my skin as they whisper things to each other while never breaking eye contact. A fourth Clown, his eyes too close together, is leering at two lovely young women seated across the lobby. I keep Collin at my side, my left arm firmly around his waist, and he scoots closer.

A young waiter arrives with a tray of champagne flutes. "Okay," he says, not unlike a kindergarten teacher. The Clowns scoot up to make eye contact, trying to intimidate him. He's of course unflappable, his pleasant face unwavering as he places flutes on the coffee table between us. "I'll be right back with the bottle."

He hurries away, and the Clowns snicker.

Mama raises the prongs. "Okay, boys," she snaps and jabs the Nike bag guy in the pecs. "Enough bullshit."

Collin and the boys giggle, and Nike Bag rubs his chest. "Hey, watch it with that, lady."

She jabs him again. "Don't you 'lady' me."

I notice a security detail gathering, eyeing the prongs.

She jabs him again, in the knee.

"Hey, c'mon."

"I'm your elder." Then she softens at a nice thought. "You can call me Mama."

"Fine." Nike Bag rubs his chest. "Damn."

"Now." She straightens a bit and stares at him. "What do you punks want with my boys?"

Nike Bag chuckles. "Lady—" Mama raises the prongs, and he jerks back, palms out. "I mean, Mama. . . . Mama, we don't want nothin' with the Robards Syndicate. I swear. We don't need no more riots in the Little Big House, or anything like that. The Clown Posse is all about becoming businessmen." He nods at the cooler between Mama's feet. "Which is why all we want is that thing there."

Mama leans forward and looks into his eyes. "And how do you know about this thing here?"

"Mr. Flanduzi gave us specific instructions." He frowns. "You ain't the seller?"

Flanduzi? Who in the hell is Flanduzi?

Mama says, "I'm the helper, you nitwit. So is Dickie here."

"Helper? We don't care about no helpers. We're representing the buyer, Mr. Huloojasper." He reaches down and pulls a slip of yellow paper from his shoe. He unfolds it carefully, looks at me, and returns to the scribble on the paper. "You don't know Bobby Flan——. . . Flan . . . duzi?"

Mama straightens and jabs him in the thigh. He cusses.

"Does he look like he knows anything?" Mama snaps. "Who sent you boys?"

"Mr. Flanduzi."

"Bobby Flanduzi? And what did he tell you to do?"

"He told us to go to meet him tonight at his house, and that he'd give us that there red thing. And then we'd need to make the sale with Mr. Huloojasper. So we were scouting Mr. Flanduzi's neighborhood—just to make sure we knew what to expect tonight—when you came out of his house with the red thing."

"Cooler."

"Whatever. And that's when we saw that the . . ." He nods to Cujo and Ernie. ". . . Robards Syndicate was involved. So we call Mr. Flanduzi, and he says, follow them. So that's what we did." He sits back and chuckles to himself. "I don't think Mr. Flanduzi is cut out for this type of thing."

Mama says, "I told Bobby Flanduzi that I'd handle the sale." She looks down, sighs. "He said, 'Absolutely not. You're nuts, stay away from my family.'" Mama rolls her eyes at the memory. "But he and Linda have enough to deal with already, so I vetoed him there."

"No one told us they changed the meet-up time and place."

Mama frowns at a thought, sighs again. "I guess I didn't. I guess I just got a little confused. When Dickie called this morning, I guess I thought we could do this at Dickie's compound."

"I'm not Dick—"

"Shut up." Mama takes a breath, steadies herself. "Now, I want you boys to listen." She taps the cooler with the prongs. "I know exactly how much Bobby Flanduzi wants for this."

"Look, Mama, we're just the brokers here. You give us the cooler, we give you this bag here, and we give the cooler to Mr. Huloojasper." He looks at his buddies, proud. "And Mr. Flanduzi pays us a transaction fee."

"Who's Bobby Flanduzi?" I ask.

Mama seems astounded. "You don't even know your employees."

"And Huloojasper?"

"We found him," Nike Bag says. "We found the buyer, we did it all."

Mama says, "Okay, let me see the bag."

He lifts it, lowers it onto her lap. "Go ahead."

Slowly, her fragile fingers work the zipper. I feel everyone in the lobby watching as she pulls the zipper flap away. "Okay, let's see," she says as the contents become apparent to everyone in the lobby.

Cash.

Lots of cash.

Bundles of twenties.

Lots and lots of bundles of twenties.

I'm hit by the ripe scent of well-circulated bills.

"Forty-five thousand," says Nike Bag. "Go ahead and have your Dickie count it."

The waiter returns with the bottle of champagne, a $485 selection that Nike Bag had made after a four-second review of the wine list. I reach to put the flap back over the cash, and Mama swats my hand. "Keep your greedy corporate paws off that."

Collin's eyes enlarge, and he rasps, "Unbelievable."

The waiter notices the cash, acts like he didn't see it, and presents the bottle to us. "Okay," he says. "We have a Pol Roger brut, Sir Winston Churchill, 1999."

Nike Bag nudges the Clown sitting beside him, nods at the waiter, and grins.

"If I could just get a credit card from the party."

Silence.

The waiter glances at the bag on Mama's lap. "Or if you'd prefer to pay in cash."

Mama turns to me. "Coming here was your idea."

Silence.

All of this, so I can hold Audrey in my arms in the middle of an English Beat set? So I can take her home and start something special? So I can quit my job, house-sit a mansion, and ditch the rat race for two years? So I can write my book and perhaps save a generation from wasting thousands—no, millions—of hours in useless meetings? So I can show my troubled nephew that the Bob Watson can (and will) change his life?

"Fine," I snap and pull out my credit card. "Here."

"Should I keep it open?"

"Sure," says Nike Bag. "But before you crack that thing, can I take a look?"

"Of course."

"I just want to make sure it's what I ordered."

"Certainly."

Nike Bag takes the bottle and makes a big deal of inspecting the label, squinting as he runs a forefinger under the text, mumbling to himself. He tosses it a little, like he's weighing it. "For buoyancy," he informs.

The waiter shifts and watches.

He jerks it around, thrusts it up in the air, into the sunlight, and peers into the bottle. "Hmm." He turns it upside down, then quickly right-sides it. "There's something about this one."

"Would you like me to cancel the order?"

"Sure," I say, "maybe that—"

"Nah," says Nike Bag. "It's probably just me."

The waiter turns and looks back to the bar, which is when Nike Bag gives the bottle a few quick shakes. When the waiter turns back to us, Nike Bag offers a sweet smile, his bad teeth showing.

"Okay?" asks the waiter.

Nike Bag hands the bottle back, so gentle. "Definitely okay."

"Shall I?"

An unapologetic groan. "Please."

The Clowns and the boys scoot to the edges of their seats, eager. Nike Bag tells the waiter, "Back in the pen, where there are no ladies, you'd do just fine. You know what I mean, sweetie?"

They giggle as they watch him untwist the wire casing.

"There you go," he says. "You've done this before, haven't you?"

The waiter can't suppress a laugh. "Okay, dudes."

"That's good," Nike Bag says. "Keep doing that there."

The waiter pulls off the casing, sticks out a foot, and begins to pull on the cork.

Nike Bag says, "I think you got it."

Waiter keeps pulling.

Someone moans.

Mama lifts the prongs. "Boys."

"Here, sweetie." Nike Bag stands and struts up behind him, his voice deep and throaty. "Let's do this together."

"No, please take a seat." The waiter pulls the cork off, and white foam shoots everywhere. Hundreds of dollars' worth of aged champagne drips down the bottle and onto the table and carpet. The Clowns roar and oooh and ahhh, and the waiter stands back and chuckles, shaking his head.

"Someone get this sweetie a towel."

What remains of the champagne, the waiter pours into our flutes. "I feel like I've just been in the weirdest episode of *Scared Straight!*" he says, laughing. "I don't think I'll even commit a parking violation."

Nike Bag lifts his flute toward Mama, says, "Good times."

Mama tries to move the bag to my lap but loses her grip, and cash pours out, tumbling onto the couch and floor. Ernie's eyes bulge. Cujo announces, "Piñata time," and drops to all fours in a mad crawl to the money. Collin and Ernie join him.

There's a loud murmur in the lobby as scores of young venture capitalists, silver foxes, and "gold diggers" watch us with strained, ashen faces.

Nike Bag says, "Hand over the goods."

Cujo is at our feet, scooping up bundles and shoving them down his jumpsuit.

"*Cujo!*"

More scooping, until Mama reaches down, grabs him by the ear, and twists hard.

He freezes. "Okay, okay."

Still gripping and twisting. "That's Flanduzi family money."

"Okay, Mama. Okay."

She presses the prongs against his throat. "Dickie's gonna count all of this right here, and if there's even twenty dollars missing, it's coming out of your allowance, wild child."

Allowance? No. That can't be—

"Okay, Mama. Please."

Collin and Ernie are frozen, watching.

She lets go, and he rolls onto his butt. "Christ, Mama." He rubs his ear, then begins to pull the bundles out of his jumpsuit, throwing them at me, hard. I feel like a bad juggler failing to handle an incoming volley of balls. Breathless, I scoop up the bundles and shove them into the bag. People are watching. The murmuring gets louder, and soon a tall member of hotel security is standing before us. "I'm afraid we've received some complaints," he says, eyeing the bag. "I think you may need to—"

"Hey, dude." One of the Clowns—another beefy bald guy, but with Prince Charles ears—stands up and stares him down. "You got a problem?"

"We do have a problem."

"I'm about to have a problem, too." Long stare. "With you. If you don't leave."

The security manager backs away, whispers into a microphone on his lapel.

Okay, five minutes before the first cop shows up.

Mama yells, "Start counting, Dickie."

Crap. I take a bundle and start fingering the twenties.

Nike Bag says, "Hand it over, Mama."

There's fifty twenties in the bundle. I start to count the bundles, pulling them out of the bag and stacking them neatly on my lap, my knees closed tight. Collin and Ernie are kneeling at my feet, watching with wonder. I can nearly feel the eyes of forty additional onlookers.

Mama takes the cooler and lowers it onto the table.

Okay, forty-five bundles, times a kilobuck a bundle. That's forty-five K.

"It's all here," I announce, and I have to admit it feels good to say it.

"Put it back in the bag, honey, and zip it up." She nods to the cooler and frowns at Nike Bag. "I want you kids to open that up. I don't want anyone saying we didn't deliver the goods."

I bag the cash, catch the waiter's eye, and wave him down. "Just go ahead and close the tab," I say. "And add fifty as a tip."

Nike Bag says, "Mr. Huloojasper said no tampering."

"Too bad," Mama says. "Open it, confirm it's all there."

Prince Charles Ears says, "That's not how it's done in white-collar business."

"Dude, in white collar, it's all digital and shit."

And I hear myself say, "Someone trusted you guys with forty-five K in cash?"

Mama's losing patience. "Open the goddamn cooler, boys." She points the prongs at me. "And use that cordless telephone of yours."

"Huh?"

"Take a photograph with your cordless telephone." She's yelling now. "A photograph of the Clown boys with the contents."

The waiter delivers the bill, with the credit card already run through. I sign the charge slip and take the card.

Nike Bag stalls.

"C'mon, boys."

"Mr. Huloojasper said—"

"You can tell Mr. Huloo-what's-his-name that this deal is off unless we can prove this transaction was completed fully and that we did give you Clowns the goods."

He sits there, looking to his colleagues for direction.

"Here." Mama is on her feet, shuffling around the coffee table. "I'll open it. Give that to me." He looks to me. "Honey," she snaps, irritated. "Get your telephone camera ready."

By the time I am ready to click off a few shots, we're surrounded by a small audience of silver foxes, hotel staff, and even our waiter. It reminds me of one of those scenes in the movies when someone's hot at the craps table and has begun to draw a crowd. I step closer and squat to get a better shot. "Okay," I announce, and Mama reaches down and flips open the tiny lid.

Everyone's silent, staring at the contents. I snap off a few shots.

Cujo breaks the silence. "Forty-five K?" He fingers his beard, thinking, staring. "For those?"

Mama looks at me. "Honey, you better get Collin to school."

Shit, she's right. I pat my pants, checking for my keys and wallet.

"Just give me your telephone," she says. "In case I need to call your tramp. Or maybe even your sister."

I hear myself laugh. "Um . . . No."

Mama says, "Um . . . Yes."

"Mama, I don't think you want to have the phone."

She squints at me, waiting for more.

"The cops will be tracking that phone soon. That phone is probably already connected to an assortment of felonies that have happened today. Break-ins. Car chases. Kidnapping—me. Illegal cash transactions. Phone calls with the loved ones of your victims. You're leaving digital fingerprints everywhere."

Her face deflates. "How does that work?"

"Why don't I keep it?" I say. "I wouldn't want anyone to find you with this phone."

Mama straightens and folds her arms.

"Think about it, Mama."

"Dickie," she says. "Would you like to meet my friend Sabine?"

I roll my eyes, defeated, and nod.

"Then give me the fucking telephone." She puts out a hand. "Now."

"It's gonna get your arrested," I say. "And the boys are gonna lose their parole."

Mama says, "Last chance for Sabine."

Fine. I hand it over.

"Take the wagon," she says, irritated. "And Cujo, too." She shuffles back to her seat, oblivious to the dozens of people staring at her. "Ernie and I will stay here with the money." She takes a few big breaths as she lowers herself back onto the couch. "The Clown boys are going to take Mr. Huloo-guy's purchase and leave us before the cops show up." She gives them the don't-you-get-it-eyes. "Right, boys?"

"Fine. C'mon, Collin and Cujo. We're gonna do an errand."

Collin gets up, but Cujo doesn't move. He's still looking into the cooler on Nike Bag's lap. "Cujo," Mama snaps. "Stop staring at the monkey drool and go."

Still staring.

"*Cujo,*" Mama roars, leans over and stabs him in the shoulder with the prongs.

He blinks hard, shakes his face, snapping himself out of it. "Huh?"

"Go with Dad."

The Clowns are mobilizing. They head toward the exit,

champagne flutes in their hands, the cooler of "monkey drool" in the protective clutch of Nike Bag.

Cujo turns to Mama, confusion in his eyes. "Dad?"

"Dickie," she snaps. "Go with Dickie and the kid, and make sure he comes back."

Cujo releases a plaintive moan. "Me? Why not Ernie?"

We look at Ernie, who seems to have gone into a trance as he stares at the ceiling.

"I want you to go."

"Ah, c'mon, Mama."

"Don't you *dare* argue with me, mister."

"Fine." Cujo gets up, his body deflated. "I get all the boring chores."

She turns to me, says quietly, "We've spoiled them, haven't we?"

"That's what I wanted to do," Cujo moans. "I wanted to stay here with the monkey drool."

Mama stiffens. "The monkey drool's gone. The Clown boys just left with it."

Cujo pouts. "Or at least stay here with the forty-five K."

Collin squeaks, "Me, too."

"Listen." Mama stands up and points the prongs at Cujo. She's yelling again. "Go take the fucking kid to school. The forty-five K isn't going anywhere."

"Whatever." Cujo heads toward the exit. "C'mon, Warden. Let's do this fast and get back to the cash."

From behind us, the sound of a dog clicker. Cujo turns just in time to snatch a mini of Thunderbird out of the air. He stops, twists off the cap, and makes a big show of pouring the liquor into his mouth, lifting the little bottle high into the air, creating a long stream. When he's done, he straightens, swallows, and allows a contented sigh. He tosses the empty to a passing bellhop, who fumbles with it before it tumbles down the hallway. "Okay." He pushes out a tiny burp. "Let's do this."

Collin looks up at him in wonder.

Onlookers provide a wide clearance.

"So, Mr. Warden," he says and unzips his jumpsuit a tad, revealing more body fur.

"I'm not the Warden."

We turn the corner and see that the bellhops somehow already have Mama's wagon pulled up, doors open. It strikes me, this metallic-blue relic "popping out" in stark contrast to nearly everything else here at the Rosewood, a defiant artifact nearly aglow in this citadel of polished, sparkling newness. Collin releases my hand and bolts for the wagon, squealing as he dives into the backseat.

"What's the deal with this kid?"

"He's my nephew."

"Oh." Cujo sounds mildly surprised. "I figured he was yours."

Maybe it's the moment. The wild moment that has me off guard. Or maybe it's the half glass of champagne on an empty stomach. Whatever the reason, I hear the words tumble out of my mouth. "Oh, no. I could never have a kid. Not after what I did."

Cujo stops abruptly. He turns, grabs my shirt, and looks into me, and I notice a depth in those eyes—could it be warmth, or even compassion?—that I hadn't seen before.

"So . . ." His voice is suddenly so gentle. "Was that really monkey drool?"

GET SIDETRACKED

The Halvaford School in Menlo Park boasts the highest percentage of "alumni" who eventually end up at Stanford or an Ivy League school. According to its website, admission for the incoming kindergarten class requires an IQ test, five letters of recommendation, a $2,000 application-processing fee, and four panel interviews (one for the parents, three for the kid). Tuition is $36,500 a year, but that does not include the annual field trips, which start with the Galápagos for the kindergartners and climax in eighth grade with a weeklong "internship" with White House mentors in the Eisenhower Executive Office Building.

I park the wagon in front of the campus and turn to the backseat, where Collin and Cujo are buckled in. Collin pulls his eyes off Cujo and says to me, "Suddenly, SAT Prep doesn't seem very important, Uncle Rick."

Cujo stiffens, grimaces, and pushes out a tiny fart.

"I've been meaning to ask you." I turn a little more so I am eye-to-eye with Collin. "Do you enjoy school?"

Collin looks at me like I'm nuts. "Enjoy? Kids who want to

get into a *good* college don't 'enjoy' school, Uncle Rick. They dominate school."

"I dominated school," Cujo says, "on the playground."

I say to Collin, "You said yourself: SAT Prep doesn't seem very important on a day like today. Not when you're in the middle of a Neanderthal adventure." Collin looks up at me, and I smile and rustle his hair. "Do you know how long it will be before you even need to take the SAT?" He looks at me. "You have more than ten years—a decade, Collin." I take his knee and shake it playfully. "You're doing just fine."

Collin balls his fists and looks away. "Sometimes, I just hate the SAT more than anything."

Cujo says, "What's an SAT?"

"Here's the deal," I say. "I kinda feel like it's okay for you to be a kid a little more often. You know what I mean, buddy? So I'm starting to feel like maybe it's my job to help you break free once in a while. So you can actually be a kid."

"Like today?"

"Yeah, like today. Or even when you're older and I'm living somewhere else, and you can feel okay about going on a un-planned adventure, or just doing something a little bit crazy."

Collin looks up at me. "Crazy? Really?"

Sitting there talking about this, I find myself wondering, when will this kid ever have a chance to do something risky? When will he ever wipe out on a bike, or meet a few assholes, or even just be—oh, don't say it—idle and bored? I mean, aren't these things important for a kid? Aren't these the things that help shape kids into healthy adults? I'm not sure parents with Over-achiever Fever understand this.

Collin seems to deflate, his body sinking as he looks down at his clasped hands. "I don't have time for crazy adventures, Uncle Rick. Not if I want to get into a *good* college."

"Well, it's true that crazy fun might not help with college admissions. But do you want to know what I think?"

He looks up, shakes his head.

"Fancy colleges are just one tiny sliver of what this big, exciting world has to offer. And you're a kid. Your job is to have fun and *not* worry about colleges right now."

"My dad says the Barnards have a reputation to uphold."

"Reputation? Don't worry about that. It's not your job to make your mom and dad look good."

Cujo says, "He's right, kid. You've got to be you."

Collin throws his hands into the air. "But how? I mean, how can I be me when I have no time to be me?"

"Sometimes," Cujo says, "I'd just tell my parole officer to chill out so I could be me for a night or two. You know what I mean, little dude? But those ankle bracelets were a bitch—didn't come off."

"Collin," I say, "the good news is that you don't have an ankle bracelet. It's a lot easier. All you have to do is pull a Bob Watson."

Collin looks at me with hope. "A Bob Watson? What's a Bob Watson?"

"It's like ditching school, only you can do it all your life."

He allows a grin. "And how do I pull a Bob Watson?"

A shot of electricity shoots through me, and I feel like I'm gonna float off my seat. "First, you need to find inspiration—a reason for ditching SAT Prep."

Collin smiles. He reaches over and squeezes Cujo's forearm, and the felon looks down at him and grins. "I've definitely found my inspiration," Collin says. "Now what?"

"Second, you need to make sure everyone sees you in class, and you need to make sure you really kiss up to the teacher. Make them feel important."

Collin thinks about it. "I can do that."

"Then comes the fun part."

Collin twinkles. "Yeah? What do I do next?"

"You need to create a distraction, kiddo. So they're not paying attention to you when you leave. Can you do that?"

He bites his fist as he thinks about it. Slowly, he nods yes.

"Then the next thing you do is even more fun."

He looks up and giggles. "What's that?"

"You leave."

Collin looks so excited—his teeth gritted, his eyes gleaming, his knee bouncing—that I wouldn't be surprised if he exploded into a cloud of shiny confetti.

● ● ●

I walk Collin to the school office and sign him in. Collin makes eye contact with the school secretary and puffs out his chest. "I'm here now, Mrs. Randolph." He says it so loudly, he's nearly yelling. "Now I will proceed to Miss Doring's classroom for an exciting session of SAT Prep. I can't wait. The journey to a *good* college continues today."

Mrs. Randolph looks up and smiles. "Okay, thanks, Collin."

Collin gives me a wink and leaves the office, and I beam with pride. This is a kid who understands that the foundation of any successful Bob Watson must include a rousing validation of your keepers, a reminder that you are "in the building," literally and figuratively.

I approach Mrs. Randolph. "I have an odd request."

She peers up, eyes thinning.

"I was wondering if I could use a phone here."

Pregnant pause. "The team huddle room is open. You can use the phone in there. Just dial a nine."

"Thanks," I say. "I can't find my phone, and I need to call Collin's nanny. You wouldn't have her number, would you?"

Mrs. Randolph laughs. "Are you kidding? Your sister made Audrey the primary contact for nearly everything here." With a few keystrokes, she pulls up Audrey's number and jots it down on a slip of paper, says, "I am going to miss her. And so will your nephew."

In the huddle room, I call Audrey. She's surprised to hear that it's me.

"Why are you calling from the school line?"

"Long story. Listen . . ."

"What happened to the Neanderthal adventure?"

"It's happening. I just thought it would be good to teach him how to pull a Bob Watson." Mrs. Randolph walks by and glances in, her jaw tight. "This place is a bit intense."

"Gee, you think?"

I turn and cup my hand around my mouth. "There's way too much pressure on these kids."

"Did you know Collin has a classmate who submitted an ice sculpture for this overnight make-a-castle project?"

"It's like everyone has to be spectacular," I say.

"Exactly. And when they aren't spectacular, what do you think happens?"

This sparks a recent memory. I'd read a magazine article about the high schools in Palo Alto, the overachiever capital of the west, where the number of wonderfully talented teenagers who commit suicide is so high that they've put fences around the train tracks—the other year, they had seven high school suicides. In San Francisco, a girl jumped off the Golden Gate Bridge because she'd lost her 4.0 grade point average.

"The universe needs you, Rick Blanco."

"The universe?"

"Yes. The universe needs you to be the crazy uncle who injects some sanity into Collin's life. Can you do that?"

I think of the Bob Watson. "What if I told you I'm already on it?"

"Then I'd say you're finally getting it."

"And I kinda feel like the universe wants us to go see the Beat tonight."

She laughs. "Call me when you have an update."

We hang up, and Cujo lumbers into the office, his massive frame filling the space, his inked-up scalp beading with sweat, his hands clasped, his eyes big and innocent. He makes eye contact with the suddenly paralyzed Mrs. Randolph.

His voice is so gentle. "I'm here for the show-and-tell."

• • •

I will say this about the Halvaford School: Yes, a large number of their students are unhappy and stressed-out, but they definitely know how to follow directions—in this case, the first three steps of pulling a Bob Watson. In a matter of minutes, my little nephew has found inspiration, he's validated his keepers, and he has distracted a critical mass of people. Like an off-balance half-court shot that somehow rattles in for a highly improbable basket, Cujo has managed to get a series of administrators and teachers worked into frothy hyperventilation without ever mentioning Collin. It culminates with Collin's SAT Prep teacher leaving her classroom so she can dash to the office and resolve this matter of the enormous, inked-up, hairy man who thinks he's here for show-and-tell in her classroom.

"Who told you to come for show-and-tell?"

Cujo offers sweet-and-innocent eyes. "My parole officer."

I don't want to leave the office—this is so fun to watch—but I also don't want to screw up my nephew's very first Bob Watson. So I head back to the wagon, where I find Collin on the floorboard curled into a ball. "You did it, kiddo." I get into the car and turn the engine. "Your teacher looks like she's about to have a seizure."

Collin pops up and bounces onto the backseat. "That was amazing."

"Feels good, doesn't it?"

"Everyone should feel this way—free," he hollers. "Including Cujo and his kind."

"Well, I think Cujo *has* been liberated. He's what they call an ex-con, meaning he was once locked up."

Collin isn't listening. "You heard him, Uncle Rick. Cujo feels misunderstood and exploited."

The vocabulary on this kid.

"Just about every single employee at Robards International feels exploited, kiddo. I'm afraid it's not limited to just Cujo and his kind—although I agree the conployees get it the worst."

"Exactly," Collin says. "*You* don't have to wear a weird uniform. But he and the others do."

Cujo arrives and joins Collin in the backseat, making the wagon bounce and tilt. I tell the boys to buckle up, and we pull out onto the road. Within seconds, we've turned the corner and are out of sight from the Halvaford School. "That was fun," Cujo says with a sigh, and offers a fist bump to a beaming Collin. "Sure beats work."

"That reminds me." I take another turn and hit the gas. "And what is it you do at work?"

"Your cleanup."

"Cleanup? Mine?"

He nods, and looks down at Collin. "Every time your uncle

fires people—like when he moved all those jobs to China and laid off those folks in Nebraska—he gives them a package."

Collin says, "What kind of package?"

"He means goodbye money and other things that will help people who've been laid off. And that's not me, kiddo. He's talking about Dick Rayborne. I do bottom-tier data transformation."

Collin looks up at Cujo. "What else is in the package?"

"Something we call free career transition services."

I instinctively kick the brakes, and we all jerk forward. "You mean, career counseling?"

"My boss calls it necessary PR. You know, like 'The Warden just doesn't dump hardworking Americans for ex-cons in the States and slave labor in China—well, yeah, he does. But he gives 'em—free of charge—assistance to help them land on their feet.' And by 'assistance,' I mean ol' Cujo here."

"And how do you help them?"

"The counseling." Cujo seems surprised that I'm not getting it. "You know, they call a number and get me, and I just follow the script. It's easier than taking orders at McDonald's."

"You read advice over the phone?"

"Sometimes I add my own stuff," Cujo says. "And I'm learning."

"Learning."

"Like, when a chick gets laid off . . . ." He opens his eyes, gives me a serious look. ". . . she isn't interested in dirty talk." He shakes his head, tickled by his apparent blind spot. "It took a few warnings from the boss to learn that one."

Collin seems to be studying Cujo's slanted forehead and heavy brow. "We still have so much to discuss."

Cujo looks down at Collin and chuckles. "Sure, little bro." Then he reaches over and shakes my seat and swats the back of my head. "C'mon, Warden. Let's jet back to the fancy place and take another look at the forty-five K. And I wanna ask Mama about the monkey drool."

• • •

In the lobby, Ernie has the cash spread out on the coffee table.

Mama looks up to us, the reflection off her glasses hiding her eyes. "I'm letting him play with it," she says to me. "I've been trying to keep him busy while you've been out doing God knows what with God knows who."

Ernie bites his tongue, this huge happy look on his face, as he shifts some stacks around and fingers through others. The silver foxes and gold diggers seem to have lost interest in the spectacle. Cujo stands over Ernie, points to the table, and whines to Mama, "You're letting him play with it?"

"I sent you on an important errand, young man. Something I couldn't have asked him to do."

Still looking at the table of cash. "I can't even fucking touch it, but he gets to play with it?"

"Watch your tongue, mister."

Ernie fans a stack of twenties in front of his face and hums to himself.

"How come I never get to play with money?"

Mama stands up and points the prongs at Cujo. "Maybe it's because he wasn't convicted of following bankers to their homes and tying them up for days on end as he slept in their beds and systematically robbed them blind."

Cujo smiles, his lids low. "Oh, yeah. That."

Mama sits down, nods to Ernie. "He's not a thief," she snaps, her voice carrying. "Making love to old ladies for money is a far cry from kidnapping and larceny." Cujo shrugs, and she adds, "This money belongs to people who need it. They're not like your puffy bankers."

I pull Collin in front of me, so Mama can see him. When Collin finally sees the cash on the table, he gasps, and his eyes bulge and widen. He steps forward, still staring.

"Sweetheart," Mama says. "Would you like to join Ernie?"

Collin looks at me, and I nod yes.

Mama says, "Just don't take any, okay?"

Collin smiles and darts to the table.

"Mama?" Cujo looks at her, hope in his eyes. "Are you gonna tell me about the monkey drool?"

"Not now," Mama snaps and settles in on me. "I need to talk to your father."

God, this is getting weird.

"Now that he's chasing another one of his sluts from the office." Mama stands and yells at me, getting new looks from the silver foxes. "Well, boy do I have news for you, Dickie. You think I've been moping around all these years, being the victim?"

"No role playing, Mama. Not here."

"Just remember this in your walnut brain." Mama reaches into her fanny pack and pulls out my phone. "If you sneak out with the kid before we're done addressing my needs, I won't call my friend Sabine Rorgstardt. But I *will* call your slut and tell her what a creep you are."

My gut tightens at the idea.

"And I need you to make a delivery with the cash. Back at that prison you call a workplace."

Cujo says, "If I promise not to pocket any . . . ?"

Mama says, "I swear, I'm gonna shove these prongs up your nose."

I stand there and watch as my nephew and a convicted

felon play with $45,000 in the lobby of the Rosewood Sand Hill. I catch Mama watching me, and she says, "This is our family, Dickie, whether we like it or not."

Our family, whether we like it or not. And just like that, it clicks—a memory from so long ago it seems nearly foreign, so distant and removed that I wonder, *Can it possibly be mine?*

● ● ●

The campfire is extinguished, the lantern is off, and finally it's quiet. The sound of the river rushes through the dark. It's soothing to hear the river, to be here in the tent with my parents and sister. That safe, warm feeling, even though we're up in the mountains. The rush of the river never stops, and as safe as I feel, I'm reminded that nature—the world, really—has its own plans, does as it pleases, regardless of any of us, and it settles into me with a shiver. The other side? The side none of us here can control? It's right over there. Always over there. Waiting. Ready for its moment. I curl up in my sleeping bag and listen to my dad snore, gazing at the long shadows of the pines crossing our tent until they become a blur.

In the far, dark corner, something scratches the fabric of our tent.

My heart skips a beat, and I stiffen, listening for more.

Another big scratch—not the scratch of something small.

Papa keeps snoring.

Another scratch.

Now my heart is pounding.

From the other side, Ana says, "Mama?"

My mom tosses and murmurs, deep in sleep.

"Ricky." Ana is nearly breathless. "Is that you?"

I choke on my spit, finally say, "No."

Long silence as we listen.

Finally, another scratch.

"Papa?"

Snoring.

In the dark corner, silence. And then, a heavy scratch. This is no animal.

Finally, I cry out weakly, "Papa?"

Snoring.

"Mama?"

Another scratch, this one heavier than any of them. Is that a knife?

I summon the courage to creep out of my sleeping bag just enough to shake Papa awake, which is when I realize his arm is extended from his own bag, clutching a long, thin tree branch, moving it back and forth for a few more scratches.

"*Papa!*" I burst out and shove him.

Papa breaks into a loud laugh, his whole body shaking.

Mama's laughing, too.

Ana sits up, puffs her chest out, releases a frustrated groan. "That wasn't funny at all." But she can't maintain the anger, and her voice softens. "I can't believe . . ."

Papa's still laughing. Hard.

"Honey. Shhh. You're gonna wake up the entire campground."

"I was so scared," Ana says. "I'm still shaking."

"Oh, come on," Papa says, sniffling and sighing. "Come over here."

Ana climbs over to their sleeping bags, which they've zipped together. She wiggles in, and Papa says, "You've never heard of the old scratch-on-the-tent prank?"

"I hope you know I was five seconds from screaming."

I sit there and watch them.

Mama says, "You okay, Ricky?"

"I guess."

Papa says, "Nothing's ever gonna bug us in here, unless you stuff a juicy pot roast into your sleeping bag."

Mama says, "I think Ricky feels left out."

"No," Ana shouts. "There's no room in here."

"Ricky, you okay over there?"

"Mama, no! He's fine."

"I think he needs a hug, too."

Mama says, "Get in here, mijo."

I clamber over Papa and force myself in.

Ana makes an Ooh-no moan.

"Come on in. The more the merrier."

It's a tight fit—with my knee pressing into Ana's back—but Mama and I are already giggling. All of our arms and legs are interlocked, and soon we're all laughing. Someone's tickling my side, and I jerk uncontrollably.

"Ow," Ana says. "Calm down."

Papa says, "I say, we sleep this way every night."

"Manny, he's gonna think you're serious."

I can't stop laughing. Papa's laughing again, too.

"Mama, I swear. His whole body is tensing up. He's trying to fart."

Papa gets a breath, sighs, and tries to sound surprised. "Ricky can fart on command? We need to find this kid an agent, Lena."

My jaw is clenched, and I'm straining. And giggling uncontrollably.

"He's trying to push one out. I can feel him. Ricky, stop it. I swear."

Papa says, "Ricky's don't smell."

"Are you kidding me? Mama, stop him."

Mama says, "Come to think of it, Manny, you're right."

I grunt and giggle and tense up.

"Okay." Ana tries to jerk free, but we've got her. "Let me out."

Mama says, "Accept your little brother for who he is, mija. Whether you like it or not, this is your family."

My grunt becomes a growl, and finally I push out a short, tight one. And I burst out laughing.

"Let me out," Ana says, defeat in her voice.

"Do you think I could squeeze one out, Lena?"

That gets me laughing so hard, I jerk back and forth.

Mama grunts and gasps. "Well, what about me?"

Ana screeches, tries to climb out.

I keep laughing.

Papa exhales, defeated. "Guess I don't have Ricky's kind of talent."

I keep laughing. Can't stop laughing. It feels so good.

Until it doesn't.

Oh, no.

Mama sighs, says, "We should get to the river early tomorrow."

Ana cuddles closer to Papa. "Do you think we could hike to that spot you promised?"

"We'll see, honey. We'll see."

My heart sinks. I try to wiggle out.

"Where do you think you're going, mijo?"

"Let him go," Ana says.

"What is—" Mama stops herself, jerks away from me. "Rick, did you—"

Ana feels the wetness and shrieks.

Mama rushes to unzip the sleeping bag and sit up. "Get out," she says, hushed. "Before it spreads more."

Ana scampers back to her bag, yells, "You idiot."

I climb out, my heart in my throat. "I didn't mean . . ."

Papa sits up, pats around. "What's wrong?"

"He peed his pants." You can hear the tension in Mama's voice. "There's urine everywhere."

"What?" Papa unzips his side of the bag. "Are you kidding me?"

My underwear and pajama bottoms are starting to get cold and uncomfortable.

Papa sighs long and hard. "You have got to be . . ."

"It's all over the bags," Mama says. "Damn it."

Ana is silent in her bag.

"Ricky," Papa snaps. "Get over here and help us figure this out."

I start to cry.

More sighs.

"Manny, he's still a kid."

Papa's voice softens a little. "I know, but he needs to—"

"Papa," Ana says from inside her bag, her voice tight. "You know it. Mama knows it. I know it. Even Ricky knows it." Long pause. "Ricky screws up everything. Always."

LOSE CONTROL OF EVERYTHING

We're parked in the Robards International lot when Mama instructs Ernie to press his barbecue prongs into the back of my neck. It's just enough to send razor-sharp ripples down my spine.

I freeze. "Dude. Chill."

The prongs press a little deeper.

"Okay, listen." Mama lifts the Nike bag between us and drops it on my lap. "It's pretty simple how this is going to happen." She's breathing hard. "Ernie is going to escort you back into the offices. Once inside, first you are going to find—now, listen to me—one of those red laser pointers. You understand me?"

More pressure from the prongs.

"Okay, fine," I say. "One laser pointer."

"Good. . . . Now . . . ." She shakes the bag of cash on my lap. "Listen. . . . Number two, you're going to locate Bobby Flanduzi, and you're going to personally . . ." She pauses, then shouts. ". . . Hand. This. Over." She drops her chin, gives me the eye.

"You're going to . . ." Another shout. ". . . *Apologize* . . ." She sighs. ". . . for your part in this. Meaning, you will acknowledge that you're the biggest reason Bobby Flanduzi had to get involved in something like this in the first place."

"Mama, c'mon. The role playing is getting really old."

"Mama?" Cujo's voice is soft and tender. "Was that really monkey drool?"

"Shut up." Mama sighs hard, looks around. "I'll be at the Playroom with the boys."

The prongs recede.

"One question," I say, and the prongs return. "This Bobby Flanduzi?" I try to look at Mama without moving my head. "Does he know who I am?"

"*Of course*," Mama yells. "You're Dick Rayborne. Mr. Paperwork. Master of the Goddamn HR Universe." She puffs, looks around for the right words. "Master stripper of benefits and compensation. The *Headcount* cover boy? The man who's made millions by lowering the average salary at Robards International."

"C'mon, Mama. Enough with the Dick Rayborne crap."

"You want me to call Sabine Rorgstardt in a sec?"

"Okay, fine." I close my eyes, take a breath. "Does this guy know that I'm going to be dropping off forty-five thousand dollars?"

Mama looks at me, sunlight reflecting off her thick lenses. "Call it a bonus."

The prongs recede, and I rub my neck, and feel blood.

Collin asks, "Can I come?"

"No, honey." Mama sweetens. "You and I are going to have some fun with Cujo in his secret playroom."

Collin brightens. "Cujo's secret playroom? Really?"

Mama bites her tongue and winks.

"Where?"

Mama nods to the large expanse of bushes to our right. "Right over there."

"The wild." There's wonder in Collin's voice, and his eyes widen as he gazes into the bushes. "Of course his playroom is in the wild."

• • •

Collin grabs his hair and pulls in opposite directions, a huge smile developing as he stands before the Playroom. It's like he's been presented a gift beyond his wildest dreams—nearly embarrassed, his legs spread wide, his mouth open. He releases an enthusiastic "wow" and laughs as he stands there and takes in the dirty mattresses, the glistening tri-tip perched over a bed of extinguished coals, the sea of empty beer cans, the dozens and dozens of strewn spare ribs and chicken bones, the tiny TV flashing a glimpse of Pops from the *Regular Show*.

"Honey." Mama yanks my arm. "Snap out of it."

I motion to Collin. "This is hilar—"

"Shut up." She points to the manhole, her hand shaking. "Grab Ernie and get in there."

Collin tugs on my arm. His eyes are serious, and his mouth is tight. "Do you realize what you've done?" His tone is hushed, and his lips are barely moving, and his eyes burrow into me. "You truly . . . really . . . truly . . . I mean, really . . . legitimately . . . have found . . ." He nods to the barbecue, where Cujo has picked up the tri-tip with his hands and is eating it corn-on-the-cob style, pulling off pieces with his mouth as he stares blankly into space. ". . . a true descendant of the Neanderthals."

"Listen, buddy. I don't think he's really a—"

"No." Collin grabs my arm, pulls it softly. "Do you realize?"

"What?"

He whispers. "Do you realize this is exactly how they lived? Minus the Cartoon Network, of course." He surveys the area again. "Caveman times? They had no concept of waste management."

"Honey, I think Cujo's never learned to—"

"Hey." Mama stands over the manhole, and Ernie's head eases out of the opening, that silent jolly look on his face. "Ernie's waiting. C'mon, lard-ass. Let's get the show on the road."

Cujo puts down the meat, wipes his hands on his jumpsuit, and slips into a tangle of brush with a deep giggle.

"No way," I say. "Absolutely no way. I'm not taking the drainage pipe back into the campus. We'll just walk in."

From behind us, snapped twigs and rustling leaves. More deep giggling.

Mama puffs her cheeks, shuffles over, and slaps me. Hard.

"Hey."

"Listen, you twerp." She slaps me again, and my cheek burns. "He's not like you. He's a conployee." She pauses as if she's waiting for it to sink in. "Conployees aren't like you suits. They can't just walk out of the office anytime they want. He's supposed to be at the—what do they call it?—the day-care place."

A jolt ripples through me. "You mean, the Robards Happy Family Work/Life Balance Day Care Center?"

She blinks hard, annoyed. "Yes, yes. That."

Gee, I wonder why that place is empty.

"If they see Ernie walking into the office with you, he's fired." She slaps again, this time lightly. "You understand? He's on third-degree probation in there. One more documented 'escape,' and he loses his job." She pokes me with a bony finger. "If Ernie loses his job, the next thing that will happen will be that his parole officer will get a notice, and then it's back to jail for . . ." She shifts into sweet voice. ". . . my little helper boy."

Crap.

"Okay. Fine."

She shuffles around, swats me on the ass. "Get in there. See how the other ninety-nine percent live."

From behind, loud rustling and branch snapping. And then, a blur. "You're it," Cujo hollers as he explodes past us. Collin spins and wobbles from the tag, his arms out for balance, his mouth open in pure joy. Cujo explodes through the empties, a wake of aluminum rippling behind him, and launches himself into the air, hollering "Collin's it" as he kicks his feet high and slaps his butt before landing on his ass, sending cans everywhere.

Collin bolts after him, giggling.

"Collin's it."

Ernie giggles, climbs out of the manhole, and darts to the action.

"Boys." Mama fights off a smile. "We have work to do. Ernie, get back in that manhole this instant."

Ernie giggles as he prances through the empties taunting Collin.

"*Boys!*"

"Collin," I say. "C'mon. Settle down."

"Document this, Uncle Rick. The Neanderthals engage in free play." He turns and chases after Ernie. "Just like us."

Cujo circles the Playroom and comes up on Collin's flank, grunting, "Time for the launch sequence." Collin squeals as Cujo grabs him and flings him up. "Liftoff."

I jolt at the sight. "Collin."

Collin windmills his arms as he sails through the air. He shrieks and lands on one of the mattresses, causing a few empties to bounce.

"Collin."

Collin picks himself up and throws his arms up, laughing.

"The boys are active." Mama puts her hands up, like it's out of her control. "And they need to get their energy out."

Ernie spins in tight circles faster than I would have thought possible, rippling the empties.

Cujo exaggerates a tiptoe attack, hands at his chin as he approaches Collin. "Gonna get ya," he says, giggling.

Collin backs up, smiles, bites his lip, and points to me. "Get my uncle."

Cujo stops in his tracks, turns, and looks at me. "C'mere, Warden."

"Cujo's it," Collin announces. "Cujo's it."

"Guys, c'mon. We've got so much to do."

Mama shakes her head, folds her arms, and laughs. "They never get tired."

Cujo slinks closer, giggling.

"Guys," I say. "Seriously."

"Life's short, Warden." Cujo explodes toward me. Cans shoot everywhere. Up close, another deep, wet giggle. And then I'm weightless, flying through the air until Cujo somehow catches me and tosses me back up, spinning me and catching me until he slides me gently into the empties.

I sit up in the empties.

Holy shit.

Everyone's laughing.

I shake my head, hoping for clarity.

Ernie jumps onto Cujo's back, and Cujo takes off.

"Rick's it, Rick's it."

Cujo zips around the Playroom, Ernie holding on.

Collin runs up to me, whispers, "C'mon, Uncle Rick." He tugs at my arms. "How many times do you get to play with a real Neanderthal . . ." He tucks his chin and looks at me. ". . . in the middle of a school day?"

Kid's got a point.

I get to my feet, pick him up, and hug him, and he squeezes me back. "C'mon, Uncle Rick." He squirms in my grasp. "We need to get them."

Cujo buzzes us as Ernie holds on, still riding his back, giggling. I lower Collin, squat, and offer him my back. "Hop aboard," I say. "And hold on." There's a tight squeal, and soon two little hands clamp on to my shoulders, legs gripping my waist, and I hear his sharp little voice in my ear. "*Turn*," he shouts, and I do, until we're facing Cujo and Ernie. "*Charge*," Collin shouts. "*Get 'em.*" I lock my arms under Collin's knees, tighten, and charge, nearly slipping on a can.

"*Get the prey*," Collin shouts, his voice rising.

"Wait a minute." I stop and turn my head back to Collin. "Prey? I thought we were playing tag."

"Same difference," Collin says. "It's just that Predator and Prey appeals to their . . ." He lowers his voice. ". . . preference for hunter-gatherer, survival-of-the-fittest games."

Cujo bounces past us with Ernie in his arms, making jet-engine noises. Ernie's arms and legs are outstretched as Cujo twists and turns through the Playroom. Collin releases and slides off my back. "Airplane rides," he gasps, the wonderment heavy. He looks up at me. "See? Here I was trying to adapt to Cujo, when he's reminding all of us that—indeed—they're perfectly capable of adapting to us."

Cujo turns Ernie for a dramatic bank. He lifts Ernie high into the air and lumbers toward us. "Dive-bomb," he announces.

Ernie makes shooting noises. *Chicka-chicka-chick . . . Chick-chinnngg.*

Cujo intensifies the jet-engine noise.

Chicka-chicka-chick . . . Chicka-chicka-chick . . . Chinnnnngggggg.

Collin tugs on my arms. "Let's get airborne. *Now.*"

What can I say? I never could have guessed any of this. I never could have guessed the ensuing "aerial dogfight" between Ernie and Collin. I couldn't have guessed reacting the way I would to Mama's subsequent clicks—"I haven't seen you boys play so well together in ages"—or asking for my own mini of Jack Daniel's. I couldn't have guessed taking a second mini after I got Collin airborne for another dogfight with Ernie that had us running out of gas quickly and making a rough emergency landing on one of the mattresses, followed by Ernie's own emergency landing, the prongs nearly spearing me in the arm. I couldn't have guessed Cujo picking up a beaming Mama and carefully lowering her onto the "family bed," where she slowly eased into the middle of the most absurd group hug I'll ever be a part of, with Cujo wrapping a leg around us all, with Ernie still making gunfire noises, with Collin in the middle, laughing uncontrollably, tears streaming down his red cheeks, with Mama saying, "Still hate families, Dickie?"

* * *

I crawl into the darkness, the Nike bag slipping off my shoulder again and again. There's no good way to carry a bag of cash when you're crawling through a drainage pipe, and kind of buzzed.

Never could have guessed any of this.

At least Mama finally called and left a message with Sabine Rorgstardt. That's progress, right? I mean, this Sabine woman still needs to call Mama back and agree to meet us, but there is hope. Right?

I stop a moment. "Ernie?" I can't see Ernie. Hell, I can't see anything—all I have is the fading sound of his scampering and grunting as I crawl up the drainage pipe. "Dude," I whisper. "Slow the fuck down."

The scampering stops, so I quicken my pace, hoping to catch up.

"Ernie?"

Up ahead, giggles.

Cujo was right; it *is* remarkably clean in here. They really did come and clean it out; Cujo hadn't been joking when he said, "Warden, what do you think would happen if one of your parole officers saw us walking around with muck smeared into our jumpsuits, old leaves stuck onto our asses?"

I crawl until Ernie's giggle seems closer. *Thank God.*

"Wait up."

He scampers up the pipe.

"Dude."

Up ahead there's a heavy *thunk*—cement on cement—and then a burst of light. I squint at the rays flooding in, can't see anything but white. "Ernie," I shush and crawl ahead. "Wait up."

Finally my eyes adjust, and I can see Ernie's legs dangling from an opening. *God, yes, the manhole.* I squat-run to the opening, growling, and Ernie's legs disappear. When I reach the opening, I can hear people talking, someone laughing, and the hum of massive air conditioners. "Ernie," I whisper-yell. "Don't leave. Tell me how you—"

"Hmmmmph." Ernie drops his head back into the pipe, grins, and puts a finger to his lips. "Shhhhhhh."

He recedes, and I rise out of the pipe, the fresh air washing over me, and I feel like a kid again. Pure wonder. A sense of magic. The pride of doing something no one else is doing, something kind of cool that makes you feel you have powers the others don't. I mean, a second ago, I was in a place that seemed so far away, in a secret "playroom" in the middle of "the wild," and now I'm transferred back into Robards, fully formed, like I've teleported à la *Star Trek*.

Beam me up, Ernie!

We're standing in a shielded area created by a dense cluster of bushes on one side and a wall on the other, and I marvel at how the boys ever found this spot, how they ever decided to go on an adventure through the pipes of Robards International. I suppose that's what cons do—look for ways out—and I realize we have more in common than I'd realized. Ernie looks at me, matches my smile, and carefully lowers his prongs back into the drainage pipe. Gently, he picks up the cement lid, and lowers it over the hole. He straightens and looks at me, puts an index finger to his pursed lips, raises a brow. He makes the me-first signal. I nod and ask, "Where exactly are we?"

Ernie creeps closer to the edge of the bushes, listens intently.

"Ernie," I whisper. "How do you—"

But he's gone.

* * *

Paralyzed in the bushes, I stand and watch as Ernie passes by twice in five minutes, each time releasing a tight, high-pitched whistle to tell me the coast is clear.

But what if someone sees me from a window?

What if someone's about to come around the corner?

How could I ever explain my walking out of a bush?

On Ernie's third pass, I realize this is insane, and I step out in midstride, as if the bushes aren't there, a hand slipped into a pocket, a determined look on my face, as if I'm consumed by the finer nuances of bottom-tier data transformation. In two strides, I'm off the grass and on the pathway that curls around the Invitation to Cooperate building—a.k.a. Cell Block A. Ernie lets me catch up, his toothy grin more crooked than ever, and offers me a fist bump. The look on his face seems to say, *Pretty cool, eh?*

"Yeah, not bad, Ernie." I bump his fist. "Adds an entirely new dimension to pulling a Bob Watson."

We enter Cell Block A. I have a guy in mind, a buddy who used to work with me during our early days in "cross-transfer subordination and documentation," when we were fresh twenty-somethings. Now David Sagan works in HR as a sort of parole officer to one segment of the Robards conployee base—the "re-habilitated deviants" population, which the company has found to demonstrate higher degrees of innovation, ingenuity, and old-fashioned pluck. David's job is to manage the "caseload," ensuring that the rehabbed deviants don't, well, deviate in ways that would expose the company to costly legal action. Of course, he has no training in criminal rehabilitation, but the company offered a 2 percent raise (the first in six years), and his size—six-foot-three, 230 pounds, with broad shoulders and long, lazy legs—afforded him some command presence with the "caseload." I'm thinking David might be able to give me some background on this Flan-duzi guy and, most important, tell me where he sits.

David keeps a small shatter-proof glass office in the center of Level 3 of Cell Block A, where hundreds of conployees sit in a call-center arrangement. Sales calls? Service and support? Career-transition support? Technical assistance? God knows, but I admit the place is buzzing with an energy that's nearly palpa-ble. A steady, edgy din permeates the floor as Ernie and I cross the call center, several conployees pointing at me, whispering, "The Warden." Having worked on the other side of campus, I had no idea so many employees confuse me for Dick Rayborne, and I wonder if my only option—assuming Ana doesn't give me the house-sitting gig and I can't quit Robards—is to shave my head or grow a beard. How would "lumberjack chic" look on me? Could I pull that off?

We approach David's office, and I have to touch the wall

to stabilize myself—probably should have declined that second mini in the Playroom. I notice David is on the phone. I ease a little closer to let him know I'm here, but he's focused on his phone friend. "Me?" he says into the headset, his voice deep and gentle. "Me, I'm a pretty large man, so naturally my genitalia are proportionate to the rest of my body."

One of David Sagan's favorite things to say.

I try to ease into his line of sight, but he swivels his back to me. "David?"

He tries to wave me away. "Well, if you're asking me," he says, "I insist on thoroughly cleaning my lover with a warm wash-cloth."

Someone taps me on the shoulder, and I jerk around. It's a perfectly normal-looking man with carefully disheveled, light brown hair, an easy smile, and intelligent green eyes. "Mr. Ray-borne," he says, his voice clear, confident, and calm, "I just want you to know how much I appreciate the opportunity you've given people like me." He nods to the expanse of conployees outside David's office. "People who wouldn't have had a second, third, or fourth chance."

"Thanks, but I'm not—"

"And I want to let you know . . ." He nods to David, who's now hunched over and whispering into his headset. ". . . I'm working with Mr. Sagan on the anger issues. I'm working on the fixation. I mean, sure, yeah, okay, I know I'm back to following Beth—she's my crush from junior high, so it's hard to shut *that* down. But anyway, I think that's just because I feel that if she finally got to know the real me—the real Wayne Hardy, not the so-called monster who's been bothering her for twenty-eight years, or the dude who killed her gerbils and lived in her attic for eighteen days—she'd see me the way you and the Robards International leadership see me: as a man who's turning a new leaf, a man who has a lot to offer." He pauses, bites his lip in pride. "A man who's going places."

David says into his headset, "It's been a long time since a beautiful woman has urinated on me."

Wayne takes a breath, opens his mouth, and—I place a hand on his forearm. "Wayne, I really appreciate you sharing this with me."

David says into the phone, "Of course I'm aroused."

Wayne says, "If you could let Mr. Sagan know that we spoke, and that you suggest the conduct reports be dismissed, I would greatly appreciate it."

David crinkles his brows. "I do like goats, but not that way, sweetie."

I look Wayne in the eye. "I try not to interfere with the individual cases."

Wayne stiffens and reddens. A vein bulges from his neck.

"But maybe I can mention this with David," I say.

Wayne eases, breaks into a smile. "Thanks, Mr. Rayborne."

David's gentle, nonjudgmental voice: "Of course I'm naked."

Wayne says, "May I shake your hand, Mr. Rayborne?"

David giggles into the phone. "How does that work? Would I lay on a tarp?"

I turn and shake Wayne's hand—it's cold and wet. "You'll see, Mr. Rayborne. I'm not the guy in Mr. Sagan's files. Not anymore." He closes his eyes, beams. "I haven't made a pipe bomb in weeks."

"Okay," I say. "I need to speak with David."

David smiles to himself and nods.

Wayne reddens, puffs his chest out. His eyes go hollow, and his jaw tightens. "I'll take care of this, Mr. Rayborne."

David soothes, "So, you refrigerate the semen?"

Wayne steps into David's office and slaps the glass wall

so hard that I jolt backward. The walls rattle, and David jerks around. Wayne leans forward and begins to pant, his nostrils flaring. "*Mr. Sagan*," he yells, his voice going acidic. "Hang the fuck up." He nods to me. "Mr. Rayborne is here." He steps forward and practically leans over David. "And you're . . ." Wayne takes a deep breath and shouts it out. ". . . *making him wait*." His chest heaves, and he bites his lip as he stares down at David Sagan.

David turns and sees me, stiffens a sec, his eyes going wide, then exhales—*Oh, it's just you*. He returns his attention to Wayne and cocks an eyebrow. His voice is soothing. "You've been doing so much better the past few weeks, Wayne." He offers him his concerned look—a rising eyebrow and a puckered mouth. "This is unfortunate."

Wayne straightens and balls his fists.

"Mr. Sagan and I can take it from here," I say. "Thanks, Wayne."

Wayne leans over David, who's still seated.

"Wayne," David says. "Remember what we've discussed?"

Wayne loosens and blinks.

"Deep breaths, Wayne."

Wayne shakes his face, blinks.

"Remember your opportunities for improvement." David's voice is so sweet and gentle. "You know, anger management? Impulse control? Overcoming obsessive-compulsive tendencies? Appropriate workplace tonalities?"

Wayne steps back, turns, and saunters out of the office, humming to himself like he's suddenly window shopping. Ernie sidesteps to avoid him.

David says into the headset, "I think I need to call you back, sweetie." He frowns. "Honey?" He pulls off his headset and swivels to face me and Ernie. "Mr. Rayborne," he announces, winking, glancing at Ernie. "Something about you looks different."

"Tell me something," I say. "Do I really look like Dick Rayborne?"

David allows an uneasy grin. I guess that means, *Yes, you do look like him.*

"What is it? I mean, I have more hair. I'm taller."

"Yeah, but you have the same hairline." David looks at me, thinking. "And general head shape."

I feel my body deflate. I don't want to look like Dick Rayborne.

"Here's the thing," David says. "I think it's a matter of workplace context. People are at work when they see you, and they are viewing everything through that workplace lens. Then they see you, and their mind automatically associates you with another Robards person—Dick Rayborne. It's like how an optical illusion works—their brains are trained too see Dick."

His logic makes sense, and it gives me a little comfort.

"Listen," I say. "I need to speak with you about something."

"Ernie?" David says. "May I ask that you give us a few moments of privacy?"

Ernie gets up and meanders out of David Sagan's fishbowl and shuts the glass door. David says, "Thanks, sweetie," and Ernie nods and stares at us through the glass. That jowly smile.

"You think *we're* horny?" David looks at Ernie, then at the expanse of seafoam green outside his fishbowl. "Just imagine how horny *they* were in jail."

"I don't want to think about it. David, listen. Dude. I—"

"You don't want to think about it because you know what would happen if you and I were in jail together." He tilts his head, enjoys the idea. "I mean, if we were cellmates."

"Dude, I really—"

"I would have no choice but to overpower you."

I nod to the Robards People Finder tool showcasing his phone friend. "David, I need you to look someone up."

"I'd be forced to mount you." He looks at me, makes his voice soft and gentle—but deep. "To get up inside you."

"David, fine, keep going on the jail scenario. I don't care. But I need you to look up an employee for me. His name is Bobby Flanduzi. With a *z*."

He swivels the screen back to him, types in the name.

"Maybe he goes by Robert."

David stares at the screen, furrow his brows. Sighs. "Because I am a good five inches taller than you, and a good forty pounds heavier."

"Flanduzi. Does that name ring a bell?"

David stares at the screen, shakes his head no.

"As far as you can tell, he doesn't have anything to do with the conployee program?"

David's reading. "It says he's in Finance. Conployees are forbidden from working in Finance. No exceptions." He looks at me. "What's this about?"

"Just don't tell anyone I was here, okay?"

David looks at the screen again, returns to me. "You're not here. Not even now." We look at Ernie, who's gazing at us, his eyes eager. "Dick Rayborne is here." We turn back and look at each other. "Isn't he?"

"Okay, fine." I nod to his screen. "What do you have?"

He rotates the screen to me, and I twitch at what I see. The salt-and-pepper hair. The bushy mustache. The prominent ears and narrow-set eyes. It's all so familiar, and I stare at his face, thinking.

Where have I—

And then, it hits me. I know exactly where this guy is.

David is looking at me. "And I wouldn't share you with anyone."

"What are the chances?"

Ernie does a few quick steps to keep up. Shrugs his shoulders at my question.

"I mean, there are probably eighteen or nineteen hundred people on this campus."

Ernie offers another so-what shrug.

We walk past the hidden escape hatch, and I sling the bag of cash over my shoulder. As we approach my building, I nod hello to the security guy stationed near the lobby entrance, and I notice four surveillance cameras pointed at us. The brochures say conployees are allowed into the normal buildings, but the reality is that they're about as welcome as vomit in a swimming pool.

"Okay, I know exactly where Flanduzi is."

Ernie nods.

We walk past the guard.

"So we're going to march in there and hand him these forty-five Gs and head back to the escape hatch. Make sense?"

He snorts, nods happily at my mention of the escape hatch.

We take the stairs. "But I may need you to lie low. You know, stay back a little."

Worry spreads across his face.

"I'm just saying, we want to do this without getting caught. Right?" We turn another corner, and I feel the eyes on us. "Okay, Ernie. Let's pick up the pace a little."

This is a crucial Bob Watson tenet. When returning from your Bob Watson, you must walk like you own the place—your pace accelerated, your eyes steely, your body language unapolo-getic. Preferably, you have props in your hands—a pen and notepad, maybe, or a folder. And you must reenter the confer-ence room in midstream—again, quick and unapologetic, as if you just darted out for a few minutes and came back as quickly as possible, as if you don't want to miss a thing.

"Okay, Ernie." We in on my cube, picking up the pace, like I'm trying to reach a ringing phone. "Let's do this." We reach my cube, I drop the Nike bag beside my chair. I pull out my chair, motion for Ernie to take my seat. I lean over my keyboard, pull up a blank Word doc. "Act like you're working on something, okay?"

He giggles, nods, and begins to type nonsense into the doc.

"Stay here," I say.

Time to pull off one of the more difficult moves in my Bob Watson tool kit—the delayed reentry.

• • •

Walking to the conference room, I begin to second-guess myself.

Is Bobby Flanduzi—this guy I've never met—really inside this room? Is he really attending the very same meeting I had ditched this morning? Seeing his photo in David Sagan's office had triggered something in my mind—a nearly dreamlike memory of Flanduzi sitting there in the conference room, his shoulders sagging, his face so lifeless it seemed to be ready to drip into his lap, his whole body slouching, as Janice from Finance opened up the J-23 Incubation meeting with the precision of an anal-retentive dance instructor.

Yes, I *had* pornolized this guy in the workplace orgy.

And I allow myself to recall a fleeting thought from this morning, an epiphany that I'd wanted to shoo away as quickly as it came, that it wasn't just me. That indeed, we were all miserable.

Time to roll.

I straighten my shoulders and puff out my chest a little, affecting that confident, assured body language that is so important for a delayed reentry. Instinctively, I reach into my pocket for my mobile phone—having it pressed to your ear is a great way to insinuate that you'd stepped out to make a call. But then I realize Mama has my phone, that she's ready to call Audrey and my sister if this doesn't work. Fine, I can pull off a reentry without props. The fact is, people don't really pay much attention when you reenter a meeting—they assume you'd stepped out a few minutes ago, assuming they even notice you (they usually don't). What they do notice is newcomers.

I approach the door, peek through the portal for a quick second. Janice from Finance is clicking through an eye chart for the ages, the conference room screen littered with tables of numbers so small I can't imagine anyone being able to read them. She's using a laser pointer to circle one column of numbers and acronyms on the screen—her audience barely awake, it seems—and I'm reminded of Mama's order to bring back *one of those red laser pointers*.

I open the door and am hit with a hot, thick waft of stale air, trailed by a faint ripe odor.

". . . which is why the Hathaway guys need to achieve a truly deeper thrust with the L-Docs in the tier six regions." As I return to my seat—my notepad and pen right where I left them four hours ago—Janice never looks up. Neither do the others. Compared with this morning, they look utterly defeated now, so tired—their skin less buoyant, their eyes nearly hollow, five-o'clock shadows emerging, makeup hardening. "Because these metrics here?" The laser circles a set of blurry numbers on the screen. "It's an opportunity to develop a truly rich hyperarticula-tion of the subcategories that need rationalization."

My heart is racing as I scan the roomful of lifeless faces, searching for Flanduzi.

"If the J-23s are ever going to meet the new BMI segmentation requirements . . ."

And then silence. I glance up, and Janice is looking at me, zeroing in.

Shit.

I meet her gaze, lean forward, and pound my fist on the table. And I complete her thought. ". . . we'll need to cross-pattern the L-Doc substantiations against the legacy process flows."

Janice stares at me—chest rising, nostrils flaring—and my heart sinks.

"Exactly," she pants, nearly breathless. "Exactly. That's ex-actly what I told the Cando guys." She looks down, straightens her pantsuit, and pivots toward the screen, the laser pointer in her grip. "I'm glad you're with us today, Rick."

I look around, and the others nod in agreement.

Okay, probably a good time to leave a final impression.

I rise from my chair, look around, and spot Bobby Flanduzi at the end of the table. He's checking his phone. I stride around the table and approach Janice. "May I, Janice?" I nod to her laser pointer, and she hands it over. "This is the problem." I aim the pointer at the screen, circle a new column of acronyms and num-bers. "This right here. This is where we must harvest true ROI. Not just the process-mitigation stuff, but the true transformative value-capture."

Janice stands back, nods again. I hold on to the pointer and meander back toward my side of the table. "Because . . ." I stop behind Bobby Flanduzi and point the laser to yet another column of data. ". . . this is the area that really concerns me, Janice. This is the area where I'm at a loss. I mean, how do we even start to document a new process over here?" There's a murmur in the room, and Janice dives into a marathon monologue. I stand behind Flanduzi—nodding at Janice, maintaining the eye contact that is so important in any Bob Watson. After two minutes, I slip the pointer into my front pocket and take a knee behind Flanduzi. Janice barks out the acronyms—nearly breathless— and I lean in and whisper into Flanduzi's ear.

"Hey."

He jerks a little, stiffens, and turns around, his eyes wide. "Hey."

I lean in closer. Whisper. "I've seen the monkey drool."

He seems confused, then concerned. His skin pales. He tries to whisper without moving his lips. "What did you just say?"

I look around. Everyone is watching Janice unleash more acronyms. I lean in a little closer. "Monkey drool."

He decides I'm crazy, that it's just a coincidence. "Dude." He frowns and pulls away. "What's your deal?"

Janice acronyms poetic. "We must cascade the L-PARs through the ROI and the SWAT metric."

"I'm sure there's a more scientific name for it."

"Dude. Seriously."

"Like, baboon saliva?"

His jaw muscles begin to twitch, and he knows that *I* know about *his* monkey drool.

"So, what kind is it?"

"What do you mean, what kind is it? And were you in my house today?"

"The 'drool' in the vials. What kind of drool is it? Mama calls it 'monkey drool,' but I'm guessing it's baboon saliva, or lemur, or orangutan." We look at each other. "No?" Another long stare. "Regardless, the Robards Clown Posse delivered the cash to Mama and me." A pause as we look at each other. "And yes, I was in your house today."

Long silence.

"And once we complete the L-PAR thrust, we penetrate deeper with HyperPHY."

"Who are you?"

"Rick Blanco. Bottom-tier data transformation."

He searches my face.

"And I need you to play nice. I need you to do as I say, because—come hell or high water—I'm gonna take the totally cool chick I've been chasing for years, I'm gonna take her to the Greek tonight to see the English Beat. And I'm gonna show my sister I can be trusted with her house. And I will quit this shithole." He looks at me like I'm absolutely nuts. "So, you *will* cooperate. You hear me, Flanduzi?"

"And we must spray the L-Docs all over the L-PAR."'

Slowly, he nods.

"Okay. So." I look for spies. "I have your forty-five K."

His lids fall. "Okay."

"So listen. This is what we're gonna do." I look around. "I'm gonna get you out of here. You just sit here, and when I tap you on the shoulder, I want you to get up and follow me out of this conference room. You understand? We're gonna do what I like to call a Dual-Op Bob Watson."

He frowns.

"I mean, I'm gonna get us both out of here. Okay?"

He bites his lip. "But Janice hates it when people—"

I raise a finger to stop him. "You want your forty-five K?"

Nods yes.

"Okay, then trust me. We're gonna do this right under their noses."

He straightens up. "Okay." Deep breath, and then a glance at me. "Mama sent you?"

"And we'll flank the Cando guys with the P-FIDs."

"She did." I look up at Janice. "Okay, when I tap your shoulder, what are you gonna do?"

Bobby Flanduzi closes his eyes and shakes his head. "I can't. I feel like I'm gonna faint. I'll make a scene."

"You think I'm gonna pull you out and hurt you?"

Eyes still closed. "I seriously feel like I'm gonna faint."

"Fine."

I stand up, straighten my back, and watch Janice as she pounds her fist to an oddly rhythmic listing of acronyms—"First, it's the R-PID, then it's the L-Docs, and then it's the L-PARs."

I watch a little longer—nodding, making eye contact—and I realize Janice is so deeply engrossed, and her subjects are so deeply hopeless (lost in their own daydreams and meditations), that this Bob Watson is a slam dunk. No need to create a distraction or a new hot topic. No need to wait for her to turn her back or for someone to get into a debate. This one's easy—for me, at least. The trick is, you just walk briskly to the door and leave, like you have every right, like you have a long-standing hall pass, and like you're obviously coming right back.

I lean over Bobby Flanduzi's shoulder. "Stay here," I say. "I'm coming back with your money, and you're going to answer some questions."

Flanduzi nods, and I walk out of the conference room as Janice says something about L-Doc enrichment.

●　●　●

I race back to my cube and see that the bag of cash is gone.

Ernie is at my desk enjoying a YouTube video of Big Bird,

my white earbuds burrowed deep into his head—his eyes huge and moist, a tiny grin dimpled into his face. He has the sound so loud, I can hear Big Bird—his back hunched, his yellow feathers radiant—as he talks to Elmo.

I scan my cube; the Nike bag is nowhere. "Ernie," I rasp, breathless.

From inside Ernie's head, Big Bird says, "A break is fun, too."

"Ernie, where's the bag?"

Music starts, and Big Bird begins to sing to Elmo.

I'm taking a break, I'm taking a rest.

I grab his shoulder. "Ernie."

I'm taking some time . . . to be at my best.

Ernie glows, hums along.

"Ernie." I pull out an earbud and speak into his hole. "Ernie, where's the cash?"

Oh, won't you take a break . . .
Won't you take a break . . .
With me?

I pull out the other earbud and yell, *"Ernie."*

Finally, Ernie looks up as the earbuds broadcast Big Bird's happy plea.

We can dream a dream
We can wonder why?
We can take the time to let the world . . . go . . . by.
Oh, won't you take a break . . .

Won't you take a break . . .
With me?

I see my hands take him by the jumpsuit lapels and shake him. "Where's the goddamn money?" He hardens, offers a growl, and I release him. "Dude," I whisper. "I asked you to sit here and watch the bag. I come back and the money's gone and you're watching *Sesame Street*."

Another growl, and Ernie swivels and opens my overhead cabinet, revealing the Nike bag.

"Boy," Elmo says. "Taking a break is fun, Big Bird."

•   •   •

Ernie and I pause outside the conference room.

"Okay, dude." We fist bump. "Let's do this."

I rest my hand on the doorknob, imagining that I can feel Janice's vibrations through the cold steel, like I'm some kind of Bob Watson maestro clairvoyant—extrasensory, open to the universe and all the information it's sending me, absorbing it all, sending it through my eardrums and optical nerves and dozens of other glands and organs, all of it funneling into my cerebral cortex as I prepare to execute yet another beautiful, luscious, perfectly formed Bob Watson.

I caress the knob, feeling cocky, like a Bob Watson badass, as I watch Janice through the porthole, reading her movements, measuring the tautness of her face, gauging her intensity, hoping for a high point that will render her—once again—oblivious to the world around her. She seems to strain her neck as she barks into the air, and she turns her back to the others as she uncaps the marker in her hand. I open the door, and my senses are assaulted once again—thick air, a ripened odor, the heat hitting my cheeks as I march into the screaming wind of Janice's acronyms.

"And we'll leverage the SysCON for a new level of P-FID rationalization."

Everyone in the room is looking at their phone, except Blake the intern, who is nodding off. And then there is Bobby Flanduzi, the only one who's noticed me as I cut through the room like I'm invisible, like I own the place. He looks up at me, his eyes hopeful, his hands clasped in his lap, his knees and feet together. His face sags a little when he realizes I couldn't possibly be carrying $45,000. He opens his mouth. "You said—"

I reach him and press a forefinger to his mustache. "Shhh-hhhh."

Janice begins to turn and face the group, so I drop to a squat behind Flanduzi.

"Of course, the P-FIDs can be reverse engineered using the 459 process."

I whisper into his left ear. "You ever want to see your money?"

Shaky, he nods yes.

"Then you will need to answer some questions."

Slowly, he cocks his head, like he's thinking about it, saying, *I'll see what I can do.*

I lean in, whisper, "Starting with the monkey drool." He jerks at the words. "C'mon, bub. What are you doing with a cooler of something like that?"

"Of course, we need to think about the Bonzo tables."

Flanduzi stares ahead, watching Janice, then turns his head back my way. He opens his mouth, thinks better of it, and folds his arms.

I lean in again. "I was in your house this morning."

He straightens, scratches the back of his neck.

"What kind of guy keeps a cooler of monkey drool—infected monkey drool, is my guess—in the family fridge?"

His chest rises, and he reddens. "Someone who loves his daughter . . ." His whisper cracks with emotion ". . . more than anything in the world."

This softens me. "Dude," I say. "What are you doing selling animal saliva on the black market?"

He's nearly panting, looking straight ahead. "My daughter."

"The money? The cash is for your daughter?"

He bites his lip, fighting off a full cry. "Mmmm-hmm."

"Your kids look young. Why does she need forty-five thousand dollars?"

Flanduzi takes a breath, composes himself, shakes his head. "I need it. For my daughter. So she can see the right doctors." He huffs and puffs, and yells out, *"The goddamn paperwork."*

Paperwork? Isn't Mama always calling me Mr. Paperwork?

Janice is frozen. Staring at Bobby Flanduzi, then at me.

Oh shit.

"Yes," she pants, nearly breathing fire. "That's right. The paperwork. The J-Configs are too much. Just way too much paperwork." She pivots and turns to the whiteboard, uncaps her marker. "Which is why the K-KARs are so critical."

Flanduzi whispers, "It's all the paperwork they make you do, just so you get your kid in to the right doctor—you know, for a treatment that could change her whole life."

I look at him, trying to follow.

"Ever heard of Kawasaki disease?" he asks. "The inflammation of arteries. Treatable, as long as you can see the right doctors. As long as the medical insurance people don't run you through a bunch of hoops—a bunch of paperwork—and slow you down."

"Insurance slowed you down?"

He nods. "More and more paperwork. More calls, more paperwork."

I feel my throat tighten.

"And finally, the wife and I decide we can't wait another day. The paperwork keeps coming, delaying coverage. They keep running us in circles—and, of course, the real reason is that the treatment's not cheap. So finally the wife and I, we say . . ." His voice cracks again. ". . . we just gotta do this right now. So we pay out of pocket, which is what insurance wanted all along— it's what keeps the Robards premium costs down, of course, and that's what it's all about." He lets out a dry chuckle. "Keep the premium costs down for Robards."

"So what you do is, you essentially milk the Bonzo tables."

"The good news is, Emma's safe and well. We're just broke."

"So the monkey drool?"

"You're right—baboon saliva." He looks around; everyone's come alive and is babbling about Bonzo tables, oblivious. "Long story, but someone's looking at some new genetic research and—"

"Huloojasper?"

"Yeah, what a name. Probably fake. Someone that a friend of a friend knows. Biomed. All I knew was, they needed someone to pick up a cooler of samples—vials of saliva from a grasslands baboon. Some type of research. They didn't want the vials to go through customs, for whatever reason, so they needed someone to retrieve the samples in Jalisco, bring them across the border, get them to this Huloojasper guy, the lead scientist at this start-up. He pays me forty-five thousand for moving some baboon saliva. Pretty tidy sum, right? But then I freaked out, worried about getting arrested or something, decided I needed intermediaries, and I had the bright idea . . ." Another dry laugh. ". . . of hiring some conployees to complete the transaction— figured an ex-con would know how to do a discrete drop-and-pay. I didn't want anyone seeing me reaching out to conployees—just in case this whole thing blows up—so I put out a Craigslist ad seeking Robards International conployees who want extra work, and I get two responses—one from the Robards Clown Posse, and one from this old lady who was Googling 'conployees' for her research."

"Mama?"

He nods. "She insists on getting involved, comes over and meets the family—says she wants to help. Before I know it, we're telling her everything. First she gets all pissed, cussing out Dick Rayborne. And then she says she has a couple of 'boys' who can do the job for us. But I already have the Robards Clown Posse set up. But I guess Mama didn't understand."

My chest hardens, and I feel my jaw muscle twitching. "All of this because of the medical coverage bullshit?"

He nods. "They have a term for it—*paperwork blitz*. Whole idea is to overwhelm a claimant with so many requirements, so much paperwork, and then countless runarounds and rejections and technicalities, that you just throw your hands up and surrender." He pauses, swallows hard. "Problem is, after four weeks, we just couldn't wait any longer." Another big swallow. "So, I guess you could say they won—we paid out of pocket. Maxed out the cards. Drained the savings."

I blink hard, try to take in deep breaths. I place a hand on his shoulder. "So basically, you're trying to save your daughter's life. How old is she?"

"Seven."

"Seven." I steady myself. "And you're trying to claim your coverage. And you get the Dick Rayborne Special?"

"Mama says Rayborne has been praised for being a trail-blazer with the practice of paperwork blitzes. In some journal—"

"*Headcount.*"

"Yeah, that's it. She shared a clipping." He bristles, looks away. "It's disgusting."

Rayborne. What a complete prick. I close my eyes and take

a few deep breaths. *Steady, big boy. Steady. Time to calm down.*
I take another breath and let it out slowly as Janice barks something, the syllables distant echoes in my head.

What kind of person does something like that?

"Now," Janice says. "Let's talk about Phase 21."

I lean into Flanduzi. "Okay, so I met the Robards Clown
Posse, and they're taking the vials to Huloojasper, or whatever
his name is." I look around again, get even closer to Flanduzi.
"And they gave Mama the cash, which I'm gonna bring to you
in a second."

He lets out a sigh of relief, looks away. "We're days from foreclosure. We need that money."

"Anyone asks? We never spoke, okay?"

He nods.

"And I've been in this meeting the entire day. Right?"

"Actually . . ." He's squinting, thinking about it. ". . . you have
been." Cocks his head, squint turning to frown as he challenges
his memory one last time. "Haven't you? But you said you met
the Clown Posse and went to my hou——"

I stop him. "Of course I've been here the whole time. I've
been sitting in here with you since this dreaded thing started." I
look away, and I'm hit with the visual memory of a naked, pissed-
off Angel chasing Ernie through this guy's house. "All those
comments I had about the J-23 and the right ROI analysis of the
FODs?"

"That's right, that's right." He stiffens, screws his eyes shut in
shame. "I'm losing it. Sorry."

"Of course, I had to step out for a few bio breaks and calls."

He frowns to himself again. "How'd you get the vials?"

I think about something. "You may want to change the sheets
on your kids' beds. Just to be safe."

"Huh?

"Time to give you your money," I say, grabbing his shoulder. "Okay." I look for spies one last time. "I'm gonna create a distraction. You understand?"

He looks like a timid boy. "What do I do?"

"Nothing. You just sit here." I look around. "Someone's gonna hand you a bag containing the money. I want you to accept the bag, take a peek inside, confirm the money is there. Okay?"

Troubled eyes. "Won't everyone see?"

"Believe me." I prepare myself. "They won't see a thing." He bristles, and I head for the front of the room. "Janice," I say, "we can talk about the K-KAR and the SysCON till we're blue in the face. But the fact of the matter is, it's up to each of us . . ." I spin and look at the room, give them the eye. ". . . to do the right thing day in and day out. We must commit." I notice a few eyes rolling, some long sighs. "So I am going to be the first one here today. To stand here and make a pledge. The bottom-tier data transformation pledge."

Someone moans in agony. Janice stares at me, her face nearly shaking.

I raise my hand like I'm taking an oath. "I promise to embrace . . ." I produce a dramatic swallow and gaze up the ceiling. ". . . the SysCON . . . the K-KAR . . . and the —DAP." I weaken my voice with emotion. "I will be open to process husbandry. If I ever live to see the day where a K-CONKAR graces our spreadsheets, I will embrace it as if it were the fruit of my very own loins."

Janice's chest rises and falls, her nostrils flaring.

"That is my pledge."

"Yes," Janice rasps, breathless. "Yes. Thank you, Rick. Yes, we should all take the pledge."

"Right here," I say and back away. "Right now."

"Yes," Janice rasps. "That's right. We're going to do this right now."

I back away, bowing, hands clasped at my chest.

Janice faces the attendees and closes her eyes. "If there is ever a day in which this company produces a K-CONKAR process, I pledge to let it suckle from my bosom." Her voice cracks and lower lip trembles. "To bounce it on my knee. To change its poopy diapers. To be the most tenacious helicopter parent anyone has ever seen."

I backpedal to the conference room door and tap three times. I step aside, and Ernie walks in, nearly strutting, his shoulders proud, his head bobbing, the Nike bag under an arm. He stops, scans the room, and Bobby Flanduzi lifts his chin to him, fingers him over. Ernie releases a crooked grin, checks with me, and I nod an affirmative. He turns and struts over to Bobby Flanduzi, and—I swear this is the truth—not one attendee of the J-23 Incubation meeting gives him a mere glance. Not with the spectacle unfolding at the front of the room.

Ernie squats beside Bobby Flanduzi, looks to me. I fold my arms, lean against the wall, and nod to proceed. The young, hairless man seated beside Bobby Flanduzi stands up and eases toward the front of the room, ready to make his ass-kissing homage to bottom-tier data transformation at Robards International. Ernie lowers his lids in a way I've never seen—feeling cool?—and lifts the flap of the Nike bag, tilting it toward Bobby Flanduzi so he can get a private view of the bundles of cash. Bobby's eyes bulge, and he nods as Ernie places the bag on his lap.

Janice sobs, "I pledge to terminate the HyperPHY process if that's what this team decides."

Ernie gets up and heads toward me. Bobby looks over and gives me the eye—*I don't know who you are, dude, but thanks.*

And like that, I'm struck by a strong emotion. Hell, I'm actually making a difference in someone's life. I'm helping a family avoid foreclosure. I feel my chest rise in pride. I meet his moist gaze and hold it, nodding, wishing I were wearing a hat that I could tip to him. Bobby turns and pretends to listen to Janice, but succumbs quickly and stares long and hard into the bag.

More ass-kissers meander toward Janice, ready to make their pledges.

I open the door, and Ernie struts out of the conference room.

Janice releases a post-sobbing sigh. "Sometimes I feel so empty."

· · ·

"Beeline to the escape hatch, Ernie."

Ernie giggles and nods.

"We did it, Ernie."

His eyes gleam.

"We helped a family today."

He makes his jowls crinkle. Smiles.

"That guy in there needed that money. For his daughter. I mean, they really needed that money."

Ernie nods.

"I mean it. You really made a difference today, dude."

His face flushes, and he stops to give me a little hug. I find myself hugging him back.

We reach the "escape hatch" in a matter of minutes, breathing heavy, limbs and faces tingling—alive. Ernie holds the barbecue prongs in his mouth as he slides the manhole cover back over the escape hatch, closing our portal to the Robards International universe. We scamper back to the Playroom on all fours, and I swear it feels so natural, like I'm a kid all over again, the magic of discovery coursing through me, a small smile spreading across my face, barely able to contain myself, reveling in that rare feeling of actually pulling *it* off—whatever *it* is, wanting so badly to tell my big sister that, indeed, I did it right, I didn't screw things up. Scampering down the pipe, I nearly squeal at the bliss of it all. I just successfully dropped off $45,000 to a fellow working stiff, right in the middle of a J-23 Incubation marathon meeting, helping him avoid foreclosure.

I did it. I really did it.

Just wait till Ana hears—

But then the reality returns. Because Ana knows the real me. She knows what happened. What I did. She knows there's no going back. Ever.

• • •

"Mama?"

"Ricky? Where are you?"

"It didn't go too well."

"Where are you, mijo?"

"I guess she was just being—"

"Ricky."

"—nice. Okay?"

"What do you mean nice? Where are you?"

"She wasn't really interested in me that way."

"What? Wait, baby. What happened?"

"It didn't work out."

There's a long silence. "Oh, mijo." She sighs that sweet way.

I'd been doing okay until I heard the sympathy in her voice. Now a ball in my throat is enlarging and dipping into my chest, and I swallow hard.

"Ricky?"

"I'm fine. Seriously, I'm fine."

"Where are you?"

"At the movie theater."

"You went anyway?"

What happened was, I was supposed to meet Danielle Meza at the theater. I took my bike, and she was going to have her older sister drop her off. I had been thrilled. I had summoned a lot of courage last week when I caught up to her as she walked alone to History and I asked her out. It was the first time I'd ever done anything like that.

I called her from the theater, and she apologized. "I think I just want to be friends."

I watched people meander into the theater, oblivious.

"Rick?"

"Yeah."

"Rick, I'm sorry. I didn't know what to say. You're such a nice guy, and you're superfunny. It's just that . . . I mean, I just didn't want to hurt your feelings."

"Okay, well, I'm at the theater."

"I'm sorry," she squeaked.

"It woulda been cool if you'd called me last night or something, but it's no big deal. But anyways . . ."

"I know, and I feel like a total jerk. I'm sorry. I'm not good at this."

"It's okay. I just have this extra ticket." I took a deep breath, let it out slowly. "I'd call Mr. Tetherman to come join me, but I've been reading that psychopath principals don't really enjoy movies."

She let out a huge laugh. "Okay, well. I better go. Christina and Jennifer are waiting for me."

I sat in the theater lobby for a long time, thinking. Eventually, I got up and went into the theater—*Jerry Maguire* was supposed to be pretty funny, and the thing had already started, so no one would see me come in alone.

"So where are you now, mijo?"

"The theater."

"Just come on home, and you can get dinner with me and Dad."

I feel my throat tighten. "That's just the thing."

"What do you mean?"

I screw my eyes shut and grimace. "I came out, and my bike is gone."

"What do you mean? Someone stole it?"

The lump grows, and my voice fails. "I guess."

"You locked it?"

"I don't know. I was so nervous—I think I did, but maybe not?"

"Ricky." She sighs, the sympathetic annoyance heavy in her voice, and all I want to do is hug her. "This is the second bike in six months."

She's right, and I can't say anything unless I want to start bawling.

Long sigh. "Ana's at Julie's house. Do you want to come get dinner with us? You, me, and Papa?"

I'm embarrassed to say yes, but sometimes you just need your mom and dad.

•   •   •

From the blackness I emerge back into the Playroom, where Mama has given me back my phone and now is teaching Collin how to use the dog clicker. Collin looks like he's having a blast, so I decide to take a seat. Soon, I find myself stretching out on the mattress, slipping my hands under my head, and staring up at the leaves shimmering in the sun. For a moment, it bothers me that I've gotten so comfortable in such filth, but then my mind settles on Audrey. I imagine her with me tonight at the Greek—in front of me, in my arms, as we move together to the Beat. That would be nice.

My cell rings. It's her.

"I was just thinking of you."

She offers a you're-hopeless laugh. "Dude, you're supposed to be bonding with your nephew."

Collin produces a click and tosses Cujo a mini.

"I am. We're having a Neanderthal adventure."

"Yeah?"

I holler and thrust the phone into the air. "We're in the wild right now, aren't we, kiddo?"

Collin hollers, "Yeah, and it's *awesome.*"

I bring the phone back to my ear, and Audrey says, "Wow. Nice."

"And my friend got ahold of the Stanford Neanderthal expert."

"Who?"

"Sabine Rorgstardt. One of the country's leading experts on Neanderthals. I think we're going to do a few more things, then go see her on campus."

Audrey seems amused. "What are you doing, errands?"

I think of the $45,000 in cash I just dropped off. "Basically, yes."

"Well, Collin sounds happy."

"He is," I say. "Compared to this morning, it's like night and day."

"This is what I wanted, so thank you."

I think about the bus. "I didn't realize he's been so consumed with this school crap."

"But it's more than that." She pauses. "Right, Rick?"

I think of Collin trying to break a leg so he can spend time with my sister. "Yeah, I guess."

"I'm sure you can see that your nephew needs you, right?"

"Needs me?"

"To balance things out for him," she says.

"You mean with the Overachiever Fever?"

"I was thinking, maybe you could intervene a little," she says. "You know, knock some sense into his parents' heads."

Suddenly, the Greek Theatre fantasy seems a million miles away.

"My sister's changed," I say. "We speak different languages, practically."

"And maybe it wouldn't be such a bad idea if she let Collin come back to the States and hang out with you this summer."

I think of the house-sitting gig, the chance to quit Robards International—I can't blow that opportunity. "Yeah, maybe Collin needs more sanity time. More normal-kid time."

"You could provide that for him." After a long pause, she adds, "I'm not sure Ana and Samson can."

I freeze with a familiar fear—I really don't want to destroy any more lives.

Her voice is so sweet. "Rick?"

That's what I promised myself.

"Rick?"

"Yeah," I say. "I'm here."

"Well, I'm excited about tonight."

I shake myself out of it, like I've done for decades. "Tonight?"

She laughs. "Yeah, I'm in. You kept your side of the bargain. You guys are still gonna see that Stanford expert, right?"

"The Sabine lady? Of course." Thinking about the Greek, I feel a grin spreading. "So how should we do this tonight?"

"I'll buy the tickets online," she says. "We can drive up to-gether once you drop off Collin at the house."

The skin on my face charges.

Finally.

Tonight.

Audrey and me.

"I'm so glad this is happening," I say.

"Yeah," she says, stretching it out. Energetic, but measured. "I am, too."

I hear myself say, "I guess you know how I've always felt about you."

Her voice lightens. "Maybe."

"I think you're very special."

"Thanks." She sounds like I just complimented her choice in rain gutters. "I consider you a friend."

The music in my head stops.

"Rick?"

I swallow and taker a deep breath. "Do you mind if I ask you a possibly uncomfortable question?"

There's a long pause. "I guess not."

"Well, I guess—I mean, we've known each other awhile. And you've always known I've kind of always had this crush on you."

"I don't know." She laughs. "Maybe, I guess."

"And you've always been very nice about it."

"Well. You're a nice guy. And I can see you in Collin."

"But you've always kinda deflected the attention."

"Yeah, I guess."

"And then today, out of nowhere, you finally say yes."

"Is tonight a date?" She laughs at herself. "I mean, I don't know what tonight is."

We both laugh.

"What I mean is, why tonight? After all these years, why'd you finally agree to go out with me tonight?"

"Well . . ." Silence. "Hmmm."

"Is it because you're no longer going to be Collin's nanny, so dating his uncle would be okay?"

Another long silence. Finally, Audrey says, "I don't know. I guess I just really wanted you to see what I see—with Collin. You know, with this being my last day—You know, I've been with the little guy since he was four weeks old." She clears her throat. "I just want the best for him. And I just really think he's gonna need you once in a while. Because, you know, I'm moving on. I need to. I can't be his nanny—his de facto mommy—anymore." Her voice cracks. "So I guess today was just a—you know—last-ditch effort."

I hear myself saying, "You love him, don't you? I guess that's obvious."

"Love him? Of course I love him. I've practically raised him. I mean . . ." She thinks about it. ". . . he'll always be a part of me."

"I think that's beautiful," I say. "This love you have for him. I mean, you're willing to go out with me tonight so I might catch a clue."

She forces a laugh.

"I mean, catch a clue about Collin."

"I like you, Rick. I do. I think you're a riot. I just . . ."

"Don't feel that way?"

"Maybe not." Long pause. "Sorry." Another long pause. "I mean, not the way I think you want me to feel."

My throat tightens. "It's okay." I take a deep breath, hoping to regulate myself a little. "Hey, it's not your fault. You never asked for all this attention all these years."

"Maybe not. But I'm flattered."

Since we're at this place, I decide to make sure I'm hearing her correctly. "So it's cool if you don't, but I think I'm hearing you're never gonna feel that way?"

She's squeaking now, embarrassed. "Sorry." Empathy heavy in her voice. "I know you wouldn't want me to lie to you. I just thought we could hang out like friends—in fact, I was thinking maybe we could bring my friend Sondra along."

"The weight lifter with the boil?"

"Yeah, if you don't mind. And my sister's friend Ben. You'd love him."

My vision blurs. "Yeah, sure."

"Or, we could just go the two of us, like we discussed. I'm totally fine either way."

For some reason, I see the bike rack at the cinema. My bike is gone.

"Rick? I'm totally fine to just—"

"No, no. I'm cool."

"I'm sorry."

"Nothing to be sorry about. I'm having a blast today with Collin. And I appreciate how much you care about him. *He's* having a blast today. So it's totally cool."

"Oh . . ." She pauses, unsure of what to say next, maybe. ". . . good."

"And so maybe we just take a rain check on the concert tonight."

"Oh . . ."

"I just don't want to be that charity case."

"Rick . . ."

"Or that platonic friend."

"No, I get it."

"Or have tonight be weird."

"I'm just—"

"Because I have so many fond memories involving you."

"And me of you."

"Maybe we just protect that and not screw with it by doing the Greek tonight."

"Whatever you want to do. I really hope I didn't give you the wrong impression over the years."

I think about that. Maybe when you want someone so bad, you can convince yourself of anything.

"If I've given you the wrong impression, or if maybe I let this thing tonight feel like a date—and I guess that's what it was, I suppose—I am really sorry, Rick. This thing with Collin has me all screwed up, and I thought maybe . . . I don't know."

"No, I understand. No worries."

"Sorry."

Protracted awkward silence.

"Okay, well . . . I think Collin just ran out of minis, so I better say goodbye for now."

"Minis?"

Collin runs up and snatches the phone out of my hand. "Sorry, Audrey. But I'm training my Neanderthal in the wild right now, and we're almost out of liquor. He might get feisty. We have to go."

And he hangs up.

And I look at my phone, and see that bike rack again.

Mama shuffles up and hands me a mini, and I think, *At this point, what the F?* I twist off the cap and down it, shuddering.

"We're going home," Mama says.

I force myself out of it. "Home?" I sit up, shake my face. "What are you talking about? Your place?"

"Don't play games with me, Dickie."

My chest tightens. "What the hell are you talking about?"

"What I'm talking about, mister, is going to *our* home."

She looks away, the light reflecting off those thick glasses. "We're bringing this family back together, and we're doing it at the house—your place." She turns and looks into me. "No more running, honey. No more running from your family, from your past. No more of that ditching you do—not with us. You hear me?"

I stare back at her, letting myself sway, my head light, my face tingling. "What the hell are you talking about?"

Her voice softens a little. "You know what I am talking about, Dick. You've been ditching and running from us since everything fell apart."

A lump forms in my throat. . . . I swallow, take a breath. "And when was that?"

"Don't waste my time playing dumb, sweetheart. You know when you started running and ditching. I know it was rough, what it did to you—hell, I was there. The point is, we're going home and we are going to confront this business once and for all. The boys are just about grown up now. But the little one?" She looks down at Collin. "You still have a chance with him. Don't blow it, Dick, you hear me? He still has a chance. You still have a chance with him, to be a part of his life."

I feel my brows turn in. "Okay, listen. Where's home?"

"Our old place. The place you ditched. The home you ditched."

I need to stay calm, so I try some deep breathing. "Refresh my memory on exactly where 'our old place' is."

Her voice shakes. "I can barely remember, it's been so long." Slowly, she digs into her fanny pack, fingering through items. "So I had to go to the library to use the computers, then the county recorder's office to get the exact address." She produces a small piece of folded-up paper, pulls it open. "Here we go," she says, more to herself. "The place in Atherton." She studies the notes. "Almendral Avenue." Then her voice sharpens. "That HR palace of yours. The one they featured in *Headcount.*"

Oh. The *Headcount* magazine pic of Dick Rayborne at his home. "Mama, come on. You know I'm not Dick Rayborne."

She weakens. "Don't you dare try and screw with my head."

"He's probably got more security in that house than the U.S. Mint."

"We *are* going to that house, Dickie. And you're getting us in."

Whatever. I give up.

Mama fingers through her fanny pack, pulls out a worn piece of paper with somethng scribbled on it. "Give me your phone," she pants, breathing hard, and for some reason I do. Slowly and carefully, she taps the number into my phone. A male voice answers, and she says, "It's me. . . . What? Yes. . . . We're leaving now."

"Who was that?"

"Wouldn't you like to know?" Then she mumbles. "Fucking deserter." She slaps the phone back into my open hand and shuffles away. "Listen . . ." She takes a few breaths. "Talk with the kid, then meet me and the boys at the wagon in five minutes, okay?"

"Talk with Collin? About what?"

Mama stiffens, looks at me. "God, you men are clueless."

* * *

The boys have turned off the Looney Tunes, packed away the TV into the escape hatch, and followed Mama to the wagon. Now it's just me and my nephew sitting on the edge of the mattress, his body leaning into mine, and I wrap him up in my arms, give him a squeeze.

"You sure seem to be enjoying Cujo."

"I wish I had my field journal with me."

"Maybe it's better this way. You can just enjoy the moment."

We sit there awhile.

"It's not right how they treat him, Uncle Rick."

"It's not right how they treat anybody here, kiddo."

"Why do they do that?" His voice tightens. "Taking advantage of the Neanderthals."

I think of Dick Rayborne and his paperwork scheme. "I'm afraid that's what people do to each other."

He stiffens. "Not everyone."

I run my hand through his soft brown hair. "You're right. Not everyone."

"I mean, we should be setting an example." He sits up, turns, and glances at me. "Leaders should think about more than themselves."

After a moment, I ask, "Do you think maybe someday this could be something you change? You know, as a leader yourself?"

Collin looks at me like I'm crazy. "Someday? How about now?"

"Collin, you're eight years old. Your job is to be a boy and have fun and play and obey your parents. That's it."

He turns in, his forehead resting on my arm, and melts into me.

"Hey, kiddo. You okay?"

He sinks deeper into me.

"Have you been feeling bad?"

Slowly, he shakes his head, scoots closer.

"You wanna tell me what's going on?"

He looks up, tears in his eyes. "It's just that . . ."

"It's just . . . what?"

He takes my hand, runs a finger around my knuckles. "It's just that . . ." Sniffle. "Well, I really really really really do appreciate the fact that you got me a Neanderthal on my last day." He looks up at me, his watery brown eyes so serious. "And I *will* help his kind. I swear I will. It's just that . . ." He looks down, picks at my knuckle, sniffles. "I guess I still . . . feel sad inside."

"You feel sad?"

He drops his head even more, grips my finger. "And scared."

"Yeah?"

"I'm really scared." He breaks into sobs. "I'm scared about not having you and Audrey." He squeezes me so hard. "You're my very best-ever friends. Audrey's my . . ." Big breath. ". . . everything . . ." Big breath. ". . . and I love her so much." He falls over into my lap, crying so hard it's silent. "I don't want . . ." He strains. ". . . anything to change."

"I know, sweetheart." My eyes water, and my breathing gets shallow. "I don't want anything to change, either. But some-times—" I catch myself, take a deep breath. "Sometimes we don't have a—" And I can't finish.

"I want you and Audrey forever and ever."

I'm quaking. "I love you, kiddo. I'm always gonna be your uncle."

"Audrey is like my real mommy."

"Oh, don't say that."

"And you're the daddy I wish I had."

"Kiddo."

"And I pretend you're my mommy and daddy."

I try to shush him. "Collin."

"But it doesn't work, the pretend."

"I'm sorry, kiddo."

"I don't want to go."

"You can come hang out with me."

"Can you work in Argentina?"

"I don't think so. But there's the phone. And Skype."

He shakes his head, looks down. "I'm scared."

"I'm scared, too."

He looks up, surprised. "You're scared?"

I sniffle. "Sure."

"What are you scared about?"

"Well . . ." I pause, consider my words. "Maybe I have a hard time when things change, and I know I might not get to see people I really really care about."

He's looking at me, thinking. "I wish we could do adventures every day of the week."

"Me, too."

"And talk about things from—you know—the middle of my heart."

"Yeah."

"Uncle Rick." He looks up at me, fights back a grin. "I like it when we go to that donut place and talk."

I have to search my memory. I think maybe we did that only once—two years ago. "The donut place is awesome."

He picks at my knuckle again. "Do you think we'll ever do that again?"

The lump in my throat rises. "I'm not sure, Collin."

He looks up at me. "Maybe we could go today. You know, one last time."

Everything comes to an end, no matter how much you fight it.

"I don't know about donuts. But how about another adventure? I mean, what if I told you we're going to a mansion?"

Collin smiles at the idea, then softens when he settles on my eyes. "Uncle Rick?" He studies me a bit more. "You look sad."

I feel a little dizzy for a second. "Oh, I'm just . . ." I shake my face for clarity. "I don't know, kiddo."

He dips his head, takes a breath. "My mom says . . . A long time ago? Something sad happened." He looks at me some more. "And that it changed you forever and ever."

I force a chuckle. "Your mom told you that, huh?"

Collin looks up at me, his little mouth puckering. "Uncle Rick?" Eyes pensive, softening. "What happened?"

What happened was, I *did* change forever and ever.

Collin nestles closer. "Uncle Rick?"

I blink to snap out of it. "Time to go?"

Collin smiles. "I love you, Uncle Rick."

"I love you, too, kid."

"Will you come see me in Buenos Aires?"

"Will you promise to be a kid?"

Slowly, he nods.

"Then it's a deal."

•   •   •

The full brunt of the liquor is finally starting to hit me.

My head is spinning a bit, but I'm keeping it together.

The wagon is so loaded down with people, we nearly scrape the bottom coming out of the Robards International parking lot. As far as Mama sees it, "we've got the whole family together for a change"—Ernie and Collin in the back, and Cujo riding in the bay like an overgrown dog. With Cujo's help, Mama has once again confiscated my phone and is now driving. I'm sitting in shotgun begging for its return.

"Honey," Mama warns. "I'm telling you—just shut up and tell me where I'm going."

I wave the piece of scratch paper in front of her. "All I have here is an address. I need my phone, so I can get directions."

"We've got about forty maps in the glove box." She's shouting now. "*Where am I going?*"

I shuffle through the glove box, cussing to myself. "I'm not going to find this place on a fifty-year-old map."

She pauses for a moment. "How soon we forget," she says. "Those maps got us to Yellowstone and back. Not that you'd ever remember that."

"You made a promise."

"And I kept it. I called Sabine at Stanford." Mama eyes the rearview mirror. "Cujo? Don't you dare touch Mama's box back there, you hear?"

I steady myself, take a breath. "I need my phone."

"And I need my husband to pay attention to his family. Meaning, no email. No calls with the home office. No flirting with the floozies. No con calls about the conployees. So, in other words . . ." She's shouting again. ". . . *no phone*."

"Listen," I snap. "I'm not—"

"Hey," she says, suddenly softening. "Not in front of the kids. Can we at least agree on that? Let's both stop."

In Atherton, Mama's old wagon sticks out like a pair of ass chaps at the Vatican. We're so out of place in this neighborhood of palatial, multimillion-dollar homes that it feels as if the Fleetwood is nearly vibrating, releasing volleys of offensive shock waves, alerting the occasional mom in black yoga pants and the countless crews of yard-service workers. After we roll up to an enormous wrought-iron gate, we sit there and gaze at the expansive, carefully manicured property on the other side. Set far back and shrouded by an assortment of majestic white oaks is a home that couldn't look sweeter, cuter, or more wholesome. A six-thousand-square-foot, single-story cottage with gray shingle siding, white trim, and endless nooks and gables. I imagine a Disney princess dancing and twirling inside with a warm plate of fresh-baked cookies.

Mama breaks the silence. "Come on, open it up."

I look over to her and slur, "This is Dick Rayborne's house?"

"Get us in there."

My head sways. "How am I supposed to do that?"

"Open the gate."

I have to do something. "I see an armed guard," I blurt. "With an assault gun."

"It's so obvious when you lie to me, Dickie. Plus, I've done my homework on this place."

"Mama, please."

She grips the wheel and revs the engine. "The next thing I will do is ram this gate." The boys howl in excitement. "And you know I'm not bluffing." Another rev.

Yes, I am superbuzzed, but I'm not so far gone that I can't still imagine cops coming to arrest us, and maybe even uncovering our illegal transaction involving substances extracted from wild baboons in Uganda. "Okay," I snap. "Give me a second."

I step out of the Fleetwood and head for the aluminum intercom beside the gate. At this point, who gives a shit? I let out a little burp. Maybe we can straighten this out. *I really shouldn't have had those minis.* And then an idea hits me—*I should walk up to this intercom and tell them to keep the door closed. Mama won't hear me, and we'll avert disaster.* I take another step, and the intercom buzzes. A voice says, "Sorry, Mr. Rayborne. I didn't realize that was you."

"No, you don't have to—"

But the gate opens inward.

Mama revs the engine.

PARTICIPATE IN A FELONY

It seems like we're on an amusement-park ride for toddlers, the Fleetwood rolling slowly along a winding cobblestone path through an enchanted world of blossoming pink and white rose-bushes, finely trimmed boxwood shrubs, tinkling water fountains, babbling brooks, Dutch Colonial birdhouses, and even a few wild bunnies hopping across a deep green lawn. We complete a final twist on the path and roll up to the house; a silver Porsche with vanity plates (CNPLOY) is parked out front, and Cujo rouses in the back of a wagon, not unlike a Labrador that's picked up the scent of the ocean. He rolls around and presses his fingers against the glass, laughing. "Mother lode," he bellows. "Mother-fucking mother lode."

Ernie snickers.

Collin straightens and shouts, "I think they have a pool."

"I want you boys on your best behavior."

They whine.

"We're going to see how Dad's been spending our money since he left us."

"Mama, are we going to get a present?"

"If I have well-behaved boys, they might get a present from the box. Yes."

"No, I mean, a present from the house." Cujo is salivating, swallowing spit. "Something we can take from the Warden's—I mean, Dad's—house."

Mama sighs. "If you do what I say?" Long silence. "Maybe."

From the back of the wagon. "What are we waiting for?"

"Mama," I say. "This is getting crazy. When they find out—"

"*Shut your hole*," Mama yells.

In the back, Cujo rocks so hard that the wagon bounces.

"Okay." Mama kills the engine and struggles to turn and look Collin in the eye. "Are you ready to be my special clicker boy?"

Collin twinkles and nods.

She reaches into her fanny pack, pulls out the clicker, and tosses it over the seat. "You keep that handy." Then to me, she adds, "Let's take a look at the love nest."

"Mama. C'mon. This has gone far enough."

She tightens, pulls out my phone. "You want me to call your sister and put the kid on the line? That could derail everything, couldn't it?"

I think of Audrey, feel that awful feeling of rejection all over again.

Then I think of living for free in Ana and Samson's compound.

Then I think of quitting Robards International tomorrow morning.

So I open the door and put a leg out. "Okay, kids. Let's do this." The wagon explodes with excitement, and I hear myself hollering as they pile out, "*Listen to your mother.*"

•   •   •

Maybe it's the liquor, but it feels like a dream.

I latch on to but a few things.

The front door is solid oak.

A housecleaner thinks I'm Dick Rayborne's twin brother.

She leads us through a series of hallways.

"I think he's in his office."

A narrow, dimly lit staircase, tiny lights on each step.

On the wall, framed covers of *Headcount*.

More steps down.

Another hallway.

And then another door. Unlocks with her badge.

She stands there. "Just follow the lights."

We descend.

So many steps down.

In this sweet "cottage"? Who would've thought?

A framed award—THE HEADCOUNT SHRINKER OF THE YEAR—
10K JOBS.

We descend more and more.

A 1930s-era photo of expressionless teens in a sooty factory.

Collin says, "I feel weird."

The tiny lights are getting dimmer.

A framed, two-page spread from a 1992 issue of *Headcount*. Dick is standing in the middle of a cluster of cars, arms folded, that toothy grin popping off the page. The headline announcing, IT'S SUNDAY MORNING, AND HIS EMPLOYEE PARKING LOT IS PACKED—HOW HE DOES IT.

Farther down we go.

A framed essay in a publication called *RIF*, the headline teasing, PEER GROUP TENSION—HOW IT CAN DRIVE NEW LEVELS OF PRODUCTIVITY—BY DICK RAYBORNE.

Collin approaches, takes my hand.

"It's okay, kiddo," I tell him.

Finally we reach the landing.

There's a water fountain. Tiny trickling.

It's dark down here, like a dungeon. No windows, of course, and very low lighting. But we can see his desk, or at least part of it, a surface light illuminating an open laptop, everything else a silhouette. At the opposite end, stock prices stream across a small TV set. Mama stands over a table of framed photos. Dick with members of Congress. Dick in front of the New York Stock Exchange. Dick on the African plains with a dead lion. Dick with a dozen or so nervous teenage Chinese workers in blue shirts.

"Sorry, Uncle Rick, but I guess he does kinda look like you—a lot."

Cujo and Ernie check behind a series of paintings on the far wall—lions eating limp, juvenile antelopes. Collin releases my hand, sneaks up on Cujo, tags him on the back leg, announces, "You're it," and tears back up the stairs. Cujo loses interest in his search, turns and chases after Collin. Ernie small-steps after them, his arms working hard, still clutching the barbecue prongs.

"*Boys!*"

Mama looks around. "Is this where you go to do your . . ." The light from the TV coats her glasses. ". . . darkest things, your most sadistic activities—your pleasures, huh? Is this where you plot to bring the employees of Robards International to their knees? At your feet?" Her voice sharpens, and she tightens, leaning in, the stock prices streaming across her lenses. "Is this where you get back at the world, Dickie, you sick . . . empty . . . sociopath?"

I know she's talking about Dick Rayborne, but I feel a little guilty.

The boys thunder back down the stairs, and Collin leads them around the corner and into some kind of walk-in closet, hollers, "*Whoa.*"

I turn to Mama. "Okay, so what are we doing here?"

She looks at me, bites her lower lip, thinking.

"And I swear, if you don't give me my phone back, I'm just going to leave."

"This thing?" She peers into her fanny pack, struggles to pull out my phone. She studies it. "Looks like your sister called another eight times." She glances up at me. "I can call Cujo over right now, have him call your sister back, put the kid on the phone, see how that goes." The glasses regard me. "No?"

"Listen, Mama. Tell us what you want, and as long as it's not too crazy, I'll help. Then I need to take Collin and get going. It's a very important day."

She stands there, swaying a little, her jaw trembling. "I want my family back." She looks away. "I want my goddamn family back." She turns and shuffles toward the stairs. "Why did it all have to change?"

"Mama. C'mon. Would it help if I played along?"

She nods.

"Okay, listen." I bite my lip, close my eyes—*okay, here we go.* "I'm sorry it didn't work out, baby. You know we tried. I'm very very very sorry."

She seems to deflate a little.

"But the past is the past. We both know we can't go back."

She nods, wipes her nose with her wrist. "But I can stop you from destroying more families." She turns angry again. "Mr. Paperwork." She considers it, then adds, "Plus, I have a new man. I couldn't wait around for you forever."

"Okay, baby." I ask for her hand. "I might not want the details—that'll always be hard. But I understand."

This seems to please her.

"Now let me show you the house."

"Boys, let's go," Mama says. "We're headed back upstairs."

They giggle.

"Quit your mischief and get out here."

The rustle of metal, and more giggles.

"One . . . Two . . ."

Collin emerges from the dark wearing a steel collar attached to three thick shackles, steel wrist cuffs, and an oversize, crotchless harness. Chortling. When it sinks in, my body tenses and I lunge forward. "Collin, what are you . . ." But I can't finish.

Cujo and Ernie step out of the dark, snickering. We all gasp.

Cujo sports a "spider gag," which has turned the lower part of his face into a giant mouth hole. In one hand, he's holding a studded spanking paddle. In the other, he's tugging on a leather leash, bringing Ernie out of the dark. Collin lets out a wild laugh as Ernie tiny-steps into our full view, his head encased by a black, openmouthed slave mask, his neck encased by a spiked steel collar, his wrists cuffed behind his back, his ankles shackled together by a short metal chain. His prongs are tucked into his jumpsuit so the fork end nearly grazes his chin.

I'm speechless.

The mouth hole frames a dopey smile.

"Actually, we shouldn't be surprised." I look around, motioning to the items in Dick Rayborne's HR dungeon. "Collin, you need to get out of that stuff right now. Put it all back."

Mama shuffles up to me, whispers. "If this was what you wanted, you should've told me. You know I was always willing to try things. Remember that time in Turlock? With the turkey farmer?"

•   •   •

Back up on the main floor, I feel like I'm walking through the Pillsbury Doughboy's house.

A plump older lady is baking cookies in the enormous kitchen, and the aroma seems to follow us as we explore deeper and deeper, discovering room after room of lemon-yellow walls, white crown molding, ten-foot picture windows, and crystal vases of freshly cut daisies, sunflowers, and carnations. A symphony of tweeting birds and babbling brooks eases out of an unseen sound system. The HR dungeon seems a million miles away, except for the fact that Cujo refused to remove his spider gag, and Ernie still sports his openmouthed slave mask, his grin more prominent than ever—those lips protruding excitedly—as Collin leads him by the hand. We'd managed to get everything off Collin except for his steel collar (Cujo lost the key).

Mama looks around in wonderment. "I couldn't have guessed this."

And then the hint of a woman's voice.

We freeze, look at each other.

My chest tightens. *He's here. That Porsche outside? He's obviously here.*

From around the corner, a woman says, "Fertilization is absolutely critical."

Mama keeps shuffling, and we keep following.

We enter a master bedroom the size of a 7-Eleven. There's no one here. Then, from the master bath, a woman says, "I know this can cause an odor . . ." I look at Mama. *Not sure I wanna hear this.* ". . . but the benefits can dramatically outweigh the assault on your senses."

"Okay." Mama yanks the prongs from Ernie and shuffles to the bathroom.

From the bathroom, a man asks, "Gloria?"

Cujo follows Mama into the bathroom, and I quick-step to catch up.

"So if you can get over the odor, they'll enlarge to proportions you never thought possible."

Mama and Cujo disappear into the bathroom.

"Gloria, bring me another bowl."

"Oh," Mama says. "This is just choice."

I ease into the bathroom. It's enormous, of course. And white-tiled with peach walls and white trim. Sunlight is shooting though a wood-framed window, illuminating a giant bathtub overflowing with bubbles. Protruding out of the bubbles is Dick Rayborne's balding head, facing away from us. Watching TV. Humming. Helping himself to a bowl of marshmallows placed on a chrome tub rack as the TV flashes an Angela Lansbury lookalike walking through an English garden. "Your noses may not love fish emulsion," she tells us. "But your roses will."

Mama takes Cujo by the hand and shuffles closer.

Dick Rayborne turns his head halfway—his chin in the air, his eyes shut—and barks. "Gloria?"

"Gloria?" Mama and Cujo step into Dick's view, and he jerks so hard the bowl launches into the air, marshmallows shooting across the tub. Mama lowers her head, glowers. "Do we look like Gloria to you?"

Dick seems so scared, he's speechless. And frozen.

Cujo takes the opportunity to tiptoe a little closer and retrieve a marshmallow from the rim of the tub. He fingers it through the spider gag and into his open mouth, realizes there's no way to chew and swallow, so he forces a cough to launch it into the bathtub. Dick's throat releases an odd noise, and he tries to recede into the bubbles, his eyes registering a look of utter horror as they settle on Cujo's seafoam-green jumpsuit, and then on Ernie, who's wandered into the bathroom giggling, wearing the slave mask, his hands out.

Another distress noise.

Mama stands over him, playing the role of an utterly baffled old lady. "Dick?" she rasps.

Collin reaches the threshold and stops.

Mama somehow succeeds in making her lower lip quiver. "Dick? I thought you were—" She places a trembling hand over her brow, lowers her head. Then she takes a peek at me, winking. "I'm so confused."

Dick eases deeper into the bubbles.

"Mr. Rayborne," I slur, swaying, "I can explain all of this."

A hand eases out of the bubbles and floats toward a drink ledge beside the tub, only, there's no drink there—just a black device with a small red button. So much for reasoning with him. Now it's a matter of avoiding arrest. "Mama?" I say. "He's trying to grab something there."

Mama shouts at the bubbles. *"You sent your little brother?"* She glances at me, winks again. "Your little brother to clean up the mess you've created?"

The hand scuttles across the tile, searching for the device.

"Mama," I say and motion to the hand.

Mama turns and huffs. She stabs the prongs into the hand, sinking the fork into the knuckles. From the bubbles, a yelp. The hand scurries back into the foam, the prongs trailing before detaching.

Mama sniffles. "You thought you could sidestep your responsibilities? Just send your bozo brother and try and fool an old lady? And not just any old lady, but the mother of your children. Come here, boys. Yeah, come over here. You, too, Collin. Someone help Ernie to the tub—he can't see. Come here. There you go, honey. Yeah, so look at us, Dick."

Dick's eyes rise from the bubbles.

"These are our children. The fruits of our loins. You prom-

ised them the world, honey. You promised me the world. You
sold us all on a vision we couldn't resist."

The scalp twitches, sinks deeper into the bubbles.

"Yeah, you sure fooled us, didn't you?" Mama sharpens,
taking an acidic tone. "Sold us—sold the world, really—on a lie.
Only they don't realize it yet, do they? But the boys and I? Your
own brother?" She snarls and glares. "We know what kind of
man you really are. We know you're the man who abandoned
the values essential to family. The man who shits on the world
so he can . . ." She motions to the bathroom like a game-show
host revealing a bounty of prizes. ". . . sit in his bathtub on a
Tuesday eating marshmallows and watching TV while everyone
else sinks deeper into a . . ." She puffs out her cheeks, bulges her
eyes. ". . . an abyss. Layoffs. Pay cuts. Benefit cuts." She lowers
her head, shows her teeth. "Paperwork."

Collin says, "Paperwork?"

"Yes, sweetie. Your dad here has created a lot of paperwork
for people at Robards."

Collin looks up to me. "Is that true, Uncle Rick? Paperwork?"

I open my mouth, and Mama says, "You bet it's true, sweetheart. Your so-called dad in the tub here—"

"He's not my dad, Mama."

"Just humor me, kid." She pulls up her pants, twitches her
nose. "When your uncle and his friends at work see a doctor—
when they have a boo-boo, or when their children have a boo-
boo—the doctor will charge them a lot of money. That's why
they pay for medical insurance through their employer—in this
case, Robards International. Most companies also help their employees pay for the insurance."

Collin blinks and nods.

"Then, when they have a doctor's bill, the insurance company pays for part and the employee pays the other part."

"That sounds fair."

"That would be fair," Mama says. "The only problem is, your so-called dad in the tub here has worked with the insurance company to create a system that makes it hard for employees like your uncle . . . or Cujo . . . or Ernie to get reimbursed."

"To get their money back?"

"Exactly."

"What did he do?"

Mama says, "He created a system of paperwork that is so confusing . . . so complicated . . . so cumbersome and flawed . . . so annoying . . . that lots and lots of people just give up, or don't give up but make a small but critical mistake along the way. And guess what?"

"Are Neanderthals covered?"

"Robards International and its insurance provider don't have to pay their share. Meaning . . ." She tugs on Cujo, who's unstrapping the spider gag from his face. ". . . employees like your brother here are effectively cheated out of their medical coverage."

Collin looks at the bubbles, then at Mama, and then back to the bubbles. "Is that true?"

The bubbles shift.

Mama shuffles to the tub and reaches into the opposite end of the bubbles, yanks hard. The sound of draining bathwater pulls me back to the evenings of my childhood when I'd take long soaks as my parents watched the *Nightly News*.

"I think it's time for Dickie to come out."

•   •   •

A few bubbles remain stuck to Dick Rayborne as we escort the nearly naked executive to a vast area that looks more like the lobby of a midsize luxury hotel—plush sofas and chairs, yellow-white porcelain lamps, large oil paintings of stately properties in England, and a seemingly endless series of crystal vases and figurines on side tables and wall ledges. I am not sure what to feast my eyes on—this grotesque spectacle of decadence, or the sight of Dick Rayborne wearing nothing but a small, peach-white bath towel, his sagging, cottage-cheese breasts and arms slick with bathwater, his belly dripping over the towel, his head hanging low, his brows down in some type of embarrassed glare.

Mama shuffles up and prongs him in the throat. He recoils with a snarl.

"When you lived with us . . ." Another pronging, another snarl. ". . . you never needed . . ." She lowers her head, forces him to look her in the eye. ". . . maids and cooks and security men."

He sways back from her and forces an uneasy grin, showing those enormous teeth. My lord, they're huge.

"And knowing you . . ." Another poke—this time in the belly—and he steps back and rubs the area with his injured hand, dots of red showing through the tissue. ". . . you probably don't give them benefits or a decent wage."

Dick offers a weak, have-mercy grin, his eyes enlarging.

"Or any vacation days. Or sick days. Or holidays."

Cujo announces, "I'm bored."

Mama returns to Dick. "Send them home, honey."

"Home?" His voice is weak and lispy—it's not what I expected. "Send who home? I'm confused . . ." He bobs his head, and his eyes enlarge again, measuring, sensing, hoping. "Do I know you?" He recedes a bit, looks at her, then at me. "Were you all part of Wave 93?"

Collin looks at me. "Wave 93?"

"Sometimes a company will tell a large group of people their jobs have been elimated, and so they kick these people out.

Robards calls these waves—endless waves. I think Wave 93 was last week."

Another forced grin from Dick. Reddening jowls. "Those things are out of my hands."

"Oh, no you don't." Mama wags a finger in his face. "No more running from your responsibilities, Dickie." She lifts her chin into the air, yells, "*Gloria?*"

I grasp a sofa to stabilize myself—damn, those minis were a bad idea. "Maybe we don't need more people right now, Mama."

"Exactly." Mama hollers into the air. "*Gloria honey? Dickie needs you in the living room.*"

From a distant room, Gloria hollers, "*Coming.*"

Mama turns back to Dick, reaches into her fanny pack, and pulls out my phone. Lifts it into the air with a trembling hand. Takes a few big breaths. Juts her jaw out. Slits her eyes. "This cordless telephone is loaded with dozens and—" She suppresses a burp, tries to catch her breath. "—and dozens of kinky photos of your HR dungeon and S and M playroom. Just the kind of photos that can go—how do you say?—bacterial on the computers."

"Viral," I correct.

"Viral," she says. "Dickie, your kinky sex toys are about to go viral."

Dick whitens.

"So when Gloria comes in . . ." She sharpens again, yells. ". . . *you're going to do exactly as I say.*"

Dick has begun to pant. He looks to me. "If you're on the Wave 93 roster, I can reinstate you." He glances at Cujo, who's struggling to remove Ernie's slave mask. "Same with the con-ployees. Not a problem."

A woman enters from the far end of the living room. I recognize her as the sweet-looking, plump lady who was baking cookies when we came in. Up close, she's older than I'd first thought—easily in her midsixties—and her expression looks more like fatigue than sweetness. "Hello," she says to us, forcing a smile. "I'm not sure we've met properly."

"Listen, sweetheart." Mama pumps the prongs in the air. "There's a very logical reason you've never met us. We're his family."

Gloria looks at me, smiles. "I can see that."

I didn't need to hear that.

"Yes." Mama seems to lose her train of thought, frowns, and whispers to herself before looking up. "Well, Dickie is hiding from his family. In fact, your boss is probably the least family-friendly businessman around."

Gloria bows her head, steps back.

"Does Dick even know about your family, Gloria?"

Gloria looks at Dick, who shoots her that uneasy grin, his eyes sinking.

"Didn't think so." Mama points her prongs skyward. "Today is going to be a family day, Gloria."

"Okay. Do you want a family dinner tonight?"

"No. Dick and I want you and the other employees here on the compound to take the rest of the day off. Okay? And spend some time with *your* friends and family. Or go get drunk or laid or whatever your thing is."

Gloria brightens, looks at Dick, who nods reluctantly.

"That includes the security team, okay, Gloria? Those guys who clicked open the gate for us. Okay?"

Gloria checks with Dick, who seems to have frozen.

"Dick says, *Do it.*" Mama shuffles to Gloria, taps her on the shoulder with the prongs. "Have a wonderful day, honey. I mean it. And don't forget to tell the security guys, okay?"

Gloria nods, removes her apron. "I'll go tell them and the others."

"You understand, right?" Mama softens. "Sometimes, a family just needs some private time."

Gloria nods. "I have a fresh batch of oatmeal-raisin cookies in the oven, but I can—"

"Go, honey. Tell the others and go. Let those cookies burn to black little balls." Mama turns to me, and nearly coos, her eyes twinkling. "It's time for some family bonding."

• • •

Dick says, "Just tell me what you want, and we can talk about it."

"What I want is, Family Game Night."

Dick gives Mama an ooooooo-kay look, eyes widening, chin tucked in.

"I've got a new game, Dickie. It's called Good News/Bad News."

Dick bites his lip.

"Can you guess what the good news is, Dickie?"

"You're not going to hurt me?"

"That's not it. The good news is . . ." Mama digs into her fanny pack and pulls it out. ". . . I brought my laser pointer." At the mention of the laser pointer, the boys go wild—Cujo running tight circles around the furniture, Ernie jumping for joy on the main couch, his little arms outstretched as he bounces higher and higher. Collin decides it looks like fun, and he gallops around the room—his knees high, his shoulders hunched, his eyes crossed—slapping his butt, hollering, "Laser pointer, laser pointer, laser pointer."

Mama smiles to herself. "They still love this game." She chuckles. "Here, Ernie. Take your prongs." She adopts the baby voice. "Mama knows you like to have your prongs when we play Laser Pointer."

Dick Rayborne sinks into his chair, clutches his towel. "Good news?"

"The boys love Laser Pointer because it involves . . ." She digs into her fanny pack, pulls out a wad of cash and two minis of Jack Daniel's. ". . . prizes."

The boys hoot and holler.

"So . . ." Mama pants and puffs as she struggles to put the cash and minis back into her fanny pack. ". . . the good news is, it's time to play Laser Pointer."

Collin tugs on her shirt and peers up. "What's the bad news?"

"Well, for Dickie the bad news is . . ." Mama strokes the laser pointer and looks at Dick . ". . . we're going to play it in his house."

Dick forces a smile. "We don't need to play Good News/Bad News. Or the laser pointer game."

Eyes closed, shaking her head, Mama tells him, "I have a lot of questions about how things work."

"Work? Where work? What do you mean, work?"

Mama looks at him, eyes twinkling. "Let's play."

"Mama." I approach, touch her arm, concerned. "Let's not get too—"

"Ready." Mama thrusts the pointer into the air, stroking the button.

Ernie and Cujo stare at the laser pointer. Collin spreads his legs and slaps his butt.

"Set."

Ernie squeals. Cujo freezes.

"Okay," Mama squeaks. "Who wants to win a beverage?" The boys bark. "And a one-hundred-dollar bill?" More ruckus, and Mama scolds, "You boys better show your little brother how to play. You hear?" She sharpens. "Stay there, Dickie."

"Collin," I holler. "Be careful."

"And . . . catch that light."

A bright red laser dot dances in front of us—across the rug and over the coffee table and right by Cujo's feet before darting away and settling on an empty yellow armchair. Cujo and Ernie nearly knock each other over as they bolt for the chair—Ernie hurdling the coffee table, Cujo upending it. Collin follows far behind, giggling.

Dick Rayborne sits up.

Ernie dives for the red dot and crashes headfirst into the armchair, stabbing it first with the prongs and knocking it over, tumbling end over end, clearing out a stand of vases near the hearth. The dot avoids him and bounces to the nearby lampshade.

"*Dude,*" I shout. "*Watch it with the prongs. Stay back, Collin.*"

Mama laughs and sings, "Weee-eeeeeeee," as the dot dances about.

Cujo cuts through the room like a charging linebacker, swatting items out of his way as he closes in on the dot, his brows furrowed, his lips twisted in determination. Ernie approaches from the opposite end—that openmouthed grin widening, his enormous blues twinkling—and dives over a couch a second too late as the red dot bounces away and the lamp is knocked off the end table, shatters on the floor. Cujo tries to adjust but ends up spinning out of control and careens into a china cabinet, shattering the glass and collapsing shelves of crystal vases and antique china plates into a heap of shards. Collin runs after the dot as it dances over a series of French Impressionist oil paintings on the far wall.

"*Help your brother,*" Mama shouts.

Dick takes an acidic tone. "Okay," he yells over the din, standing up, clutching his towel. "Come on."

"Oh yeah?" Mama directs the laser dot onto Dick's forehead. It takes but a second for the boys to correct course and head for him. "You have a problem?"

Dick sits down, Mama sends the laser dot back to the paintings, and the boys correct course yet again—but not before Cujo clears out a table of framed photos and sideswipes a vintage grandfather clock, the bells issuing a series of *dongs* as it crashes down.

Mama seems so pleased. "I saw this on a TV show called *Too Cute*." Cujo slams into a painting, and Ernie swats at another lamp. Collin giggles as the dot dances around his feet, avoiding his stomps. "Only . . ." The dot leads Cujo into a canary-yellow wall, and the floor vibrates with his impact. ". . . it was with kittens."

The carnage continues.

Dick pleads.

"Tell me," Mama says. "Who's Emma Flanduzi?"

Dick pulls at his face and wails. "Who?"

"Exactly." Cujo slams into a hutch with porcelain piglets. "You nearly killed her with your goddamn paperwork, and you don't even know who she is."

"Wave 42?" Dick rubs his temples with open hands. "Was she on Wave 42? The one we laid off the day after her husband died?"

"Wrong."

The dot leads the boys into the adjoining dining room, where Cujo takes down a chandelier and crashes atop a long table, wrestling with the fixture like it must be subdued. Mama keeps the dot on the chandelier and reaches into her pack, produces a click. "You did it, Cujo. You captured the dot."

Cujo hoots, tosses the chandelier aside, and races to Mama. Collin and Ernie join, and all three slide to a stop, facing her—panting hard.

"Lady." Dick's so red, it's like he has a rash. "Come on. Let's be reasonable here."

Mama's digging into her fanny pack. "Cujo wins Round

One," she announces and hands him a mini and then a one-hundred-dollar bill. "But you two still have a chance. In fact . . ." She returns to her fanny pack, fingers moving slowly. ". . . Mama's gonna give you each a five-dollar bill." They jump up and down, and Cujo drains the mini. "For effort."

The boys back away, keeping their eyes on her pointer.

"Okay," Mama says. "Round Two."

The red dot zigzags across a far wall, teasing the boys.

Dick says, "Let's talk about this."

The boys crash and slam and launch.

Mama suddenly doesn't sound so senile anymore. "Tell me, Dickie. Why did have your computer whizzes cook up a software code that makes it so hard for employees to sign up for benefits that twenty-one percent of them now give up?"

Dick snarls, "You're crazy."

"Really?" Mama points the laser back to the oil paintings, and Dick yelps. "Is that why you recruited a select group of conployees to create your own 'Special IT Projects Group'? Those young conployees—just boys, really—who've been planting glitches in your open-enrollment website for benefits. Little glitches that target one out of every fifteen employees who log on thinking they'll enroll for medical, dental, and life insurance? Little glitches that follow said employees like herpes. It doesn't matter if they switch out computers or file a ticket with IT, does it, Dickie? No matter what those poor souls do, where they go, or what kind of scan or scrub or vaccine—whatever you call it—their computers keep freezing over and over and over, every time they try to sign up for benefits, until most just give up." Mama glowers at him. "And Robards International keeps the money."

I'm not sure Dick hears her. He slips his fingers into his mouth and pulls down on his jaw as Cujo, Ernie, and Collin swat at the paintings—one after the other—in hot pursuit. The dot glides under the Steinway to the left, and Cujo scurries under the piano and takes out the far leg when he emerges from the other side, making the piano crash to the floor with an off-key slam.

"*Dickie.*"

"Okay, fine." He shakes his face, balls his fists. "Fine. I hired a group. Yes. Fine. A couple of hackers. You happy?"

"They call themselves conhackers," Mama says and points the dot at the peach drapes—Ernie charges into the drapes, gets tangled up, and pulls the whole mess (including the rod) off the wall. "Okay, next question."

Dick Rayborne gets up, catches himself, and sits down. He snarls.

Mama sends the dot back into the dining room.

Dick pleads, "Just tell me what you want."

Mama jerks the dot around, and the boys crash into each other before plowing into a serving cabinet—I hear splintering. "An employee must complete eighteen steps in order to sign up for 401(k) matching from Robards International." She sends the dot back to the living room and settles it on the white mantel, then leads the boys from one end to the other—silver flutes and framed photos and crystal candleholders are either crushed or sent flying. "The launch sequence of the space shuttle was easier than the process you created, Dickie. A mind-numbing amalgamation of phone calls, computer forms, and old-fashioned paperwork—not to mention the heavy volume of slight procedural infractions that allow you to reject half the people who actually do complete the process, who are then instructed to start all over."

Cujo plows into a giant bowl of potpourri, and Mama issues a click. "Boy, you are good at this game, aren't you, Cujo? Come get your prize." And then to me, she adds, "I found the laser is better than the bouncy ball. The laser keeps the action going."

The boys are still panting.

Dick Rayborne seems woozy.

I still feel way too buzzed.

Mama says, "You're a modern-day robber baron, you know?"

Dick surveys the damage and swallows hard—it looks like a pack of hyenas tore through the place. Hyenas on meth and N D z. Furniture in splinters. Broken glass. Ripped paintings. Shattered porcelain and china. At least a dozen cracks or indentations in the drywall. Stabbed or shredded fabric on the chairs and sofas.

Dick opens his mouth, makes a weird noise. Mama shuffles to him and stands over him. "The bottom line is, each time you prevent a hardworking employee from claiming her benefits, your bonus gets a little fatter." Mama waits. "Doesn't it?"

Dick shrugs.

"Answer me."

Another shrug.

Mama sighs, reaches into her fanny pack. "I didn't think we'd need to play another round of Laser Pointer."

The boys stir, and Dick straightens. "Fine," he snaps. "Fine. Yes, the bonus is higher. The less we spend on benefits, the higher my bonus." He puffs out, chokes on his spit. "We live in America, you know."

I hear myself saying, "America isn't about ripping off hardworking employees."

Dicks offers a mild sneer.

Mama says to Dick, "And it all stops today."

He chuckles and reddens.

"You think I'm crazy, Dickie Boy, but here's the truth." She lowers her head, waits for him to make eye contact. "You're going to hold an emergency meeting of the Robards International board of directors." She looks at him. "Today."

"Me?" Dick laughs and snarls. "You think I'm—"

"You're an officer of the company, which means you can call a meeting."

"Of the compensation subcommittee." Dick is amused. "Not the entire board."

"You'll start there," Mama says. "You'll call the HR subcommittee of the board."

"Compensation," Dick corrects.

"Whatever you call it."

Dick seems to brighten as it settles in. "I'll need to come in to the office for that," he says. "Solo."

Mama studies him a moment. "I think it's time for another round of Good News/Bad News."

"That's not necessary."

"But you don't seem to understand, Dickie."

"I'm sure I can figure it out."

"Let me help you." Mama closes her eyes. "The good news is, Dick Rayborne will indeed go to the headquarters of Robards International this afternoon. And I won't be there."

Dick can't suppress his grin.

Collin looks up at Mama, his eyes wide. "And the bad news?"

Mama turns to Collin. "Well, the bad news is for Old Dickie. That's because we're sending in a new and improved Dick Rayborne. That means Old Dickie—well, I'm afraid he's not going anywhere for a while."

Dick whitens. Collin crinkles.

"I don't understand, Mama."

"You see, honey, we're sending in your uncle. Dickie's brother." She bites her lip, shakes her head as she thinks about it. "I just don't trust Old Dickie."

My stomach tightens. "I'm not impersonating this guy."

She turns to me and softens. "Now listen, honey. You want to make a true difference in your lifetime? A real difference? You know, change the lives of tens of thousands of people—and their families?"

"It's not that simple."

"Oh, it is. It's as easy as walking into his closet, putting on one of his suits. Taking his badge. And his car. Using his phone to call his secretary, or whatever you call 'em these days. And then just marching in there and convincing the subwhatever to take a new approach." She pauses, cocks her head, and sticks out her chin. "Otherwise, the boys and I might be forced to cancel your six o'clock meeting with your sister. Or we might decide to join you. Or stay out really late with Collin." She sighs in mock concern. "Really late."

"I can do it," Dick says. "You don't need him."

I think about losing the house-sitting gig. It makes me want to throw up. "Mama, you want me to do something that is very illegal."

"Listen," she snaps. "What he's doing is illegal—spiritually, in terms of what is right and wrong—regardless of what the lawyers say."

Collin approaches, takes my hand in both of his. Looks up at me. "She has a point, Uncle Rick. Those things Mama was describing? They're just wrong. Nobody should be allowed to exploit Neanderthals this way."

Dick says to me, "You leave me here with them, you're fired."

"Maybe that's not such a bad thing," Mama says.

A deep chime echoes throughout the house, and I search for clues.

"Doorbell," Dick says with hope in his eyes.

Shit. The police? Or maybe Dick's security team didn't go home after all?

Mama says, "Ignore that for a moment." She glances at Dick. "We're still playing Good News/Bad News."

"That's okay," Dick says.

"Why do you get so stressed out?" Mama says, irritated. "It's like I'm torturing you or something. Jeez. What a baby. I mean, every round starts with good news, doesn't it?"

"She's right." Cujo finishes off his mini of Jack, shivers, and tosses the empty over his shoulder. "Stop the whining, dude. Mama, can we have a headlock party?"

"No," Mama says. "Okay, so the good news is—"

"I think the good news would be if we get the hell out of here," I say. "You know, before the police show up."

"I think the good news would be if you shut your hole." Mama turns back to Dick. "So, the good news is, I'm not going to make you come back to me. I'm sure you're happy about that, since I'm certainly not what you want now that you have all this robber baron money and probably have this place brimming with young tramps. Yeah, I give up. After all the lies. After all those years of taking care of the kids while you're out sucking the world dry. After feeling alone and neglected for so long, I give up, Dickie. You happy? I'm sure you are, because that's what you wanted all along, isn't it?"

Dick shrugs.

"So that's the good news, honey. You've finally got me off your tail. No more nagging. Aren't you happy?"

Dick looks at me, says, "Help me here."

I give him my *I'm-powerless* look.

"Of course . . ." Mama raises a brow, slows down. ". . . the game is called Good News/Bad News. So . . . I *do* have a bit of bad news."

Dick clamps onto his bath towel with both hands.

The doorbell rings again.

"The bad news is, when you leave a vibrant woman alone like that, she begins to appreciate—how shall I put it?—previously unwanted male attention. If you know what I mean."

"Of course I do," Dick says, "That's fine with me, lady. Seriously. I haven't been around, so you hooked up with a few fellas."

"I don't think you fully understand." There even seems to be a bit of compassion in her voice. "Yes, I have taken a lover. But that's not the bad news."

The doorbell rings a third time, followed by three tight knocks. Mama looks to Ernie. "Will you get that for me, sweetie?" Ernie yanks his prongs out of the leather armchair and meanders around a corner toward the front door. "And let me tell you, he's really kind of a dreamboat. Such a nice body for an older fella. Looks like he could be in a magazine advertisement for cologne or teeth brightener. And sharp as a tack, too." She squinits at a thought, whistles to herself. "Crazy smart. And not conniving smart like you, but a-thousand-thoughts-a-second smart."

"That's fine," Dick offers. "I mean, it was inevitable. Yes, I'm hurt. But I'll get over it."

We can hear Ernie open the front door.

"Yes, good for me. And good for my body, too, because let's face it. My lady bits have been hungry. I mean, *really* famished." She looks at Collin, turns back to Dick with a sneer. "They've been malnourished for a long time." She lowers her eyelids, looks at Dick with satisfaction. "And let me tell you, my new fella knows how to hump a lady." She looks at Dick, waiting for a reaction. "He knows how to feed those ravenous lady bits." She smiles, winks, and whispers, "How to make a tired old woman scream."

Dick seems happy. Relieved. "Well," he says, quick and nearly jovial. "That *is* some bad news. I have to admit. I don't like the idea of another man having you—whoever you are. Umm, what I mean is, it's hard to let go." He shoots me a look—*This lady is crazy.*

Around the corner, footsteps.

"He doesn't like pillow talk," Mama says. "But after a good fucking . . ."

I twist Collin around by the shoulders. "Go see if Gloria left any cookies in the kitchen."

". . . I really just want to talk as I wait for him to recharge— that is, if he's not on Viagra. Well, anyways . . ."

Collin scampers away, and I holler, *"Don't go too far."*

". . . he prefers to sit there in bed smoking his pipe, thinking, and I—Well, I guess I got to talking one afternoon. Because, we hump in the afternoon."

Ernie quick-steps back into the living room, and Mama says, "Was that him, honey?"

Which is when he appears. An older guy—sixty, sixty-five— walking slowly toward us in flip-flops, a skin-colored Speedo, pukka shells, and an opened blue dress shirt. Lots of oil on his legs, stomach, and chest—and I'm hit with an oddly soothing waft of cocoa butter.

"Larry," Mama gushes. "Speak of the devil."

Larry has thinning, dirty-blond hair and a tightly manicured beard. He looks good—fit, spry, and handsome—and yet I can tell there's something terribly wrong with him. Maybe it's those deep brown eyes that seem to look right through you. Or maybe it's the empty grin. Or the twitching fingers. Or the fact he has a buck knife strapped to the side of his Speedo—his *skin-colored* Speedo.

Dick Rayborne squirms.

Mama looks at Larry and beams. "Come over here and plant one on me."

Larry just stands there, so Mama shuffles over to him, wraps her arms around him. Larry doesn't respond—just stares at Dick with that creepy look on his face. "He does this sometimes," Mama says. "I think it's just because he's got so many big thoughts racing through that brain of his. I don't push him—I just let him think."

Larry looks at Dick. "Is this him?" he says, his voice sharp and even. "The individual from Human Resources?"

Mama runs an open hand down Larry's stomach. "That's him, honey."

Larry seems to vibrate as he stares at Dick.

"You remember, right, honey?" Still stroking his stomach, watching his face. "My ex. The one who abandoned his family."

Larry says, "The individual who likes paperwork."

"That's right, baby. The one who drove me to you."

"Paperwork."

Mama releases Larry, turns to me. "The paperwork thing really bothers Larry."

His voice is tight. "I don't like HR."

Mama studies Larry. "I wanted you to confront Dick as my lover, baby. Tell him what you've been doing to me. Tell him what a jerk he is."

Larry seems to have gone stiff as he gazes at Dick Rayborne.

"He gets—I don't how you'd describe it." She looks at Larry. "I'm afraid Larry gets—how shall I say?—activated."

Dick's eyes are troubled. "Activated?"

"Yeah, see? Look at him." She turns to Dick. "He's activated."

"Activated?"

"He really didn't like it when I told him about the paperwork."

Dick forces an uneasy grin. "It's business."

"It's people," Mama says.

"I do not like . . ." Larry's voice is so light and thin. ". . . those who create unnecessary paperwork."

"So they can cheat people out of medical coverage," Mama adds.

Larry hums as he stares at Dick.

"Oh yeah," Mama says to me, nearly amused. "Larry's activated."

Ernie and Cujo circle Larry as if he's a curious ice sculpture. Finally, Cujo looks to Mama. "What do you mean, he's activated?"

Mama says, "Do you remember when you were just a little squirt and Daddy brought home that lizard?"

Cujo looks at me and grins. "Sure."

"And do you remember how Gustav reacted?"

"Gustav?"

"Gustav," Mama snaps. "The goddamn family cat."

"Oh yeah," Cujo says, giving me the eye, smiling. "That's right. Sorry, Mama. I can't believe I forgot that rat Gustav."

"*Cat*," Mama yells.

"Yeah, right. Cat."

"You don't remember?" Mama smiles at a memory, shaking her head and closing her eyes. "Your dad over there bringing that lizard home, and you kept it in that cage? And every time you'd let Gustav into your room, he'd just go sit on top of the cage and stare at the lizard—What you'd name him?"

"Suzie?"

"No, that wasn't it. Anyways, any time we'd try to touch Gustav, he'd swipe us with the claws. And then he started spraying and hissing. And then finally we brought in that veterinary student from down the street, and she said the lizard—the reptile—had 'activated' the predator inside Gustav."

"So . . ." Cujo scratches his crotch. ". . . the reptile 'activated' the cat—I mean Gustav?"

"For Gustav, seeing the reptile just flipped a switch." Mama says this so empathically, it's like she's talking to a weeping toddler. "There was nothing—not a cotton-pickin' thing—anyone could do to deactivate Gustav. He wanted that reptile so bad."

Cujo looks at me, grinning. "It's okay, Mama. I understand."

"And yes, Gustav eventually did eat that lizard."

"That sucked," Cujo declares with a smile. "I was bummed."

"Which is why it's important to understand what's happening here. Larry's activated right now. Think of him as Gustav. And Dick here as the reptile."

Cujo gives Larry a long look. "What happens when he's activated?"

"There are some things," Mama says, "that you don't need to worry about, you hear? And there are some things regarding your father and me . . ." Mama rests a frail hand on Cujo's shoulder. ". . . that you boys don't need to know." She gazes into space. "You boys should be enjoying your childhood. You should be focused on being kids." She shuffles to Ernie, puts an arm around him, and squeezes. He produces a giant smile—fat folds everywhere. "It's your job as healthy, rambunctious boys to challenge the rules—to push back. To test us and see where the limits are."

"We like pushing the limits, Mama."

"I know you do. And it's your dad's job—and my job—to deal with adult things." She turns and twinkles at Larry, then at Dick. "Things about lovers and such." She blinks and turns back to the boys. "So why don't you go explore? I understand there's a nice pool in—"

"*Pool?*" Cujo bellows.

Collin comes tearing around the corner, cookie in his mouth. "Pulllll?"

"Yes, a pool."

The boys tear out of the house.

I holler, *"Just be safe."*

Mama says to Dick, "The funny thing is—this carnality that Larry and I share? This passion? The lust? The animal nature of our relationship?" She zeros in on Dick, squinting. "It's not like anything you and I had—ever."

Dick tries to reason with Larry. "I don't know this woman."

Larry stares.

"I suppose you're right," Mama says. "In a way, you really don't know the new me. I've changed, honey. That's what happens when you neglect a woman in her prime."

"I'm sorry, lady." Dick seems to be getting really annoyed. "I'm really really sorry, okay?"

"Do you remember my fantasies, Dickie? How sometimes I wanted to experiment a little? How at first I gently suggested but then begged you to try some new things, to have a little fun?"

"Lady, come on."

"How I'd tell you I'd be okay if . . ." She whispers with a giggle. ". . . we brought someone else into our bedroom?"

"I don't remember that."

"Yes you do. And how you'd always say there was something wrong with me? Well, listen." She leans in, raises her voice. "There was nothing wrong with me. I just wanted to explore."

Dick gives me the please-help-me eyes. "Well, I was wrong, apparently. And I'm sorry."

"Good, because today . . ." She giggles. ". . . you make up for it."

"Lady—"

"Because Larry here? He likes to watch."

"Watch?" Dick seems to freeze. "Who watch?"

"Larry watch."

"Larry watch? Larry watch what?"

Mama shuffles to Dick, takes his hand, and pulls. "You and me," she says and tugs again. "Larry's a watcher. And he's gonna watch you and me do it one last time. Because, hell, you owe me that much."

"If you think I'm going to bed with you guys . . ."

Larry pulls out his buck knife, approaches Dick Rayborne.

"And yes," Mama says. "I still get gassy when things get hot, when I get a little stretched out. But that doesn't slow Larry down. He says it's natural—means I'm really turned on. So I suppose you're just gonna have to deal with it."

Dick looks to me. "Help me," he snaps. "Or you're fired."

But what the hell can I say? I'm in a tough spot, too.

Collin wanders back in, tugs on my shirt. "Uncle Rick," he says. "Cujo's doing a number two in Dick's rose garden."

Mama turns to Larry. "I'm gonna get myself started in the back bed." She digs into her fanny pack, pulls out a small baggie of brown pills, and tosses it to Larry. "Make him swallow one of those, and bring him back there in ten minutes."

Okay, this is getting *weeee-ird*.

Larry takes the bag and examines the pills. Slowly, he nods.

"Uncle Rick?"

Mama says to me, "Come."

I bark out a "ha" and fold my arms. "I'm not getting you started."

Collin says, "It's good to care for your elders."

Mama gives me the eye. "I'm talking about the closet back there, you twerp. You need to familiarize yourself with his wardrobe."

"What the hell are you talking about?"

"But once I do get going," she says, "be sure to keep the boys out back in the pool. I don't want any interruptions."

"You think I'm going to dress up as Dick Rayborne?"

She stops and pokes me in the chest. "Not 'think.' I 'know' you will."

"You're nuts."

"Actually, Uncle Rick. I don't think she's nuts at all." Collin peers up at me, zeros in with those eyes. "Did you hear everything she was saying during Good News/Bad News?"

I just look at him.

Collin adds, "Or in the bathroom? All those people he's being mean to? He doesn't play fair. Someone needs to step up."

Mama lowers her head, searches my eyes. "What do you think this has been about? You think we're all just screwing around here?"

Collin tugs on my sleeve again. "You didn't realize this was about something much, much bigger than fun with Neanderthals?"

"I . . . I just—"

"I—I—I—I." Mama crosses her eyes, mocking me. "Listen. You're going to put on one of his suits, take his Robards badge, get his cordless telephone, grab his keys, and you're going to drive yourself over to that dump, and you're going to call a meeting with that subcommittee of the Robards International board of directors, and you're going to confess everything—all the tricks, all the games, everything. You're going to get their approval to dismantle Dick's 'paperwork' system. And then you're going to resign—as Dick."

"You're crazy. I'm not—"

Collin grabs my arm and squeezes. "Uncle Rick, don't you understand?"

I pause to take a breath and let it out. "Understand what, honey?"

"That this is your moment." He leans in. "In your *life*."

This hits me, and I stand there. *What did he just say?*

"What do you mean, in my life?"

Collin says, "In leadership, they call this a defining moment."

"In leadership?" I squint down at him. "Defining moment?"

"My dad always talks about his defining moment. When he came in and told these bosses they should fire ten thousand people. He says that was his defining moment, because it boosted profits and they created new jobs in China, and they gave him more money. He says it was his opportunity of a lifetime. He's very proud." He stops and thinks about it. "But I'm not sure I'd be proud. And I know *you* wouldn't be."

"Well . . ." I choose my words carefully. "Your dad and I are different folks, kiddo."

"Exactly." He squeezes again. "Which is why I think this is *your* moment. This is *your* chance to doing something big. Something that will help lots and lots of people—people who need help. My dad helped the bosses, but I think you can help even more people."

I start to feel something. Deep inside me.

Mama says, "The kid is one smart little shit, wouldn't you say?"

I'm kinda frozen, but I manage a slight nod. The kid *is* special.

"And take it from an old gal with too many regrets. You have a choice. I mean it. And I'm telling you—you will always look back at this moment. You will go back and think about it. And it will come out of nowhere and hit you. This moment will become a part of you. Because you know you have this opportunity. And if you don't do the right thing, you will be filled with regret."

My emotions are swelling. *Holy shit, they're right.*

"Do the right thing, Uncle Rick."

I look into Mama's eyes, realizing, *She's the last thing from crazy. Has she been fooling me all day?*

"Seize the moment," she says. "Do the right thing, and never regret this moment for as long as you live."

A bolt of electricity shoots through me, and I feel my chest rise.

Collin pulls on my shirt again. "Uncle Rick?" He peers up at me, so earnest. "Can I do cannonballs in the pool?"

● ● ●

When I walk out of Dick Rayborne's enormous closet, Mama is already under the covers. Her glasses are off, and her eyes are half closed. It sounds like she's nearly purring, and I notice her clothes piled beside the bed, her fanny pack on the nightstand. "Listen, honey." She's nearly breathless. "Go tell Larry and Dick to get in here."

Despite it all, I take a look at myself in the mirror—and what I see shocks me. Dick's dark blue Italian suit and light blue collar shirt look pretty good on me. And I realize, I look more like Dick Rayborne than ever before.

"Hey," she snaps. "Stop gazing at yourself and tell Larry I'm ready." She lowers her head back onto the pillow, pulls her shoulders up, and closes her eyes, a grin forming. She allows a little moan, says, "Mama's all—mmmmmm—warmed up."

What the hell am I doing?

"And tell him to go to the kitchen and fetch some cooking oil." Another moan. "We do the ancient Japanese art of body-to-body sliding massage."

"Mama, let me ask you something."

"That body? Maybe you noticed. Larry's a juicer. A big juicer. I swear, that man juices five or six times a day. Gives him lots and lots of energy for all kinds of home projects." She giggles and whispers. "It also gives him lots and lots of great big boners."

I turn to her. "How am I supposed to call an emergency meeting with the compensation subcommittee?"

"You're Dick Rayborne." Mama twitches. "You have your badge, your cordless telephone." A gasp. "You have everything you need. Figure it out, honey." She quakes. "Now go fetch my fellas."

I head for the bedroom door, stop, and turn back one more time. "You're not senile and confused. You've been mapping this out for months."

"Honey." Another twitch. "I'm seizing the moment."

Whatever. I turn to leave.

"No regrets for me, Rick."

"Okay, whatever."

"Because we're never gonna survive—and I mean it—unless we get a little crazy."

I stop in my tracks.

Was that Seal?

"Mama's ready," she rasps. "And tell Larry to bring that mouth-gag thing."

FETCH A RANDY GRANY SOME WESSON OIL

I find the keys to Dick's car hanging off a wall in the kitchen. It's also where I find Dick. And Larry, who's shoving tomatoes and beets and watermelon and spinach into the hatch of a spotless stainless-steel Omega juicer.

I hear myself announce, "Mama's ready."

Larry stops, looks at me, and turns to the pantry. He opens the door, pokes around, and emerges with an enormous bottle of Wesson vegetable oil.

"Oh, there you go. Sounds like you two've—"

Larry turns and stares at me, those hollow brown eyes burrowing.

"Anyways." I turn to Dick. "Mr. Rayborne, I'm afraid Mama wants me to borrow your car for a bit." I look down at myself. "And this suit. And I think I need your briefcase and all that. But I promise I'll bring it back."

Larry flips on the juicer, puts a crystal glass under the spigot.

"Dick?"

Deep red juice drips into the glass. Larry stares at me.

"Dick? You okay?"

On closer inspection, Dicks seems a bit out of it. He offers a lazy sneer—his eyes slothful as he sways to and fro, holding an empty shot glass. His fine, thinning hair is pointed in different directions. Larry shows me his knife, says, "It's important to be loose . . ." He looks at me, reaches over the counter island, and lifts a bottle of Pappy Van Winkle bourbon. ". . . when you're about to share your lover with another man." Larry lifts his glass. "I have juice. He needs medication."

I look at Dick. It's like he doesn't give a shit. Check that—it's like he's not capable of giving a shit. About anything. I look at the bottle again. Pappy Van Winkle? I've heard about that stuff—some of their bottles go for something like two thousand dollars a pop. Figures Dick would drink two-thousand-dollar bourbon. Then I notice the small Rx bottle placed beside the Pappy. "What's this?" I say and swipe it up. "More pills?" I spin the bottle, so I can read the label. The prescription doesn't list a name, but it does specify the drug—something called sildenafil. I look up at Larry for clues, and he says, "Tijuana."

"What are you talking about?"

"Tijuana Viagra."

Oh. I look down at the bottle, put it on the counter, and wipe my hands. "Did you give him this?"

Larry inhales me with the eyes. Allows the slightest of nods.

Dick gazes into space, swaying even more.

"Dude," I say. "You have to be careful."

Larry puts away his knife and picks up the Wesson oil. "I'm preparing him."

"Yeah, but—" I stop myself. "Who are you?"

He turns and faces me, devours me with those eyes.

I look away and mutter, "Okay, never mind. But those other pills Mama gave you. What were those?"

"Juárez."

"The city?"

"Discount sedatives." Larry says it so delicately. "From Juárez." He picks up the Wesson oil and takes Dick by the hand, leading him out of the kitchen—he reminds me of a zoo trainer on a talk show, leading a chimpanzee offstage. I stand there and watch them, adding a final comment.

"No more Juárez, Larry."

Larry stops and looks at me.

"Or Tijuana," I say. "Okay?"

Larry says, "Leave us."

I ask Dick, "Where's the briefcase and badge?"

Dick gazes into space.

Larry says, "Think."

•　•　•

Think. Think, Rick. Think.

Finally, it hits me. His briefcase and badge are probably going to be where he works: that basement office of his. I make the journey down there, creeping myself out all over again. The place just oozes dark, cold energy. I snoop around Dick's desk area and find a black leather briefcase leaning against the side. I pull it up to the desk, where the light is, and start fingering through the inner pockets and pouches, and eventually find his white clip-on badge, which I might need in order to get through security at Robards International.

Am I really going to do this? No, I'm not really going to do this. No way. But let Mama think I will? Keep her away from my sister? Preserve the house-sitting gig so I can quit Robards and have the kid visit for a few months of normal childhood? See how I might be able to sabotage Dick's paperwork machinery? Yeah, sure. I can play along a bit more.

A soft white light flashes on his desk, and I realize it's a cell phone. I lean over to read the screen—the caller is "Shelley—Office," and the accompanying photo reveals a face I've seen for decades. Round cheeks with dimples and a nice smile. Short silver hair. She's an executive admin; I know that much. And suddenly, my heart begins to pound. What if Dick has sent out an SOS and Shelley is calling to do a welfare check or something? Now my heart is racing. I stare at the flashing phone. If I don't answer it, maybe she'll call the police or Robards security. Hell, maybe she tried to reach Dick's home security team, and no one answered.

I snatch the phone off the desk and answer it, trying to sound rushed. "Yes?"

Shelley says, "Sorry to bother you, sir."

I try to channel my inner Dick, forcing an irritated sigh. "What is it?"

Shelley sounds a little weak. "I wanted to see if you're still coming in today? I can clear all your meetings if you'd like."

I think about it.

"Dick?"

Am I really going to do this?

"Dick?"

"Cancel all my meetings," I bark.

"You sound—"

"But I think I am going to come in."

"Absolutely," she says. "Are you feeling okay?"

"I'm fine," I snap. "Just a sore throat."

"Oh, Dick." She sounds like a very bad actor, pouring it on thick, trying too hard. "I'm so sorry to hear that."

"I'm fine."

"I'm ordering you a bouquet of balloons. Right now. I know that always makes things better for you."

I'm about to stop her, but then I realize that would only raise more suspicion. "Thank you," I say. "I'd appreciate that."

"Of course," she soothes. "Would you like the vibrant colors, or the ones that look like flowers?"

"I don't care," I mutter, cringing—I hate being a dick, even when I'm pretending to be one. "Listen, how hard would it be if I wanted to convene a meeting with the compensation subcommittee?"

Did that really just come out of my mouth?

Long pause. "Today?"

"Yes."

Longer pause. "It's later in the day, of course. And half of the subcommittee lives outside of California, as you know. But we could try to get everyone on the phone, and depending on schedules for Robert, Joyce, and Murray, we might be able to get them in the office. Is it okay if people call in?"

I have no idea. "Let's just see what's possible," I say, "and we can decide."

"When would you like to have this meeting?"

"Let's try for five o'clock."

"Absolutely," she says. "I'll get those balloons to you ASAP."

"Good."

"And I'll start making calls about this meeting."

I let a little bit of me slip out. "I appreciate all the help."

Shelley's voice brightens, and she sounds surprised. Maybe even shocked. "You're very welcome," she says, nearly emotional. "Very welcome."

We hang up, and I think, *There's no way I'm ever meeting with that subcommittee.* Then I have a disturbing vision, and

I shudder and jerk at its very possibility—Mama and the boys paying a little visit to my sister and brother-in-law. Then I think of Bobby Flanduzi and the 75,000 other employees of Robards International who've been jerked around by the Dick Rayborne approach to comp and benefits. Then I think of getting arrested, and jailed. Then I think of disappointing Mama and losing my Years of Rick house-sitting gig. I think of not being able to instill some sanity into my nephew's life. Then I think of Larry getting his hands on me.

Crap.

I swallow hard and gather Dick's things, including the laptop computer on his desk. Whatever I end up doing, it won't be down here.

• • •

In the kitchen, I gather my things—whoa, I mean Dick's things—and try to decide what to do. One thing I know is, I sure as hell don't want to be inside this house. Who's to say Mama and Larry won't grow bored of Dick after the ancient Japanese body-to-body massage? Or what if the Tijuana Viagra doesn't kick in and Dick is useless? What would stop Larry from coming to look for me?

Oh, yeah. I need to get out of here.

My hand vibrates, and I realize I'm holding Dick's phone. I squint at the screen; it's Shelley again. I force a gruff voice, try to take on an annoyed tone. "Ye-es?"

"Dick, I have been able to secure Murray and Robert for the five o'clock. I have a call in to Joyce's assistant. I'm still waiting to hear back from the others. Oh, and the balloons are on their way."

The top of the house shakes.

I mumble, "Fine."

"You can use Alcatraz."

It sounds like something very large has landed on the roof. I'm taken by the sound of splintering wood and creaking joints and crossbeams. I squint up at the ceiling and cock my head, listening.

"Sir?"

It sounds like the Jolly Green Giant is on Dick's roof.

"Yes," I snap.

"I got you Alcatraz."

Above, thunderous footsteps pounding across the roof.

"Sir?"

I squint and listen.

"Sir?"

The pounding is gone. I shake my head. "Excuse me," I say. "Alcatraz?"

"The conference room," she says. "I reserved you the Alcatraz conference room. San Quentin and Rikers Island weren't available." She weakens. "Sorry, sir. I know how much you prefer the other two." She pauses. "I can look into the availability of Sing Sing or Tower of London."

I decide to mutter. "No, that's fine."

"Anything else for the moment, sir?"

I listen for roof noises. Nothing.

"Sir?"

"Actually, yes."

"Absolutely, sir."

At the far end of the house, on the roof, a heavy thump.

"Those guys," I say. "Those IT guys who are doing those skunkworks projects for me? The conhackers?"

"Sir?"

"Those guys we're using to freeze up the computers of random employees who try to sign up for benefits?"

"Oh," she says. "The Benefits-Control Tiger Team led by Peter Randell?"

"Yes," I bluff. "Exactly. Have Peter plan to attend the meeting as well."

"Sir?"

"Peter," I snap. "I want him at this meeting with the sub-committee."

Long pause. "Sir—I mean . . . Sir, I know you don't usually have 'jumpsuits' present to—Sir, I guess what I am asking is, do you want him to change out of his jumpsuit for the meeting with the board members?"

On the roof, something lighter scampers from one end to the other.

"No," I say. "Have him come in the jumpsuit."

"Certainly, sir."

"Thanks, Shelley."

There's silence. And then, "Sir, I did want to discuss something with you."

I listen for roof noises—nothing.

"Sure."

"Sir, this is difficult for me to say." A new series of thumps. I go to the kitchen window and look out, craning my neck for a view of the roof. Nothing. "But I need to say it. I need to let you know that I can no longer lend you cash from my purse."

"What?"

"Sir, I'm sorry. And I know you've said you'll reimburse me. But I'm sorry. I can't afford to lend you any more money. I know you're very busy and can't get to the ATM, or you forget your wallet and whatnot. It's just that, after two years, I've lent you nearly eight thousand dollars, and I just can't afford to keep—" Her voice weakens, and she gasps. "I'm sorry to get emotional, sir. It's just that as a single mom, I just can't—"

"Shelley, don't worry about this. He's going to repay you every cent, with interest."

"I'm sorry." She sniffles. "But who's 'he'?"

I shake my face. "Did I say 'he'?"

Sniffle. "Yes."

"I'm sorry, I meant, 'I.' . . . I will pay you back. . . . Today. With interest."

She cries. "I'm sorry to bug you about this, sir. It just means a lot to me. I'm behind on payments, and—" She stops, takes a few big breaths. "Just, I really appreciate it, sir."

I'm so mad, my vision narrows and the thumps on the roof seem distant. "Tell me, Shelley. What's your salary?"

She sniffles. "Sixty-one."

In the Bay Area, this not enough for a single mother.

"I can't believe—I mean, I'm sorry about this, Shelley."

"Sir, I just . . . I mean . . . Are you okay?"

●　　●　　●

Outside, there are howls of laughter.

I meander around the house and head for the backyard.

"Guys?"

It sounds like someone's dumped a refrigerator into the pool. Collin shrieks.

I turn the corner to find Dick Rayborne's backyard pool. It's long and inviting, with simple, classic lines and crystal-clear water sloshing everywhere, spilling over the lips and cascading across a slick deck of vintage red brick. I come a little closer and see Collin in his underwear wading in the shallow end of the pool, splashing and hopping and laughing. Bouncing beside him is Ernie, wearing fogged-up goggles and a faded orange life vest, a long strand of pool drool swinging off his chin.

"You guys," I say. "What the hell are you—"

"*Freeze*," Collin hollers.

I do. The thumps grow louder, coming up and above me, and then I freeze like a startled rodent. Collin smiles as a large dark object sails over me, and I jolt back, only to see massive, hairy legs and arms and buns flying through the air and over the deck, and then crashing into the water so violently—so authoritatively—a shock wave seems to percuss through the air. The subsequent watercourse shoots across the pool like a horizontal geyser, missing Collin and Ernie but drenching the deck, nearby chairs, and shrubs. The swells in the pool hit a good two or three feet, soaking the boys.

And I'm thinking, *I can't get my—er, I mean Dick's—suit wet.*

Collin and Ernie can't stop laughing, and I rub my temples, trying to soothe my postbuzz headache. Cujo darts around the deck in a brown banana sling thong, launching himself into the pool—over and over. The water is choppy and rough. Ernie and Collin ride the swells until something ascends from the depths, ensnares Collin, and launches him high into the air. Collin screams with delight as he sails across the pool and lands in the deep end, cannonball style.

"Dude," I say to Cujo, but he's already resubmerged. In the shallow end, Ernie hops about, giggling, looking beneath him. But his goggles are so fogged, he's practically blind.

I say into the phone, "The boys are completely out of control."

"Boys?" Audrey asks. "Did you arrange a playdate?"

Ernie explodes out of the water, a toothy grin on his face as he sails through the air—his arms doing the chugga-chugga choo-

choo, his white boxers riding far too low—as he comes down for a splash landing at the center of the pool, arms flopping.

"Long story," I say. "Listen, I think I'm about to do something really crazy."

"Rick, I'm totally cool about going to see the Beat with you. Just us."

Ernie executes a belly-flop swan dive, and Collin follows.

"No, it's not about that." I hope it sounds like our screwed-up date means nothing to me. "I just have to make a big decision, and I'm not sure who else I can ask."

And that's true.

Cujo pulls himself out of the pool, and enough water drains off him to fill a kiddie pool. My lord, he's hairy. The water beads and glistens, giving his fur an odd sheen. He backs up to the edge of the pool, reaches down, and executes an impressive backflip into the water. Collin shrieks in amazement.

Audrey says, "Try me."

So I do. I tell her everything—about Mama, about the break-in at Bobby Flanduzi's house, about the forty-five K, about Dick Rayborne and his paperwork schemes, about the tens of thousands of people who are getting screwed over. I tell her how much I'd like to house-sit my sister's place for two years so I could quit Robards, write that book, and maybe give my nephew a few tastes of a normal childhood. I tell her that no matter what I decide to do—go into Robards as Dick Rayborne or walk away now—my feeble career there is over. I tell her that I'm confident Mama is willing to ruin—and capable of ruining—my house-sitting gig with my sister.

"So what do you think?"

"This probably sounds nuts," Audrey says, "but maybe you just do what she says. I mean really, all things considered—seriously, Rick—does your job really matter at this point?"

It doesn't. Hell, I'm hoping I can quit.

"Does it matter if they realize you're not the real dude, and they call the police or something?"

"Yes, that part does matter." I laugh. "I don't think Ana will—"

"Ana doesn't have to know if you get arrested. I'd come up with an explanation for your no-show tonight, and you could have that house-sitting talk with her on the phone next week. It's not like she has a ton of other house-sitting options right now. Maybe it's better to keep this Mama lady happy."

"I suppose."

"And keep the Larry guy and the ex-cons away from your sister."

As silly as it sounds, she has a point.

"Or . . ." Cujo takes Ernie and Collin for a ride on his back, cutting effortlessly through the pool. "I guess the other option is, you could just take Collin—like, right now—and get the hell out of there. Take your chances with Mama, hope she doesn't call your sister or show up at their house. I mean, it sounds like Mama is a bit distracted at the moment."

I scan the area. "I could easily take Collin and leave." I look down, feeling kind of crappy for even considering it. Call me foolish, but the idea of leaving this benefits crap unfinished? The thought of escaping before Shelley gets her money back? The possibility of letting things resettle so Robards can continue to rip off tens of thousands of hardworking employees? The idea of going through all of this—all this insanity—for nothing of any lasting value? It just sits heavy in my gut. Too heavy.

I mean, will I ever do anything special in my life? Ever?

Audrey says, "Maybe this is what you're supposed to do. So maybe you just go for it."

"Go for it?"

"Maybe you just go for it. Channel you inner Dick what's-his-name. Make a few calls. Have that meeting. Screw with people a little." She laughs. "You know it probably won't work. But hell, have you ever had a day like this?"

"No."

"Will you ever again?"

"No."

"So maybe, you know, just go for it."

There's a pause, and I say, "That had been my plan for tonight at the Greek—just go for it."

We laugh.

"You thought this was about getting to the Greek with me," Audrey says. "And I thought this was about getting you to pay attention to Collin. But maybe we were both wrong."

I can't help saying, "I know I was certainly wrong."

"Maybe this is what it's really all about. Maybe the universe is saying, *This is Rick Blanco's chance to make the world better, to make a real difference.* Maybe it's about going a little crazy."

Crazy?

Why can't this woman like me back?

Crazy?

A bedroom window opens, and Mama announces, "We need more oil."

Yes, crazy.

* * *

Mama says from the window, "I'm gonna send Larry out there. I need some alone time with Dick." Her voice goes raspy, lingers on the words. "One last romp—just the two of us. Things are starting to kick in for Dick here. Just keep the boys busy, will you? And keep them off the roof."

Dick's bedroom window sits in the shade behind a large rose-bush, directly behind the pool. With the sun in my eyes, I'm having a hard time seeing Mama and her fellas. I squint at the window and try to make sense of the figures within. Finally my vision corrects and the shapes begin to make sense. Mama is in front, topless—maybe fully naked, for all I know—with her glasses off, and she's glistening in vegetable oil. Behind her is Larry—shirtless—slathered in oil, caressing her arms, smearing his beard against her neck, eyes lidded.

I didn't need to see that.

"Don't worry, Dick's fine." Mama's so shameless there in the window—in all her sagging, wrinkly imperfection—and I find myself admiring her freedom. You know, Mama actually is pretty cool. "Larry babe, why don't you put on your bottoms and take a dip?" She adopts a guttural tone, slows it down, nearly moaning. "Dick and I . . . We need one last time. Okay, babe?" She slows, trying to be sensitive. "And don't get me wrong. The Nuru massage was nice, just the way I like it. And then—babe, I swear it—you were *won-der-ful.* You gave it to Mama real good, just the way she likes it. But . . ." She sighs as if she's thinking about it. ". . . a gal deserves one last time with her husband, don't you think? You know, for the road. And plus . . ." She releases a dry chuckle. ". . . I guess Mama wants more."

Larry doesn't seem to care. "I will photosynthesize," he says. "And think."

"That's right, babe," Mama soothes. "Soak up the sun and do your thinking."

"About the paperwork," he says.

"Of course, babe. Now why don't I see you in a bit, okay?" They ease back into the shadows and return to the windowsill with Dick Rayborne, and I gasp. Dick still has that not-capable-of-caring look—slathered in vegetable oil, staring into space, his upper lip curling on one side, his eyebrows frozen in disharmony, his shoulders hunched forward, his hair shooting in all directions. He sways far left, takes a step to stabilize himself.

"Of course," Mama says, "he resisted at first. But we got him revved up after a while." She presses into him, their Wessoned bodies slipping and sliding as she hums suggestively and runs her bony fingers up his belly, pinches his nipples. "He might be a little subdued here and there, but I'll tell you what—there's one thing here that's definitely *not* subdued." She turns to him, pulls back to look him in the eye. "Although I *do* recall you being a lot bigger."

· · ·

Dick's bedroom window is closed, and the shades are drawn.

I'm reclining in a chaise lounge watching the boys. Ernie has put Collin on his shoulders, and now Cujo is swimming underneath Ernie to put *him* on *his* shoulders.

I glace at Larry. Is he meditating?

Cujo surfaces, and Ernie and Collin rise out of the water.

Larry is seated upright in a pool chair—hands on his knees, chin up, eyes on me—sunning himself. His golden skin is moist, like an overheated glazed donut. The only thing on him that isn't glistening is his Speedo.

I think he's just chilling.

The Cujo-Ernie-Collin stack eases across the pool, teetering.

Or is he looking at me, as in, You're next?

Like a felled redwood, the Cujo-Ernie-Collin stack plunges into the pool.

That's nuts. He's just superfocused on the paperwork.

Larry's eyes seem to burrow deeper into mine.

"Okay, boys." I sit up. "Everyone towel off. Time for a snack, and then we hit the road."

They ignore me.

I think of what Mama and Audrey said: Time to get a little crazy.

Just don't get arrested.

"Boys—out."

They splash around.

"Boys? I say. "Get out. *Now.* C'mon."

They whine and mope.

The bedroom window opens, and Mama sticks her head out, looks around. Sweat is streaming down her temples, and she seems winded. And pissed off.

"Some things never change," she huffs. "What was that? Five minutes? Three minutes?" She grimaces, snarls, and grips the window ledge, staring into space. "There's a reason I always called him the Three-Minute Dick."

Larry stirs, announces, "Time for some paperwork."

•   •   •

Leaving Dick's cottage compound is quite the production.

Mama has the boys buckled and ready and bouncing in the wagon. She sticks her head out the driver-side window and hollers, "C'mon, Larry. Show on the road, babe."

Larry's own station wagon—a brown Chevy Malibu and not much newer than Mama's Fleetwood—is backed up to the entry path of the house, idling. Finally Larry saunters out of the house in his Speedo, flip-flops, and opened dress shirt. He scans the compound and reaches back to the doorway to pull out an oiled Dick Rayborne in a bath towel, leading him toward the waiting

Malibu. Dick zigzags toward the wagon with that lazy sneer, those slow eyes.

I stand next to Dick's Porsche, his briefcase slung over my shoulder as I press my fingers against his suit. I will admit it feels good to be in this suit. And that bothers me, considering everything.

"Listen, Larry." I take a few steps but stop when Larry gives me those eyes and pulls aside his shirt to show me the buck knife holstered to his Speedo. "Listen, Larry . . ." He freezes, tenses his body, and devours me. "What are you gonna . . ." Those eyes, burrowing deeper and deeper. "Okay, never mind."

"Okay," Mama says, irritated, and gets out of the Fleetwood and heads toward us, zeroing in on me. "Listen, kid. Don't worry about Larry and Dick, you hear? You just worry about that meeting with the subcommittee."

Larry pops the back hatch of his Malibu and leads Dick into the bay, where the *Headcount* darling reclines slowly into a full sprawl, letting the bath towel slide off. Larry shuts the hatch, adjusts his Speedo, and turns to give me one last stare.

"That was the agreement," Mama says. "If I get to have a little alone time with Dick, so does Larry."

"Yeah, but—"

"No yeah-buts." She slaps my face, light but firm. "Dick's gonna be fine."

"How do you know that?"

"Hey," Mama says. "Do you think I'd be sleeping with a homicidal psychopath?"

I open my mouth, but nothing comes out.

"Listen, kid. Larry isn't a killer." She cocks her head, gazes into space, thinking. "As far as I know. You see, he's a teacher."

"Please don't tell me he teaches kindergarten or something."

"Or, better—he's an artist."

"Artist? Maybe."

"Only, instead of clay or watercolors, Larry's medium is people." She looks down, shakes her head. "People like Dick. Or, I should say, Old Dick. Someone like the New Dick?" She points at me, smiles. "Larry couldn't care less about the New Dick."

"I'm not New Dick. I'm Rick Blanco, and I don't even know why I'm—"

"Listen." Mama shuffles closer, leans into me. "You're my New Dick, and you're wonderful." She reaches out, straightens the lapels of my—I mean, Dick's—suit, and gives me a playful punch in the arm. She lifts her chin and smiles. "You're going to do just fine today, honey. And as your wife—because I of course get New Dick as part of the package. As your wife . . ." She inches closer, adopts that low, raspy voice. ". . . it's only fitting that I get a little kissy-poo goodbye."

I push her away, and she grabs my head, pulls it in, and sticks her tongue in my mouth. I jerk away, reeling from the taste of cocoa butter—Larry's cocoa butter—and spit onto Dick's cobbled driveway. Mama wipes her mouth with the back of her hand. Smiles. "And as the loving wife of New Dick, it's only fitting that I'm there for you today at Robards. The boys and I. We'll be there. Maybe we'll start out at the Playroom, but you will let me in so I can help you."

I'm still spitting. "Absolutely not."

"Absolutely yes," she says and heads back for the Fleetwood. "I suppose big-shot executives like you can bring in anyone they want. Which reminds me—I want you to include an employee at the subcommittee meeting tonight. His name is Carl Blakenship."

Larry gets into the Malibu, shuts the door, and shifts it out of park.

"And remember what we said, right?"

"And that was?"

"We're never gonna survive unless—"

"—we get a little crazy," I finish.

"You got it." Mama gives me wink and whispers, "Go get 'em."

I stand back and give her one last look as she chuckles silently, bites her tongue in that old way, and winks. And I fold my arms, realizing that there's so very little that I *do* know, and that my world—my life—is forever changed. That no matter what happens next, I have indeed already gone 129 percent crazy.

Crazy?

Fine.

And then—*Oh, yeah. Crap.*

I run after the Malibu, waving. Mercifully, it stops. The side window descends, and I squat to meet his cold gaze. "Actually, Larry." I reach into my—I mean, Dick's—briefcase and pull out the personal check I'd written to his admin, Shelley, and show it to him—thirteen thousand dollars, to reflect interest on his original debt to her. "I need Dick to sign this. He's been forcing his admin to pay some of his personal expenses the last few years."

Larry looks at the check, then at me, and then back at the check.

"Just a little signature from our buddy back there."

Larry seems to be studying my jugular.

"Larry."

The back hatch pops.

It takes five minutes—and a visit from Larry—to make Dick sign.

•   •   •

Dick's Porsche handles well, but I really don't see what the fuss is all about. There are so many other things I would rather do with this kind of money. The Bluetooth is nice, though. I've Googled

"Crazy" on Dick's smartphone, and now the song is thumping thick and sweet as I cruise down El Camino Real, leaving Atherton.

Miracles will happen as we trip

I turn the volume up, feel my head bopping, and punch the gas.

But we're never gonna survive unless
We get a little crazy
No we're never gonna survive unless
We are a little
Cray cray crazy

I speed past Teslas and Mercedes and Toyotas as the beat shifts into a deeper groove. My chest swells, and I breathe in through my nose, let it out slowly.

Miracles will happen as we speak

I pull a left onto Willow, heading for U.S. 101, and the music quiets. My dashboard screen lights up, announces that I have an incoming call from "Shelley—Office." I fiddle with the steering wheel buttons until I can hear Shelley.

"Sir?"

"I have your check," I sing, a little too happy.

"Sir?"

I force a tight voice. "Your check. To pay you back." *Okay, channel that inner Dick.* "The loans you were moaning about."

Silence.

"Shelley?"

"Yes, sir. I'm here." She clears her throat. "I really appreciate that. Really."

"Just remember what I'm saying here. Moving forward, if I ever ask you for more money—for lunch, for dinner, for whatever—I want you to say no. Okay?"

"Ummm."

"Consider it a test. You need to learn to say no."

"So. . . . In the future, when you say you're too busy to run to the ATM and need some dinner money, you really aren't?"

"Exactly."

"You're just testing me?"

"That's it. No matter how much of a dick I am, I want you to stand up to me. You hear?"

Long silence.

"Sir, are you sure that cold didn't turn into a fever?"

"I'm fine. Listen, Shelley, I need you to reach out to someone for me. Is that okay?"

"Of course."

"And I need this person to attend the five o'clock, okay?"

"Sure."

"His name is Carl Blakenship. Does that name ring a bell?"

"Sounds familiar," she says. "Let me look him up. . . . Oh. Looks like he's in the Invitation to Cooperate program. He works in customer support under Russell Hampton. Is that him? Carl Blakenship in customer service?"

"I assume so. Mama just said she wants him to attend."

"Sir?"

Mama? Crap. "Sorry, Shelley. That's just a nickname I have for someone."

"So, should I invite Carl to the meeting?"

"Please."

"And, sir, I was calling about the catering."

"What are you talking about?"

"For the five o'clock. Would you like the usual?"

"The usual?"

"The Brie and crackers and bottled water with a carafe of fresh guava nectar?" She waits, and I search for words that don't come. "Or . . . I could have them bring something new. Like those goat cheese pockets."

"Oh." *I can't believe this guy.* "You know what, Shelley? Let's skip the catering this time."

"Sir?"

"Yeah, let's keep it really simple."

Long pause. "So, no catering?" She sounds shocked. "Really?"

"Really," I say. "No catering, okay?"

"Absolutely, sir." She pauses. "And I just want to say I really appreciate how respect——I mean, how nice you're being today."

I accelerate onto the 101 and unleash the Porsche. "Today's today. I can't make any guarantees, but . . ." I think of Dick Rayborne splayed out in the back of Larry's station wagon. ". . . something tells me things will never be the same."

INCITE A RIOT

It's dark when I call the house again and get the answering machine.

"Mama?"

Nothing.

"Papa?"

Nothing.

"You there?"

The silence is so thick, it buzzes in my ear.

"Can you pick up?"

I begin to walk home, along the boulevard. The traffic is thinning, but the cars still come up from behind, screaming up on me—so ambivalent and mindless. I am nothing, really. The world doesn't care. Am I even here? Is this real? All I know is, *I kinda wanna be home now.*

A new set of headlights floods from behind, illuminating the sidewalk in a cold wash, casting a long shadow before me. An engine shifts down, and a Toyota coasts by, slowing before picking up again and gassing away. I decide to pick up the pace. The

Toyota veers into the left lane, slows, and pulls a U-ie around the divider. Heads back the other way. A little odd. I decide to pick up to an easy jog, the cool air jagging deep into my chest as I try to regulate my breathing. I look around, hoping for our wagon, searching. Hoping against reason. Because logic tells me something's really kind of wrong.

Where are they?

Far away, a siren.

Another set of headlights from behind, getting closer, and I recognize the sound of the engine. I glance back—*yep, the Toyota*. My heart stops a moment, descends, and I gasp for a breath. Pick up the pace. Look back again. The Toyota is slowing, pulling to the curb, and I feel myself creating distance, fading to my right. The Toyota rolls to a stop ten feet ahead, and the shotgun window jerks down. I stop, waiting. A woman's voice carries out of the car.

"Rick."

I meander over, staying wide.

"Rick. Honey. It's Lillian Carmichael."

I stop. *Who?*

"Steven Carmichael's mom."

I know that kid. Grade below me. Wild child. Very physical. I take another step, peer in, and her face looks familiar—round with high cheekbones and a delicate, pointed chin.

"Honey, listen." She lowers her head to look over her glasses. "Why don't you let me take you home?"

"I'm okay, Mrs. Carmichael. Thank you."

"Honey." She pauses. "I really think you should let me take you home."

"There was a mix-up," I say. "My parents were supposed to pick me up, but I'm just gonna walk home."

"Listen, I really really really think you need to get in the car, and I can take you home."

Ah, screw it. What is she going to do, lunge for me in the Toyota? I could take her.

I get in the car, and she smiles at me, hits the gas.

"Where do you guys live again, sweetheart?"

"Juniper."

"Oh, that's right." We head down the boulevard. "What were you doing out there?" Her voice seems a little shaky and shallow. "It's late."

"I was at the movies with a friend, then I was waiting for my parents."

Her voice slips. "Yeah?" We ride in silence a few minutes, and then: "You still playing soccer, Rick?"

"No, I play baseball."

We come to an intersection, and I say, "This is the turn."

Lillian slows well before the intersection, pulls a U-ie.

"Mrs. Carmichael. We were supposed to take a left there."

She guns the Toyota, and I turn back to the intersection, hoping for clues. Nothing.

• • •

The Carmichael house smells like marjoram. I think every family has a different scent, and I'm not surprised their house has this sharp, spicy odor.

I'm sitting on their couch, staring at a *Baywatch* rerun with Steve Carmichael, that overgrown wild child, his thick blond hair shooting in all directions—always—and big, thick arms always moving. He's on his back in front of the TV throwing a tennis ball against the wall, catching it—doing it over and over. Mrs. Carmichael returns to the TV room, looks down at her son, then at me, then back to her son. "Honey." Her tone is so helpless—begging. "Please. Don't do that. It's making marks. Honey. C'mon. Please."

Steve keeps throwing the ball.

Mrs. Carmichael turns to me, the TV lights flickering over her glasses, and I realize she's actually a pretty woman—a sweet face, an elegant neck, and long, slender legs. "I made a few calls," she says to me and bites her lip, like she's confused. "Someone's going to pick you up."

I close my eyes a moment, breathe in marjoram, and try to deny what's happening. I can see the look of defeat on Mrs. Carmichael's face as she stands there and gazes down at me, hands on her hips, jaw tight, while her son bounces the tennis ball off the wall over and over and over. But I close my eyes one last time and squeeze hard, trying to shoo away this feeling—this dark, oozing mass of dread.

The doorbell rings, and a chill descends to the pit of my stomach.

And just like that, my life is never the same.

It's my next-door neighbor Felix Ochoa and my sister, red-nosed and puffy-eyed. Sitting on the couch, both of them. Even Steve is sitting up now, holding the ball, watching. Felix tells me, softly, that my mom and dad were in a car accident tonight, and—*I'm really sorry, Ricky—I'm afraid they're gone.*

I feel light-headed and weak, and I want my mom.

"They were supposed to be at dinner," Ana sobs and looks at me. "Where were you?"

I feel my mouth move. "They were coming for me."

Ana stares at me, her mouth open.

"It was a drunk driver in a Lincoln," Felix says. "And he's also dead."

Ana says, "Your so-called date?"

I nod, and stare into space.

They're dead. . . . Gone. . . . I can't even . . .

I blink and try to focus, my eyes falling on a framed picture of the Carmichaels—all of them—standing in front of the family station wagon, a campground behind them. They all seem so happy.

"The movies?" Ana is scowling, and her voice is rising, getting sharper. "I thought you had your bike."

I turn and screw my eyes shut.

Why did I ever chase after Danielle Meza on her way to history class?

Why can't I remember to do things?

Why am I such a screwup?

I open my eyes and look to the ceiling, tears streaming.

Ana's nearly yelling. "A girlfriend? This is because you wanted a girlfriend?"

* * *

Pulling into the Robards International parking lot in the Porsche 911 Carrera, I smile to myself as a realization sets in and spreads through my body: *All of this craziness, because of a date.*

A date I won't even have.

Rolling to a stop, I realize I need to take a left. I have to. I have to take a left, then follow that little path there that veers even farther left and takes me to that executive parking area with the fourteen-foot security fence and its endless spiral of razor wire. I come to another stop, roll down the window, and press Dick's badge to the gray reader, and the gate begins to slide open, providing a view of the executive parking lot. Burly men in dark blue suits. A variety of silver, gray, and black luxury cars shimmering in the sunlight. Do I—I mean, does Dick—have a designated spot? The guards study me and nod as I roll in, and I decide to take the farthest-away slot, figuring it's probably the least likely to belong to someone. I turn off the motor and push myself out of the Porsche, feeling really awkward. I shut the door and realize I've left my—I mean, Dick's—briefcase on the shotgun seat. I look back at the guards, meet their smiles, and nod before quickly turning away. I open the car door and stoop in to retrieve the briefcase, thinking, *These guys. They must realize I'm not Dick. How could they not realize?* I shut the door again and head toward them, looking for an entrance. They look down and ease away, like I might select one of them for an unsavory task. The youngest one, a redheaded guy who looks more like an Army recruit, rushes to a modest entrance, swipes his badge, and pulls open the door. His head bowed, eyes focused on the cement before him as if I might snap at him. He offers a polite "Sir."

I force a sharp "Hey" and enter the building, wishing I knew where I was going.

Inside, the icy air cuts down my neck, into my suit. I stop, look around. It's just a long hallway with about a half dozen shut doors, each with a gray badge reader mounted beside it. I've never been to this part of the building. *The executive area. Where in the hell is it?* I stop and look around, searching for clues. Nothing—the doors are unmarked. Screw it. I'll just start using the badge and opening doors, looking in, maybe even going on a few "strolls," meandering around until I find my—I mean, Dick's—office area. I'm pretty certain I can recognize Shelley if I see her.

I come to the first door and swipe my badge, but the lock doesn't unclick. The second door does unclick, and I yank it open. Inside is a windowless, dimly lit room packed with large monitors and tower computers. In the middle are two young men in dark slacks and white collar shirts. When they see me, they sit upright, then stand with forced grins. The shorter one fists his hands and puffs out his chest. "Mr. Rayborne," he says, forcing a smile. "What a surprise. What I mean is, it's an honor to meet you."

I look around, scanning the screens for clues. "What is this?"

"Sir?"

"I mean, how's it going here?"

"Sir, may I just say, it's going well. And we both just want to say thank you."

"What are you talking about?"

"You know. Just thank you. For giving us second chances—sex offenders are lepers, we know. But like you said, that doesn't mean we're thieves, and it doesn't mean we can't contribute to society."

Sex offenders? My stomach sinks.

The taller guy says, "And we also want to thank you for allowing us to wear regular clothes." He looks at his cohort, and they exchange proud looks. "The jumpsuits? We think our work transcends normal jumpsuit jobs. Like you said, it's us two against all those employees—all those, hyenas, as you call them—surrounding our benefits fund, ready to ravage it to the bone. It requires smarts, strategy. Thinking that must go far beyond those other jobs."

"Oh yeah?"

"Sir," says the shorter one. "Have you seen the latest reports? The results are astounding."

"Eighty-seven percent." The taller one is beaming. "An all-time high."

"What do you mean, all-time high?"

"Eighty-seven percent, sir. The percentage of targeted employees who eventually give up."

"Give up?"

"Give up trying to enroll for benefits. You know, the fifteen percent of the workforce we target from Day One, whose systems always crash whenever they try to enroll?"

"Oh, yes," I say and grind my teeth. "By the way . . . Out of those fifteen percent, why wouldn't all of them give up?"

They exchange worried looks. "Well, sir. We're like you. We know you've been disappointed about that less-than-perfect score. And yes, eighty-seven percent is not one hundred percent. But you know, some people are just plucky. They find loopholes. Or the system for some reason—that one time, it inexplicably works for them. And we're trying to fix those bugs, sir. But we just want you to know that we're not happy, either, sir. Not until one hundred percent give up."

"And then maybe, sir. Maybe, we can talk about increasing the IT-headaches target to seventeen or nineteen percent of all new hires."

I look at the shorter one. "Would you happen to be Peter Randell?"

They laugh. "Of course," Peter says. "You're funny, Mr. Rayborne."

And I say, "I'd like you to present all this to some big shots today, okay?"

• • •

When I finally find the executive area, it's easy to spot my—I mean, Dick's—space. There's Shelley sitting at her station, in front of Dick's glass office, and there's a bodyguard sitting right outside my—Dick's—door.

My stomach tightens, and a cold bolt shoots to my extremities.

Why is he *here?* I stop and survey the scene, thinking. *They know.* I try to steady myself. *They know, and he's been waiting.* Shelley straightens and gives me a long look—her mouth tightening, an eyebrow lifting. The guard looks up, stiffens at my sight. "Sir," he says. "You look . . ."

"Different," Shelley says, staring, eyes thinning.

I try to change the subject. "I have your check, Shelley."

The guard tries to smile, make the moment lighter. "Your face looks . . ."

"Younger," she completes.

I summon my inner Dick, force a squint at Shelley—as I imagine this is what he probably does every day with this poor woman. I point a thumb at the guard. "What's he doing here?"

She pulls back, eyes enlarged, like she's just heard a demon. *Oh yeah.* I tighten. *I don't sound anything like him.*

The faintest grin spreads across her face as she takes a quick look and glances away. "He's always here," she murmurs, her chin tucking and eyes enlarging, locking on to mine, like she's saying, *Play along, goofball.* "Just the way . . ." Saucers her eyes again, raises her head. ". . . *you* like it. You know, on account of all the death threats you get from—you know—the employees."

"We've got two new ones today," says the guard. "But like you always say, if you didn't get threats on a regular basis, you wouldn't be doing your job."

Shelley looks away, that grin growing.

"You *do* look different," the guard says, brows wrinkling. "And sound a little different."

I frown, and walk past him and into Dick's office. "I had some work done," I say and let that sit for a moment. Then I sharpen my voice. "And it's screwed up everything. I'd rather not talk about it."

Shelley covers a chuckle.

"Well," the guard says, "you look good, sir."

I turn, and there's Shelley—in my office, still smiling and looking away to avoid eye contact.

"You okay, Shelley?"

She picks on her fingernails, says lightly, "You're not Dick Rayborne."

"What are you talking about?"

"First on the phone you were Bizarro Dick." Finally, she looks up, her eyes consuming me for a quick moment, trying to solve a peculiar problem. "Saying crazy things. Saying them in a low tone."

"Like I said." I offer my most serious eyes. "The plastic surgery screwed everything up."

Looking at her hands. "Okay."

"And I'm not myself."

"Sir?" She looks up, allows a friendly smile. "I'm not sure what's happened to the old Dick Rayborne."

My heart is pounding. "We're going to do something important today, Shelley. For real people."

"But, sir? I think the new one is better."

There's a tap on the door, and the guard is looking at me. Behind him is a balding, middle-aged white man in a jumpsuit. "Sir," says the guard. "There's a Carl Blakenship here to see you."

A minute later, Carl and I are seated across from each other. We lock eyes.

"Do you know Mama?"

Carl squints, shakes his head no. Gives me a suspicious look.

"Mama wanted me to speak with you."

Carl searches my face, hoping for clues. "Mama?"

We look at each other a bit more, and I notice his really bushy mustache. Finally, I decide to take another approach. "Carl, can you tell me why I called you in here today?"

God, I hope he has an answer.

Carl shifts his weight as he considers me. "I have a pretty good idea."

"You do." I sit up, relieved. "Good. I want you to tell me, Carl. I want you to feel completely safe with me, okay? You're free to tell me everything."

He freezes, looks away. "But you're Dick Rayborne."

"I'm not the Dick Rayborne you think I am."

Soon, Carl is telling me that six years ago he was a happy, successful accountant at Robards International—a ten-year veteran of the company, doing his thing and chugging along just fine—when everything changed. What happened was, the company's annual enrollment process was re-architected by a newly arrived HR executive—that would be me—er, I mean, Dick. The new process required every employee to reenter all of his or her benefits decisions within a three-day period—no exceptions. Benefits elections from the previous year were no longer loaded into the system as a default. In the past, if the employee did not go into the system, his choices from the previous year would continue for the following year. Not anymore. Under the new rules, if you failed to get into the system and reenter all your choices within a three-day window, you'd lose all your benefits.

"You see, Mr. Rayborne, I followed the rules. I thought it was weird that my choices wouldn't roll over—everyone felt that way—but I was ready to go in there and reenter my choices within the three-day period. No big deal, right?"

"Right."

"I never could've guessed it would change my life."

"I'm not following."

Carl looks up, stares into space. "It was supposed to be a simple, ten-minute exercise on the benefits system." He looks down, and his eyes glaze over. "The next thing I knew, I was chasing that asshole in the truck and plowing the minivan into that 7-Eleven." He slumps his shoulders, looks away in remorse. "Getting hauled off."

So. The question is, What do you do?

What do you do when you're Dick Rayborne for a day? When you learn that the benefits-sabotage system "you" designed with your conhackers did its job so well that it drove a highly rated, law-abiding employee to a new kind of road rage? When it turned a man with a spotless record into a felon convicted of attempted murder with special circumstances? When the system you created kept freezing and shutting down on this poor soul— time after time after time? When a good employee logged on to the system a total of seventy-eight times in three days in a desperate attempt to retain basic benefits for his family? When said employee submitted no fewer than fourteen urgent tickets with the Help Desk within a seventy-two-hour period, and the newly arrived conployees who staffed this Help Desk failed to even call him back? When, on his seventy-eighth attempt to make his elections online, the screen on his laptop went dark and flashed an alarming series of metallic orange and green colors before shutting down forever? When the defeated employee heaved his laptop at the office wall, turned over four filing cabinets, and tore through the floor in a rage he never before knew, heading for his minivan, knowing he must leave before he did something he *really* regretted? When he was soon speeding through Santa Clara—ring-eyed and mumbling to himself—as some prick in a Ford Super Duty F-350 XLT cut him off, and our unwell employee decided to chase him all the way through the front doors of a nearby 7-Eleven, coming to a stop near the forty-ouncers, nearly killing four people and breaking the legs of three others? When he was convicted, sentenced, and released early on good behavior with the completion of extensive psychoanalysis (diagnosis: something called triggered insanity)? When Robards International graciously offered him a new, lower-paying job in the greatly expanded Invitation to Cooperate Program for ex-cons with "limited" benefits (all he needed to do was log in to the benefits system, select his choices, and click Submit)?

What you do is, you say you're sorry. And you promise to change things.

"Carl, I'd like you to stick around, if that's okay. I'd like you to share your story with some suits I have coming in. All right?"

"Sure." Carl looks up, says it as pleasantly as possible. "And since we're here, I was wondering if you could help me."

"Of course."

"You see." Carl turns his shoulders in, picks at his fingernails. "The open enrollment came and went, as you know. And, well, the system kept freezing on me again. And I was wondering—Well, first I want to let you know this time I was able to control my anger a lot better, even after the forty-five attempts. But I was wondering if you could connect me with someone in IT who might be able to help me sign up for the basic medical coverage?"

"I'm gonna have you meet some guys, okay? They're in a room not too far from here, and I'm gonna have them take care of you, okay?"

Relief spreads across his face.

I think about the two conhackers I met downstairs and decide it's prudent to add, "Just don't show them any photos of your wife and kids, okay?"

● ● ●

I send Carl downstairs to meet with the conhackers and try to formulate my thoughts for this subcommittee meeting. I actually open up Dick's laptop and poke around in his PowerPoints, even find a few troubling charts tracking our increasing inability to retain top performers. Then I find a few more slides highlighting the company's plummeting quality metrics. Maybe I can use several of these for the meeting. Then I seem to crumble inside. *What the hell am I doing? I can't pull this off. Hell, I don't even know what it is I am trying to pull off.* I take my hands and cover my face, and try to summon Mama and her courage, her vision.

Go crazy.

I can do this.

I have to do this.

Keep Mama happy a little longer.

Convince my sister I can be trusted with her house.

Help the families of Robards International.

Let my kid nephew be a kid once in a while.

I glance at my—Dick's—watch. It's nearly go time.

Shelley pops her head in. "The guys in the lobby called. You have a visitor."

Mama.

"Can you have her brought up?" I frown at the slides. "I'm trying to figure this out."

"That's the problem. They say she's refusing to sign in. They can't get her to provide a name or anything."

I look up at Shelley, offering a grin. "Signing in as 'Mama' isn't good enough?"

"Mama?" Shelley chuckles, straightens. "She's actually claiming to be your wife."

"Well," I say, grinning, "I've been meaning to tell you . . ."

She smiles, folds her arms. "I think if you went down there and got your 'wife' yourself, they wouldn't make her sign in."

A few minutes later, I'm rush-walking into the executive lobby of Robards International, my heart pounding at the possibility of being spotted for who I am—an impostor, an accomplice to executive kidnapping who's now bringing in another accomplice. Thank God the lobby is empty except for the security guards behind the desk and—of course—Mama standing in the center, her neck glistening in vegetable oil, her pelvis pushed out.

"Sweetie," she announces, stretches her arms, motions me to her with her fingers. "There you are. These fellas won't let me come up and surprise my own husband. Come over here and give me some sugar."

The security guards watch as I let Mama wrap me up in her arms and slide her open mouth across my face. I strain and turn to avoid a direct hit, and her teeth and tongue trail against my jaw. I look at the frozen guards and force a smile. "Sweetie," I say. "You're here." Mama holds me close and groans. I push her off and turn to the guards. "I'm taking my wife upstairs."

"Yes, sir."

I take Mama's hand and lead her out. "Where are the boys?" I ask.

"Relax," Mama snaps. "You're such a helicopter parent—jeesh. Besides, we need to talk about this meeting."

She's right. "Actually, I was thinking. I spoke with that guy you mentioned—Carl Blakenship."

"Good."

"And I spoke with Peter Randell, the conhacker."

"Even better."

"They're all going to be there, and that's great. But when the subcommittee sees me, they're going to know I'm not the real Dick. You know? They've worked with the real Dick, the Dick who truly knows this stuff. You know?"

Mama struggles to get up the stairs—panting, gripping my forearm hard. She looks up at me, grimaces.

"So I'm wondering if it makes sense for me to even be there? You know? Maybe I just bring them together, bring you and Carl and Peter in, and then I step out? You know? I just think you all might be able to tell the story better than I ever could."

Mama stops and looks at me.

"I mean, maybe we could even get Bobby Flanduzi to attend and tell his story."

Mama reaches into her fanny pack and pulls out my phone. "Take this," she says. "But just so you know, I copied your sister's name down. So, any funny business with me, mister, and I'll call your sister right now and tell her everything."

I feel my jaw pulse. "She wouldn't believe you."

"Well . . ." Mama shakes her head and takes a few more steps. ". . . if you want to take that risk, honey, just try it."

I tighten. "Listen," I plead. "I'll do what you want with this meeting. I'm just telling you, they aren't going to believe I'm Dick. And I think hearing from the real victims, and hearing about the conhacker project—that *has* to be illegal—will be more effective."

Mama huffs as we reach the top of the stairs. "Just take me to the conference room." She stops, looks around, trying to catch her breath. "I need to collect my thoughts, and figure this thing out. Because I think you're right. You'd screw it up."

I feel a lump at the bottom of my throat. Because I know she's right.

I always screw things up.

• • •

Once Shelley and I get Mama, Carl, and the conhackers into the Alcatraz conference room, I realize it's nearly time for the five o'clock meeting. Mama takes my hand and leads me out of the room. "I want you nearby, you hear?"

Dick's security guard approaches with a walkie-talkie pressed to his chin. "Sir, we have an SOS from Bob Irvman."

"Who's that?"

"Bob from Security in Cell Block A. You know, the guy who took care of that, you know, that . . . that solicitation problem for you in Dallas." He pauses, presses his lips a little, and steps back. "I'm afraid we have a Class Three situation over there."

"What the hell is a Class Three situation?"

"Sir, it's a Class Three riot. That's as bad as any prison riot you've seen on TV. Sir, we have this building secure, and we're locking the other buildings, per procedure."

I think of dozens of squad cars speeding onto the Robards International campus. "Are they sure? I mean, are they sure it's that bad?"

"It's bad, sir."

"Do we need to call the police?"

"If we can't contain them. If they get out of Cell Block A, we'll have nine hundred ex-cons rioting across the entire campus."

Ricky screws up everything. Always.

"And you're sure it's that bad?"

"Sir, come with me a second." He leads me to a small office around the corner. Inside, two other security guards are seated at a desk analyzing the grainy screens of no fewer than ten displays, each of them providing a live feed from Cell Block A. "Let's take a look."

"Holy shit."

"Exactly, sir. That's why we can't—we really shouldn't lift the lockdown. This thing is far from quelled. Bob and his guys are getting ready to do a floor-by-floor."

I lean in and scan the screens, and what I see makes me choke on my spit. The screens are buzzing with black-and-white feeds from dozens of security cameras placed throughout Cell Block A. Each screen flashes scenes of absolute mayhem—conployees turning over desks and chairs, conployees kicking walls, conployees punching and kicking each other, conployees taking whizzes on desks, conployees attempting to rip flat-screen displays off walls. But most of all, conployees pumping their fists in the air, in unison, as they chant something over and over and over.

"It's bad, sir."

I scan the screens, hoping to make sense of it all.

"Most have congregated, sir."

"What do you mean?"

"You know, sir, an unsanctioned assembly. Take a look." The guard leans over and clicks a mouse. The top screen—the largest of them all—blinks and flickers until a new feed flashes into clarity. Hundreds of jumpsuited conployees have encircled a center table in the cafeteria. They're pumping their fists into the air. Some of them are skittering off to wreak havoc elsewhere, but most remain congregated around a main table.

"We have an agitator, sir."

"Agitator?"

"He's right there in the middle."

I lean in and squint at the grainy forms on the screen, and soon I find the agitator—my nephew, standing on a cafeteria table, stomping his feet, pumping one fist in the air and using the other to shout into a bullhorn.

I freeze, and my bowels weaken.

"Sir, we understand the chant is a bit odd—*We're humans, too. So whatchya gonna do?* Clearly this agitator has planted some ideas into their heads, got them thinking about their second-tier status at the company."

Someone seems to reach for Collin, and my stomach goes ice cold.

I turn to the guard and grab his lapels. "What's your name?"

"Jeremy, sir." He looks at me, his eyes huge. "Sir, do you want to go to your safe room and wait this one out?"

I release his lapels. "Jeremy, this is an order. I need them to unlock every single door in that building. You hear me?"

"Sir, we'll have—"

"Jeremy, I'm not going to say it again. There are innocent people in there, and they're trapped in there with nine hundred felons until we unlock those doors and people can disperse. Now, Jeremy. I'm telling you one last time. Open. Those. Doors."

"Sir, we're talking about hundreds of thousands of dollars in dam——"

"Jeremy." I'm grabbing his lapels with both hands, shaking him. "I'm going to fire you and every single member of your crew here unless you tell them—right now—that Dick Rayborne wants those doors opened this instant."

I release him, and he brings the walkie-talkie to his chin. "Bob, this is Jeremy. I'm here with the Warden, and he wants all doors in Cell Block A unlocked. I repeat, the Warden has reviewed the camera feeds, and he wants all doors unlocked."

Long silence, and then, "Ten-four."

I run back to the Alcatraz conference room, pop my head in. The subcommittee isn't there yet, fortunately. I get Mama's attention. "They're in Cell Block A," I snap. "The boys took Collin to Cell Block A."

Mama gives me an exaggerated so-what? look. "He'll be fine."

"He started a riot," I yell, pull my head back out, and slam the door.

Back in the security office, Jeremy announces, "Lockdown on Cell Block A has been lifted. The conployees are pouring out, and we have all the other buildings in a strict lockdown."

"Show me the cafeteria again."

The cafeteria appears on the top screen. Thank God, I can see Collin. The kid is still on the table, still leading a group chant, still pumping his fists, still stomping his feet. The mob is thinning as more and more conployees march out of the room, their fists in the air, heads bobbing. I'm relieved to see Cujo standing close to Collin, even pushing a few conployees back.

"Sir, we're getting a new report. The agitator is leading them in a new rallying cry. Something along the lines of 'We're no subspecies.' Does that make any sense to you, sir?"

I stare at the screen, my mouth open.

"Regardless, the mob is mobilizing, sir. Are you sure you don't want to go to your safe room?"

"Jeremy, I want you to track the movements of the agitator. With the security cameras, okay?"

"Yes, sir."

"Just give me one of those radios—a walkie-talkie. How do I use this?"

"Sir, here. Just . . . There you go. Turn that like this. And then, yeah. Press this if you want to talk."

I turn to leave the room. "Just let me know if they leave the cafeteria, okay? Tell me where they're going."

"Sir, you're going out there?"

"I need to get him."

"Sir, I should come with you."

"No," I say. "I need you here. I need your guys telling me

where he's going, and I need you to make sure that meeting in Alcatraz actually occurs."

Silence.

"Okay?"

"Yes, sir. Brandon will track the agitator and keep you coordinated."

"Perfect."

"But, sir. I really think you should change."

"What are you talking about?"

"Your clothes, sir. If you run into Cell Block A like that right now, they'll rip you to shreds."

I stand there, look down at my—I mean, Dick's—suit, and it clicks with me. Jeremy's right; the last thing I can do is look like Dick Rayborne right now.

"Follow me, sir. Your safe room has a jumpsuit for this very purpose. You really did think of everything, sir."

. . .

Outside, scores of conployees rush past me hooting and hollering. They're like thirdgraders released from class on the last day of school, headed in every direction, crisscrossing each other as they embark on a hundred different adventures. To avoid getting plowed over, I have to dart from side to side. Some already have reached the main professional building and are congregating at the doors, kicking on the presumably shatterproof glass, trying to bust through. I press the radio to my chin and holler, *"I need a location update."*

The radio crackles. "He's at the back of the primary mob, sir."

"Where?"

"Right ahead. And, sir?"

"What?"

"Sir, the agitator is a child." It's like he can't believe it. "A child, sir. The agitator is a little boy."

Finally, I see the mob, but not Collin. "He's not here."

"He's at the back of the mob, sir. The agitator was leading them, but his friend pulled him back. Straight ahead, sir."

The conployees are packed in tight, clapping and yelling at the tops of their voices, and it really unnerves me. Their war cry sends shock waves down the narrow pathway and seems to rattle the windows in the adjacent buildings. All of it makes me want to turn around and head back to the executive building—but I summon every muscle in my body to press forward.

We're no . . .

Clap-clap-clap.

Subspecies.

Clap-clap-clap.

We're no . . .

Clap-clap-clap.

Subspecies.

Clap-clap-clap.

I step out of the way as they begin to pass. I yell as loud as I can. *"Collin."*

All I can hear is . . .

We're humans, too.

Clap.

So whatchya gonna do?

Clap.

Finally, I see them at the back of the mob. "Don't let them take advantage of you," he hollers under the war cry. "Don't let them treat you like dumb brutes. Because you never were, and never will be." He's nearly crying. "They never understood you." Cujo is trailing behind—watching, smiling. I rush to them, take

Collin by the arm, and pull him back a little so he's with Cujo and me.

"Hey."

"Collin, what on Earth are you thinking?"

Cujo says, "Dude, you're wearing a jumpsuit."

"Uncle Rick, I can't believe you've allowed this to happen. Treating Neanderthals like subhumans. Doesn't this bother you?"

We're humans, too.

Clap.

So whatchya gonna do?

Clap.

Collin yells, "What we're going to do is fight for liberty."

"Collin, you've started a riot. This is not—"

"The time for change is now."

My phone rings. It says my sister has called ten times in the last forty minutes.

"Collin, this is a company. This isn't a city or a state."

The call goes to voice mail.

We're no . . .

Clap-clap-clap.

Subspecies.

Clap-clap-clap.

A new call comes in. It's an unknown 650 number. What the hell is going on? I swipe and answer the call.

"Yes, this Sabine Rorgstardt from Stanford University."

"Oh, hi. I'm sorry, I'm a bit frazzled at the moment."

"I'm doing a favor for a friend." She sounds like a robot, so serious. "I understand you wanted to arrange a brief visit for a certain someone who is passionate about Neanderthals."

We're no . . .

Clap-clap-clap.

Subspecies.

Clap-clap-clap.

"Yes, I'm sorry, Sabine. Can I call you back?"

"Of course," she says, and I hang up a little too quickly.

I turn to Cujo. "I need to get him out of here," I say. "Pull a left up here and wait at the door. I'll have them buzz him in." Then I bark into the radio. "They're coming to the bottom-floor entry. I want you to let the boy in immediately—as soon as you see him at the door."

A new call comes in—my sister.

"Yes, sir."

I swipe at the screen of my phone. "Ana," I say as pleasantly as possible. "What's up?"

Ana sounds acidic. "I simply can't . . . believe you."

I fall back some more, try to cup my hand over my mouth as I speak into the phone. I try so hard to sound pleasant. "What do you mean?"

Long pause. "You know exactly what I mean."

I watch as Cujo leads Collin away from the mob and toward the door to the executive building. A few conployees linger back with them. The door opens, and the conployees rush the guard, pull him out of the threshold, and toss him onto the sidewalk. They charge in, and Collin and Cujo follow suit. I feel my stomach tighten, and I decide to hightail it over there.

"Actually, Ana, I don't know what you mean."

"His body-language coach?" She waits, hoping it will register. "The body-language coach. He was waiting for Collin, and he never showed. I'm gathering you two ditched him?"

How about the entire second half of the school day?

"Do you have any idea how important these things are? You know, if you want to get into a *good* school?"

I want to say, *How can you care so deeply about things like your*

kid's body-language tutor and yet neglect this kid so thoroughly?
Instead, I say, "I'm sorry, Ana."

I help the guard up, and he opens the door with his badge.
We enter.

"This is the kind of thing, Rick. I'm sorry, but this is exactly
the kind of thing that worries me—you know, about taking care
of the house, about Collin coming out and visiting."

The guard and I take the stairs up to the executive floor,
where Mama hopefully is holding court with the subcommittee. "Listen, Ana." I feel like I'm about to explode, but I hold it
together, take a deep breath. "In terms of having command presence and earning the confidence of followers, I think Collin's
body language is just fine."

• • •

By the time I reach the executive area, the meeting with the
compensation subcommittee is in progress in the Alcatraz conference room. I stop twenty feet short and marvel at the sight
before me. An empty-nesting granny with no affiliation to the
company is holding an emergency meeting with the compensation subcommittee of the Robards International board of directors. And the guest speakers include one benefits-sabotage IT
geek, one sabotaged employee-turned-conployee, and one very
passionate, opinionated, and confident eight-year-old.

Never mind me pretending to be Dick Rayborne.

Shelley is pacing outside Alcatraz. When I approach she
says, "Mama wants you gone."

"I know. I just wanted to make sure you guys are okay."

"I just heard the tape," she says.

"Tape?"

"Is that your nephew there? The agitator?"

I nod and smile.

"The security guys just played the tape," she says. "It was nuts. One minute, he's simply asking them about the rules for conployees, and the next thing, he's telling them they're oppressed, that they're being discriminated against, that they're humans, too. That they never were the brutes—the subspecies—that the world thinks they are." She looks away at a thought, shakes her head. "It was amazing. Conployees started coming over and listening. Then more guys came over. Then he's suddenly leading these protest chants, and that only got them more worked up. It was crazy to see."

I glance into Alcatraz. Collin is at the head of the table, his arms thrust out in exclamation, his head cocked sideways in a plea for reason. It looks like he's got a lot to say, his jaw jutted out, his eyes saucered, his jugular popping. And I have to say—I'm not too surprised that the three members of the subcommittee are sitting there listening, equal parts curious and entertained. I also have to say I'm more than a little proud of Collin's vision, his leadership. Okay, so maybe this is what they teach at the Halvaford School—how to change the world.

And then I realize, *Collin was always this way.*

I glance in again. Collin is still lecturing. I turn to Shelley and say, "I need to find a way to excuse ourselves early enough so I can get to get to my sister's house by six."

"Well then . . ." Shelley looks at her wristwatch. "You have fifty-three minutes."

"I have to stop this," I say and ease the conference room door open.

Collin is saying, "Every assumption modern society has made about these people—and yes, they *are* people—is wrong. They never were subhumans. They've just had too many people dismiss them as . . ." Collin thrusts his fingers up to make the quotation sign. ". . . 'dumb Neanderthals.'" His voice quavers, and his jugular bulges. "It's just that no one ever gave these poor guys a break. The world expected them to act like subhumans, so a lot of them have done just that. And yes, many of them—like my Neanderthal, Cujo—do have pronounced brows and large bones, like an ape or early human, but the truth of the matter is, those features have no correlation at all to intelligence or lack thereof. In fact, the History Channel says . . ."

I look to Mama, and she's shooting me a nasty glare. The subcommittee members—two men and one woman—notice and turn to face me. I can't remember their names to save my life. The two men smile uneasily and nod. One of them says, "Is that your honorary jumpsuit, Dick?" and laughs.

Oh, shit. That's right. The jumpsuit.

"We just have a little situation outside, and I needed to—No need to worry about it. Just stay in here, and you should be fine."

Collin hasn't stopped talking. ". . . which just goes to show you that they are capable of doing much more than anyone has ever guessed. But more importantly, this Invitation to Cooperate program doesn't allow them to assimilate into normal society. The program is dividing classes, widening the divisions, and creating even greater problems, if the revolt downstairs is any in-dication. And if you ever stopped to look at the fossil record . . ."

Mama says to me, "I need you to get Bobby. Remember?"

Oh, crap—Bobby Flanduzi. In the next building. Stuck in an all-day meeting with a huge bag of cash as hundreds of conployees go wild a few feet away. "Okay," I say. "I'll go get him."

"Thanks, Dick." Mama turns to the board. "Mr. Rayborne is going to get an employee who has an important story for you. A story you must hear."

The board members lean back and roll their eyes. The woman

says, "This has got to be the strangest meeting I've ever—" She turns to me, squints. "And you're not fooling anyone."

"Huh?"

"You're not Dick Rayborne," she snaps. "Where's Dick?" She leans back, looks at her mobile phone, thumbs over her screen. "Where's his number?"

Mama says, "Dick's going to get Bobby Flanduzi. In the meantime, we're going to thank Collin here and introduce you to Dick's computer boys, and then Carl."

My—I mean, Dick's—phone rings in my pocket. The female board member looks at me, scowls. "Why do you have Dick's phone?"

I say to Mama and the board members, "I'll be right back with Bobby Flanduzi." Then I meet the woman's eyes. "Give us a chance, okay? As an officer of the company, it's really important that you hear this."

Mama says, "Because it's not just the conployees who are being mistreated, but nearly every single employee at the company. And it's your ass that will be thrown in jail."

I close the door, and Shelley pulls on my arm. "We have visitors," she says, so calm. "Over there." Across the empty office, dozens of conployees are fanning out. One short, massively broad-shouldered conployee with a red bandanna tied over his nose and mouth has collected three laptop computers and is meandering through the office, scanning desks and cabinet tops. Others seem to be sightseeing as they stroll across the floor, their heads down as they try to avoid clear shots from the security cameras. Jeremy approaches us, says, "Don't worry, sir. The majority of the mob is next door."

My real building.

Where Janice from Finance is holding her all-day meeting.

Fantastic.

I turn and grab Shelley by the wrist. "I want Jeremy to never leave Collin out of his sight." I look at her. "Okay?"

She nods, says, "*I won't let him out of my sight.*" We stand there, watching the conployees. Finally, Shelley whispers to me, "You know, if they hear these stories. The board? If they hear these stories, if they are officially disclosed regarding the tactics Dick and the company are using. And they *are* illegal. Then the board is legally required to act. Did you know that?"

Slowly, I shake my head.

Shelley nods to the conference room. "Your wife is a lot sharper than she lets on."

Something just can't allow me to accept that Mama planned all this.

"Go get Bobby Flanduzi," Shelley says, "and let's see if we can do something kinda big today."

●   ●   ●

By the time I reach my real building, hundreds of conployees have poured in through shattered glass doors and windows, and hundreds of normal employees have streaked out, car keys in hand, screaming into their cell phones, the whites of their eyes showing. On each floor, including mine, conployees are yanking displays off desktops, or stacking laptops neatly in their clutches, or simply lounging in the break rooms and coffee areas. Distant sounds of breaking glass, splintering wood, cracking plastic, and baritone hooting bounce off the walls. Some are still yelling Collin's war cry. One conployee sits in a cube, his feet on the desk, with a desk phone cradled to an ear as he chats with an old friend who seems to be living in Barstow. "First we need to store it in my cousin's garage," he says. "Then we talk numbers with the Stockton guys."

I don't see one regular employee. Anywhere.

I turn a corner and approach the conference room. I stop and take a breath, looking at the closed door. Considering everything that's happened, one would think they couldn't possibly . . . I mean, we're in the middle of a melee—a looting, a riot, an uprising. Of course, Janice loves her meetings. And yes, she hates to stop any meeting early—in fact, she resists early stops with every fiber in her body. And yes, Janice never loses sight of things. There is never any doubt she's a tireless corporate soldier who will grind you to pulp. And yes, that conference room is a bit removed—kind of tucked away. And yes, these walls are thick, the door solid. But still—what about those conployees over there holding an impromptu donnybrook? What about those guys on the other end marching through the adjacent hall, chanting and pumping and clapping? What about the red-alert alarm that's just sounded, slashing deep into my skull, blaring long and hard with ruthless precision—over and over and over—like we're a submarine that's taken a direct hit?

Blang . . . blang . . . blang . . . blang . . . blang.

Don't they hear all of this?

Apparently not.

I approach the door and peer in through the porthole. Janice from Finance is at the whiteboard, her back to the attendees, each and every one of whom is staring into space, thumbing through a mobile phone, or slumping his head in utter defeat. Only Hank seems to be taking notes.

Poor souls.

And then I realize, at least they're safe in their J-23 Incubation meeting. At least they're missing the stress of a full-blown melee. At least they can sit there, bored off their asses—daydreaming about sex, or planning dinner, or finalizing to-do lists—instead of rushing to their cars with the knowledge that a felon is riffling through their desk drawers. *Okay, time to get cranking.* I scan the room for Bobby Flanduzi. There he is, still in the center of the room, still staring at his zipped-up Nike bag, still seeming a bit dazed. Time to spring him loose, get him and his money to Alcatraz and then into his car and headed home with the cash still in his possession.

I get ready to do a reinsert—a basic, unapologetic Bob Watson maneuver of walking back in, preferably when heads are turned in the opposite direction. Then I realize I'm wearing a jumpsuit. Now, that *would* cause a commotion. I back up a little and unzip the jumpsuit and step out of it, wondering if anyone in there will notice my new eight-thousand-dollar Italian suit. At least I left the suit jacket back at Dick's office. I peek in, and Janice's back is still facing the attendees, who are still in their own worlds. I open the door, slip in, and head to my seat, where my notepad and pen lay undisturbed.

"So . . ." Janice scribbles a concoction of acronyms onto the whiteboard. ". . . the K-KAR acts as a virtual filter for the P-FID, which means we must R-Doc every single L-27 in the system so we can run B-PODs across every division, whether it is . . ." Her whiteboarding becomes more aggressive, more passionate, as she really puts some mustard into it. ". . . the FG, or the YTA, or the PGT or even the guys in EDG."

I look over to Bobby Flanduzi, who's still staring at the Nike bag. I wait for him to look up.

Janice turns to face us. "So, the question is, how do we architect a system for P-FIDs when all we've ever done are K-KARs?"

I raise my hand.

Janice nods, and I stand up and walk to the whiteboard. Gently, I relieve her of the marker, and I begin the scratch out the most ridiculous thing I've ever put on a whiteboard (during a real meeting, at least). I sketch out an insanely intricate matrix of lines and arrows and boxes and—of course—triangles and cylinders, and then I begin to label each of them—a flurry of K-KARs and P-FIDs and B-PODs and L-27s. I really have no idea what the hell I am suggesting, but I also really don't have the time to care—all I must really do is provoke them. When I finish, I turn and jam the cap onto the marker and meet Janice's gaze. "This, my friends . . ." I force my voice to quake, and I tense my jaws and neck and arms. ". . . is the future of the K-KAR optimization process." I pause again and try to choke on my spit. "The future of bottom-tier data transformation. The future of . . ." I drop to a near whisper. ". . . the future of everything."

I hand the marker back to Janice and slowly return to my seat, my head bowed like I'm leaving an altar. Janice stands there, her chest rising, nostrils flaring. "To suggest that the K-KAR might someday be directly fed into the B-PODs is nearly offensive." She takes a huge breath, looks down, and lets it out slowly. "And yet . . ." Her voice lightens. ". . . there is something nearly poetic to the suggestion. Something . . ." She uncaps the marker, turns, and attacks the whiteboard, scribbling furiously. ". . . possible." She tightens her jaws and loops long lines over my drawing. "What if—Now, consider this. What if . . ." She loops another long line across the matrix. ". . . we introduced a Tri-B-POD Process—call it a TB-PODP—and strung it through the K-KAR?"

I sit there, lean back, and fold my arms, nodding in quiet satisfaction.

Imprint? Done.

Distraction? Done.

Ditch? They'll never even miss us.

• • •

By the time I send Bobby Flanduzi and his Nike bag of cash into the Alcatraz conference room, the red-alert alarm seems to have gotten much louder. Collin and Jeremy the security guard are waiting for me. "This building is cleared and secure," Jeremy says, and the alarm finally stops. "Most conployees have either returned to their desks, left for the day, or are loitering in a few professional buildings. The rest of the executive team is huddled in Rikers Island, waiting out the storm." He lets his shoulders sag. "A few employees called 911, but we were able to turn back the police at the gates. As you've said before, a police response would be a publicity nightmare." He cracks a grin. "I knew you'd be happy to hear that, sir. Like you said, sir . . ." He blinks, looks down in embarrassment (or maybe shame?) as he recites ". . . employee terror lasts only a few minutes, maybe an hour, but bad publicity lasts forever."

I close my eyes, wait for the anger to dissipate. I control my breathing. When I open my eyes, Mama is sticking her head out of Alcatraz. She's smiling, her eyes twinkling. "I had Shelley come in and take official minutes so that it would be on the record." Her voice lifts in excitement. "With all of this in the minutes, they're legally required to act—that is, unless they want to go to the big house."

I nod and Collin beams.

Mama looks at her wristwatch. "Now it's time for you and the kid to get out of here. I know you have your own important meeting."

I look at the clock on my phone—it's 5:34. *Holy crap.* I have twenty-six minutes to get Collin home, and it's rush hour, which usually takes forty minutes. I tense and spin around, trying to think clearly. *What do I need?*

"I need my wagon." Mama says it so sweetly. "Why don't you get your briefcase . . ." She gives me the eye. ". . . and your keys for the Porsche and just go?"

I leave the check for Shelley on her keyboard, facedown, and soon we're racing out the back door and into the gated executive parking lot. I'm not sure I knew what to expect, but I certainly didn't expect the gate to be jammed open with a two-by-four, and I didn't expect to see an old white pickup truck idling inside the lot. I didn't expect to see several dozen conployees using hydraulic tools and crowbars and wrenches to strip down the executive fleet of Mercedes, Teslas, Karmas, and BMWs. And I most certainly didn't expect to see Ernie and Cujo working a jack under my—I mean, Dick's—Porsche.

I run up to the Porsche. "Hey."

Ernie keeps cranking the jack, lifting the Porsche off the ground. Cujo lowers his wrench and looks up at me. "I've gotta say," he says, his eyes so alive. "This has got to be the best fucking day at work ever."

"Guys. C'mon. I need the car."

Cujo begins to wiggle off a wheel. "Sorry, dude. You know how much these wheels go for on the black market?"

"Guys. Listen. I'll give you this Porsche. I promise. I mean, forget the wheels. You can have the whole thing."

Cujo stops with the wheel, and Ernie peers up at me.

"Just put this car down, get those lug nuts, and tighten them back on. Please. Just please let us get the hell out of here, so I can convince my sister—I mean, do you want Collin to never be able to come back home and visit? Do you think some vegan chef named Luke should babysit Collin for six weeks?"

Cujo looks at Collin, then at me. "You serious, dude? Some weed eater is gonna babysit our little buddy in Mongolia—"

"Argentina."

"—unless you hightail it to your sister's crib in twenty minutes?"

"That's it. Exactly. C'mon. I need your help."

Ernie is already lowering the Porsche, and Cujo is wrenching a lug nut onto one of the wheels. "I'll get these two on this side," he grunts. "Ernie will do the other two over there—You hear that, Ernie? The Egghead needs to get to his sister's." He looks up at me. "You just get in the car and start the engine, and we'll have you two peeling out in a second. Just wait for my tap on the window."

Only problem is, Ernie is just standing there looking at me with the saddest face. Cujo notices, releases an annoyed sigh. Then he looks at me, says, "You have to understand, Warden. This kind of thing is tough on Ernie."

"What kind of thing?"

"Saying goodbye." He looks at Ernie, then at me and Collin, his voice softening. "Mama says Ernie has some 'loss issues.' All I know is, it's hard for the little guy to let go." He studies Ernie some more. "I think he's worried that he's never going to see you two again. And he likes you both."

I turn to Ernie and meet his wet gaze. "You think you're never going to see us again?"

Ernie blinks away a tear. Nods.

"Well, what if Mama and I set up a playdate—I mean, some time for all of us to hang out?"

Ernie sniffles and nods.

Cujo works the lug nuts. "I'll do the other wheels real fast so you three can hug it out."

Ernie grins at us, sniffling, and opens his arms.

• • •

Racing up Interstate 280 to Woodside, weaving in and out of relatively light traffic, I hit speeds nearing ninety miles per hour. All I know is, I'm glad I don't have my commuter car this afternoon. I scan my rear- and side-view mirrors, hoping I don't see the flashing lights of a California Highway Patrol car. Not that I would stop if there were any. We just have to get there by six. No exceptions, especially not today.

Finally, at 5:51, I shift down on the Woodside Road exit. I scan my mirrors one last time and feel my shoulders relax as I realize we now have more than enough time to get to Ana's house by six o'clock. From this spot, I usually can get there in five minutes, which now gives me four cushion minutes to slow down and think about what to say to my sister and how to say it.

Collin's breathless. "That was amazing."

"Don't tell your mom." I pull a right onto Woodside Road and head down the hill. "I need to clear my head, kiddo. It's just spinning right now."

"Put on some music," Collin says. "Music always helps."

I fiddle with the stereo, and like a miracle, I'm able to get SiriusXM Radio. Apparently Dick Rayborne likes his love songs—Channel 17 ("Love") appears on the screen, and suddenly I'm listening to "When a Man Loves a Woman." I pound on the buttons until I land on Channel 33 ("1st Wave")—and just like that I have the English Beat, of all bands, thumping through the car, the saxophone wailing, the bass thunging, and the horns twisting and winding to "March of the Swivel Heads," the instrumental version of "Rotating Heads."

Maybe the universe really does want me to go to the Greek tonight?

I downshift as I approach Southgate Drive and pull a right, my head bopping to the beat, the trumpets popping.

Bup-bup bup-pup
Bup-bup bup-pup
Bup-bup bup-pup
Beeeep bup-bup-bup

We take a quick left on Eleanor, and it feels like I ran over a bag of sand. The Porsche wobbles and swerves, then drops with a loud crack, and I see one of my—I mean, Dick's—wheels rolling past me and onto someone's manicured front lawn.

Crap.

I pull the Porsche to the curb, come to a loud stop. I grip the steering wheel, screw my eyes shut, trying to think. I open my eyes, glance at the clock on the dashboard—5:54. Eleanor Drive is a giant circle, and Collin's house is on the opposite end. If we walk it, or even run it, I'm not sure we'll get there in time. But what options do I have at this point? I get out of the Porsche, remove my—I mean, Dick's—jacket, and throw it into onto the driver's seat, shut the door. I call Collin out, and we start trotting along Eleanor.

Six minutes. We can do this.

A car approaches from behind. I crinkle my face, waiting for a quick blast of siren—but there is none. Instead, a black Mercedes-Benz G-Class SUV rolls past us, and I feel a wave of relief spread across my body—until I realize it's Ana's SUV, and that is Ana in the driver's seat. She seems to slow down at the same moment I realize that it's her. She lowers her head a little to get a better look at us through the rearview mirror, so I yank Collin and we make a hard right and leap over some shrubs and onto someone's lawn, realizing that unless we get to the house now, we're hosed. I won't be able to explain any of it, and it will all unravel from there—no house-sitting offer, no Summer of Sanity with Collin. I just can't leave him with Luke the vegan chef for six weeks.

Luckily, there's a pickup truck approaching—more yard workers (the area is packed with them).

"Dude," I huff.

"Yeah?"

"You wanna make sure you can come back this summer and hang out with your uncle? Maybe even see Cujo and Mama and Ernie?"

His voice cracks. "More than you'd ever know."

"Okay." I step out onto the street, waving for the truck to stop. "Get ready."

The truck rolls to a stop, and I reach for my wallet, rifle through the bills, pull out sixty dollars. Three young Mexican immigrants look at me with amusement. I nod to the back of the truck, which is packed with bags of clippings. "Can you give me and my nephew a lift down this road?"

They glance at each other, look back at me, and scan the surrounding area. The driver tightens, nods to the back the truck—*Go for it.* I offer the money, which seems to annoy him. "No." He smiles, nods to the back again. "Let's go."

Soon Collin and I are sunken in the bags of clippings, giggling as the truck rolls down the street. I peer out to see where we are, and there's my sister in her Mercedes; she's idled on the side of the road, talking to a mom in yoga pants holding a giant Starbucks latte. Ana glances at the truck, and I duck with a laugh, the horns still popping in my head.

Bup-bup bup-pup
Bup-bup bup-pup
Bup-bup bup-pup
Beeeep bup-bup-bup

After another block, I tap on the cab window, and we slow down.

"Come on, kiddo. Let's do this."

"But we're not there yet."

I help him out of the truck, and I thank the guys one last

time. They're laughing and exchanging comments in Spanish as the truck rolls away, waving to us.

"We can walk the last bit here," I tell Collin. "This is better than your mom seeing us pile out of the back of a yard truck."

I look behind us, and there's Ana's Mercedes again.

Shit.

I grab Collin and yank him into a stand of bushes. The Mercedes rolls past, and Collin says, "Now what are we supposed to do? We're supposed to be there."

I look around and take his hand. "Follow me, kiddo. Time for one last adventure."

"What do you mean?"

"We need to cross the backyard of this house. Do you know these people?"

Collin takes a look at the house—it's enormous—and shakes his head.

"Let's do this."

I help Collin up onto the fence. Then I clamber over. My—I mean, Dick's—pants catch and tear as I tumble to the other side. Collin lands on his feet unscathed—somehow. The yard is giant and very sparse, which seems odd to me until I see the ostrich galloping toward us. We scramble to our feet, turn, and run for our lives as the ostrich closes in, its head low, its wings spread out. I suddenly recall a comment from Audrey about a neighbor with an "attack ostrich" in the backyard, but I'd thought it was a joke.

I certainly don't now.

Collin screams—not in excitement, but in terror. I scoop him up and sprint as the sound of the bird's disturbingly enormous feet gets louder and louder. Collin buries his face in my shoulder, and I let out a tight shriek. I pull a hard right, trying to lose the bird, and failing, so I course-correct and make it to the opposite enclosure, a Cyclone fence covered with vines. I lift Collin onto the fence and scramble up and over as the ostrich jabs its beak into my ass. Collin and I tumble into a carefully manicured and—more important—unpopulated lawn and race across it, realizing at last that I'm approaching my sister's side fence. We slow down, gather ourselves, and take our time climbing over that last enclosure.

On the other side, we stand in my sister's bushes as I try to catch my breath and watch the proceedings inside the house. Fortunately, Ana and Samson James Barnard IV had the entire house remodeled three years ago so that the family room and kitchen look out to the backyard through expansive floor-to-ceiling glass walls and sliding glass doors, which now give me a clear view of Ana walking into the kitchen, purse in her clutch, greeting Audrey, who's slicing an apple at the counter. Taped-up moving boxes are everywhere.

Ana looks at Audrey, then at her wristwatch.

I know what we need to do. I take a knee and look into Collin's eyes. "Listen, kiddo. About today—maybe we don't tell her about the riot."

He nods, so serious.

"Or about Mama and that guy Larry."

Another nod.

"And maybe we don't mention the laser game at Dick's house."

Collin says, "We better get in there."

I take his hand, and we dart from the bushes to the sliding glass door connecting us to the kitchen. I force a smile and tap on the glass. Ana and Audrey turn to us, surprised. I think Audrey is most surprised, judging by the frozen look on her face, but fortunately she recovers and beats Ana to the door, unlocks it for me, and opens it with a smile. "There you are," she says.

The clock on the stove says 6:01.

Ana's face darkens. "You're late," she snaps.

"You're right," I say. "I'm sorry."

Half her mouth is turned up, teeth showing. "What were you doing out there?"

"I just wanted to see if I could find that pin."

Ana looks at me like I'm crazy. "Pin?"

"My pin for twenty years of service at Robards International. I think I lost it here the other week."

Ana's still looking at me like I'm crazy. "You hate that place."

"Still." I look away, embarrassed. "Twenty years is a lot of—"

"What happened to your face?" Her look has switched from bafflement to disgust. "Did someone scratch you?"

"No, I just got tangled out there."

"Rick." She has that disappointed tone I've heard all my life. "I mean, what the hell is going on here?"

"Mommy," Collin says. "I met real-live Neanderthals today."

"Collin, I'm talking to Uncle Rick."

I clear my throat, force a peaceful look onto my face. "What do you mean, what's going on?"

"I mean . . ." She points to the spiked metal collar still locked around Collin's neck. ". . . I thought I told you, no more dress-up things for Collin."

"That's just—"

"Rick." She's talking in that sarcastic, whispery, why-don't-you-get-it tone. "The point is, you don't listen to me. You don't respect my choices as a parent."

Collin looks at me, then at her, and then back at me. He moves to hug her, but she redirects him to Audrey, who's waiting with open arms.

"Maybe I'm not as bad as you think—What I mean is, it's good for kids to spend time with people who love them. People who are outside the nuclear family."

Ana studies me and finally turns to Audrey. "Can you take Collin to his room for a bit? You can do the Mandarin flash cards with him, okay?"

"Come on, kiddo." Audrey takes Collin by the hand, leads him out of the kitchen. "Your mom and uncle need to talk."

"But, Mom," Collin says. "We played tag in a bunch of empty cans."

"Collin, have you done your Mandarin flash cards today?"

"No," he mumbles.

"Exactly." Her voice hardens. "Get in there and do your cards."

Once they leave, Ana looks down at her Peruvian hand-scrubbed granite countertop, sighs hard. "I just don't know, dude."

I try to be oblivious. "What do you mean?"

"The whole house-sitting thing," she says. "Today was exactly what I *don't* want—forgetting the body-language coach, neglecting the Mandarin flash cards—I even gave you a set to keep in your car. All this fantasy crap with the Neanderthals. All the screw——" She stops herself.

I explode. "What? Screwups? Is that what you were going to say? I'm always screwing up?"

"That's not what I meant, Rick."

"It's exactly what you meant." My face burns, and my heart aches. "That's what I am to you, huh? All these years later. Still a screwup."

"No."

"Your little brother who's always screwing up. Who screwed up his whole life—got yours screwed up, too. Your little brother who got Mama and Papa killed."

"I've never said that."

"Yes, I screwed up, Ana. I screwed up really bad that day, and Mama and Papa got killed. It was my fault."

"It wasn't your fault. I was a kid when I said that. When are you going to forgive me?"

"And I'm probably gonna screw up again. Hell, I screwed up today. Big-time."

Ana snaps, "You always nail me for that, every chance you get."

"Forget me for a minute, because . . ." My chest softens and my voice fissures. ". . . screwups are actually good. For kids. For adults. For everyone."

She can't look at me anymore. "I don't know what you're talking about."

"So yes, I screw up. Deal with it, because your son needs me, Ana."

"Needs you? I think that's overstating—"

"No, it's not." I steady myself and go for it. "Ana, you know what today taught me?"

She folds her arms and stares at the floor.

"You and Samson are negligent."

She looks up and stares at me. Eyes thinning.

"Collin needs a lot more than you seem willing to give. Today made that abundantly clear."

Her chest rises, and her face darkens. "You don't know the first thing about kids."

"I do know that this kid needs support."

"We have him at the most exclusive school on the peninsula. And his scores are extraordinary. What do you mean, he needs support?"

"Ana, what happened to you? Where in the hell is my sister?"

"She grew up." Her chest rises and her nostrils flare. "She got married, had a kid, and became an adult." She glares at me. "Do you realize what an amazing little boy Collin is?"

I was ready to shout something, but this gets me. I let out a bunch of air, my shoulders sagging. I get a flash of Collin lecturing a room of executives, leading the conployee revolt, talking me into doing the right thing. Changing the course of a company. Impacting tens of thousands of lives.

She's right—this kid is amazing.

"Don't you realize? Everything we do, we do for him. Don't you realize, he's going to blow this world away? All those crazy things we do with him—it's not about me or Samson. He's going to change the world."

He just might.

"Okay," I say and look away so I don't have to meet her eyes. "Maybe I've been a little shortsighted."

She's looking at me.

I hear myself say, "Maybe I've made some of this about me, and didn't even realize it."

Her face softens. "There are the plans and ideas you have *before* you are a parent. And then once you actually *are* a parent and you're deep in it, there's the reality."

I let out another long breath and bite my lip. "Maybe I've been a bit idealistic and shortsighted. But what I do know for sure—what is an absolute certainty—is that he needs another kind of support from you."

She looks away, her chest rising again, her eyes moistening.

"Ana." I wait for her to look me in the eye. "I think you got scared. I think after Mama and Papa, you got scared of ever giving yourself the way you did back then."

She shifts her weight and shakes her head.

"A busy husband. A big, all-consuming house in Woodside. Overachiever Fever. Hiring Audrey to take care of Collin. Did you ever think that maybe it was all about creating some kind of protective layer? Never getting too close to anyone again? Never getting destroyed like that again?"

I wonder if Ana is going to heave something at me. Instead, she gives in to a spasm of sobs. She holds herself, her chest heaving. "I miss them so much."

"I do, too, Ana." I close my eyes and try to ground myself. But I lose control of my breathing, which turns to short bursts of panting. And I break down, too. "I miss them every hour. Of every day."

I come over, and she lets me hug her. We cry. And hug and squeeze. The torrent builds.

"I'm so sorry. I'm sorry what I did, Ana. It was all my fault."

"No."

"It hurts so bad."

"You didn't kill them."

"I did."

"Tom Morrison did."

Tom Morrison was the drunk who blew through a red light and plowed into our Mama and Papa.

I sniffle and sigh. "But now we have Collin, and he needs us."

"I try," she squeaks, "but sometimes it's just too much. It feels too . . ."

"Ana, your son needs you."

She sniffles, nods.

"And I say this because I'm your brother and I love you. I'll always tell you the truth when everyone else is blowing smoke up your ass. So I'm telling you—you need to do whatever you need to so you can let go of that fear. I mean, find someone who can help you do that hard work."

"This, from a man who's spent his whole life avoiding loss."

"I'm totally screwed up," I say. "But right now, it's your turn. You have a son who needs you, so here's what you're going to do. First, you're going to find help in Buenos Aires. Not just a really good person who can help take care of Collin, but help for you and these issues. I mean, you guys have the money—get the best person down there to help you change, like, now."

She closes her eyes, nods.

"Second, Collin will come spend some time with me. I'll try not to screw up too much, and you will use the time to find that help. Your hear me?"

Ana says nothing.

"Ana Theresa Blanco."

This surprises her. It's like that old name slices into her.

"You're going to get help."

Ana pushes away from me, straightens her blouse, and sniffles. "Okay. But you have to promise me you'll do the Mandarin cards."

My sister might have turned into a crazy gringa, but she's *my* crazy gringa.

And right now, I love this crazy gringa more than anything.

• • •

By the time Ana and I have doped out the house-sitting details, Audrey has fed, cleaned, and prepped Collin for bed. She's reading him one last story, her voice a little weak. I loiter near Collin's door, not sure what to do. I want to say goodbye to my nephew and tell him about our Summer of Sanity, but I want to give him and Audrey some space. So I return to the kitchen and have a glass of pinot with my sister. Samson James Barnard IV sits three feet away, ignoring us, tapping away on his ultrathin laptop, his icy blue eyes devouring a seemingly endless array of tables and charts and graphs.

Ana and I talk about Mama and Papa, and it's actually fun.

Samson never looks up.

When I finally return to Collin's bedroom door, it's quiet

in there. I poke my head in. The lights are dimmed, putting a soft glow on all the moving boxes. Ana's in the far corner, in a rocking chair I've never quite noticed. Collin is cradled in her arms—far too big to be cradled, limbs dangling—as she rocks him back and forth, back and forth, running a finger along his hairline, looking down at her sweet sleeping child. When I try to withdraw, she looks up. Her cheeks are wet, her eyes puffy.

I don't know what to do.

She whispers, "Help me get him in bed."

I tiptoe over and lift Collin out of her arms. His limbs and head are so heavy when he sleeps; it's like they melt into mine when I bring him close and hug him one last time, kiss his forehead, and lower him into his bed. He gathers up his favorite lovey—Totty—and rolls and curls, and I slip the comforter over his little body.

I'll see you real soon, buddy.

I turn and nearly slam into Audrey, and she asks for a hug. I bring her in, wrap her up in my arms.

"It's gonna be okay."

"I love him so much," she gasps. "He's a part of me."

"You'll see him again."

"I know."

"This summer," I whisper. "He'll come up, and we'll all have a fucking blast."

"I just worry about him."

"I know."

"I wanna go down there with them, but I can't do this forever."

"I talked to my sister. She's gonna work on some things."

"Is he going to be okay?"

"I'll just have to make sure."

She pauses a long while. "Me, too."

I lead her out of the room, and we collect ourselves in the hallway.

"They're getting drunk tonight," Ana whispers. "They usually do. Hell, I might have my own bottle." She brushes the hair off her forehead, looks away with a sigh. "This day's too much."

"I might just have a bottle in my future, too."

"Oh." She reaches into her back pocket, pulls out a slip of paper. "That Mama lady called me right before you showed up. I have no idea how she got my number."

"Mama knows everything."

"Apparently so." Ana studies her note. "She needs you to check in on that Larry guy."

"Larry?"

"She wants you to make sure he's not getting carried away."

Carried away? I gaze into the air, thinking, and my mind freezes.

"I guess he's got that HR guy at his place."

Oh, crap. I stiffen. *Larry's had Dick for hours.*

"This is his address. She just wants you to do a welfare check. You can use my car if you want."

"I'll just take Uber. Thanks, though."

"And I'm totally cool if you wanna check out the Beat tonight."

"Nah." I'm smiling. "I'll just end up lunging for you, and you don't want that."

She laughs. "I don't. Sorry."

"No, I'm sorry for being such a pest all these years."

She smiles it off. "But we can be buds?"

"I'm sorry, but I am not sure I can be your bud. Maybe someday."

She nods. "Fair enough."

I look into those giant green eyes. Those gentle and peaceful eyes. This beautiful creature who makes me feel like it's gonna be okay?

Of course she doesn't like me.

I shut my eyes a moment, tell myself to stop it. I open them and look at her and allow a tired smile. I lean in and kiss her on the cheek, maybe with a little extra lip.

"You take good care."

•   •   •

It turns out Larry doesn't live too far from Woodside. His home is only ten minutes from my sister's place, but even in the dark the differences are stark. Whereas my sister has lived in a sprawling $5 million property in tony Woodside, Larry keeps a modest, single-story house in a cute neighborhood of smaller homes in nearby San Carlos.

My Uber driver parks the car, and I look at the house, double-check the address.

That's it.

The lights are out, and I wonder if anyone is home. Then I see a red ember brighten in the dark hollows of his porch. I step out of Mama's car, shut the door, and head to the house. The ember fades.

"Larry?" I walk a little closer. "Mr. Rayborne?"

Inside his closed garage, someone slaps a service bell.

The ember brightens again, and rises. I squint into the darkness until my eyes adjust, and I see Larry—he's naked, save the Speedo, and drawing off a tobacco pipe. He stretches and turns for the front door, opens it. The interior seems to be lit by a dim orange glow, and a slice of jazz eases out of the house, all bass and tight, popping horns. Smart and fast jazz.

I think he's looking at me.

"Larry?" I wait, get nothing. "Mama wanted me to come check on Dick."

Larry turns and saunters into his house, leaves the door open.

"Larry?"

From the garage, another *ding* from the service bell.

I can see Larry in his kitchen, pouring himself what looks like whiskey or bourbon. Then I realize it's Dick's two-thousand-dollar bottle of Pappy Van Winkle, and I find myself climbing the steps of his porch and entering his home. The jazz is loud in here, and the orange glow is everywhere. I didn't think they made orange lightbulbs. I pick up an odd hybrid aroma of cocoa butter and vanilla-scented tobacco.

"Larry?"

Ding.

His home is sparsely furnished, with ceramic-tile flooring and very few lights, all of them orange. I notice a variety of African tribal masks mounted on his walls as well as several framed and seemingly faded photos of large power plants. I reach Larry in the kitchen, and he turns with two glasses of bourbon, offers me one. I glance at the bottle on the counter—yes, it's Dick's Pappy Van Winkle.

"Larry, I just need to . . ."

Larry lifts his bourbon to me, and we clink glasses. I try to look Larry in the eye, but the orange lights are so low and Larry's brow so pronounced that all I see are two black holes. The bourbon goes down warm and wonderful, and the jazz curls into me. I take another sip, and he joins me.

"Yeah, so I'm sorry to bother you, Larry. But Mama wanted me to make sure Dick is—"

Ding.

"—you know, that he is okay."

We stand in silence awhile.

"Tell me." His voice is cool and even. "Do you enjoy paper-work?"

We look at each other.

"No, Larry. I don't particularly like paperwork."

Long silence.

Ding.

"Neither do I." He sips his bourbon. "What bothers me most, however, is unnecessary paperwork."

"Yeah, I remember you saying that."

"I have read lot about Mr. Rayborne and his paperwork."

"Yeah, Dick does like to create more and more—"

"So perhaps now . . ."

Ding.

". . . Mr. Rayborne is in heaven."

"Heaven?"

From the garage: A *tzzzt*, followed by a yelp, followed by a hastily slapped *ding.*

Larry sways and hums. "Paperwork heaven."

"You see, Larry, I just need to make sure Dick's okay."

"Mr. Rayborne is fine." Larry shifts his weight, leans against the counter, and takes a sip. "As long as he keeps up."

"Keeps up?"

Tzzzt—yelp. Growl. Ding.

"With the paperwork. He fell behind right there."

"He's doing paperwork?"

The slightest of nods. "Would you like to see him?"

"Well . . ."

Larry leads me through his family room to the back door that connects to his garage. I ease a little closer and listen—there's a flurry of paper shuffling, heavy panting, and even a some stapling and hole punching. And then . . .

Ding.

Larry says, "He doesn't have time to complain."

I step away from the door. "I guess I don't need to . . ."

"I've been preparing for Mr. Rayborne for some time." Larry cocks his head, hums along with the jazz. "I wanted to create an experience for him. Something that he would never . . . ever . . ."

Tzzzt—yelp. Ding.

". . . forget."

We listen to Dick Rayborne and his paperwork.

"You don't wanna just let him go?"

The hollow sockets regard me. "I'm afraid we've only just begun."

Ding.

SEIZE YOUR NEW LIFE

By the time my Uber ride pulls into the Robards International parking lot, it's just after 7:30 P.M. My plan is to pick up my Prius here, drive home, and write my resignation note, which I'll send to my boss tomorrow morning—I can't believe I'm going to quit and get paid to live at my sister's place.

Of course, all of this is assuming there isn't a warrant out for my arrest.

Cruising past the mangled executive parking gate, I notice a cluster of security sedans idling inside the private lot. I have my driver slow down so I can lean over and squint for a better look. Four security guards seem to be standing in a loose circle, legs apart, one of them talking into a radio. And in the middle of them is Mama, her arms wrapped around a bundle of papers—it's as if she's expecting the guards to rip them out of her clutch.

Crap. Totally forgot about Mama.

When we roll into the parking lot (stripped luxury cars everywhere), the guards are surprised to see that it's me—I mean, Dick Rayborne—in the backseat. Jeremy straightens, puffs out his chest, and walks to my side of the car. "Sir, I'm so used to seeing you in the Porsche or the Hummer or the Expedition."

I try to sound annoyed. "Long story."

"Sir, your . . ." He says it in the tone of a question. ". . . wife here?"

I look away, blink. "Yes."

Mama shuffles to her nearby Fleetwood, opens a back door, dumps the files onto the seat. "They don't believe we had a life together—a long life." Then she adds, cheerily, "Set 'em straight, Dickie."

"Sir, we didn't know you were married."

"Well, common-law wife."

"Yes, sir."

Mama gets into the Fleetwood, shotgun side, and I can't help but smile at her. "Drive me home," she hollers.

I turn to Jeremy. "I guess old Dick's been kind of neglectful. Lost sight of his family. Lost sight of the people who really matter. Got too caught up in himself—in the money."

Jeremy looks at me, bites his lip, and nods. "We found her in the back making photocopies of documents. She said you told her to do that."

I blink. "I did."

"So Cory was doing another sweep and saw that she was still out here." Jeremy bites his lip again, steps in, and whispers. "Looking maybe a little confused."

"I've got her now."

Jeremy forces a smile. "Have a good night, sir."

I begin to pull away, but not before I tell Jeremy that I don't think I'll be coming in to the office for a few days, if not longer, and please let everyone know.

Mama lives in the hills—actually, not too far from where I grew up. Her house is a simple one-story rancher—the kind I lived in, the kind all my friends lived in. The exterior looks like crap now, and I wonder if anyone has painted it in the past thirty years. The wood-shake roof seems to practically drip onto the sides of the house, and nothing appears to have been washed in decades. But the flower pots and planter boxes are exploding with life.

When we come to a stop, I turn to her. "How long have you lived here?"

She shakes her head, huffs. "Help me bring in those files."

Her house smells stale and spicy, and I imagine it has smelled that way forever. Mama shuffles around, grunting and panting as she flips on the lights in her tiny kitchen and family room, where it appears she spends most of her time. There are other rooms and halls—places where I imagine the family gathered, where kids ran up and down, where neighbors came over for drinks, where the cousins visited for Christmas dinner—and they seem dark and closed down, like no one's ever going to come here again, like Mama is the only person who's ever here anymore. And it puts the biggest lump in my throat.

Mama motions to a side table loaded with framed photos. "Those are my boys," she says. "My real boys." She keeps shuffling, panting. "And their families." I lean in to give the photos a respectful look. Her sons are men, of course, and they seem decent enough, their families healthy and chipper. I scan the table a bit more, and I notice a blurry photo of Cujo and Ernie clipped to a framed portrait of a grandson—the boys seem to be enjoying ice cream at a parlor.

"Steven and his family live in Manteca."

I study Steve's face—God, he looks familiar.

"And Eddie lives with his new wife and stepchildren in Brentwood."

"That's close," I say. "Kinda."

Mama shuffles over, shakes her head. "Sometimes I think they wouldn't visit if they lived across the street."

"Nah, I'm sure they're just superbusy. You know, with the jobs and the kids and the new wife and all that."

Mama touches my shoulder, says, "Rick, you don't know where you are?"

This gets me. I look at Mama, then at the photos. I take in a breath, trying to recall something—that spicy odor, so oddly familiar. Marjoram? *Why does that* . . . I look at Mama again, hoping for a clue, but all I see are the lights reflecting off those thick glasses. I turn back to the photos, and Mama seems to wait as I scan them all once more. Then in the back of the arrangement, I notice it.

It's an old photo. A family of four standing in front of Mama's metallic-blue Cadillac Fleetwood station wagon, a campground behind them. They all seem so happy. I lean in for a closer look. There's Eddie and Steve—I went to school with those wild boys—a man I've never seen before, and there's Mama, so young and slender and beautiful and brimming with happiness, her arm around Steve, her eyes trained on her husband.

Mama looks at the photo, nods. "I can't tell you how much I wish we could go back to that day, Ricky."

My head is spinning.

I've seen that photo.

I've been here.

I knew her son Steve.

Why is my heart sinking, my throat tightening?

I swallow hard, look to Mama. "Steve Carmichael? Your son is Steve Carmichael? The wild child?"

Slowly, Mama nods.

"You're Lillian Carmichael?"

She takes off her glasses, offers a gentle smile.

I feel my voice tighten. "You're the mom who picked me up—who insisted I—You're Steven Carmichael's mom." My mouth fills with saliva, and I struggle to swallow. "You saw me . . . and you came back and picked me up."

Mama comes a little closer, rests a hand on the back of my neck. "I have thought about you, Ricky. I have thought about you every single day."

I look down. I can't even fathom this.

"I never forgot you, honey. I always kept an eye on you, even when you and your sister moved in with your grandma over there in—where was it—Fremont?"

I stand and stare at Mama's brown shag carpet for a long while. I look up at her. "I mean, today? You planned all this?"

Mama laughs. "How could I ever plan this? *You* phoned *me*. Remember?"

"But this is . . . This. I don't know."

"Sometimes I've wondered." She looks away. "Maybe a part of you knew who I was, but another part of you didn't want to go there."

"And you've been planning for all of this in your head? Like, for months?"

She nods. "Just been waiting for my opportunity. Because I decided it wasn't just a coincidence."

"Coincidence?"

"That you look so much like Dick Rayborne." She smiles to herself. "I decided the universe wanted *something* to happen."

"The universe wanted Dick in Larry's garage?"

Still smiling. "Maybe."

Lillian Carmichael? It sinks in a bit more, and my brain slows down. I take another look at the faded family camping photo from so long ago. There's Mr. Carmichael, and there she is gazing at him. My chest tightens and my eyes water.

"Your husband. He really did . . ." But I can't get myself to say it.

"Left me and the boys? Yes." She's looking at the photo. "He could be a real prick."

I look at the photo again. They all seem so happy. They *were* so happy.

Mama says, "I know it might sound nuts to a young man like you, but it makes me feel good to look at that photo." She bites her lip, trembling. "There comes a time when you realize how fleeting those great moments are. Then they're gone forever."

"I think I understand."

"That there was *my* best time. All of us together. Even though he turned into an asshole."

"You gotta appreciate the moments, that's for sure."

"He croaked ten years ago. I'm not sure anyone cared. But I guess I'm still working things out, as crazy as that sounds." She looks away and takes a big breath. "I guess it still stings."

"Some things will always be a part of us."

"That's right." She shakes her head and squares herself to me. "Which is why this thing with you has bothered me for so long. I never let you know it was going to be all right." She looks down. "That I was going to keep an eye on you. Hell, I never even gave you a hug. I just let you sit there."

"It's okay. We all did the best we could."

And I really mean that.

"Can I give you a hug?"

"Of course."

"And tell you that your mom—I knew your mom, honey. And she was an amazing, smart, and beautiful woman who loved you very much."

"Okay, we don't need to—"

"And Rick? Can I tell you one last thing?"

"It's okay, Mama. Seriously."

Like a gift from God, the doorbell rings. "You want me to get that?" I say as I race out of the room with a huge sigh of relief. "You expecting anyone?"

"I get three visitors a decade," she hollers. "So what do you think?"

I open the door, but the porch light is out and I can see only the outline of a long-haired woman holding something. I'm obviously not what she expected. She blurts, "Who are you?"

I take a step back, searching for a light switch. "I could ask the same of you," I say lightly, running my fingers across the wall.

I detect a slight Nordic accent. "Is Lillian home?"

Still searching. "Of course. Trying to find the light here."

Her voice is tight. "I received an unusual call from her today. And then I had an even more usual conversation with someone named Rick Blanco. Is that you?"

Finally, I find the switch and the porch is aglow—and my jaw drops.

She squints into the blinding light. "I'm Sabine."

I just stand there.

"I am a friend of Lillian's."

Paralyzed.

"It was all very unusual, so I thought I'd stop by and check in."

It's not simply a matter of pure beauty—granted, her strawberry-blond hair and full cheeks, and piercing, intelligent eyes are not lost on me. It's just that having her here in front of me is like being reunited with an old friend.

Her brow creases in amusement. "Are you okay?"

Finally, I say, "Yes, come in. Of course."

I step back, and she takes a few steps in, pauses to give me another look. Her cheeks redden, and she plays with her hair.

"I just wanna say." I give her my serious eyes. "I'm not a specist."

"Specist?" She looks at me again, laughs.

"I don't discriminate against Neanderthals, contrary to what my nephew might suggest."

"Well, that's good to know." She mocks concern. "Because I called earlier, and you essentially hung up on me."

"Sorry about that." I admire her hands. "My nephew was instigating a riot for parolees. But I thought it was really cool you'd be willing to meet with us."

"Well . . ." She shrugs with a smile. "Lillian is cool."

I pull out my cell phone—8:21 P.M.—and think about traffic and parking and opening acts and encores. And I hear myself ask, "Have you ever heard of the English Beat?"

She's looking at me, and I feel like everything's gonna be okay.

POSTSCRIPT

From: "AUTOMATED-DO NOT REPLY" <rewards@
robardsinternational.com>
To: "Rick Blanco" <rblanco@robardsinternational.com>
Sent: Thursday, April 21, 2016—12:01 AM
Subject: Congratulations—You're recognized!!!

Dear   **Rick Blanco**

Congratulations. . . . You have been recognized!!!

Janice from Finance   has used the Robards International
Happy Workers Who Work Together Recognition Tool to recognize
your special contribution.   **Janice from Finance**   has awarded
you a spot bonus for   **"exemplary contributions
to a meeting"**   . . . </-BB-:—%!>

At Robards International, we take superior pride in rewarding positive
assistances in the workplace, which is why THE MANAGEMENT is
pleased to honor you with a financial reward. By using the below
code, you are eligible for a 10% discount on a regularly priced
super burrito as listed on the "Last Meal" menu at the Robards

International "Sing Sing" Chow Hall, with the purchase of a large-sized drink and medium bag of chips at regular price.

Thanks to teammates like   **Rick Blanco**   , the best will come soon at Robards International.

-THE MANAGEMENT

REDEMPTION CODE: ~~error~~

ACKNOWLEDGMENTS

So lucky. . . . So lucky to have David Hale Smith and Inkwell Management on my side. Lucky to have had gotten Cal Morgan's yes, and his guidance. Lucky to have been paired with Eric Meyers, who infused this project with thoughtful insight and important momentum. Lucky to have the support of Emily VanDerwerken, Kathryn Ratcliffe-Lee, Laura Brown, Keith Hollaman, Bob Alunni, Jamie Lynn Kerner, Jennifer Heuer, and many others at Harper. Lucky to have the faith of Shari Smiley of the Gotham Group. Lucky to enjoy the friendship and wisdom of Al Riske and Mark Richardson. Lucky for the reality checks from Jürgen Bürger, Jenny Allen, John Williamson, and Jennifer Bardsley. Lucky to have Carmen Bardsley's unconditional love and support. Lucky to be the proud father of Jack Bardsley and Dylan Bardsley, whose rambunctious Nerf wars and water play some years ago as young boys provided a formative spark for this book. Lucky to have the love, support, and patience of Nancy Tourkolias Bardsley, without whom none of this would be possible.

Lucky for every reader.

And lucky to have once worked with the real Bob, whose example of stealth rebellion in the face of useless meetings stuck with me all these years.

ABOUT THE AUTHOR

Greg Bardsley is the author of *Cash Out*, which was listed by the *New York Times* as one of five notable novels written about Silicon Valley. His award-winning short fiction has appeared in numerous journals and anthologies. A former columnist and speechwriter, he lives in the San Francisco Bay area.

ALSO BY GREG BARDSLEY

CASH OUT
A Novel
Available in Paperback and E-book

"One of those novels that begs for more adjectives: relentless, madcap, polished, lean, vivid, warped, original, horrifying and hilarious in equal measure."
—Marcus Sakey, author of *The Two Deaths of Daniel Hayes* and *The Amateur*

It's 2008. In three days, family man and Silicon Valley speechwriter Dan Jordan will see his start-up stock vest. He'll cash out with $1.1 million, turn in his frenetic Valley life in for a slower one on the beach with his wife and two children, and finally live the life he's supposed to live. Or so he thinks. Before he can collect his cash and get outta Dodge, all hell breaks loose...

Side-splittingly funny and full of larger-than-life characters, *Cash Out* is a sly caper gone outrageously, unforgettably awry.